Acclaim for *Hong Kong On Air*

"A frenetic, obsessive, compulsive tale of people from all ends of the world who converge on a congested, self-absorbed epicenter of political upheaval. Muhammad Cohen's tale about the chaos in the lives of players during Hong Kong's handover in 1997 brought back many memories to an old hat TV anchor like myself ... it's uncanny how much of my own dysfunctional life I saw in his prose."
—**Bernard Lo**, veteran Hong Kong news presenter

"*Hong Kong On Air* captures the soaring pulse of Hong Kong ahead of the handover and China's rise from the crash that followed. It reveals timeless truths about television news as seen from the hot seats on both sides of the camera."—**Lorraine Hahn**, broadcast journalist

"Muhammad Cohen's cast of Chinese and expatriates is alluring and exotic, yet completely accessible and wonderfully human. Combining real history and captivating characters with insider knowledge of media, finance and mainland manufacturing, leavened with cynicism, wit and genuine heart, *Hong Kong On Air* is the great American Hong Kong handover novel."—**Laurence E. Lipsher**, past president, American Chamber of Commerce of the Pearl River Delta

"Muhammad Cohen was a well-placed insider during the tumultuous Hong Kong handover. Only a thin veil separates his account from what really went on during that historic time."
—**Dalton Tanonaka**, veteran Asia journalist

"A witty, clever and all-too-accurate peek at personalities in a (barely) functional television station."—**James Chau**, television news anchor

Hong Kong On Air

Muhammad Cohen

BLACKSMITH BOOKS

HONG KONG ON AIR
© 2007 Muhammad Cohen
ISBN 978-988-99799-7-3
Published by Blacksmith Books
5th Floor, 24 Hollywood Road, Central, Hong Kong
www.blacksmithbooks.com

Typeset in Adobe Garamond by Alan Sargent
Cover art by Harry Harrison

Printed and bound in Hong Kong
First printing August 2007

ACKNOWLEDGEMENTS

Many people have helped me with *Hong Kong On Air* over the past decade of observing and writing.

First, let me thank Pete Spurrier and his crew at Blacksmith Books for taking a chance on an unpublished novelist.

Special thanks to three writers whose works you should know: Kathryn Chetkovich, Diana Darling, and Richard E. Lewis. Each read a first draft of *Hong Kong On Air* and offered a raft of suggestions that thankfully didn't include pulling the plug.

Thanks also to Raman Krishnan of Silverfish Books in Kuala Lumpur and his editor Sharon Bakar. They published my first work of fiction since grade school, inspiring me to keep at it. Raman is also the driving force behind the stellar KL International Literary Festival.

Jack Lynn, a great newsman who died obscenely young, contributed one of my favorite lines in the book and stands in for all the colleagues who gave me the rundown on TV newsrooms. Jack also, quite literally, got me out the door on my first trip to Hong Kong. I would never have made it this far without you, pal. Wish you were here to have a laugh about it over a cold frosty.

Further thanks go to:

Felix Chang, Paolo Conconi and Tim Morrissey for inside glimpses into mainland manufacturing. (There are too many people to thank for inside glimpses into lingerie.)

Rick Pollard for tales of Indonesia during *krismon* and more than a quarter century as my overseas role model.

The eRaider.com pros—Aaron Brown, Deborah Pastor, Gustavo Bamberger, Michael Levin—for insights into currency trading.

Charlene L. Fu and Twila Tardif for help with Chinese.

Bangkok novelists Christopher G. Moore and John Hail, inspirations in their own ways for more than a dozen years.

Mark Hanusz of Equinox Publishing for views from the other side of the table in contract negotiations.

Brian Diamond, my tennis partner, who volleyed manuscripts across the Pacific.

Tim Noonan and Tracy Quan for trying to hook me up with literary agents.

My niece Ika and sister-in-law Cheri, who sent dozens of query letters and sample chapters around the world. In the end, naturally, I found what I was looking for right here at home.

Speaking of home, I thank my wife, my best editor and my best friend, who works better in her second language than I can in my first. In 2007, my first novel and first child have come into the world. Without my wife, I'd have neither, and I dedicate this book to her.

One irony of covering the news is that you don't always witness the events that create it. Because of my assignments on June 30, 1997, I did not see many of the ceremonies depicted in this book. Sincere apologies if my fictionalized versions commit injustice to actual events.

Muhammad Cohen
Hong Kong
July 1, 2007

CHAPTER I

Television is My Lie

I T'S 5:58:43 A.M. HONG KONG STANDARD TIME, and Laura doesn't have her script.

What's gone wrong now? she wonders.

"Is anyone planning to bring me my fucking scripts?" Deng Jiang Mao asks from the news set behind her, his voice booming through the intercom into the control room on the other side of the glass. "Laura. . . ?"

She pushes the A-1 lever on the panel that still reminds her of a race car, an out-of-control race car, leans toward the microphone, and says in a throaty whisper, "Go with prompter." At that moment, Ashrami walks onto the *Asia Market Morning* set in a saffron sari, gold bracelets past her elbows jangling, and hands Deng his scripts. Leafing through the pages, he says, "This lead is from yesterday after-fucking-noon. . . ."

"Open in three, two, one. . . ." Quickie the cross-eyed director counts down, as if for a space shot or nuclear bomb test. He pronounces the first number as "flee," which always seems like a good idea to Laura at this moment of the day, then says, "Roll open."

"Let's hope someone commits news during the show, f'crissakes," Deng shrugs.

"Hi ho, stupid," Laura says without pushing the intercom lever as the first bars of *The William Tell Overture* blare over aerial photos of Tokyo, Hong Kong, Sydney, Seoul, Shanghai, and Singapore, separated by time-lapse stills of stock market trading floors, beaming to 42.3 million cable and satellite households from Melbourne to Mumbai. In all but a handful of television sets outside the studio, the signal dies unseen and unheard.

Few hear the voice of the Franklin Global Network's US nightly talk show host Grant Prebo say, in a much too bright and insufficiently authoritative voice as the music recedes, "Good morning, Asia, and welcome to FGN's *Asia Market Morning* . . . all the news Asia needs to get the market morning off and running . . . and much, much more." The music rises to a final crescendo, and Quickie says, "Camera one . . . cue."

"I'm Deng Jiang Mao in Hong Kong, and this is *Asia Market Morning* for January ninth, 1997. . . . *Jo saahn,* good morning. . . . Our top story. . . . "

Laura sighs, scrolls through the show rundown on her computer terminal, then picks up the phone. "Helios, Laura. How you doing on the back half of the show?. . . Message me as soon as they're done, each one, so I can check. . . . Yeah, better. Still a few problems with 'was' and 'were' . . . and the US Treasury Secretary is a man. . . . No, that's Robert*a*. . . . Okay, thanks." She hangs up as the taped US market wrap rolls, the blond, rabbit-faced Lisa Ford in New York responding to the intro with "Jo sarn, Ding," to give the illusion of live conversation.

"When's that bitch gonna get my name right?" Deng complains, as he does every morning.

"Not today, Deng," Laura replies with the intercom microphone lever down, speaking into Deng's earpiece called an IFB, abbreviating something she can't remember. "Don't forget to thank Lisa in the tag. . . . "

"For what, screwing up my name? Maybe I should call her Linda Buick. Stupid bitch."

"Her, right?"

"Yes. This time," Deng says with a smile. "Laura, I was looking through the scripts and on B-4 we've got 'Tiananmen Square massacre.' Let's just say sanctions were imposed in 1989. . . . "

"Oh, come on. . . . "

"Sometimes you just don't understand . . . and 'massacre' is overkill."

"I'll settle for 'crackdown' this morning."

"Deal. Fix it in prompter," Deng says, and changes his paper copy. "And what is this bullshit about the 'prime minister of China' again? Li Peng is the premier."

"Same as prime minister, again."

"Is not, again."

"Is." Laura releases the lever. "Ashrami, get the dictionary from Lamont's desk and bring it to Mister Deng next time you go on set."

Laura returns to editing Helios' scripts for the show's C and D blocks, unbreaking his broken English, until Quickie says, "Back in ten."

"You ready?" Laura asks Pussy, the graphics operator who speaks no English. They call her Pussy because she really knows dick, Laura thinks, as she does every morning, and suppresses a giggle. The teen's body geometry, however, is no laughing matter. With a waist that small, a bust that big, and no ass, why doesn't she just crack in half? Maybe that's why all those old ladies with the umbrellas on the escalator have those humps: they all looked like Pussy when they were seventeen. While Laura wears her standard worried expression throughout the broadcast, Pussy wears a brilliant, vacant smile along with a tube top that makes her pert teenage breasts seem suspended in mid-air, nipples like pencil points in the frigid control room air, and a pair of shorts inches long. Laura is dressed in jeans, running shoes and, for warmth over her blue knit top, a red flannel shirt she might've bought used at a Nirvana Fan Club meeting.

"Is she ready, Ashrami?" Laura asks her production assistant who helps Pussy type the words and arrange the graphics she can't read.

"Ready, yes," Ashrami replies. "I think the guest is here" she adds and leaves the control room, just in case she's thought wrong about Pussy's preparedness.

"Don't forget the dictionary for Deng." Laura rolls her chair a few inches toward Pussy and looks at her console. The graphic for the New Zealand stock exchange is loaded on the left screen, with the currency board waiting on the right screen. "Looks good," she nods and rolls back to her spot to edit scripts.

Deng reads the intro to the New Zealand stock report, the only market trading at this hour. Laura glances up from her computer screen to see the stock index graphic appear on cue, then looks out the 25th floor window with a view of Chai Wan harbor. Chai Wan leads Hong Kong Island in grime, home to dozens of auto repairs shops, each loaded with a couple million US dollars worth of Lamborghinis and Ferraris (where do people drive them? she wonders). The district is a throwback to when they made things in Hong Kong besides money: industrial laundries, food processors, metal bashers, bus depots, cemeteries, a fire department training ground with a four story tower for simulated rescues, and clusters of identical white concrete public housing towers. But the sunrise panorama from the FGN Asia control room window shows only blue water and a small green island awaiting a solitary castaway.

The chorus from *One Moment in Time* beeping from Pussy's mobile phone snaps Laura back from this five-second tropical vacation. Laura has anticipated this moment and is pleased Pussy is the culprit. She grabs the phone from the counter, declares, "Pussy is busy right now. She'll call you later. *Bai-bai,*" and ends the call.

Pussy looks shocked, then nods. "Okay, okay."

"Phones off during the show," Laura announces, and Quickie commences simultaneous translation into Cantonese. "Company rule, not mine. Next time it happens, I won't be so nice."

She turns back to the monitor and hears Deng say, "In currencies, as you see, the US dollar is.... Well, you'll see as soon as we get that currency graphic for you...."

"Currency board!" Laura screams.

"Stuck," Quickie says, then barks instructions in Cantonese to Pussy, who shrugs and diffidently pushes buttons.

"When he says, 'In currencies,' you take the board. Okay?" Laura says to Quickie, while waiting for Pussy's fix.

"Okay-aaah," Pussy sings, and three seconds late, the currency board fills the broadcast monitor.

"Maybe you lock button when you talk on phone," Quickie tells Laura. "Or maybe she."

"Phones off," Laura repeats. "Off."

Deng, relaxed because today's graphic board glitch is out of the way, gives an especially lively rendition of foreign exchange prices. He then flatly reads a short lead in for a package on Bangkok's subway construction that takes the show to the end of Block A and the first commercial break.

"What the fuck is wrong in there?" Deng yells as the studio camera's red light fades. "How many times do I have to fuckin' tell you to change the board when I say 'in currencies'? What is the fucking problem?"

"Sorry. Better next time," Quickie promises.

"'In currencies ...' This is not fuckin' brain surgery. Every time...."

"We're sorry," Laura apologizes. "We had a problem in here...."

"No shit. But you have a problem in there every fucking day. My ten o'clock doesn't have as many problems...."

"That's because they dupe all the scripts we write and edit, roll all the tape we cut. . . ."

"I've got to be the producer and the director, too, which is damned difficult from the fuckin' anchor desk. If I have to. . . ."

"Anything you'd like to do to assist is welcome and needed," Laura says, "except for screaming at the director. Scream at me. I'll scream at the director." She slips a smile Quickie's way, then turns to snarl at Pussy.

"Fuck you both," Deng says.

"Thank you. Back in two-thirty."

"Where are the second-half scripts?" Deng says.

"Coming."

"It's frequent industry practice to let the anchor see his copy before reading it on air. That's standard procedure in professional television operations." Deng gives a mock shrug. "I guess it was different at the *Financial Journal,* Laura. You're not the only one here that ever worked on a fucking newspaper. But you know what? This is not a fucking newspaper. This is television, and it's live, and there are no second chances. So instead of doing whatever the fuck you're doing during the show, it would be nice if you tried to pay attention to what's going on. Is anybody bringing me coffee, or is that something else I need to do myself? Two sugars."

"Ashrami?" Laura implores, but she's still out of the control room, living up to her nickname G-Spot, because she can be so hard to find. Laura messages Helios to find Ashrami (as if that pimply Chinese nerd could find a G-Spot) and get the anchor some coffee, and her, too, and the dictionary. Laura can't decide whether she'd prefer her coffee with valium or strychnine, though neither would likely work fast enough to make the remaining 112 live minutes of today's show tolerable. She glances at that little island in the sunrise, imagining the soothing feeling of smashing through the control room windows and flying toward tropical paradise rather than plummeting 25 floors toward the Chai Wan pavement soaked in oil from minibuses and *dim sum.* Or the joy of watching Deng take the leap.

Every morning, Laura imagines she's not flying but drowning, that it will be impossible for her to produce a show, to find enough news, write enough scripts, choose enough tape, fix enough of Helios' copy, to fill two hours of live television time. She thinks each day will be the one where she's pushed over the edge by the tension to make a hard deadline, by Deng's carping, by technical snafus. But so far, each day, Laura has survived and come back for more.

Ashrami appears on set, placing Deng's C and D block scripts on his anchor desk and then handing him the dictionary. He eyes her curiously, and she turns her head toward the control room. Laura watches via the monitor and wonders why this control room (and control rooms at other stations, Richard the next show producer has told her) faces away from the set, so the producer can only see what's going on via monitor or by turning away from the console. Inside the control room, the machine receiving the real-time data for graphics and the market price crawl across the bottom of the screen on later shows, the tape playback decks, and the teleprompter operators are also scattered behind her, providing an unruly audience of under-25s for the director, producer, audio technician and the graphics operator in the front row. Like everything in television, or at least at FGN Asia, the control room is backwards, overly complicated, too heavy on technology and light on common sense.

"Are we going to play dictionary?" Deng asks, his voice echoing around the control room. "Or have you thought of something else I can do while I'm reading the news, correcting your copy, timing the show. . . ."

"We haven't missed a time cue in three weeks," Laura protests.

"Then you're really overdue. . . . Shove a broomstick up my ass and I can sweep the fuckin' floor while I'm. . . ."

"Please look up 'premier,' " she says through the microphone into his ear.

"Okay, I'll play," he intones, flipping pages. "Got it."

"Please read the definition, aloud," she says, delighted that she's finally nailed him in full view.

Deng reads it to himself first. "Would you like me to wait until we're out of break and read it to the folks out in television land, or just for our studio audience?"

Laura feels a twinge of guilt because he's being such a good sport. "Studio audience will suffice."

"Premier, noun, prime minister, generally reserved for the head of a communist government."

"Thank you. Now that we've resolved. . . ."

"Yes, I hope that clears this up once and for all," Deng says, slamming the book shut. "Premier and prime minister are the same fucking thing. I don't want to have to tell you again. And we should use prime minister because premier is loaded. Until we call John Major the fucking Premier of England, we should call Li Peng the Prime Minister of China. "

"Back in ten," Quickie says.

Laura is so angry she wants to scream at him or walk onto the set and slap him, but 112 minutes of an empty anchor chair would surely damage her career. She remembers what Old Hartman wrote in the issue of the *Rabbit Ears* newsletter faxed to her in New York before she came to Hong Kong: "Rule 1: On the set, the anchor is always right. Rule 2: When the anchor is wrong, see Rule 1." That doesn't diminish her desire to rip out Deng's vocal cords, but it does remind her what a bad idea it is. She resolves not to speak to him, except in necessary monosyllables, for the rest of the show. By the time she hears Deng close with his standard, "That's all for this edition of *Asia Market Morning*. Stay tuned as the *Money-Go-Round* starts turning with my pal Kathleen Trang, next on FGN Asia. Thanking you for your time this time until next time, I'm Deng Jiang Mao, saying, 'Buy low, sell high,' and have a profitable day," she is almost back to normal.

"Two, one, clear," Quickie says.

"Good show everyone," Laura says, as she picks up her scripts and, before she can repeat the "phones off" edict one more time, sneezes because Richard Yakamoto, producer of the eight o'clock show has entered the control room, wearing his usual overdose of cologne. Laura wonders if he uses fragrance as an alternative to bathing.

"It fuckin' sucked. Like every fuckin' show fuckin' sucks with you fuckin' clowns," Deng announces as he whips the IFB out of his ear, unclips his microphone and places it on the anchor desk adorned with the FGN golden eagle logo, and strides across the set, holding the door for Kathleen Trang, Melbourne's Miss Little Saigon of 1992, as he exits.

Laura follows Deng to his cubicle, anger boiling up again, but before she can articulate it, he speaks. "I know," Deng sighs as he drops into his chair. "I know it's hard. I know you're doing the best you can. Everybody is. I don't want to say half the things I do in there. . . . Marvin, can I get some coffee here, buddy?" he yells past Laura, smiling to soften his order to the intern named Joseph. "Two sugars."

Back in the US, Deng was a city reporter in Los Angeles. As a guest on TV news chat shows, producers immediately noticed the camera loved him, nearly as much as he loved it. He anchored for more than five years, the last three on a network affiliate in San Francisco. His Chinese identity—though his face could easily pass for *gweiloh* and he didn't speak a word of the language until he picked up *jo saahn* here—made him a star in that market. FGN paid handsomely to lure him to Hong Kong for its new Asian business network, though not as much as a US national network offer, Deng claims. In the Secret Santa gift pool last month, Deng received a tee-shirt proclaiming, "I walked away from US network millions to get back to my roots." Laura knows that whenever there's a problem, management won't blame Deng. She also knows that as FGN Asia's only Chinese male talent, he's certain to anchor the Hong Kong handover ceremony—though nothing's been announced—and, as much as she can't stand him, Laura wants to be in the control room at that historic moment. Otherwise, what is she doing in Hong Kong?

Her journey eastward began on a gray January morning in the *Financial Journal* newsroom in lower Manhattan, the kind of day that makes you wonder if the sun will ever shine again. After sending her feature on the growth of computer bulletin boards to the copy desk, she scanned the news calendar to try to think up a juicy assignment before Dick Holmes—Dick my editor—provided another boring one. She saw the Hong Kong handover coming up in July 1997 and thought that might be an interesting thing to cover. The more she thought about it, the more she saw interesting angles. She'd interned at a Washington news-paper during the fall of the Berlin Wall and remembered how the newsroom buzzed then and how exciting she thought it would have been to be in Berlin as a reporter, as well as the deference, esteem, even awe, afforded reporters who witnessed that piece of history by those stuck stateside. Excitement and deference were two things Laura felt her life needed a year ago.

She'd grown up comfortably as the only child of a pair of mild-man-nered federal bureaucrats, her father an analyst in the Bureau of Labor Statistics and her mother an interagency coordinator in Department of

Transportation, in Rockville, Maryland, a dozen miles beyond the Washington, DC, border. Their neighborhood was mixed, a smattering of Catholics and Jews, blacks and Asians, living out the American dream of escaping the urban jungle for the good schools and blooming azaleas of the suburbs. The big issues of Laura's adolescence were property taxes, removing *Huckleberry Finn* from the junior-high-school reading list (but, as a compromise, keeping it in the school library, where everyone tried reading it; so boring), and funding drives for the girls' soccer league. She was a vice president of Students Against Drunk Driving, but that never stopped her from having a beer at house parties since her teetotaler friends Amir and Atika made convenient designated drivers. She edited the high-school newspaper, wrote poems for the yearbook ("At Rockville High /we reached for the sky. . . .") and, when Harvard and Princeton and even her namesake Wellesley didn't say yes, to her parents' secret relief at dodging those tuition bills, Laura went to the University of Maryland and stayed on track for a journalism career. She landed the job with the *Financial Journal* right after college and moved up from desk assistant in the Washington bureau to general assignment in New York to features, holding her own among the journalism school graduates. Life at the *Journal* in New York put her in the middle of things that should have been exciting, but up close, it all seemed so ordinary. That made Jeff so refreshing. He was different, not ordinary. He had a sailboat, he was his own boss in a business that went to the heart of intimacy. He knew who he was, and he wasn't competing with her. He glamorized her the way his shops glamorized underwear. He thought the things she did weren't ordinary. He didn't know that her business was so petty. He didn't know that reporters seemed, almost by creed if not pathological need, to reduce every story, no matter how important, to a bad joke that degraded everyone involved, including the reporters. The substance of the stories, of these daily first drafts of history, seemed far less important who got the lead over how many columns, who got the travel, who had lunch with whom.

That grind made Hong Kong and its handover so appealing on that gray morning before she met Jeff. The story was undeniably important: the fall of the Berlin Wall in reverse, in a city the size of New York with a supporting cast of a billion people. The story included all the things the *Journal* stood for—freedom, justice, choice—and she could tell it that way, and shine far removed from the maliciousness of the newsroom on Liberty Street. But when Laura inquired about covering the Hong Kong handover, she didn't do it solely because she thought it would be good for her career. Laura thought it would be good for her to get away for two or three weeks, maybe a month, and get immersed in something interesting for a change. Laura had not yet heard the Chinese curse: may you live in interesting times.

"Listen, can we do something about the open, and about the name of the goddamned show?" Deng says, tying a white bib around his neck and looking in the mirror on his desk to see if he needs to adjust his makeup before his next show. Stuck in the top edge of the mirror, there's a magazine cartoon of two surgeons standing over a patient on the operating table. "C'mon," the caption reads, "this is brain surgery, not television."

"I agree, *AM Asia* is better," Laura says, "but Lamont says we can't get a new voice track from Prebo until the next quarterly. . . ."

"Who the fuck needs a track from Prebo? He means dick here. No one in Asia has any fucking idea who that prick is. I'll make the fucking track. I have a voice."

"Okay. I'll mention it at the meeting." Laura hesitates, as she does whenever she talks TV to people who know more about it than she does, which she believes includes everyone but the janitor at FGN Asia. "Wouldn't it be weird, though, for you to voice the open then anchor the show?"

"You think I'm going to keep waking up at four o'clock forever?" Deng barks, before conceding, "You're right. Ask Old Hartman to do it. He's done everything else in television." Deng smiles at Laura, then beads sweat from his face with a tissue. "Oh. . . . I'm sorry about the Tiananmen thing," he adds. "I know you had 'crackdown' in the prompter. 'Incident' just came out. That's what we call it," we being Chinese patriots.

"When I'm perfect, then I'll complain about you." She smiles, then sighs. "But what about 'premier'?"

"I'm glad we got that cleared up. The dictionary was a good idea."

"But I was right, you were wrong."

"What do you mean?"

Laura sighs again. "I said premier and prime minister were the same thing, and you kept saying they weren't. . . ."

"Oh, I guess I misunderstood," Deng says.

"Well, understand now: I was right, and you were wrong."

"As I said, it was a misunderstanding. Apparently, we were both saying the same thing, but at that hour. . . ."

"We were not both saying the same thing. You kept insisting prime minister was not the same as premier."

"But they are. Why would I say they're not?" Deng studies the mirror to make sure the sweat hasn't ruined his pancake foundation. "I know there's a lot going on out there, a lot to deal with, and sometimes it's hard to communicate clearly."

"The way you humiliated me was pretty clear."

"Oh, I didn't mean. . . ."

"There was no mistaking the way you berated me."

"Then maybe you know how I feel when there's a fucking error in the copy, or a graphic doesn't come up."

"That's different. Inside the control room, the only thing that prevents chaos is the respect you manage to. . . ."

Deng shakes his head. "How long have you been here?" and continues before she can answer, nine weeks, producing their show for six. "You still don't understand television. What do you think the anchor's job is? It's all about respect, and every time there's an error, it makes me—and the whole network—look like fools."

"But those people don't know you," Laura says, resisting the temptation to say she probably has a bigger audience in the control room than he has out in television land.

"I don't know them, but they think they know me. They invite me into their homes. They rely on me for critical information that's more important than pushing a couple of buttons and rolling a tape. They may make decisions about their life savings, their future and their children's futures, based on what they hear from me. So they damned well better think they know me and that they can trust me. Every fucking error you make undermines that trust. It doesn't matter to them—or to me—whether it's your mistake or that other pair of tits doing graphics. . . ."

"But this was your mistake, and you undermined my credibility. . . ."

"As far as your credibility goes, worry about earning some before you worry about losing it. And as far as mistakes go, like I was trying to explain to you—try listening and you might learn something—nobody gives a shit who's right and who's wrong. What matters is that we eliminate the mistakes. And we're not going to make that fucking premier mistake again, right?"

Laura nods, too angry to speak.

"Good. Tomorrow, check your fucking ego at the door when you do my show. Now, I've got to make a phone call and read in before I'm back on the air," Deng says, lifting the receiver on the phone, indicating it's time for Laura to leave. As she walks across the newsroom, he yells, "Don't forget about the open. Let's try to get that fucking right."

Almost shaking with rage, partly because she would have forgotten about the open without his reminder, Laura reaches her desk across the newsroom, where she finds nine a.m. *Money-Go-Round* production assistant Honest Ho seated, collating rundowns. With more people than newsroom seats, Laura and *Market Wrap* producer Sara Fergis share a desk. Sara begins working on her rundown around one p.m., *Market Wrap* airs at six, and their cohabitation causes no conflict. If not for the 12:30 daily staff meeting, they'd never see each other.

"Sorry-aah," Honest says, without looking up from her sorting. Laura walks past the row of anchor offices to the front wall of the newsroom, where morning supervising producer Edie March is in the slot, a raised platform like the sergeant's desk in a police station. Edie leans between her two computer screens and three televisions assuring a translator from Taiwan that she shouldn't fear deportation on July first. Edie nods at Laura, and, seeing she's waiting to talk to her, launches into her closing remarks for the translator: "This network will not let any government interfere with our freedom to deliver the news as we see it, to whom we want to deliver it, utilizing whatever personnel we deem appropriate. That is FGN policy, from the top, and it has been articulated to the very highest levels of the Immigration Department, and indeed, to the very highest levels of the incoming Hong Kong SAR government through our contacts here and in Beijing. And they have assured us that nothing, absolutely nothing, will change with reference to our ability to obtain working visas for all necessary personnel, regardless of origins. The letter to that effect from the Hong Kong government, signed by the chief secretary for administration, is on file in Human Resources up on 28, if you want to see it for yourself. So sign your lease, Wufen, darling, and don't worry about a thing." The translator smiles and walks back toward the tapes area. "Good show today," Edie tells Laura.

"Deng said it 'fucking sucked like every fucking day with you fucking people.'"

"At least you're consistent, darl'."

"That's really something about the letter. Maybe it's a story."

"Letter?"

"From Anson Chan herself—she's the chief secretary, right? See, I'm learning. . . ."

"Oh," Edie shrugs, and scans the newsroom to make sure the translator is out of earshot. "I made that up. I don't expect they'll kick out everyone from Taiwan after the handover, but who knows? I can't even be certain about my visa—never needed one before. I suspect there's a greater chance they'll throw out us *gweilohs* before they evict their wayward brothers and sisters from Taiwan, but I don't reckon that they've even decided yet. The story to watch is the air transport agreement—Hong Kong's travel treaty with Taiwan is up for renewal and if the SAR government renews it, that's a sign things won't change regarding Taiwan even while pressed to the warm bosom of the big motherland. But until then. . . . What was I supposed to tell Wufen?"

"What if she's goes to HR and asks. . . ?"

"Laura, of all people you should know that no sane person goes there of their own free will."

"True enough," she agrees, thinking of the ongoing mess HR has made of her work visa application.

"Besides, you know what I say. . . ."

"Television is my lie."

"It used to be my life, but the 'f' got worn out from the lot of fucking shit I endure for it." Edie smiles and shakes her head. "Let's go have a fag." She bolts out of her ergonomic padded chair, a supervisory perk. "I can't believe they won't let us smoke in the newsroom. What's the third world come to?"

Laura, who doesn't smoke, follows Edie past the elevators and through the heavy metal door to the open air concrete fire stairway that

looks away from Laura's fantasy island toward the public housing high
rises, the cemetery that depresses local property values, a dilapidated
pier, and far in the distance, the towers of Central Hong Kong peeking
above the clouds. The newswomen sit on the concrete steps, overlooking
cigarette butts, three days of Edie's wire service printouts for her morning
read-ins, and the dregs of her five a.m. cup of coffee from yesterday
glistening like a biology experiment despite the chilly air. Laura shivers
and pulls her flannel shirt around her. "Hong Kong is the same latitude
as Havana, so why am I freezing?"

"Same latitude, perhaps, but quite different attitude. You'll pine for
this cool weather during the eleven months of inferno," Edie says,
lighting up. "What's up, darl'?"

"Deng wants to change the open and the name of the show."

"Well, whatever Deng wants, Deng gets."

"He says we can ask Old Hartman to record a new track, but what
about the name? Can we change that?"

"I'll check, but I'm nearly certain we produced the font here—oh, yes,
I remember . . . misspelled 'morning' twice—so just put in an order to
graphics." Edie explains how tape editors will recut the open, depending
on whether the music and voice were laid down separately or tracked
together, and how they can try some different effects with the show title.

Laura's mind wanders when hearing these technical details. Instead
of being a journalist—chasing stories, meeting fascinating people, craft-
ing elegant prose—she thinks, I'm whacking out 35-word stories that
end with [READ BOARD], worrying about mobile phones ringing
during the show like a movie usher, and now supposed to tax my brain
to find the best way to superimpose six letters over a bunch of pictures.
Television is my lie, too, now.

"By the way, what's the name he wants?" Edie asks, since she supervises
Laura's show.

"Name?"

"Of the show."

"Oh, *AM Asia.*"

"Lovely."

"What about CK? What's he going to say about all this?"

"As if he'll know, *mei-mei.*"

Laura likes it when Edie calls her *mei-mei,* little sister in Cantonese. When Dick her editor told Laura she could be in line for a transfer and needed to call FGN Asia, Edie picked up the phone. Right away, Laura liked Edie's British accent—it sounded classy and authoritative to Laura, particularly with its sprinkling of clearly articulated four-letter words— and Edie convinced Laura that Asia was the center of the universe. "Europe is yesterday's news, America is hanging on for dear life," Edie said. "The Asian tigers are driving the world's economic life. The Asian century has already begun, and we want you to be a part of it. Fuck, FGN Asia needs you to be a part of it, to come ride the tiger with us, if you're half the journalist and have half the soul that they say." Later, Edie admitted she'd never heard of Laura before that conversation.

Laura had assumed from the accent that Edie was Oxbridge, but she was actually FILTH: Failed In London, Try Hong Kong. A school leaver—as they call UK high-school graduates—at seventeen, Edie (as she told Laura as they became the day's first customers at Oscar's in Lan Kwai Fong one afternoon) headed east looking for adventure and men who could provide sex, drugs and travel funds. After two years, she'd reached the Andaman Islands, staying at a five-star resort with a studio musician she'd met at an ashram in Sri Lanka—"You wouldn't know his name, but he played riffs you do know, like the 'dat-dat-dat-dat-dah, dat-dah, dat-dat-dah' from *Tommy*"—and walked in on him bonking a maid, who screamed "Rape." Edie closed the door and charged a plane ticket to Hong Kong—"first place that came into my mind with higher fare than Bangkok"—to the room account at the front desk. She returned to the room—"Rape still in progress. Longer bloody ride than he'd ever given me"—to grab her clothes and all the cash she could find before taking off.

Even then—"getting on twenty years, I'm afraid"—the money was incredible in Hong Kong—"scads of it"—still mainly in the hands of Brits. She bought a respectable outfit and found a job in a British law firm as a secretary to a partner. They began screwing "bloody hell, right on the desk after he took me to lunch at the Wankers—I mean Bankers—Club my first day." He set her up in an apartment and plied her with cocaine. "But I wanted more, and he was married to a very proper wife." The lawyer specialized in deals across the border—"things were just starting to open up." From typing his documents and taking

notes at meetings, Edie realized she could do the partner's job at least as
well as he did. So, when they crossed the border to Shenzhen for a
meeting, "which he'd made into an overnight trip for a change of pace
from afternoon delight," she mixed a horse laxative into his cocaine then
begged off due to a stuffy nose. "He was cemented to the toilet for twelve
hours," so Edie took the meeting and made the deal. She expected the
firm to hail her as a heroine and make her a lawyer, too—"I didn't
understand about Inns of Court and all." But the partner must have
squealed. Back in Hong Kong that afternoon, she found the firm had
already cleared out her things and hired her replacement—"Some fat
old thing; they sussed him out, too, I reckon." She told the partner to
find her a new job, or she'd tell his wife and the firm about all of his bad
habits. He sheepishly called his banking clients and placed Edie as a
trainee currency trader—"Just like TV: watch a screen for trivial details
in real time." She also "made the bastard pay two years rent on my flat
in advance, and told him to fuck off whenever he wanted to come by
and check the plumbing." Edie moved off the trading floor—"some
people are born for it, but it was just a silly game to me"—to junior
analyst and wound up writing everyone else's reports—"only native-
English speaker in the shop"— getting nice raises along the way "but
the bloody MBAs got the promotions and serious money." Sharing the
elevator with a television crew doing an interview in her building
changed Edie's life. "I always thought people in TV were giants, like
basketball players. In the elevator with this silly English girl and two
Chinese guys, I realized, bloody hell, they're just like me." She called
TVB and talked herself into a job on the business desk and shot up the
ranks. "It's amateur hour here still. Show up regularly and sober, and
you're practically a star. Still I was devastated when, six months on, I still
wasn't presenting the evening news." Instead she moved to producing
daily financial cut-ins, then launching a weekly business news show and
finally running TVB's entire English news operation before signing on
as the third employee in the FGN Asia newsroom, after CK and Lamont,
the afternoon supervising producer, who came from FGN in New York
and technically outranks her—"Each job for more money than I ever
imagined I'd make in my entire life." Edie's biggest complaint is her love
life. "Nothing's taboo anymore, and how can you compete with these

little China dolls? If I were a man, I'd want one, too." At least that's what Edie told Laura.

"One more favor for *mei-mei,* please," Laura says, as Edie's cigarette, the hourglass for this staircase session, winds down. "Would you ask Old Hartman to do the voice for the open?"

"Sure. I'll tell Mike Pussy's grandmother is getting a divorce."

"She is. . . ?"

"Oh, *mei-mei,* I hope you're a bit more shrewd when it comes to that husband of yours in ladies' pants. Are you sure ladies' pants aren't his lie?"

"Jeff's good as gold," Laura says, punning on his name.

"Perhaps, but consider what might have happened to the 'f' in his case." Edie giggles.

"Did you see Pussy's outfit today?" Laura says.

"Barely."

"She looks like she came straight from working the street."

"But remember what I told you. . . ."

"That she goes to gay bars all night to stay up because she can't wake up. . . ?"

"No," Edie says, tossing away her butt. "These Hong Kong girls all dress like hookers. . . ."

"But," they say in unison exiting the stairway, "none of them mean it."

Honest Ho has vacated Laura's desk when she returns. She thanks Helios, a fresh graduate of Chinese University—everyone at the station who's not a producer or anchor seems so young to Laura—for his work on this morning's scripts. "Your English is much better," she tells him, more a wish than a fact. Then Laura starts calling banks and brokerages for tomorrow morning's 6:45 and 7:35 guests. Despite the hour, fund managers generally jump at the chance for exposure to FGN Asia's audience of dozens. She fills in the pre-interview forms and scripts questions and answers for Rahesh Rimza of Bank of Reckoning's discourse on currency rates (stable for the next twelve to eighteen months, he forecasts, as long as the handover goes smoothly), and she dials Alex Berkeley of Hilgerman Funds, an expert on Taiwan equities. Good variety, plus he's cute and single; Edie will like that. Trying my best for *jie-jie,* big sister. While typing, Laura eats an apple from the plastic bag on her desk. She brings a load of fruit every day to eat while she works—it's about all her stomach can take at three a.m.—and she puts it out for others to share. But her newsroom colleagues prefer those disgusting sweet buns, greasy *dim sum,* or instant noodles—nothing but chemicals and carbs. Yet the Chinese all seem so slim, Laura thinks, while I'm dragging ten extra pounds around like a caboose. I've got to get to the gym today, she swears, and wonders whether she'd agree to be a dumb bitch like Pussy in exchange for a body like hers. Not if I had to let Chinese guys touch it, she concludes.

Laura checks the AP news calendar for events ahead this week, clears today's stories out of her show rundown and slots in some potential items for tomorrow. She sends a message to Edie about Alan Greenspan's testimony to Congress that will be happening during the US morning. Laura walks back to the editing area to track down Nancy Black, the thick Australian woman in charge of tapes who keeps changing her hair color. Black, with orange hair this week, is in an editing bay with two Chinese editors, attempting to eat *dim sum* from a sheet of glistening brown paper, giggling along as they chide her ineptness with chopsticks. Nancy sees Laura, turns serious, and says, "What do you want?"

"Alan Greenspan is testifying. . . ."

"Who?"

"Alan Greenspan, the chairman of the Fed . . . the US central bank. He's testifying today, morning US time, and we may get a package overnight. If it's up on the bird. . . ."

"If it's on the bird, you'll get your bloody package. And if it's not, you won't."

"If it's not on the bird, can't we take it off the US air check?"

"We can, if you can tell me when it will run."

"I don't know," Laura admits. "Wait a minute. His testimony begins at 9:30 p.m. our time. I'm sure the US network will take it live. . . ."

"Do you want the testimony, or do you want the package?"

"I want both, if we can."

"We? So you're going to be here at 9:30 so my overnight man doesn't have to roust himself from his *kung-fu* movie and his girlfriend to roll the tape?" Before Laura can answer, Black says, "I didn't think so. I'll see what I can do." Nancy readies her chopsticks for another stab at a *siu mai,* then asks, "What is it we're going to do with this testimony if we get it?"

"I'll watch it and cut a couple of sound bites."

"Oh, so you cut SOTs, too."

"I mean, I'll choose a couple of SOTs, and ask you to cut them."

"Thank you. Happy, happy, joy, joy." Nancy pushes the *dim sum* toward her editors. "You ruined my appetite, 24 hours in advance. That's a new record for you bloody producers." The editors giggle, though Laura's never seen any evidence they understand English well enough to pick up Nancy's sarcasm. "We won't have time for breakfast tomorrow, boys, so build up your strength now. Thanks a lot for stopping by, Linda. A real pleasure."

"Laura. Thanks. See you at the meeting."

Laura returns to her desk and calls Jeff.

"Hello," Jeff says.

"Hi, sweetheart. I've got my meeting in a couple of minutes, but I wanted to say hi, and tell you I love you."

"Thanks. I love you, too. Who is this?"

"Very funny."

"How's show biz?"

"Pretty awful. I'll tell you when I get home. We're going to change the name of the show."

"But not the time. . . ?"

"No, I'm afraid not. One step at a time."

"Right. I was afraid we were going to be like a normal couple again."

"Fat chance. Love you, and see you at dinner. And after."

"Love you. Bye."

She never imagined things would turn out this way while she stood banging on the door of the lingerie store in Bethpage that windy morning last March. The sign on the door said "Back in 5 Minutes" but it had already been seven when she started knocking. On her way to interview Senator Alphonse D'Amato's mother, Laura spotted a major hole in her pantyhose—back when work wasn't hand-to-hand combat, she wore hose and heels, makeup and jewelry; these days the only accessory she'd consider is a helmet—so stopped the car at the shop. She could hear something going on inside, but no one came to the door. Then this little Spanish teenager unlocked the door, straightening out all her parts, especially this push-up bra that lifted her boobs out in front of her chin, giggling. Jeff stood on the sales floor, his brown hair messy, shirt misbuttoned, and fly open, radiating postcoital contentment across his broad face.

"Sorry to keep you waiting," he said. "Can I help you?"

"It looks like you know how to help yourself," Laura replied.

"Rosalinda and me were just taking inventory in the back."

"I hope nothing came up short."

Jeff chuckled. "The key is rotating your stock properly."

"Right. Oldest items on top, I'd guess. But I'm only here for a pair of pantyhose."

"You're in luck," he said, pointing to a rack in the back. "When my pop ran this joint, he didn't stock pantyhose, believed they subverted the natural order of foundation garments."

"And I can tell you're a man who believes in nature," Laura said, selecting a pair and walking toward the dressing room. "I'll just put these on now while you zip your pants."

When she came out of the dressing room, Jeff was very apologetic and said he wanted to buy Laura a coffee or give her some underwear to make up for her inconvenience. Laura said she was in a hurry, "I'm interviewing Senator D'Amato's mother."

A giddy smile bloomed across his face. "I'm your best source," he said. "High waist half-girdle, 42X, extra stiff in the front, back support panels. But she has the behind of a woman half her age." He handed Laura a little sachet to bring to Estelle—Mrs. D'Amato—told her his name was Jeff, and that she should come back after the interview, in case he could fill her in further.

"Filling in women seems to be one of your specialties," she said, leaving.

Laura did come back after the interview, and he filled in details about himself over a bottle of white wine at the marina overlooking the water and his boat. The Golden Beauties shop and four others nearby were his father's, and he'd quit college to run them when the old man died suddenly nine years earlier. He said it was nice to finally meet an intelligent woman who didn't need a girdle. They dated that summer, went sailing on his boat in Long Island Sound, had backyard barbecues with his mother, who boasted, "All the men in this family do very well in ladies' underwear," and had extraordinary sex, as new lovers do.

When the Hong Kong transfer came, Laura figured that would end the affair. But instead, Jeff said he'd love to go. "Ma can handle the business, and half the stock is made in China. We can beat the pants off the competition buying direct, maybe source for others. What an opportunity." Laura thought, why not? Although she spent most of the next morning badgering Human Resources to see if they absolutely had to get married to get him a plane ticket and bump up her housing allowance, she knew she would say yes the minute he asked. Jeff was the first decent guy she'd dated in a long time, the first one who wasn't always trying to top her—except where it mattered—and she thought it would be good to have some company in Hong Kong. She took him to Rockville to meet her parents, who felt better about Laura bringing such a charming young man with her so far away, and his mother was also a hit. They signed prenuptial agreements—their parents insisted—held a small wedding at her family's house in November, and days later went to Hong Kong as wife and husband. Looking at the dating prospects in Hong Kong and listening to Edie complain, Laura is glad that's one thing she doesn't have to worry about.

From her desk, Laura sees producers and anchors filling the conference room for the 12:30 meeting, which takes place while FGN Asia runs two hours live from its FGN Europe sister network. CK Leung, station manager and cousin of KS Lau, the president and general manager of FGN Asia who resides in the plush 28th floor corporate suite, emerges from his office. CK is a small man with a crew cut that never went out of fashion in Hong Kong. His round eyeglasses reinforce the image of a mole burrowing behind his closed door, guarded by his secretary Iris Wong. Instead of heading for the meeting room, though, CK walks across the newsroom toward the control room, nods at Laura as he passes her desk, and pushes the button for the elevator. Laura shakes her head and grabs a pad and pen for the meeting.

She takes a seat in the conference room next to Edie. Producers, directors, supervisors and anchors are scattered around the oval table. Chinese who don't speak English cluster around Quickie, who provides simultaneous translation in a stage whisper. Lamont Chan, afternoon supervising producer, opens the meeting. He's a Chinese-American who wears his short hair slicked into a part, looking like the well behaved elementary school student he undoubtedly was, the kid who suffered through those late afternoons of Chinese school while his neighbors played stickball, but who'd parlayed his Cantonese into a big job in Hong Kong while the stickball players now run the family restaurant. Or, in Deng's case, make a dozen times more money than him and still consider Lamont a hopeless drip.

"Okay, let's settle down. First of all, CK wants you all to know how much he regrets not being able to be here. . . ."

"For the 17th consecutive day," Laura whispers to Edie.

"He has an important meeting in Zhuhai about our Chinese service that we plan to launch in April," Lamont continues. "So you've got me." Lamont flashes an angelic grin. "First, let me ask Edie for her notes on this morning's shows."

"Thanks, Lamont. The shows looked good." Edie then scans her notes, looking past the minor glitches for something significant. "We're using this story about the nude bank robber in Belgium too much. It was funny once. . . . The technical stuff is looking better. . . . There's a good package from Reuters about the fifth anniversary of the US base closing in Subic Bay. Maybe Iggy . . ." Ignatius Fernandez, idolized back in his native Philippines and a regular on the Friday 7:45 p.m. flight to Manila, not quite so regular on the Monday 9:05 a.m. flight back, ". . . can voice it. Let's get it cut. That's all on the shows.

"Looking ahead, there's the HK-Taiwan air agreement negotiations next week. Fiona," Edie says, looking at Fiona Fok, the news editor, "the talks start Wednesday, and we should have a crew for that. Possible live shot, all shows, plus *US Prime News.*"

"I'll see what I've got booked," Fiona says. "You say Wednesday?"

"We can wait, if you want to review your crew sheets. . . ."

"I'll see. . . ."

"Fiona, dear, we need to get this footage, for us and for the US network. Missing it is not on, just not on. . . ."

"Well, I can't invent crews, and Wednesday is a. . . ."

"This meeting is a priority."

"Isn't everything?" Fiona shrugs. "And if we get the shots, what's the assurance that tapes will be able. . . ?"

Nancy Black leans forward, her bulk contrasting Fiona's lack of it. "The only tapes around here we don't cut and feed are the ones we don't get. . . ."

"All right everybody," Lamont says. "Fiona, we have your assurance that the air agreement talks will be a top priority in terms of crew assignment?"

Fiona frowns and nods.

"Great. Thank you, Fiona. Anything else, Edie?"

"Just a heads up for the late shows. The US Fed chairman, Greenspan, is testifying US morning about the economy. Play it up. It's big news in the US, for US markets. And the Nikkei and the rest will likely take their cue from it tomorrow. We expect to get a package from the US, and maybe a clean feed of the testimony. Nancy, please let Laura know what comes in. . . ."

"Will do, dear," Nancy says, answering the dirty look Laura shoots across the table with a smirk.

"Thank you, Nancy," Lamont says. "I think that covers all of the show issues. The floor is open. . . ."

Old Mike Hartman, a longtime FGN US anchor, jumps in. "Lamont, two things. What kind of progress are we making on the handover countdown series? And, what's the latest from New York on what we're up to?"

"Mike, thank you. I'm glad you asked both of those questions. Last thing first, let me say that New York is completely supportive of everything we are doing, not just on the handover, but on all fronts. The feedback I get is extremely positive. They are genuinely excited about the progress we have made and the track we're on. We're trending in the precise direction and at precisely the pace forecast when corporate began the planning process for FGN Asia some eighteen months ago. New York has also assured me that this operation remains one of FGN's top operational priorities—there's that pesky word again—and that, especially regarding the handover, but overall as well, we can count on getting whatever resources we need to continue to create, expand and maintain our role as the preeminent business news network in Asia, part of the best global business network in the . . . the . . . in the world."

The downcast eyes and shaking heads among producers and anchors, even among staff that can't even understand English, reveal they know Lamont is babbling nonsense. He rolls ahead unperturbed.

"As for the handover series, we've made substantial progress. Shirley and I have come up with the graphic for it, though we're still undecided about using a live countdown clock like they have in Tiananmen Square. Maybe May can give us an update on what stories she's working on."

Pang May Pau, FGN Asia's only staff reporter, is a Hong Kong native, short and curvy with a full round face who speaks perfect English in an unlikely smoky voice with a trace of a British accent. "We're working up a series of vox pops on different issues, everything from the currency peg to border controls. And Fiona," upon whom she relies for her crew everyday, "has been extraordinarily helpful."

"Are people scared?" Old Hartman asks.

"I don't think scared is the correct word, Mike," May says. "Somewhat apprehensive, perhaps. But mostly just uncertain. For example, no one expects Hong Kong to adopt the one-child policy, but many of my friends are pregnant now, just in case."

"Your doing, Mike?" Deng asks.

"No, Deng, I'm too busy shorting the Taipei market," Old Hartman parries. "Last thing from me, the next issue of *Rabbit Ears* will be out in a week, and based on what I've been hearing and seeing in scripts, we'll focus on action verbs. Nothing enlivens writing more effectively than the proper active verb."

"We'll be. . . . Excuse me, we anticipate this edition anxiously, Mike," Lamont sniffles, giggling at his own joke.

With none of the other anchors speaking up, protocol permits producers to take the floor.

"Deng has suggested," Laura begins, largely over her anger by now, "that we change the name of the morning show to *AM Asia,* and Mike has agreed to voice a new open for us." She turns toward Shirley Hung, the graphics manager whose English is little better than Pussy's. "I'll put in the graphics order after this meeting, and I hope we can get it all done by Monday."

Quickie translates for Shirley, who tells the group, "Sure, sure. Just spell everything correct." She makes the last word sound like reversing the charges on a long distance call.

"You've signed off on this, Edie?" Lamont asks.

"Of course. Do you imagine Laura could use 'voice' as a verb without my help?" Edie says with a smile.

"Well, then it's good by me," Lamont says. "I don't think we need a sign-off from New York on that. Thanks to Deng and to Mike. And to Shirley."

Bobby Ching, the two p.m. producer, asks, "What's happening with distribution?"

"I'm glad you asked that, Bob," Lamont says. "As you know, CK isn't here because he's working on distribution in Guangdong Province. That's why we have the translation staff geared up here, for distribution inside China. . . ."

"But Guangdong's less than a half a million households at most," Ching, whose first job in TV was in distribution for MTV Asia, interrupts, "in a regional universe of half a billion. What about Japan, Korea, even Australia and other markets where we don't need translation, like Malaysia, India. . . ?"

"I'm even more glad you mentioned that, Bob," Lamont says. "Distribution right now is very important, but we have to be product driven, quality driven, not sales driven. The people up on the 28th floor are handling sales. We have to provide them with the very best product in the market to sell."

"But if a tree falls in the forest. . . ." Bobby says.

"In five years—and the people in New York talk in terms of these time frames, five years, ten years, FGN is establishing a long-term presence in Asia through us—in five years, distribution in the conventional sense won't even be an issue. Except in China, which is why it's so critical for CK to keep pressing there. In a year—two years at most—people will be able to watch our programming on their computers, wherever they are. The Internet and online video are going to revolutionize this business, change all the parameters, forever and, I believe for the better, as long as we're on the right side of the revolution in electronic media."

"So the revolution will be televised, after all," Deng says.

"We'll be busting out of the box and into people's lives," Lamont continues, oblivious to his skeptical audience, "wherever they happen to be. Remember Dick Tracy's two-way wrist TV—that's going to be a reality with computers and mobile phones that act like computers. The technology is right around the corner.

"That's not just for the better for viewers, it's going to transform the business of television in profound ways. Today we have to pay a ratings service thousands of dollars for their best guess about how many people are watching, and rely on them for details about who those viewers are. We're captive not only to their data but to their system of data collection. Let's say we want to know how many of our users—that's the terminology for the new paradigm, users, not viewers—how many users own a small business. Well, maybe Nielsen doesn't collect that information in our markets. With the Internet, we won't need Nielsen. With a mouse click we can not only count our users, we can induce them to tell us all about themselves—where they live, how much they earn, what business they're in, what they're shopping for this month, this week, today. And we can mine that data—data mining, digging for demographic gold—to make sure that we deliver not just the broad demographic groups, but the absolute individuals an advertiser wants. Furthermore, we can tailor ads to discrete users. Want to reach all the expatriate CFOs of UK companies in Asia? In a year or two, we'll be able to do that, in an absolutely verifiable fashion.

"The 20th century was the era of broadcasting. The 21st century will be the era of narrowcasting, and a whole new ballgame that very few networks are ready for.

"That's one of the great things . . . one of the greatest things about being part of FGN. We're not only at the cutting edge of financial journalism and television news. We're at the cutting edge of 21st century communications technology.

"No place on earth is more ready for this trend, for narrowcasting, and more suited to it, than Asia. That's why I'm so excited about it. FGN Asia is establishing the beachhead for the whole network in this field, and that means we'll be the trailblazers for the entire global television industry. We're going to bring this medium into the 21st century. And for Asia, the 21st century begins on July first." Lamont smiles and sighs. He takes off his glasses and wipes them, which Laura suspects is his way of checking whether his nose grew during that speech.

"Anything else?" Lamont says. "All right then, let's go out and make great television. Thanks, everyone."

As the overflow crowd leaves, Edie says to Laura, "We're already narrowcasting. Our audience couldn't get much narrower." Laura giggles and walks back to her desk, where Sara Fergis has already begun settling in. Laura sees Richard Yakamoto heading for the door, so she sits at his desk to write her *AM Asia* graphics order. She also fills out a request for audio studio time for Old Hartman. Well, at least I've fixed something today, she thinks, even if wasn't particularly broken.

Then she thinks, everybody knows, except CK. He won't care, but as a courtesy, I should tell him. Otherwise, he'll never know, she giggles. She logs on to the computer and writes him a memo.

To: CK Leung, Station Manager
From: Laura Wellesley
Re: Asia Market Morning Name Change
Date: January 9, 1997

After consulting with the anchor and getting consensus approval at today's 12:30 meeting, we have agreed that the name of the morning show will be changed to "AM Asia," effective as soon as possible, provided you have no objection. The graphics have been ordered, and Mike Hartman has agreed to voice a new open. Thank you.

CHAPTER 2

Looking for Mr. Goodbra

JEFF GOLDEN CAME TO HONG KONG searching for opportunities in women's underwear but still hasn't found the right opening. This afternoon's second meeting with Winston Lam of Glorious Morning Apparel followed the usual script. Last week, Jeff gave Lam basics of the lines he wants: underwear and bras, separates and sets, with rough design ideas on cuts and colors. He came back to the dingy office on the third floor of an industrial building in Sham Shui Po, past a reception Nazi who barked at him in apparent English, and into the conference room with a pair of mannequins in cowl neck sweaters and yellowing samples of ancient undergarments mounted on the wall, to sit at the long table, take the tea tossed at him by the tea lady, and wait twenty minutes for Lam.

When Lam and his production manager, Mr. Tan, showed up, they had bunch of ludicrous samples—full-metal-jacket underwire padded bras, girdles like his father sold back in the old days, panties big enough to cover a Honda. All synthetics with poor stitching, all white. Oh yes, they had looked at his specs, but these goods were popular with their western customers, Lam said. When Jeff convinced them that he really wanted the items he'd asked for and prices for them, the Glorious Morning team disappeared, the tea lady returned to refill his cup and he had to confront the reception Nazi to find the men's room.

Returning fifteen minutes later, Lam said he'd checked with their factories and that they could, because they are very skilled and know-ledgeable suppliers, deliver precisely what he wants. All Jeff needed to do, Lam said, was place an order with them and they'd see it through from patterns to the shipping container. Then they quoted him price estimates, FOB Hong Kong, higher than Jeff paid for the same goods in New York. Jeff thanked them and told them he'd be in touch after checking with his home office.

Now riding to the subway on a yellow and green minibus that smells of school kids in uniforms and their greasy snacks, Jeff admires Lam's *chutzpah*. But the part that either charms or annoys Jeff most, depending on his mood, always comes when he asks about production facilities. Like others in this great wall of Hong Kong garment wholesalers he's met, Lam gave him the "what does stupid *gweiloh* know about China?" look, combining amusement, pity and contempt. Jeff has gotten the same look from each of the dozen suppliers he's visited, along with bad samples, bad prices or both. Golden Beauties is definitely on the slow boat to China sourcing, and, at this moment, Jeff figures he might as well laugh about it.

He gets off the minibus with everyone else at the MTR station—MTRoo they call it—and puts his fare card through the slot to enter. Jeff enjoys this portion of the otherwise frustrating search, riding the clean, sleek, stainless steel trains and rubbing shoulders with Hong Kong. The place feels alive, has a pulse, a rapid one that reminds him of Manhattan, which Laura had reintroduced to him, so different from the quiet suburbs where he'd spent too many years. And he feels that beat—a buzz in the air coming from all directions, around every corner—wherever he goes.

As in New York, the subway jams all types together, from guys in suits and women in fashionable outfits to repairmen in greasy clothes with their tools and a computer or air conditioner that has to go back to the shop balanced precariously on a luggage carrier. Clutches of junior-high students in school uniforms spin themselves and conversations around the train's poles, oblivious to the hazard their backpacks present to those outside the circle. Grandmothers talk to each other while trying to induce inquisitive grandchildren to stay seated beside them. Filipina maids traveling alone seem focused on the grim prospect of more cooking, cleaning and errands ahead, but in groups they turn the train ride into a party on wheels, gathered around oversized woven plastic red, white and blue striped shopping bags, the only adults aboard laughing. Nervous looking young women in skirts too short for sitting anywhere but a table for two in the corner adjust their makeup, talk into a mobile phone, or both. He can't imagine how anyone can hear or be heard on a phone over the clatter of the train, the bilingual stop announcements, or the piercing "doot-doot-doot-doot-doot-doot-doot" closing door warning. But maybe the racket here is no worse than at home with three generations, mahjong tiles, something frying in the wok, Cantonese opera pots-and-pans music on the radio, and two other conversations next to you. When a phone rings, half the people in the train reach for their pocket or bag. Jeff can't even understand why anyone would want a mobile phone. Laura agrees, and they've made a pact to shoot on sight if either one of them gets one.

Jeff exits at Central Station and walks down Queen's Road past the doorman with the turban and white coat at the Lane Crawford department store toward the Midlevels escalator, Hong Kong's greatest urban transport innovation and one of the few things in town that's free. In the subway, on the streets, at the bus stops, and on the escalator, everyone strikes Jeff as busy, driven, moving up, in sharp contrast to his own lack of progress. In elevators, people instinctively reach for the "Close" button first. Even taxi doors shut automatically.

Although most people he sees are Chinese, they come in an array of shapes, sizes and physiognomies: dog faces, cat faces, moon faces, duck faces . . . this middle-aged woman blocking his way on the escalator could play the Lion in *Wizard of Oz* without makeup. No, contrary to the old saying, they don't all look alike. Add in the expatriates— westerners, Indians, Africans—in their various shades, and it seems to Jeff as if the whole world was given a shake and whoever wasn't firmly enough rooted or decided they wanted to let go, landed in Hong Kong, walking slow and talking fast.

Jeff is from the tribe that came by choice. He was the envy of his pals back on Long Island, but Jeff thought it was a dead-end street, and not even a street he'd picked. His father, Murray Golden—Murray, the Golden *Gotke* King—keeled over at age 56 from a massive stroke while playing pinochle at the beach club just before Jeff was about to begin his junior year at SUNY-Buffalo. The only child, Jeff decided he'd take some time off from school to pitch in at the five outlets of Golden Foundations and help his mother adjust to the loss.

Jeff's grandfather Isaac had been a tailor back in Russia and kept at the trade when he came to America. Murray tried, but lacked the dexterity for his father's craft. So he started selling what the old man made and, once he started mucking in *schmattes,* discovered that women's undergarments carried big margins. A girdle that cost two dollars wholesale retailed for twelve. Jeff wasn't sure about the chicken-and-egg question of whether Murray met his mother, the daughter of a brassiere maker, because he was in the business, or got into the business because he met her. In any case, the family moved to Long Island, and Murray opened Golden Foundations in Bethpage, in one of those shopping centers that sprung up around the tract developments in the 1950s with a supermarket, dry cleaner, bakery, pharmacy, hardware store, and takeout food—Chinese or Chicken Delight or a pizza parlor—along with a couple of other specialty shops, like a pet shop or jeweler.

Jeff hardly ever heard his parents talk about the business during his childhood, even though his father spent nine hours a day at it, twelve on Thursdays, six days a week, and his mother kept the books. Most evenings, his mother carried the conversation, telling his father about the doings among the neighborhood housewives and children. Jeff's mediocre progress in school and athletics got extensive hearing. They were also remarkably casual about his baby sister, Faith, who died during a flu epidemic when Jeff was two. "Things happen," his father said at the time, and often in the years that followed, "whether you like it or not."

Over the years, Murray opened more stores, five in all, but his routine never seemed to change. Leave the house at 8:30 every morning, come home by seven (9:30 on Thursdays), watch the news while eating dinner, then read a library book, usually biographies, while his mother alternately cackled at the television and expressed disappointment that nothing was ever on. Jeff did his homework or watched his own TV in his room. On weekends during the summer, they'd go to a beach club on the south shore, Jeff and his mother on Saturdays while his father worked, the three of them on Sundays. During the winter, they'd visit friends and family, or have other couples over for card games while Jeff and their children, always around his age, played Monopoly, Strat-O-Matic baseball, or doctor, depending on the company.

Jeff can count on one hand the number of times he visited the stores before he began working with Murray on Saturdays his first year of high school. Outside, it was the 1980s with purple hair, yuppies, and Victoria's Secret ("If it's such a secret, why is she sending out three million catalogues?" Murray always asked), but inside the stores The Beatles hadn't appeared on *Ed Sullivan* yet. Brassieres (Murray always said "brassiere") that endowed the wearer with a pair of torpedoes on her chest, girdles with hooks at the bottom for stockings on headless beige mannequins cut off above the knee standing atop the high-riser drawers holding the stock. Formica counters ran half the length of the store on each side, foundation garments on the left, soft goods like stockings and underwear on the right, with dressing rooms and fitting areas at the end of the store. The walls were white, the drawer units eggshell lacquer, the curtains beige, the fluorescent lights bright, the ambience clinical. "This is the way my ladies like it," Murray said. He always called the customers "my ladies."

All goods on display were white, off-white, beige or peach. Murray did have black and even red "undergarments" socked away in the drawers. "I sell a lot of black to the sisters from the Dominican order," he explained, but there wasn't going to be a whiff of anything sexy showing in the shop. That matched the sensibilities of his "mature" clientele, aging along with Murray. Jeff's friends in high school envied his professional opportunity to see women in their underwear, but he brushed that off saying, "It's bad enough seeing them dressed." Murray modeled himself after the reliable neighborhood druggist: you could trust him with your intimate details and he'd find something behind the counter to fix it. He knew most of his ladies by name, asked about their families, and never chided them for pounds and inches the years had added. "Comfort is what we sell," Murray explained to Jeff. "That starts with the customer feeling comfortable in the store, with the storekeeper."

During one of his many moments as a teenager when Jeff—never especially studious, smart or popular—was wondering what he was going to do with his life, he asked his father about his choices. "Choices? I had to go out and make a living. Period," Murray said. "You're lucky you have that luxury, to choose something that you like, something you want to do, something for which you maybe have a passion."

"Do you have passion for what you do, pop?"

"I have passion for making a good living for my family. I'd dig ditches if I had to do that. And every day when I open door to the store, I'm thankful that I can do it like this instead of digging ditches." The stores never seemed especially busy on Saturdays, maybe $300 turnover, and the Goldens lived modestly in their three-bedroom split level, but there was no denying that Golden Foundations had made Jeff's childhood comfortable.

Murray's sudden death kick-started Jeff's adult life. His mother knew only the bare bones of the store operations. His father had run the store in Bethpage, the original, and the other four were managed by ladies like Murray's customers, "like family," she said, and like herself. Jeff felt that if he could handle the business for a few months, maybe the whole year, his mother would sort things out, maybe get another manager or bring in someone else to do the books so she could take Murray's old role, and he'd finish college. But from the start he could sense his mother was comfortable doing what she did, staying home, keeping the books as something to do between Hadassah meetings and canasta and going into the city for a matinee with the girls every couple of months. She wasn't going to change without a push. Whatever was going to happen, Jeff would have to make it happen.

At first, Golden Foundations wasn't just a job for Jeff, it was an adventure. He took on responsibility, made decisions about what to order, and hired people. And he had money, unlike his friends who were still in school or just getting started. His mother showed him that his father had drawn $500 a week in salary, "So now that's what you'll be getting." As a tribute to his father, Jeff resolved to earn it. He began paying so much attention to the books his mother said, "Are you trying to put me out of a job?" Instead of being a distant flower whose fragrance lightly perfumed the Golden home, the business became almost the sole topic of conversation between him and his mother. From the books, Jeff saw that sales were barely covering costs, and that the trend had been steadily downward for several years. Murray's ladies were dying, moving to Florida, giving up their girdles, and no one under 50 wore foundation garments anymore. "We've got to change things, Ma," he said. And he did.

First, he wrote a letter to all of Murray's ladies: the stores always collected names and addresses. The letter, from him and his mother, thanked customers for their patronage over the years and for their expressions of condolence for Murray's untimely death. The ladies could be assured that the business was remaining in the family, under the leadership of Murray's wife and son, so customers could expect the same custom service and attention that Murray and his staff had always given them. There may be changes in the appearances of the stores, but inside, they'll always find the personal attention that has made Golden Foundations the "foundation of your comfort" for more than 25 years. For two weeks, Jeff and his mother spent their evenings handwriting customers' names on the 3,000 letters, signing their own names to each, and addressing the envelopes. "A personal touch never goes wrong," he said, sounding like his father.

Then Jeff set about figuring out what changes to make. After work and on days off, he'd drive to Victoria's Secret outlets—that clicking was the sound of his father spinning in his grave—department stores, even sex boutiques, to check out the merchandise and the customers. In the stores, Jeff ripped out the old drawers and counters, put most of the merchandise on racks where people could see it, put in glass display counters, carpeted the floors, and added display windows at each store done up professionally like a window at Tiffany's and changed weekly. (Five windows were created, then moved from store to store to get maximum bang for buck.) While his mother conceded shops she liked had these features, she griped about the cost.

"We can get a loan from any bank on the island," Jeff assured her. "Our credit is good."

"A loan," she clucked. "That would kill your father." Though Jeff had sufficient grasp of the company finances to know it didn't have the capital for these renovations, the bills all got paid without him visiting a banker. "Thank your genius bookkeeper," his mother would say whenever he asked for details.

He changed the name of the stores from Golden Foundations to Golden Beauties. He expanded the lines to include swimwear, sexy lingerie, sachets, exercise clothes, even pantyhose. He took out an ad in *Newsday* to promote a special men's night just before Valentine's Day. When that worked, he tried workout nights, petite nights, swimsuit nights, even a Father's Day night ("Give the man in your life what he really wants, in a gorgeous wrapper.") While business didn't boom, Jeff's changes reversed the downward trend and boosted the cash flow. Just as important to Jeff, it gave him a sense of command and pride of ownership. The stores were his Golden Beauties now.

That was the first two years. He'd shaken the dust off a 25-year-old business that needed freshening. Running the stores then settled into a dull routine, and a time consuming one. Sure, he could sneak out for a couple of hours to go work out or even see an afternoon game at Shea Stadium, but he had to show up everyday. One by one, Murray's ladies managing the other branches went the way of the clientele they embodied: retired, moved, died. The new managers, in two cases Murray's ladies' daughters, were good, but they needed to know he was watching. More merchandise and bigger turnover had raised the stakes from his father's day. Jeff had to stay on top of things more carefully.

And he was still living at home. At first, he never thought about moving out. His mother needed him and wanted him there. She said she'd never spent a night in that house, or any other, by herself. Even if Jeff didn't always make it home by dawn (when they couldn't use a date's place, he'd suggest a motel, which really turned on some women), she felt reassured knowing they still lived under the same roof. She liked the company, and she always kept three placemats on the kitchen table, just like when Murray was alive. Jeff thought of the house as corporate headquarters, another reason to stay. As he was sure his father must have, he learned to tune out his mother when she recited the latest neighborhood gossip or banalities she picked up from television. After three years of running the stores, and spending another year taking evening courses for his certificate, Jeff used his savings and the money from his father's insurance policy to buy a sailboat, which cost almost as much as a house, was more interesting than a girlfriend, and gave him a place to call his own. He named the boat *Golden Beauty*. In the stores, he hired young women, usually community college students, as sales clerks based largely on how much he thought he'd enjoy screwing them and how likely it seemed they'd let him.

Laura had caught him at that game when she came in that morning almost a year ago for a pair of pantyhose. When she gave him shit about it, he discovered he enjoyed it, figured they could have fun together. She was good looking enough, too, with dirty-blond hair cut short and parted to the side and that pixie face with sparkling eyes, narrow chin, and a thin nose that sloped up at the end. She was about his size—a change from these small, dark and handsome numbers like Rosalinda—and, it turned out, about his speed.

Dating Laura reminded Jeff of what he'd been missing in his suburban shopkeeper's routine. She lived in Manhattan, so he drove into the city regularly for the first time since he was checking out the competition the year after his father died. Although he saw lots of people in the stores, he didn't really connect with them, except to sell them panties or a leotard. The help rarely stimulated him above the belt. Jeff and Laura went to trendy restaurants, parties with interesting people, reminding Jeff how little was happening in his life. He found Laura a bit too self-absorbed, competitive, and impressed with herself, but he did appreciate the way she kept him on his toes and had opened his eyes.

Then came her Hong Kong announcement. As she told him about Franklin Global Networks, owner of the *Financial Journal,* giving her a transfer, his first reaction, silently, was, "What are the chances Golden Beauties is going to transfer me to China?" Then his mind started racing. What if I told her I wanted to go with her? Marry her? Sell the businesses? He told Laura the news was a big shock, so he wanted to sleep on it before reacting. As he drove home, he thought, half the stuff in the stores comes from China. After almost ten years, he knew the merchandise.

He could try exporting from there. He'd still be in ladies' damned underwear, but ladies' underwear had been good to him and his family. Whatever they got for selling the stores would give him a little stake to get started over there. His mother might take it hard, but if he said he was doing it for love, for his new wife, she couldn't complain, even though Laura was a *shikse*. Ma was after him to get married, start a family, repeatedly pointing out that the house was big enough for a wife and kids.

When he got home, his mother was already asleep. He called Laura and told her, "I didn't need to sleep on it to know how much I'd miss you. I want to marry you and go with you."

"You know, Jeff, ever since I was a little girl, I dreamed my Prince Charming would call in the middle of the night to propose to me. At least tell me you're on your knees."

Yeah, she'll keep me on my toes, Jeff thought, and he actually knelt on the floor of his bedroom. "I'm digging my knees into the shag carpet here, honey. Will you marry me?"

"Now I need some time to think. Call me in the morning. But thank you. It's lovely of you to ask, Your Highness."

Jeff talked to Laura's office voicemail three times that next morning before she called him back and said yes. Jeff phoned several business brokers, and, after sketching out the state of the stores for each, heard their largely depressing assessments. Specialty stores in old shopping centers weren't worth much, so he'd be lucky to get someone to pay one times sales for them, probably less if he wanted to sell five as a package. A little back-of-the-envelope figuring told Jeff the deal might clear $1 million, which had a nice ring to it, but wasn't nearly as much as he'd hoped for. Naturally, the brokers said, they'd need to take a look at the books and talk to his mother. One broker mentioned something didn't sound right about the net versus cash flow: "I'm not saying someone's stealing from you, more like maybe you're stealing from someone."

Jeff called his mother to make sure she'd be home that night so they could talk, and when she said she was making lasagna, he stopped at the bakery to get garlic breadsticks and some of those flaky butterfly pastries she liked for dessert. He even bought a bottle of Chianti with straw wrapped around the bottom. He arrived home as usual at 7:20 and washed up. She had the lasagna on the kitchen table, the breadsticks in a basket, and the corkscrew ready on the table when he sat down.

"You know, your father and I had this wine when we went to Italy. Oh, that was lovely, the summer after your sister died," his mother said, as Jeff opened the bottle. "You stayed with the Milkens."

"Let me pour you a little, Ma."

"You can pour me a lot. I'm not driving."

"To your health, Ma. *L'chayim.*" They both took a gulp. She dished out lasagna, Jeff took some salad, passed the bowl to her, and had another sip of wine.

"That was a lovely place, Italy. It was really beautiful, colorful. I don't just mean the place, the museums. . . . Oh, that was all fantastic, but the people. They were what was really different. They knew how to live. Not like your father, *al'eva shalom.* Worked himself to death. No, in Italy, they know how to live, la duchy vita, they call it. The good life." She sighed, and took a sip of wine and held her glass toward Jeff. "To the good life."

"Ma, I think it's time Golden Beauties went international. . . ."

"Open a store in Italy? You wouldn't get home until much later. . . ."

"Ma, you know Laura. . . ."

"Oh, yes, the *shikse,* she's a . . . a newspaperwoman—that's her, no? Lois Lane, I call her."

"Ma, we're going to get married . . ."

"It's about time. A Jewish girl would be better, but your mother would never. . . ."

". . . and we're going to live in Hong Kong."

"In Hong Kong? Hong Kong in China you're going to live?"

"Yes. Laura's job is transferring her there. They're giving her an apartment, and they'll pay for her, and me, to move there."

"You love this girl?"

"Yes." Jeff sipped wine. "Of course. Otherwise, why would I marry her and go to Hong Kong . . . to China?"

"Then, *zei gesundt.*" She dug into her lasagna in earnest and grabbed a breadstick from the basket. "I love these garlic ones."

"I've also thought about the business, and about you, Ma."

"I'll be fine. I have friends. With Suzanne, a trip to visit you I could make."

"Of course you'll be fine, Ma. If I didn't think you'd be fine, would I do this?" His mother looked up from her plate and smiled. "But about the business. . . . You know, most of the merchandise now is made in China and around there. I think it's time that we got into wholesaling. . . ."

"You know, that was what your grandfather did, my father Schmuel Rabinowitz, a very big man in brassieres. . . ."

"I think there are a lot of opportunities there. To begin with, we could supply our own stores. Cut out the middlemen, really cut our costs." He thoughtfully chewed a small bite of lasagna, then asked, "But, Ma, do you want to run the stores?"

"Oy, Jeffrey, you know how it is. Your old mother is comfortable staying home, doing the books. Let somebody else be out there in the public."

"Then, I think we should sell."

"Sell?"

"Yes, sell the stores."

"The stores we should sell?"

"Yes. I spoke to a couple of brokers and. . . ."

"To brokers you spoke?"

"Yes, Ma. They said that, depending on the leases and a few other things, we could probably sell for gross annual sales, maybe a little more, depending. . . ."

"Ah . . . depending."

"So, the stores might bring two, maybe two-and-a-half million. After taxes, we could have maybe three-quarters of a million . . . dollars."

"Three-quarters of a million . . . dollars we could have." She nodded and took another forkful of lasagna.

"I think it's the most sensible thing to do, if no one is going to look after the stores. Like pop always said, 'The eye of the farmer makes the hen grow fat.' We could write into the contracts that we—our wholesaling from China—would be a preferred supplier for the stores, guarantee a certain percentage. . . ."

"That all sounds very simple. And very logical."

"All right. Then tomorrow. . . ."

"But it wouldn't work."

"Wouldn't work? Why not?"

"Ah, Jeffrey. You don't really understand your father's business."

"Of course, I don't know it as well as you and him. I don't have 30 years experience, but from running the stores. . . ."

"Jeffrey, it's not the stores. For your store, I'll get another manager. My friend Irene's daughter is looking for a job. Nice girl. If you weren't already attached to this *shikse,* I'd try to make a *shitach.* A beautiful girl, with a very nice figure, like Rita Hayworth. The stores will be all right."

"But the headaches, Ma. There's a lot of things you don't know that go on, and you have to watch. Even your cousin Thelma, she used to steal. . . ."

"The stores are just a little bit, Jeffrey."

"A little bit? A little bit of what?

"The stores are a loss. Since you fixed them up, they're not such a big loss, but still a loss."

"How are they a loss?"

"Listen to your bookkeeper. A good week, you gross fifteen hundred, the others gross a little less. All told maybe six thousand a week. Payrolls are almost half of that. Cost of goods is a third. Overhead, accountants, electricity. . . ."

"So, if they're a loss, why keep them?"

"Because they're anchors."

"Anchors?"

"Yes. Your father believed they drive the business, they drive the traffic."

"The traffic? The business?"

"For the shopping center."

"So we take a loss for that? Let the owner of the shopping center worry about that."

"I do."

"You do?" Jeff chuckled. "Ma, why should you worry for the owner of the shopping center?"

"Because I am the owner. Of the shopping centers." She took a sip of wine. "I never told you. Your father never told you, so why should I? I thought what you did with the stores was very nice. It was clever, and I was very proud of you."

"But I don't understand. . . ."

"Your father opened his first store and, in those days, he worked by himself, he made a living. But he didn't really know ladies' undergarments, not like my father did, but he knew with the stores he was never going to make a big living. But real estate he knew. Don't ask me how, but he knew. He had a head for what's a good location for retail, like some people have a head for music or drawing. It's little things, he'd say, where are the schools and train stations in relation to the houses so which way do cars go, especially in the morning, where do you get foot traffic. . . . You went somewhere with him, he'd say, 'I'd never put a store on this road. There's not enough lights, so people don't stop, they think they'll just keep going home, or god forbid they're on the wrong side of the road, they take their life in their hands to make a left turn into the parking lot.' He knew, just from looking. The first shopping center, where your store is, he got a loan from my father and your Uncle Ben, and he bought it. The ladies' undergarment business is very good for a shopping center. First of all, it was ladies who came there. So they'd also go to the supermarket there, the dry cleaner. When they'd come in to Murray, and he'd do the measurements and order a garment for them—one trip. They'd come back for a fitting, and he'd tell them he'd fix it for them—he hardly did a thing mostly, but always said he would—that's two trips. Then they'd come pick up the garment—three trips for one girdle. A seven-dollar profit on the girdle and seven happy tenants."

"So what about the other stores?"

"Once he had the one shopping center, he could borrow from a bank. He'd find a good location, then look into the owners. A widow, maybe with children who didn't get along, partners fighting, a bankruptcy once in Plainview. He'd come in, open a Golden Foundations, and look for other tenants to generate traffic. A ballet school or a place for music lessons. The mother brings the kids, has an hour to kill, doesn't want to go home, so she does a few errands. Always nice tenants like that. No record stores or those dope shops where you might get a rough element. Family places. . . ."

"And you run this?"

"Now I do, yes. I have a very good manager. As a matter of fact, he's Chinese. His parents have the takeout place in the shopping center in Syosset, and your father knew him since he was little, Jerry Liu. Jerry Lewis, I call him."

"You own five shopping centers?"

"We own five shopping centers. You and me. When you finished college, your father thought maybe you would come in on that side of the business, like Donald Trump did with his father. . . ."

"But. . . ."

"But your father died, and who could think straight?" His mother sighed. "You seemed interested in running the store, the stores. The real estate, with Jerry Lewis, it runs itself. When there's vacancies, he finds a tenant, collects the rents, makes the contracts. . . . He's a lawyer. It's funny, no, a Jew with a Chinese lawyer. But, you know what they say, 'Pretty clever, these Chinese.' I guess you'll find out for yourself over there in Hong Kong."

"So, I could. . . . While I was running the stores. . . . I didn't have to run the stores."

"Nobody forced you, *tateleh*. But you seemed to enjoy it. And I thought, well, the girls come in and talk to him about their underwear. . . . On *Sally* last week on the television, they had a guy. . . ."

"I thought I was doing something important, for you, for pop. . . ."

"And you were, you are. Somebody had to fix up those stores. Even my friends thought they were too old fashioned. You seemed to be very happy. . . ."

"I was, but I didn't realize. . . ."

"Your father always said, 'If you wanted to do things different, why didn't you?' Nobody forced you to run the stores. And you did very well, you learned a business, and now you can try the business in China. I think that's wonderful."

"The real estate. . . . You want to keep that?"

"Of course. I hardly lift a finger. Jerry Lewis takes good care of it, of me, of us. The taxes things, when your father died that could have buried us, forced us to sell like some of the people your father bought from. But Jerry Lewis fixed it up. I don't know all the details exactly, but it's in the Caribbean, the company. When I die, there will be nothing for you to worry about."

"But now. . . . You don't want to sell?"

"Why should I? I have no headaches with the properties, and they throw off very nice cash," she said, picking at her salad. "No. The time to sell would be, your father always said, when one of those big chains comes sniffing around, like Kmart, either to buy us out or to build someplace else in the area. The supermarkets, they're always looking to buy, but we give them a good deal and they stay. They don't want to move, and they don't want to build. Besides, where are they going to build? One thing about land—they're not making any more of it, especially not on Long Island."

"What—you know, if things were different—what did pop want me to do?"

"Oh, who knows? But I think he was always looking to go further out. People keep moving further out. Riverhead was potato farms when we moved out here. Now, they're getting an outlet mall, I hear."

"So, instead I was running an underwear store. . . ."

"Nobody planned for your father to die like that. You're telling me you're disappointed. . . ?"

"No, I just. . . ."

"Who wasn't disappointed that your father died? He was my husband, you know. But his main concern was always that we were well provided for, and we have been. We are." She took a forkful of lasagna and washed it down with a sip of wine. "It was a circumstance, a situation beyond our control. We did what we all thought was best back then. We can't go back and do it over. We did what we did, what's done is done." She refilled their wine glasses, mostly hers. "I think this thing in China could be a wonderful opportunity for you, on top of getting married. I know you're not a little boy anymore. You know women's undergarments inside and out, and I think you'll do very well for yourself over there. And, of course, we can keep you on salary while you're there, as our sourcer, to help get you started. I'm sure in time you'll be the biggest man in Chinese underwear."

Jeff had promised to call Laura after he spoke to his mother. But he sat in his room with a half glass of wine, trying to figure out what to tell her. He'd wanted out of Long Island, but he'd discovered a good reason to stay. There was real money here, the kind of money he only imagined getting close to when he saw those 60-foot yachts on the Sound bounding past his little sloop. Jeff figured he could learn shopping centers like he learned ladies' underwear. After all, he'd spent more time in shopping centers than he had in ladies' underwear.

But his mother hadn't said what he now realized he wanted to hear. She hadn't said, "Stay, Jeffrey. Don't run off to Asia with this *shikse* you barely know. Stay and let me and Jerry Lewis teach you our multimillion-dollar real estate business." One of her favorite expressions was "It's not what you say that counts, it's what you don't say." Still, it could be worth talking to Jerry Liu. Maybe he'd be interested in marrying Laura and moving to Hong Kong.

He let his mother answer the phone when it rang, even though he knew it was Laura. "It's my future daughter-in-law," his mother called to him.

"Hi, Laura."

"Hi, darling. So I guess you broke the news to your mother. . . ."

"Yeah, and. . . ."

"She seems to be taking it pretty well," Laura said. "Not losing a son, she just told me, but gaining a guest room. Two guest rooms, here and in Hong Kong."

"She told me. . . ."

"I spoke to my parents, thanks for asking, and they're delighted, if somewhat bewildered. But bewildered is pretty standard for them. Listen, they want us to come down this weekend. They want to meet you, and your mother."

"Well, I. . . ."

"And they insist on having a reception or something at the house, their house."

"There's. . . ."

"I told them there's no need, but they insist. We can get the licenses here, or we can do it there. They even said they'd find a rabbi, or at least someone with a beard, for the ceremony, if you want that. It would have to be on the sixth. At the same time, I can pick up whatever things I need from there and bring them back with me for the movers. I scheduled them for the eighth, at my place and yours. But you'll have to call them to confirm the address. And I asked about your boat, but HR said there's no way they'd pay for moving that, and that we couldn't afford a dock in Hong Kong anyway. But a guy in the office says he'd be interested in buying it, if you decide to sell it. That's my report."

"Sounds great," Jeff sighs. It had all gone too far to stop now. "I'll call the mover. The number's at the store. I'll call tomorrow."

"Okay. Listen, I've got a million things to deal with, and everything's less than a month away. So I'm going to get off the phone here."

"Yeah. Me, too."

"Tomorrow night, Rita wants us to see her opening. . . ."

"Right."

"I can meet you there, that gallery on Spring. Around seven. Then you can see your fiancée's opening. It's been a while. . . ."

"Okay. See you tomorrow.

"I love you, Jeff."

"Yeah. Love you. Bye."

Jeff sighed. He'd created his own situation beyond his control, like what his father did by dropping dead. But tomorrow morning, after a night to sleep on it, he could talk to Laura, explain things to her, call the whole thing off, and stay here to get his share of those shopping centers, grow that business the way he grew Golden Beauties. In a few weeks, since his mother hadn't started hemorrhaging when he mentioned moving, he'd even begin looking for his own place. He'd restart his life, but here, as the next Donald Trump, the way his father had wanted it. Ladies' underwear wasn't going to stand between Jeff and what he deserved anymore.

CHAPTER 3

Proper Gardens

B Y THE TIME JEFF CLIMBS THE ESCALATOR past Gypsy Café, where a HK$900 bill—that's like 120 US bucks—for two salads, a pasta and a bottle of Australian wine had turned him against eating out, even though Laura paid, and the lime-green mosque that lends its name to their building's cross street, he's not just awash in the urban floorshow of Hong Kong, he's dripping with sweat inside his raincoat. This morning's cold and clammy has turned sticky.

He leaves the escalator at Mosque Junction—*Mo Lo Miu Gai*—and turns right and then left at the corner of Peel Street—*Bai Li Gai*—for the short, steep climb to their building, an eighteen-story needle that the escalator wraps around on its climb to Robinson Road, the York Avenue of Hong Kong's expatriate lifestyle. When he first saw the tall, skinny building perched on a 60-degree incline, Jeff was reluctant to enter. The landlord, Kennedy Kwong who'd lived in the US and Canada before returning to Hong Kong, noticed and assured him, "It's been here nine years and hasn't fallen down yet."

"That might mean it's due," Laura replied that day.

The name of the building—every building in Hong Kong has a name, which, annoyingly, people tell you before the address—is Prosper Gardens, written in English and presumably its Chinese equivalent—though for all Jeff knows, the characters could say, "Stupid *gweilohs* pay $15,000 a month to live here"—on the faded brown tiles above the entrance. The "s" in Prosper is missing, but the comparatively clean spot in the tile makes the name easy enough to read.

The name reminds Jeff of his business struggles as he opens the metal gate into the concrete courtyard with a rusting tricycle, under the alcove past the attendant asleep at the wooden desk guarding the gate to the lobby. He opens that gate and walks up the stairs, checks their empty mailbox, then down the stairs to the elevator. Dew flecked with dirt has condensed on the tiles in the hallway. Jeff doesn't see any greater evidence of prosperity here than he does of gardens. As he rides the elevator to fifteen, instinctively ducking away from the scrape just above eight, Jeff seethes about the Winston Lams of the world making it so tough for him to prosper. He belongs back on Long Island, back home where the only Lam of interest would be on a souvlaki spit, putting his feet up and letting the dough roll in from five shopping centers. As he unlocks the gate to apartment 15A, pulls the silver ring through the lion's nose to open it, then turns his key in the door, and pushes it open until it jams against the wicker chair, just enough room to squeeze inside, he's ready to cry.

Laura has beaten him to it. She's sitting in the middle of the love seat with her legs tucked under her, sobbing quietly, her head in her hands, a glass of red wine on the dollhouse-sized coffee table. She looks up, then drops her head back into her hands. He sits next to her, hugs her and says, "Sweetheart, it'll be all right."

"Oh, Jeff," she sniffles. "I'm sorry. I just . . . I don't think I can do it."

"Do what?"

"This job. My stupid job" She breaks out of his embrace, wipes her eyes and sits up. "It's not like being a reporter. It's like being a traffic cop. A traffic cop at the Indianapolis 500."

"But it's just been a few weeks. . . ."

"It's been more than two months," she says after a sip of wine. "There's so much to remember. A million details that have nothing to do with the news, nothing to do with journalism. It's all for television." She pauses for a big sniffle. "The almighty god of television. Technical details, like I can't go from a tape to a box, but I can go from a box to a tape. Or that a package without a sig-out needs a tag. I'll never remember all of it."

"Well, just listening to you, I see you've learned a lot in two months," Jeff says, managing to smile. "I don't have the slightest idea what you're talking about. You can already speak TV."

"And in the control room," she continues, unappeased, "there are like a dozen people. I still can't even figure out what everybody does. And, of course, I can't ask them, because none of them, except the director, speak English. My graphics girl, this teenager, can't speak English, and she has to write the fonts and spell them correctly. And she doesn't know English, except for 'okay, okay' when she screws up." Laura takes another sip of wine. "I have to watch the show and pay attention to fifteen other things, too, plus talk to the anchor and the director. They should call it the out-of-control room." She allows herself a brief smile.

"The other thing is that it takes me so long, still, to put the show together, do the rundown. I have to know everything that's going on. When I was writing for the *Journal,* I just had to know the story I was writing. I could concentrate on that. As the producer, I've got to know every story on my show, plus all the stories I've decided not to do, along with all that technical stuff. It still takes me six hours to get the show together. Sara, the *Market Wrap* producer, she does hers in four. I'm in the middle of my first hour, and I'm still working on the second hour. And I'm still making mistakes in the rundown, missing directions in scripts, and writing stories way too long. Every block, I'm in constant terror that I'll miss the time cue. . . ."

"You'll get the hang of it," Jeff says, hitting his time cue.

"Maybe. But do I really want to? I mean, is this what I want out of life? Go to bed at six and get up at midnight? I can't even sleep with my husband because we'll wake each other up and both be useless."

Jeff hugs her again. "We'll find a way to make it work, sweetheart. We'll get in a routine. Have a little workout, then dinner. . . ."

"Damn it, I'm sorry," she says, breaking away from his hug. "We were supposed to go to the gym. . . ."

"We still can. Just put your cocktail aside, young lady, and. . . ."

"It's not my first." She sighs. "Now that I've had my cry, I want a nap. How about if you come tuck me in, mister, a little workout in the home gym? After a day like today, I can use a good tucking."

"Afternoon delight," Jeff says. They kiss and move to her bedroom, where the air conditioner always runs to block out the humidity and the blinds are always closed, blocking out the view of the escalator below and the massive white brick apartment building across Robinson Road.

For Laura, sex with Jeff is the one time she doesn't think about television or the nasal drone of Cantonese offending her ears or the smell that seems to follow her everywhere these days, the burning rubber aroma of that stuff they call stinky tofu, one name around here that—unlike "Proper Gardens"—makes sense. Even with the excitement—and it's always exciting for her with Jeff, to the point where she sometimes babbles uncontrollably without any idea what she's saying—it's the one time of day she feels relaxed. It's the one place she feels completely competent, able to fulfill everyone's expectations, including her own. When she reads things in magazine or hears other women, like Edie, talking about new positions and such, she allows herself an inward snicker: if it ain't broke, don't fix it.

"Lovely tucking," she tells Jeff. "After my little nap, let me take you out for dinner."

"I can just go down to Wellcome and get something to wok up," Jeff says. So far, she's been paying for eating out, "just until you get your feet under you here," but he's worried that could change with the next bill. His mother's US$500 a week doesn't go very far divided by HK$900 dinners. Besides, it doesn't feel right, Laura paying, especially Laura signing the dinner bill while everyone seems to be watching.

"Oh, you're so sweet." She's glad the most competent cook in house has volunteered.

"That's why you married me."

"When I get this all under control, I'm going to take you away for a weekend at one of those hotels up at the Gold Coast," Laura says. "Forty-eight hours of eating, drinking and screwing."

"We can try that here, any weekend you're ready," Jeff says.

"I suppose," she says. "Consider that a warm up."

They embrace. Jeff gets off the bed and gathers up his clothes.

"Wake me up in time to get a good night's sleep," Laura says as he closes the bedroom door, thinking, no, I married you because ... because you were the most different and interesting guy I knew and because you were willing to come to Hong Kong. It's the biggest decision I've ever made, and, unlike the hundreds of decisions I make everyday in the control room—the out-of-control room—it's one I don't have to analyze or reconsider. She nods off thinking, "If only I'd told Dick my editor I wanted to cover *Carnivale* in Rio or South African wines instead...."

Jeff tosses his clothes onto his bed and turns into the bathroom between their bedrooms to wash up at the sink sized for a bus restroom. He steps out, turns, and he's in his bedroom, precisely the length of his bed plus headboard *cum* night table, with a built-in closet along the opposite wall, and just enough room to walk sideways between them. He positions himself between the closet doors and swings them open to pull out jeans and a tee-shirt. As he crabwalks to the door, he thinks he sees someone in the window of the next building. Why not? It's about three feet away. You could have dinner with the neighbors without anyone leaving their apartment.

One step to the left, two steps to the right across the living room, and he's in the kitchen, big enough for two if one of them stands in the sink, which Kennedy nearly made them do to confirm the "partial sea view" his ad promised: "I want you to trust me," he said, pointing out the sliver of Victoria Harbor between the highrises though the window over the two-burner gas cooker. "Only expats on big packages have ovens," Kennedy assured them convincingly. At HK$15,000 a month, almost $2000 US, Jeff's calculated the place costs $100 per step. He takes the rice cooker, a handy item Kennedy included in the furnishings, from the top of the refrigerator, puts it on counter next to the sink, then repositions himself to open the freezer door. He takes out the rice—in a cupboard, the roaches get it—and scoops out two cupfuls, enough for them tonight plus Laura's lunch tomorrow. He covers the rice with boiled water from a redeployed wine bottle on the refrigerator door, closes the cooker, plugs it in, checks the fridge for anything useful for dinner, then takes the elevator down, ducking away from the scrape above eight.

He turns left outside the gate and walks up the concrete stairway under the escalator to Robinson Road—*Loh Bi Sahn Do,* according to Kennedy, who taught them the street names in Cantonese so they could get home by taxi. Jeff hardly ever takes taxis, but he practices the names for when he's rich. The stairway always smells of dog shit and, with the escalator above, smooth concrete walls along the sides and a broad apartment block in front, is a sound tunnel for the noise of buses grinding around the curve above. Yet there's an old man sitting on a concrete bench on one landing and a pair of Filipina amahs chatting in their "badda-barrang" language on another, one of them holding the leash of a three-foot-tall Doberman and a plastic bag for cleaning up after it.

He reaches Robinson Road and illegally crosses Seymour Road, tiptoeing along the iron pedestrian fence on the far corner until it ends at the bus stop. Elsewhere, he's learned to respect pedestrian fences. At first, he dismissed them as a crutch for amateurs and old ladies. But then, trying to avoid climbing a pedestrian bridge in Causeway Bay, he hopped a fence and got caught in the middle of the six-way intersection plus tram tracks. He's also discovered the hard way that old ladies, with their deceptively wide elbow spans and umbrellas, deserve respect, too.

He enters the red and yellow themed Wellcome supermarket with tonight's menu sketched out in his head. He cruises supermarkets in other neighborhoods—they have free telephones and he takes advantage when he's out; the phone company allows unlimited local calls, and he's even found a restaurant in Wanchai with a phone on the sidewalk that passers-by can use—and knows this Wellcome abounds in exotic expatriate items such as cheese and pasta supplementing Chinese staples such as noodles—a full aisle of them—and dried squid snacks, too salty for Jeff's taste, by the dozens.

In the crowded produce aisle, he bypasses the California iceberg lettuce at HK$30 a head—four bucks!—for a bunch of the local green leaf, finding one that's not too brown at the bottom or top. He skips the Dutch hothouse tomatoes at HK$48 per kilo and surveys the Chinese cellopacks until he finds a threesome with one ripe enough for tonight. He moves to the fresh meat cooler. He considers the portion-packed spicy ginger chicken, complete with onion, green and red pepper, scallion, garlic and ginger, all pre-sliced, plus two packets of hot bean sauce, convenient, but HK$80. It's like you're paying someone a US dollar a minute for slicing and dicing. Boneless chicken breasts are HK$65 for two. They must be kidding. Here's a pack that expires today, marked down to HK$40. That's fine; it'll get cooked today. Back to produce for a bunch of scallions, and—HK$68 a kilo for red pepper? Ouch. Here's four green ones that feel crisp in a package for HK$18. Enough garlic and onions in the fridge, he's not crazy about ginger, and, at HK$25 for the tub, these white mushrooms aren't outrageously expensive and they'll soak up the sauce nicely. He swoops down the condiment aisle for vinegar, passing up the HK$45 bottles of salad dressing. In the wine section, Jeff sees the red Laura's drinking costs HK$146, a violation of his $10 rule. Here's a nice Bulgarian on sale for HK$25—$3.50, can't beat that. He puts two bottles in his basket and heads for the checkout. He hands over a couple of red HK$100s, still funny money to him, except there's nothing funny about how little of it he has, and gets surprised when his change is coins only. Oh, well, still beats HK$900 in the restaurant.

Jeff carries his plastic bags around the curve, down the stairway and the hill, through the Prosper Gardens gates, up and down the stairs and up the elevator to the apartment. He writes "J" on the shopping receipt and puts it in the envelope on the refrigerator door for them to settle up at the end of the week, then slices, dices, spices and wok-fries the chicken and vegetables in a soy and vinegar sauce, to be served with the jar of chili sauce on the side since he likes it hotter than Laura. He shakes up a slightly different version of the soy and vinegar for a salad dressing, moves the washed leaves from the colander to a bowl and tosses tomato wedges on top.

It's just past six o'clock when he wakes up Laura. After a day featuring shades of gray exclusively and intermittent drizzle, the sun has ducked beneath the clouds, streaming light through the living room window, onto the food spread on the glass-top table. Laura sits in the single chair, picks up the fork and spoon and fills her plate and wine glass. Jeff takes small portions of each dish with chopsticks, pours a glass of water, and shuffles food around his plate. Especially with the sun finally out, it feels way too early for dinner.

"This is nice," Laura says after her first forkful. "Really nice. If underwear doesn't work out, you have a future as a cook." She takes a sip of wine.

"I'm sure there's a big shortage of people who can make stir-fry here," he says, smiling past the "if underwear doesn't work out" that seems increasingly likely with every meeting in Sham Shui Po or Kwun Tong.

"Maybe it would help that you're white."

"There you go. A *gweiloh* working at the *dai pai dong.*"

"Is that what this is called, die by dong? Sounds like a version of *Fatal Attraction.* Makes me wonder what I'm eating."

Jeff chuckles. "That's funny. *Dai pai dong* is one of the little local restaurants on the street. The one near the bottom of the escalator makes really nice *jok,* rice porridge."

"You eat that stuff?"

"It's cheap and filling. Like oatmeal for breakfast."

"Better you than me, mister," she says, chewing. "Where do you pick up this local color?"

"While I'm dashing around town, meeting the men in ladies' underwear," Jeff says, pushing his food around the plate. "On the train, I read that *HK* magazine. It's kind of like the *Village Voice. . . .*"

"If only this was kind of like the Village," Laura says, taking a sip of wine. "It's not bad enough that it's Hong Kong. I have to work with people who hate me."

"I'm sure they don't hate you. . . ."

"No, they do. At least my anchor does," Laura says. "Whatever happens, whenever anything goes wrong, he blames me."

"You just have to realize that some people. . . ."

"You see, Deng Jiang Mao has never made a mistake. The other day, he calls the leader of North Korea Kim Jong the Second, then he insists that's the right name. When I finally proved that he was wrong, he said it was written wrong in the copy. . . ."

"My pop used to say, sometimes it really doesn't matter who's right."

"That's fine for sizing girdles, I'm sure, but in real life, and especially in journalism, being right ought to count for something." Laura takes another sip of wine. "God, do I really want to keep doing this?"

"What do you mean?"

"I mean the getting up at midnight, this mindless TV stuff, shoveling shit upstream to make a show that nobody sees. Even our station manager can't be bothered to watch. . . ."

"Well you don't have to," Jeff says. "I mean, we could go back."

"Go back?"

"Yeah," he says, holding his chopsticks with the tips pointing up and looking straight at her. "We could go back to New York. . . ."

"I couldn't go back to the *Journal,* not after asking to come here—sort of—and all the trouble. . . ."

"Maybe you could. Have you asked? They like you," Jeff says, trying to be delicate.

"No, you don't understand the way things are at the *Journal.* They'd never. . . ."

"So you could get another job. And meanwhile, I've got the stores. It's not like we'd starve. . . ."

"And live out on Long Island and play *hausfrau. . . ?*" Laura takes a sip of wine, smiling. "Chai Wan dawn patrol is sounding better and better."

"We wouldn't have to live on the 'gIsland. We could get a place in the city. . . ."

"Don't think I haven't thought about it, thought about it a hundred times a day, sweetie," Laura says. "But I have to stick it out here. I made a decision. I wanted to come here to see history, to be part of history with the handover, and that's what I'm going to do. It's a once-in-a-lifetime opportunity, and you're right, I'll get the hang of it. All the other producers manage, and it's not like they're any smarter than me. They just have more experience. And, boy, am I getting experience. . . ."

"Whatever you say," Jeff sighs. "I just want you to understand that whatever you want to do, stay or go, quit or whatever, I'm with you all the way."

"That's very sweet. Thank you." She leans over and kisses him, then takes a forkful of salad. "How's business going?"

"I had meeting in Sham Shui Po with another *goniff. . . .*"

"I thought you were meeting underwear makers. . . ."

"Yes," Jeff says, then realizes why she's confused. *"Goniff* is thief in Yiddish, and. . . ."

"Today at our meeting, CK, the station manager, he didn't show up again," Laura says, as she eats. "It's really awful the way he makes it so obvious that he can't be bothered to pay attention to what's on our air. I could lead with the freakin' football scores and he'd never know."

"But you wouldn't. . . ."

"If they insist we have these stupid meetings, then we should do something useful, talk about the news and what's going on. Instead, we just listen to Lamont spout off about New York's vision for the station—at least the people in New York pay more attention to what's going on here than CK does—then Old Hartman spouts off like he's some journalism professor and we're his students, and then everybody else tries to show how much they know about everything that doesn't matter. If it wasn't for that meeting nonsense, I could get out of there before noon and keep my workday under twelve hours. It's so unfair." Laura shakes her head and takes a drink of wine, then looks at the clock on the living room wall. "Oh Jesus, look at the time." She cleans her plate and drains her wine. "I've got to get to bed and so I can get up for the sausage factory—that's what Sylvia calls it." She leans over and gives Jeff a big kiss.

"I'll clean this up," he says. "Sweet dreams."

"I feel like a five-year-old, going to be bed before dark," Laura says, walking around the table. She stops in front of her bedroom to say, "Good night, sweetheart," before closing the door.

Jeff takes his plate to the kitchen, covers it with plastic wrap and puts it in the refrigerator. He spoons rice and chicken into one tray of Laura's plastic stacking lunch containers with Japanese cartoon characters on the cover and salad into the other tray. He dumps the rest of the leftovers into smaller bowls, covers them with plastic and puts them in the refrigerator. He'll wash the dishes later or tomorrow to avoid disturbing Laura. They're both such light sleepers, and both need at least six uninterrupted hours, that when Laura first started her shift, they found that his getting into bed with her, or her waking up, left the other staring at the ceiling in the dark for hours in resentful wakefulness. The solution is that Laura sleeps in her room, and Jeff in his, and neither dares open the other's door once it's closed. It's not his vision of perfect marital bliss, but he thinks it might have worked nicely for his parents as a substitute for tuning each other out in the living room every night.

He goes to his room, puts on his sneakers and packs his gym bag with shorts, tee-shirt, *Asiaweek* magazine that Laura liberated from the office last week, and Walkman for a workout at the Jewish Community Center on Robinson Road, a block past the Wellcome, closing the door and gate gently as he leaves the apartment, confident the scrape above eight won't awaken Laura.

He laughs about how Laura almost blew the deal on the apartment over the Jewish Center. He did the house hunting when they arrived, the TV station's real estate agent towing him to apartments renting for 30, 40, 50 thousand Hong Kong dollars a month, way beyond their budget, or to absolute dumps within Laura's HK$15,000 allowance, places with the refrigerator in the living room, plumbing fixtures ripped out the wall, the entrance through a Chinese restaurant, no windows in the bedroom. "You sleeping," the agent said. "You no look at view."

They found Prosper Gardens through a newspaper ad. It stood out from other places with its fresh paint and light, airy feel, including a good breeze through the kitchen and the living room. It was small, but so were all the other places they could afford, and Kennedy, with his fluent English, seemed very helpful: "Ask me any questions about Hong Kong. I want to be your friend, not just your landlord."

After showing them the flat, Kennedy said, "Golden, that's a Jewish name?"

"Yes," Jeff replied.

"The Jewish Center is very nearby on Robinson Road," Kennedy explained. "It is brand new with a gym and a very reasonable restaurant. . . ."

"He's Jewish, I'm not," Laura snarled. "I don't think we came to Hong Kong to join the Jewish Center."

"There are many rich Jewish people in Hong Kong," Kennedy said.

"A lot of rich Chinese, too," Laura retorted. "Would you consider lowering the rent?"

Back in their FGN Asia-paid postage-stamp-size hotel room—opening a suitcase required one of them to leave—Laura conceded Kennedy's place was the best they'd seen all day by far, "But I really didn't like that Jewish remark of his."

"Oh, he was just trying to be helpful. And friendly. I think he really. . . ."

"It was ignorant and stupid, is what it was, and even this *shikse* was offended. But listen, we're not living with Kennedy, we'd just be living in his apartment."

So they took the place, and, after checking out the gym, swimming pool and jacuzzi, Jeff took a couples membership at the Jewish Center. The club occupied the lower floors of a massive new twin-tower apartment building named Robinson Place. Jeff heard the story that two of the big Jewish families in Hong Kong—some of those rich ones Kennedy talked about—made their first fortunes in the opium trade and bought the property in the late 1800s, when this hillside was still the outskirts of town. They built the Ohel Leah temple—its two domed towers linked by an arch at the front remind Jeff of a chess piece—along with a recreation club for the Jewish community that once included a governor of Hong Kong. With the property boom in full swing, the Jews leased the land to a developer to build the apartment houses, with the stipulation that it include a new Jewish Community Center with restaurant, library, classrooms, banquet area, swimming pool (indoors, exclusively for the club; the developers put another outdoors for residents only), and gym, which the club shares with residents, probably the best of its kind in Hong Kong, definitely the newest, opened just a month before Jeff and Laura arrived, and at HK$3500 for a couple per year, the most affordably priced.

Jeff rubs his ID card over the sensor to gain admission and takes the elevator down to pool level where he's issued a thick white bath towel and a locker key. He changes into his workout clothes and buzzes himself back into the elevator to the gym level. It's early evening, prime workout time, which he generally tries to avoid, so he's stuck on the universal gym while waiting for the stepper to be free for his 25 minutes of pounding the pedals to The Ramones. He checks his weight on the scale—167, getting close to where it was in high school thanks to low-fat eating and exercise. Back home, his only exercise was weekends on the *Golden Beauty*, which was really a floating cocktail lounge interrupted by occasional heavy lifting.

He goes back to the pool level and does laps in the bath-warm water, then takes a seat in the jacuzzi, pushing the button to activate the whirlpool, doing his best to keep the *Asiaweek* dry. He resolves to get one of those waterproof Walkmans with his first underwear score to drown out the Israeli elevator music in the locker room. Otherwise the thick doors, low ceiling and warmth make it feel like a perfect isolation bubble from business disappointments, money worries, visa problems, and overarching weirdness of a wife who goes to bed before dark.

Over the elevator music, Jeff hears voices—speaking Hebrew, he's learned to recognize—in the locker area on the other side of the showers. The motor for the jacuzzi stops, so he puts his magazine on the shelf overhead and is about to slosh through the thigh-high water to restart it when he notices a couple of burly guys in towels with short, black hair and pasty skin, already at the button on the wall, the one with the beard apparently instructing the other about pushing it to restart the jets in the pool. Jeff says thanks and resettles himself into the corner of pool opposite the stairs as the pair hang their towels on the wall hooks and descend, giving him a nod as they wade in. The pool measures about three feet by four feet, so fitting three adult males requires delicate arrangement, particularly given the distastefulness of uninvited contact with another naked man. The two men speak more quietly in Hebrew as they position themselves in the far corners of the pool from Jeff.

"So, new here?" the one with the beard asks Jeff.

"A couple of months."

"A couple of months in the Jewish Center, or a couple of months in Hong Kong?"

"Both."

"Well, welcome. I'm Avi, and this is my partner, Moishe."

"I'm Jeff."

"Nice to meet you," Avi says.

"My English not so good," Moishe says with a smile. "From Israel."

"We are both," Avis continues. "So, you're Jewish."

"How could you tell?"

"Possibly the way you walk," Avi jokes. "You're from America, yes?"

"New York."

"What you do here?" Avi asks, the typical Hong Kong question.

"I'm in the garment business, or trying to be."

"This is interesting," Avi says. "We are also. What goods?"

"Back in the US, my family operates a chain of lingerie stores, five stores. My wife came here for her work, so I came over here to try to source, since most of our goods came from China in the first place."

Avi gives a rapid translation to Moishe, who nods and smiles. Then Avi asks, "You have found suppliers?"

"Not yet. We've only just gotten settled. . . ."

"We are also selling garments, women's wear, and Moishe and I often go to the factory in the mainland. Possibly they can make lingerie also."

"Hey, that would be terrific," Jeff says.

"If not this factory, maybe others," Avi says.

"If we can find something, I'll make it worth your trouble," Jeff says.

"It's no trouble for another Jew in Hong Kong trying to sell *schmattes* from China." Avi says, then confers with Moishe in Hebrew.

"It's good to make in China," Moishe says. "You don't go broke with the money."

"What do you mean?"

"In Israel, we imported goods from Europe," Avi explains, "take shekels and pay out European money. But the shekel falls from four to one dollars to nine to one dollars, and we have to pay so many shekels for our bills, we went broke. His brother-in-law, he was an exporter, so he paid shekels and received dollars. He became rich."

"If we know from money like we know from *schmattes,* we could be rich also then and stop with the *schmattes,"* Moishe says.

"Here, with the money set to the dollar, you don't have to worry about that," Avi says. "You don't have to be expert in money, only *schmattes."*

"That's good for me," Jeff says. "What about in China. . . ?"

"Same thing in China. The money stays with the dollar."

"I didn't know that."

"Still a *greener,"* Moishe says. "Fast off the boat."

"We are planning to go next week for one day to China," Avi says. "You can come also, and we can look together for sourcing."

"That would be great," Jeff says. "Maybe you can tell me about a visa. I've been trying to figure out what kind of visa I should get for. . . ."

"A visa?"

"You know, to travel to China? I have the application for a business visa, but. . . ."

"At the border, for 100 renminbi—100 Hong Kong dollars—you make a stamp that's good for 72 hours."

"Oh really," Jeff says. The motor on the jacuzzi stops. "I'll get it," he says, standing and mounting the stairs toward the button.

"Give me your card, so we can get in touch," Avi says, following him out of the jacuzzi. Jeff goes to his locker and gets a card from his wallet.

"Golden Beauties," Avi says, reading the card, as he opens his locker and extracts his for Jeff. "I like this name." He flips over Jeff's card. "You don't have Chinese on the back," he says, half asking, half scolding.

"Should I?"

Avi flips the card back to the printed side. "And you don't give your mobile phone number," he says in the same tone.

"I don't have one yet. My wife and I. . . ."

"Boychick, you really are a *greener."*

CHAPTER 4

The Second-Biggest Story

"I WANT THIS, I WANT THIS, I want this," Laura insists, stamping her feet in front of Edie's slot. "I need everybody—everybody—in here working on it," she tells the mostly empty newsroom.

"They are," Edie says, holding one phone to her mouth and left ear and another on the right ear with the mouthpiece pointing up.

"I want it on *US Prime News* back home, Eugene Mason saying we broke the story and showing the tape of *AM Asia,* and being able to call my mom and say, 'That was my show.' I want to kick CNN's butt. . . ."

"As soon as we have it, you'll have it," Edie assures her.

"Should we call Lamont? Get him to talk to New York. . . ."

"I've already talked to them. . . ."

"But, you know, his connections. . . . He's always talking to them. Maybe. . . ."

"Laura, Lamont is the last thing we need here now. Can you imagine Lamont in the midst of a breaking news story? And you must stop believing Lamont's New York tales. 'Television is my lie' isn't our exclusive."

"You mean. . . ."

"He makes it up, I suspect."

"Wow. . . ." Laura takes a deep breath and looks at her watch. Three minutes to air. "Did you call the China bureau?"

Edie shrugs, *"This* is the China bureau."

Laura shakes her head. "Nobody at the *Post* or Radio Hong Kong? The paper's not here, yet. That's got to mean something."

"It means the paper is late, *mei-mei,"* Edie says, hanging up one phone. "I'm trying everyone and everything I know. . . . You have no idea how many men over the years would have given one of their bollocks to hear me say that, under somewhat different circumstances, of course."

"All the boxes are made? We've got the package set? Both packages?"

"Yes, yes. Stop worrying. You're right to keep the rundown flexible and hold the packages until something is certain. Deng can handle changes, he's a pro. Keep things moving, and don't get caught waiting. May be minutes, may be hours, may be never. . . . Speak of the devil," Edie smiles as Deng approaches the desk.

"What the fuck is this rundown?" Deng roars.

"You always scream for news, and now that we have some. . . ." Laura roars back.

"I was just telling Laura," Edie interrupts calmly, "you're a pro, you can handle a little excitement on the set. We're waiting for confirmation, and we want to be flexible enough to put it on the air the second we have it. When we do, if we do, then you go to Block X."

"What about breaks?" Deng asks Edie.

"Quickie says he can work around them. He'll cue us both," Laura answers. "I just hope we'll have enough time to go into the package after we break the news."

"If we break the news," Edie says.

"Listen. This is a big story, and it's my ass out there," Deng says. "I want to hear this from you," he tells Edie. "This is no time for amateur hour."

"Jesus," Laura screams. "How is Edie supposed to. . . ?"

"Listen," Edie says, "Laura may be new to television, but she's not new to news. I trust her judgment on news, the network does, and you're going to have to. Everyone in the newsroom, everyone in the network, is working to get a confirmation. It's most likely to come to Laura through here, through me, but maybe not. In any case, it's Laura in the control room, and that's who you'll hear it from. That's how it has to be. Good luck."

"No offense," Deng tells Laura as they walk toward the set. "It's a big story, and I want to get it right, that's all."

"I appreciate that, and we're all glad you care," she says, holding the door to set for him. "I just wish you'd realize you're not the only one who cares. I want to get it right. We're both on the same side."

"I know, I know," he says, as the door seals crisply behind him.

"Okay," Laura announces in the control room. "Days like today are why they call this the news business." She nods to Quickie for his translation. "Everyone's looking for confirmation on the story. As soon as we get it, we put it on the air and go to Block X, and Quickie will decide when we break. Everybody got that?" Quickie translates and, amid shuffling of show rundowns, he assures Laura that everyone's got it. "Okay, here we go. Second-biggest story of 1997, we hope," Laura says to Quickie as she settles into her chair. She even manages a smile for Pussy when she glances that way.

"In ten," Quickie says.

"Go with A scripts until we get the confirmation," Laura tells Deng through the microphone. He nods.

"In three, two, one . . . roll open," Quickie says.

"Live from the Franklin Global Network broadcast center in Hong Kong," Old Hartman's voice booms gravely over those same market and city stills from the old open, "this is *AM Asia*. Everything you need to know to profit from the business day."

"Cue."

"Good morning, *jo saahn*, and welcome to *AM Asia* for Thursday, February 20th, 1997. I'm Deng Jiang Mao in Hong Kong. Our top story this morning. . . ." Deng turns to camera two on his right, and over his left shoulder, a box appears with a black and white photo of an age-spotted man with the text "Deng Dead?" in the upper left corner. "Unconfirmed reports from the People's Republic of China say paramount leader Deng Xiaoping has died. Deng is considered the mastermind behind China's economic reforms and the upcoming July first return of Hong Kong to the mainland. The FGN news team is currently investigating this developing story, and we'll bring you details as soon as they become available."

"Perfect," Laura whispers into the microphone to Deng. "Now A-2." She releases the lever and tells the control room, especially Pussy, "Get the New Zealand stocks loaded." She glances at the monitor on her console showing CNN. They don't have confirmation yet either.

"The passing of Deng, if he has passed away. . . ." the anchor Deng continues, deviating from the rundown and scripts.

"He still go, I keep box," Quickie says.

"A-2, A-2," Laura says firmly into the intercom microphone, holding down the lever.

". . . would be a great irony, just eighteen weeks before Hong Kong's reunification with its motherland after a century and a half of colonial rule. Deng's innovative 'one country-two systems' policy has laid the groundwork for this historic reunion, mere months from now. For some statesmen, this. . . ."

"Stop," she implores her anchor. "It's all in the package. Read A-2."

". . . would be the pinnacle, but for Deng it pales in comparison with his other achievements in a long, stormy career that truly transformed the world's largest nation. Reunification with Hong Kong is certainly a jewel in Deng's crown, but it is his brilliant economic reform program that will be his greatest legacy. Deng's implementation of 'Socialism with Chinese characteristics' has changed China. . . ."

Laura's computer beeps. On the top line, she reads a message from Helios in the newsroom: "Deng dead, Radio Beijing. My brother hear."

Laura picks up the hotline to Edie. "Helios says Radio Beijing confirmed. . . ."

"Go with it," Edie says.

She hangs up the phone and leans into the microphone, pressing the lever. "Deng dead. Radio Beijing report. Confirmed. Deng dead. X-1. X-1. Now. X-2 package intro next." She turns to the director. "Quickie, load the obit package, tape 417. We'll do 695 in the bottom half, and figure out the rest of the show while we're in the package." She glances at CNN, still clueless, then looks at the clock and sees she can get to break from the package, then shift the rest of A block to the next segment, and drop D for this hour. She picks up the phone. "Great work, Helios. We'll shift D block to next hour. Check the other blocks for anything that needs updating. The package intros, for instance. Top them with he's dead. Maybe steal a line for two from the X block obit. Thanks."

". . . made China the fastest growing economy in the world and the focus of dynamic foreign investment," FGN Asia's living Deng continues. "And for China's 1.2 billion citizens, it has meant a tangibly better, more comfortable life. For many, it has meant riches beyond their wildest dreams. . . ."

"X-1. He's dead," Laura screams into the intercom microphone.

"China today, thanks to Deng's reforms, now boasts greater wealth than at any time in its 4,000 year history. The Middle Kingdom is in the middle of the Asian boom, the center driving economic growth for the next millennium. . . ."

"What is wrong with him?" Laura says to no one in particular. "Quickie, change the box to the obit." It's the same picture, fringed in black, with 1905–1997 in the top left corner. "Maybe he'll see that. . . . Can you try telling him?" Quickie punches up his microphone for Deng on set and relays the news.

". . . a tiger economy, given its teeth and claws by this elfin genius, thrice imprisoned, whose vision for a strong, glorious China never wavered. . . ."

The hotline from Edie rings. "Yeah, I told him, but he's still babbling on. . . . Yes, it sucks. . . . We have it, and this knucklehead. . . . Okay, I've got an idea."

She hangs up the hotline just as *One Moment in Time* beeps from Pussy's mobile phone. Well, at least one break today, Laura thinks. She grabs the phone from the counter before Pussy can and drops it into Pussy's mug of tea. "Phones off during the show," Laura calmly announces, having rehearsed this moment many times. "That's the rule."

Pussy removes the phone from the tea and looks at the caller's number flashing on the screen. "My cousin in Xiamen. I ask to call if hear Deng dead. I try help. You break phone."

". . . those comparisons miss the point. It is not only the leadership style, the policies and the underlying philosophy that makes. . . ."

"Oh god, I'm sorry. Quickie, tell her I'm sorry."

Waving translation, Pussy says, "You say sorry. You no like Pussy. You no like Chinese. You stupid *gweiloh*. You new phone Pussy. You go home."

"Okay. Tell her I'll get her a new phone." Laura scans the monitors, and sees CNN reporting the death of China's paramount leader. She's fighting back tears as Deng drones on.

In anguish, she rips off the top page of her scripts and writes on the back: *Deng dead, Radio Beijing reports. Confirmed. Go!!! X-1 NOW!* "Ashrami, take this paper to Deng, now. Walk right onto the set and hand it to him." Ashrami nods and takes the paper, her bracelets jangling as she walks.

". . . an escape route from poverty and into the global economy for hundreds of millions. . . . Ah, our lovely production assistant Ashrami

Rao is on the set." Deng nods for Ashrami to come on camera. She averts her face from the red light and hands him the paper. "Yes, it is confirmed by Radio Beijing. Deng Xiaoping, architect of China's economic reforms and the driving force behind Hong Kong's reunification with the motherland, Deng Xiaoping is dead at age 92. And now, I believe we have a report from Mike Hartman about the extraordinary career of this hero of the Chinese people and the Chinese economy."

"Roll that goddamned tape," Laura says, then holds both hands over her face. She takes a deep breath and punches the microphone for Deng. "What the hell happened?" she yells.

Deng shuffles his scripts as the obituary package plays. "Let me know where we're going out of the package, please" he asks the control room.

"What happened?" Laura screams with lever down again. No response from Deng. She thrusts out both arms, slides back her chair, storms out of the control room and onto the set. "What happened?"

"I don't recall the memo saying this was visiting day on the set," Deng says with a grin. "First Ashrami—and that was great television, her handing me the paper—now my beloved producer. . . ."

"Why didn't you follow the rundown? Why didn't you respond when I talked in your ear?"

"You did?" Deng looks under this desk and says, "Oh, would you look at that? My IFB must've gotten unplugged. Maybe I hit it. . . ." He reaches under the desk. "Quickie, give me a check. . . . Okay, it's back in now. We've got to get maintenance to take a look at that. So go back to the control room and tell me what script is next. . . ."

"You did that on purpose."

"What did I do?"

"Unplugged your earpiece, so you could do your Deng shtick."

"I didn't do it on purpose. But I will say that more people were probably more interested in my 'Deng shtick' than in New Zealand stocks this morning. And we got the news, so no harm."

"No harm? NO HARM? We had the story two minutes ahead of CNN. But you unplugged your IFB so CNN got it on air first. How's that for 'no harm'?"

"Well, I was here. What took you so long. . . ?"

"I was screaming it in your ear. . . ."

"Well, why didn't you send in Ashrami sooner? What could have been more important than this major news story. . . ?

"We'll talk to CK about this after the show."

"You can talk to. . . ."

"No, WE will talk to CK."

"No, thanks. How about if you go back to the control room and shut up and do your job, and stop telling me how to do mine?"

"You ... you ... louse. You'll be anchoring a tugboat when I tell CK. . . ."

"How about a little less provoking and a little more producing?"

"Whether your IFB was in or out, you had the rundown and the scripts. You knew what the plan was. . . ."

"One minute in package," Quickie announces on the control room loudspeaker.

"How much time in the block left after package?" Laura yells.

"About fifteen seconds," Quickie says.

"Just dissolve to the obit still to break," Laura says, then turns back to Deng. "You didn't follow the rundown and you unplugged your IFB. We'll see what CK says about that. What I say is that, if you ever do that to me again, I will kill your mike, then I will come out on the set and kill you."

"Oh man, I'm shaking. I may be too nervous to finish the show."

"I'll take the network to black as a tribute to the great hero of the Chinese motherland. Go ahead and walk. I dare you. . . ."

Deng sighs. "Listen, I know this is difficult for you. Let's just finish the show, and talk about it later. It's a shame that on this historic, tragic day, you manage to find some petty thing. . . ."

"There is nothing petty about letting CNN break the story ahead of us, about an anchor disobeying the rundown and ignoring a producer on air. . . ."

"Ignore, as in ignorant. Think about it," Deng says, giving Laura a smug smile, and resumes shuffling his scripts. "Now get the fuck out of here, or I will walk. That'll give you something to discuss with CK. Second-biggest story of the year, and your show's in black."

Laura returns to the control room, and announces, "Out of the break, we use X-1 instead of A-1, then go rest of A block to the bottom of the hour, fill to the break with the Deng obit still, then Y obit block at the bottom of the hour as scripted to break, then B block. Next hour, X plus stocks to break one, then C block, Y block, and D block. Ashrami, help whoever needs it getting their scripts organized, tell Helios, and let Richard and the other producers know what we're running. Thanks."

The hotline rings. "Laura here. . . . He says his IFB unplugged which I think is total bullshit. He had a rundown. . . . That?. . . Well, yes. Her phone rang in the middle of it all, and the rule is. . . . Yes, yes, I'll get her a new damn phone. . . . But this Deng thing, I'm talking to CK after the show. . . . No, it is. Whether or not he did it on purpose, he didn't follow the rundown, and that's the issue. . . . I think I have to. Will you come with me?. . . Okay, I understand. Bye."

After reshuffling the rundown in the computer and telling Ashrami to print it out, Laura sits with her face in her hands for the next 90 minutes as FGN Asia reports the second-biggest story of 1997, the one CNN broke.

After the show, she meets Deng at the studio door. "Okay, let's go talk to CK."

"Listen, I'm sorry you had a problem in there, but that's not my problem," Deng says. "And you take it out on the poor graphics girl's mobile, Laura? That's really inexcusable. If you want to talk to CK about your mistakes, I shouldn't be there. In fact, maybe it is a good idea for you to talk to CK, engage in a little self-criticism. It seemed to work for the late, great paramount leader. . . ."

Laura mutters "screw you" as she turns and walks through the newsroom to CK's office. "I need to see CK," Laura tells his secretary, Iris Wong, who scans CK's appointment book. "Now," Laura barks. Iris nods and dials the phone. Laura hears the ring through the thin door, then hears CK responding in Cantonese. Iris hangs up as CK reaches across his desk and opens the door. "Linda, come in, please," he says, pronouncing the "l"s as "r"s.

CK Leung, the station manager, wears a shiny dark blue sport coat and a v-neck sweater over his blue shirt with a white collar and yellow striped tie. His crew cut has grown out into the beginnings of a Beatles mop top. Laura can see dandruff flakes on top of his head and shoulders as she enters the long, thin office like a bowling lane, nothing on its white walls but four muted monitors showing FGN Asia, CNN and the two Chinese-language feeds of the local stations, TVB and ATV. The blinds in the big window with the tropical island view behind his desk are down and half closed. He has an ergonomic chair like Edie's and an idle computer terminal on the right side of his desk. He ushers Laura to the chair in front of his desk, retakes his seat, folds his hands on the desk, tilts his head slightly to the right, and says, in a voice barely above a whisper, "I glad you stop in."

"Did you see the show this morning?" Laura asks, realizing that's a stupid, unwelcome question as soon as the words come out. "We had Deng Xiaoping's death confirmed two minutes before CNN, but Deng kept babbling and we didn't get it on the air until after CNN broke it. Deng says his IFB was unplugged. I think he did it on purpose. But, in any case, he didn't follow our rundown. I made a rundown that had options for what to do if we got or didn't get confirmation, but he just ignored it and went on for four minutes about Deng Xiaoping's career— repeating stuff in our obit packages—and let CNN beat us on the story."

"Linda, you cannot expect us to beat CNN," CK says. "CNN have hundreds of reporter. We just start up. Someday, we gonna beat CNN on a big story. . . ."

"CK, we did beat CNN on a big story, on this story, today. But Deng screwed it up. He didn't follow the rundown, he didn't. . . ."

"Deng is very experience TV man. He know TV. You know, he turn down millions to come work here, because he love Asia, he love Hong Kong and China, he want FGN Asia successful. We very lucky to have presenter like Deng."

Laura realizes her bigger mistake. The anchor is always right—and the Chinese male one is always always right. But it's too late to stop. "CK, I know Deng is good. I work with him everyday. But sometimes he's not a team player. On the air, people can't just do whatever they want, somebody has to be in charge. The anchor has to follow the rundown."

"Producer also must be team player," CK says, shifting from his angled glance and looking straight at Laura. "That is why I want talk to you, Linda."

Damn it, Laura thinks. How the hell does CK know about Pussy's phone already? That bitch. These Chinese always stick up for each other anyway, but this—violating a Hong Konger's mobile phone—that's the cardinal sin. He'll really let me have it. And maybe I deserve it. Maybe

I was being a bully: if Quickie's phone had gone off, would I have dumped it into his tea? Maybe I let the fact that I don't like Pussy get the better of my judgment. It was a pretty childish thing to do. There's nothing to do now but take the consequences like a grown up.

"You send CK memo," CK says, which strikes Laura as an odd lead-in to discussing Pussy's handphone. CK reaches into a plastic folder on his desk, pulls out a copy. He glances at it, then places it on the desk and turns it for Laura to read. She sees it's her memo from four weeks ago about changing the name of the show to *AM Asia* and redoing the open. "This your memo, right?"

"Yes, CK. And the changes were made about three weeks ago."

"Who say you can make change? I say?"

"Well, no. But a week went by and there was no objection so. . . ."

"Who say okay?"

"Everybody said okay. Edie, Lamont, the experienced Mister Deng, who asked for the changes. . . ."

"CK say okay?" he asks, raising his volume.

"No, but like I said. . . ."

CK pulls a yellow legal pad from his desk and shows her a page with some scrawling in Chinese. "This my response. Drafting today. Very busy. Too much meeting in mainland. You cannot make change behind my back."

"I didn't make it behind your back. I wanted you to know. That's why I sent you a memo."

"But you not wait CK answer. . . ."

"I'm sorry CK, but I thought. . . ."

"You not understand. Have to check with New York"—he pronounces New "loo" like the British term for bathroom—"on big change like this. Have to make sure, okay. New York not like, maybe."

"What did New York say?"

"I don't know, I don't check yet. Too much meeting."

"Well, nobody has complained about the changes," Laura says, whether or not anybody saw them.

"This my station, my responsible. You cannot change and not tell me. . . ."

"I did tell you!"

"You tell, but not wait. My memo explain procedure to make change. You not follow procedure. You just do. That not right way," CK says. "Cannot this way."

"Well, we can't change it back."

"I no say change back. Do not try to tell me what I say again," he says, raising his voice further. "I know my English not perfect but I know what I say." He mutters something in Chinese, then continues at a lower volume. "Done is finish. But next time, must follow procedure. This memo explain procedure."

"All right, CK, next time, I will."

CK takes off his glasses and cleans them on his sweater. "Linda, I know you come from big newspaper. Newspaper different. I also much time newspaper. Different. I hearing people say you not see different sometimes, say you have problem for TV. . . ."

"Who says. . . ?"

"They say you not listen sometime." CK puts his glasses on and cracks a slight smile. His voice is back down to barely audible. "I know is difficult. I know not easy. Much things to learn. They say you learning. They say you make good show. But have to listen. You not know everything. Must listen and learn. Deng, he know TV. You, not yet know." CK glances at the monitors beyond Laura's shoulder. "I have many things to do, but I still very not happy about not follow procedure. Everybody make mistake, but too much mistake no good. You no make mistake, you good." He glances at the monitors again, picks a pen out of the cup on his desk and grabs the legal pad, poised to write.

"Thanks, CK. I'll try not to make any more mistakes," Laura says, standing.

"Good," CK says without looking up from his pad. As he hears her open the door, he looks up. "Good for us to talk. Wish I have more time for talk, know people better. Too busy, too much meeting in mainland. You keep try, Linda."

Laura feels dizzy as she walks across the newsroom toward Edie's platform. She hopes it's time for a cigarette break so Edie can talk her back from this trip through CK's looking glass. Lamont sits beside Edie on the platform, phone cradled on his shoulder, typing. Advertising that he's come in early, Lamont's hair is wet, the top button on his shirt is undone, and a tie hangs unknotted around his collar.

"You are one lucky girl," Edie says to Laura. "Pussy's phone still works. She said it cost 2000 Hongkies and came from. . . ."

"Screw Pussy. . . ."

"If I had bollocks, I reckon I'd try."

"I just came from CK's office. . . ."

"You sound as if it didn't go well."

"Look, can we. . . ?" Laura says, motioning her head toward the stairway smoking lounge.

"Not now," Edie says, flicking her head toward Lamont. "What did CK say?"

"He started by calling me 'Rinda' and it went downhill from there. He said, 'Deng know TV.' You know, the anchor is always right."

"Of course."

"But then, he starts giving me a hard time about changing the name of the show and the open."

"What?"

"He says that I didn't follow procedures."

"How did CK find out there's a new open? Surely, he's never seen the show."

"Undoubtedly. But, as a courtesy, I sent him a memo about it."

"You what?" Edie gasps. She spots Deng walking across the newsroom and yells, "Deng, Deng, come here. You must hear this."

"Edie," Laura mumbles, "he is the last person. . . ."

Lamont puts down the phone and says, "Since you made me come in early, you have to let me in on the fun, too."

Deng sidles up to the platform, squinting disdainfully at Laura. Half the newsroom has its ears turned toward them while pretending to work.

"Laura," Edie says, "tell Deng about the *AM Asia* open."

"CK is pissed about changing the open."

"How did he find out?" Deng and Lamont ask simultaneously.

"Here's the punch line," Edie says.

"After the 12:30 meeting when we agreed to change it," Laura explains, "I sent CK a memo to let. . . ."

Lamont begins laughing through his nose, honking as if he was snoring.

"You did what?" Deng roars and shakes his head.

"I thought I needed to let him know," Laura says, breaking her pledge to never speak to Deng again off the set.

"Deng, how many years have you been in television?" Lamont asks.

"Too many."

"And how many memos have you sent to management about something other than your pay, your vacation, or a vendetta to get someone fired?"

"One. When I anchored the eleven at KOSF, I asked all senior management to stop at my desk before going home to leave their change in a basket for the soda machine."

"Laura," Lamont says, "we don't write memos to management. They write memos to us."

"And we assiduously ignore them," Deng adds.

"I know you meant well," Edie says. "But if CK wants to know something about your show, let him try watching it."

"So what did CK say about the open?" Lamont asks.

"He said we—I mean, I, I took the bullet on this one—I didn't follow procedure. And he's writing a memo, now, about what the procedure is."

"Excellent," Lamont says. "Then we'll know exactly what we need to ignore."

"Laura, Laura, Laura," Deng says, shaking his head and walking back toward his office, "with our help, someday you'll understand television."

Laura finds herself gripping the platform for support. She tries to remember what she needs to be doing for tomorrow's show. "Do you think we'll be doing more Deng-is-dead stuff tomorrow? I mean, for my guests. . . ."

Lamont says, "That's an interesting call for you to make. On the one hand. . . ."

"But fortunately, it's been made for you, *mei-mei,*" Edie interrupts. "We have a currency trader to talk about the renminbi in the first hour, and in the second, a political scientist on the impact on relations across the strait. Pre-interviews are in for both."

"Thanks. That's a big help, but you didn't have to. . . ."

"We wanted them both today, but they couldn't," Lamont says. "Luckily for you, they're early risers."

"We know this hasn't been a day you want to save for the scrapbook," Edie says, "but *US Prime News* did run the Deng announcement from your show. We cheated a little. I gave them the tape from the bottom half of your hour, although they rather liked Ashrami and advised that we get her on camera more often."

"Man, if only we'd have. . . ."

"Mei-mei, you did quite well. You spared us sending the US network pictures of Old Hartman."

They glance at the monitor overhead, where the veteran anchorman appears flustered, fumbling for a page of copy. "Yes, here's more on the paramount leader, who died in the predawn hours this morning in Beijing." Old Hartman peers at the camera, waiting for the package to roll, but his image stubbornly remains on screen. He glances imploringly beyond the camera toward the control room, then at his face reflected in the monitor on the set.

"Switcher's broken," Lamont says. "Of all days. . . ."

After a tortuous five seconds, master control puts up the "We are experiencing technical difficulties, please stand by" animation, showing a satellite spinning in space beaming squiggly lines toward earth.

"Switcher?" Laura asks.

"It's what we use to go from one camera to another," Lamont explains, "or from the set to a tape or a remote shot. The director controls it. Sometimes it just freezes up. This happened once before, during the shakedown. We should be able to fix it in fifteen or twenty minutes."

CK comes bolting out of his office flinging the door open, and rushing toward the control room. "At last, CK's paying attention to what's on the air," Laura thinks. Maliciously, she wonders what kind of memo he'll write about this mishap.

But CK runs past the control room and out of the newsroom, toward the elevators. "Is CK going up to master control?" Laura asks.

"I doubt it," Lamont says, glancing at his watch. "He's got a meeting in Zhuhai, and he's already late."

CHAPTER 5

Enter the Dragon

J EFF MEETS AVI AND MOISHE in front of the JCC on a Monday morning for his first visit to the mainland, fully outfitted with his passport and business cards, as they'd reminded him. His two companions have a half-dozen identical plastic shopping bags with tins of butter cookies inside and ask Jeff to carry a pair. "You can't meet Chinese suppliers without presents," Avi explains.

"Oh. You should have told me," Jeff says, taking a pair. "I could have...."

"You're lucky. They're trying to get your business, so they'll maybe give you a present. But if they give you a present from us for a present, you give it back to us, *boychick?*" Avi says, smiling, and translates for Moishe, who chuckles.

They walk to the escalator, flowing down until ten o'clock, and rapidly descend. The escalator isn't crowded, but riders standing rather than walking impede their progress. For all the talk about working so hard, and Laura to the contrary, Hong Kong doesn't strike Jeff as an early-rising town. From what he's seen, people tend to stay late rather than start early. When the escalator ends, Moishe leads the way along a series of ramps and steps through Central Market, smelling of chicken shit and diesel fuel, over the high speed road, across the elevated walkway in front of the stock exchange, with its statue of a bronze bull in the plaza and a corrugated metal fence masking a vast construction and landfill site beyond it—people like Jeff's mother who say, "They're not making new land," have never been to Hong Kong—around a corner to a grubby concrete platform overlooking the brackish harbor, where about a dozen men, mostly elderly, sleep on mats made from cardboard boxes cut open beside shopping carts holding their possessions. Across the harbor, a series of hills are visible in distance in the cool, clear

February morning air. A narrow stairway smelling of urine leads them down to the Star Ferry entrance. Moishe springs for the HK$2 first-class fare for all of them at the collection window, and they trot, shopping bags flapping against their legs toward the green light on the left, indicating a ferry loading at that pier. Jeff stands at the back of the upper deck cabin, admiring the Hong Kong Island skyline—a majestically angled black glass tower, an erector set assemblage with the Hongkong Bank logo on top, a white box with round windows like portholes, and a building shaped like a rocket ship ready to blast off, stand out among dozens, maybe hundreds, of other skyscrapers elbowing for space. Even though 80 percent of Hong Kong's population lives there, the Kowloon side looks like a small town from the harbor, with the low-slung Cultural Center dominating the waterfront—the building with the best view in town but no windows—and a squat box in front of the pier with a neon sign on top so prominent that you'd think you were arriving in a land called Motorola.

As the ferry approaches the dock, Moishe and Avi lead Jeff to the scrum of passengers gathering around the exit. Crew members in powder-blue sailor suits that look more appropriate for Gilbert and Sullivan than this grubby circuit toss fat lines toward the pier, most landing in water for the shore crew to fish out with barge poles. The ferry jerks a few times, and the scrum jerks with it, churning starboard toward the dock over the choppy water. Lines secure, a whistle blows, and a crew member lets out the line to lower the gangplank. Passengers begin crossing before the ramp hits the gray concrete pier.

"We hurry, we can make the 8:15 bus," Avi says, so they hustle around the semicircular sidewalk enclosing a gaggle of buses, minibuses and taxis, past the McDonald's—"World's busiest," Avi notes—then turning left onto Canton Road with low, grimy shopfronts across the street, and on their side the modern Ocean Terminal shopping and hotel complex that eliminated a half-dozen cross streets from the grid. The bus terminal, across from a tower covered in pink stone, is little more than an empty lot. "I wouldn't have found this place without you," Jeff says. They buy tickets at an unmarked shack, board, and find separate seats in a nearly full bus that reeks of fried dough and tobacco, pushing past vendors in the aisle hawking snacks and newspapers.

The guy in the window seat next to Jeff could be eighteen or 48, dandruff flecks dotting his casually parted dark hair. He nods at Jeff, makes a show of rearranging the plastic shopping bags between his legs without actually moving them, and closes his eyes. Jeff is seated too far from Avi and Moishe to ask all the questions he has ahead of his first crossing into the mainland. He settles his shopping bags on the floor between his legs and leafs Laura's most recently liberated *Asiaweek*.

The bus lurches through traffic in parts of Kowloon he's never seen, enters a tunnel through a mountain and emerges on a modern freeway in the New Territories, which he visited during his travels to the unaffordable with the FGN real estate agent. Apartment tower clusters fill in flat spots between hills, and the tracks of the Kowloon-Canton Railroad sporadically run alongside the road. A stream appears on the left, widening into a river as the bus drives north, then a magnificent bay dotted with craggy islands, birds majestically swooping between them, and mountains with green slopes on the other side. Jeff thinks this must be the Pearl River delta he keeps reading about.

Within an hour, the bus reaches the Lo Wu border crossing. Jeff joins the crowd leaving the bus, bringing his bags with him as Avi and Moishe do. They're waiting for him outside as the passengers are herded into a building with molded orange fiberglass walls and a high roof. The checkpoint has a temporary feel, as if built for easy disassembly after the handover. Avi puts Jeff in the right line to get a stamp from a Hong Kong officer in a blue uniform then pay $100 Hong Kong to a People's Republic of China guard in dark green for a 72-hour visa good within the Shenzhen Special Economic Zone, while he and Moishe use a different line for visa holders. They meet past the checkpoint windows and pile back onto the bus, everyone returning to their same seats, riding for another 35 minutes on another modern highway. Long two-story buildings in pale shades without apparent windows line this road. In the background, Jeff sees so many construction cranes he thinks they must be built or stored there because there can't be so much building going on in one place.

The bus stops in an unpaved lot remarkably similar to the one they started from in Hong Kong. Before Jeff's foot hits the ground from the last step off the bus, skinny men in shabby clothes try to grab his shirt, reaching for his sleeves, shoulders, collar, and pull him their way. "You go me," they insist, "you go me," until Moishe and Avi shoo them away and lead Jeff to a reddish-brown four-door car.

"Taxis," Avi says, anticipating Jeff's question from his puzzled look. "Or pickpockets," he adds, and Jeff pats the pocket that still holds his wallet. Avi motions Jeff into the backseat and gets in next to him. Moishe sits in front and launches into a lively conversation with the driver in Chinese. "See, I have a reason for keeping him around," a smiling Avi tells Jeff.

"What kind of car is this?" Jeff asks.

"Don't be offended," Avi replies, then fakes spitting, "feh, ptui—a Volkswagen." He smiles. "They just made a factory in Shanghai, and it's the best car they get without import tax."

They ride for just a few minutes to the gate of one of those windowless boxes, this one painted light gray. A uniformed guard lifts the barrier, and they park in a virtually empty lot among a pair of Toyota Land Cruisers, a Mercedes, and six more of these VWs in dark colors. They get out of the car and a uniformed security officer unlocks the building's wide metal door. As it swings open, a Canto-pop tune pours out. Jeff follows Avi and Moishe through another set of doors where the music is overwhelmed by the whining and beating of hundreds of sewing machines. Women, most of them young, all of them Chinese, sit behind the machines under fluorescent tubes, their arms covered from wrist to elbow in sleeves sewn from scraps. The women slide collars, hems and trim under their machine's needle then drop the finished pieces into plastic boxes. One team assembles women's tops in what looks like a synthetic silk. Another sews back pockets onto blue jeans.

"In a Chinese factory, smell for smoke to find the bosses," Avi says, repeating it twice until Jeff finally hears him over the racket.

"They're in the showroom?" Jeff asks.

"Boychick, these guys make stuff for guys that have a showroom."

The trail of cigarettes, past and present, leads them to an office built along the back wall of the factory. The door is open but a long glass window along the front wall for supervising the factory floor is covered by a drawn curtain. Inside the room—four or five times bigger than our living room, Jeff notes—with dark wooden paneling, one man sits behind a large desk and two others, one in a military uniform, sit on a beige, fake-leather couch watching television, their feet on the glass coffee table in front of them. Jeff recognizes the logo of a Hong Kong station in the top right corner of the screen.

When Moishe speaks, all three men stand to greet them. "That's Mister Xu, the big boss, Mister Wian, and Constable Zao," Avi explains, as the two groups exchange handshakes and the guests are motioned to the couch and offered cigarettes in a red box as their three hosts light up. Xu, the man behind the desk wears a suit, the label still on the sleeve of the jacket, white shirt and thick, elegant-looking tie. Wian also wears a suit, the jacket flung over the back of the sofa, a white shirt with short sleeves, a cheaper-looking tie, and a pocket protector holding a pen, pencil, small ruler, and other instruments. He leaves the office and returns with three plastic chairs. An elderly woman carrying a tray follows and puts it down at the edge of Xu's desk. The tray holds short glasses and two tall, red metal thermos bottles. Avi and Moishe present their plastic bags to Xu and Zao who nod vigorously and smile broadly but make no move to examine the contents. His fellow travelers motion to Jeff to give his bags to Wian. Zao leaves the room with his bags. Xu removes the plastic stopper from the less-dented thermos and pours tea into the glasses, passing filled glasses to each of the men. The three guests sit on the couch with Xu and Wian opposite them, looking down from the taller plastic chairs.

Moishe hands Wian a magazine with a few pages dog-eared. Wian looks at the pictures, removes a magnifying glass and small pad and pencil from his shirt pocket, writing and sketching meticulously. Xu and Moishe talk, with Avi occasionally making a comment in Hebrew to Moishe. After about five minutes—Xu refreshes everyone's tea and Avi nudges Jeff to tap his index finger on the table while Xu pours—Wian passes around his sketches and notes. The only parts Jeff understands are the dollar signs and the numbers that follow them. Xu pulls out a paper folder, puts the drawings inside and closes it as Moishe and Wian leave the office. Xu pulls out a fresh file and looks at Jeff.

"Did you bring any samples or drawings?" Avi asks.

"Uh, no," Jeff says. "I thought I'd just see. . . ."

"That's okay," Avi says. "Just tell us what you want."

"Ladies' lingerie."

"Yes, yes. . . ."

"For starters, T-backs, bikinis. . . ."

"High legs?"

"All cuts. . . ." Jeff says.

"Lacy? All cotton?"

"I'm sorry, I didn't think we'd get so far right away," Jeff says. "I have spec sheets I can bring up next time."

"You can fax from our office," Avi says.

"We also want bras, swimwear. . . ." Jeff says, then asks Avi, "What will these guys do? I mean, what are the steps in ordering and production?"

"Usually, we rough out ideas with Wian, then they make samples. We say okay or send back for changes, then we price and they start production. If you don't buy, you pay for samples. If you buy, then 50 percent advance, balance on delivery. Minimum lot 3,000 pieces mostly, but flexible. Depends on item and amount, but usually three-four weeks from okay to container."

"That sounds good," Jeff says. "Sleepwear?" Avi nods. It sounds too good to be true, and his pop always said those things usually are, so he'll slow it down until he finds out what really matters. "Listen, I think what makes the most sense is for me to talk to New York first, see what they want now and then I can ask for samples. . . ."

"Can FedEx sample New York two days," Xu says, surprising Jeff with his English.

"Sometimes, it stops problems for people over there to see the item," Avi says.

"Especially when Mister Xu pays," Moishe adds, just back from the factory floor.

"Just to give me some idea. . . ."

"On price?"

"Yeah. Take the Bali bra, R-106, retails $18.95. . . ."

Moishe translates Jeff's description to Xu who gives a lengthy reply— Jeff figures that's a danger sign—then translates back to Avi in Hebrew, who tells Jeff, "They make like this with two hooks instead of S-clasp, more lace, and convertible straps. FOB six RMB, about US 75 cents."

"You're kidding." Jeff says.

"And that includes lunch," Avi adds. Xu nods and leads the way out of his office. Constable Zao rejoins the group at the outside door. He rides in a Mercedes with Xu and Wian while the guests follow in the VW to a parking lot opposite the bus stop. The restaurant entrance has rustic log rails that, on closer inspection are painted concrete, and, inside, a waterfall flowing amid gray, fake rocks into a pond with large goldfish and white statues of princesses. They're greeted familiarly by the hostess in an elegant long red dress with, Jeff notices, long slits up both sides exposing bare legs. You could make a fortune selling pantyhose here, he thinks, if they ever started buying it. A short man in a suit, label still on his sleeve just like on Wian's and Xu's, shakes hands with Zao and leads the group through a maze of crowded tables and carts piled with plates and straw baskets of *dim sum* to a back room with a round table, a lazy Susan in the center. Another woman in a matching dress seats the group and hands Xu a nearly full brandy bottle for inspection, apparently his private stock, while the man flips the switch starting the room's waterfall. "Like the JCC jacuzzi," Jeff says.

"Wait a while," Moishe says, smiling.

Waiters load the lazy Susan with plates of dumplings, vegetables, and soups, along with tall bottles of beer. "Don't worry, all strictly kosher," Avi says, and, when Jeff chuckles, he adds, "Everything vegetables." Xu pours beer into Avi's glass, while Avi taps the table with two fingers. As Xu begins pouring for Jeff, Avi nudges Jeff and he taps the table. Xu smiles.

Whatever the stuff is, Jeff thinks it tastes great and keeps eating until Avi tells him through the side of his mouth, "They need to go, but waiting until you finish." Jeff puts his chopsticks down.

"Ho m ho sikh?" Xu says. "Do you like?"

"Yes," Jeff says.

"Ho ho aah," Avi says.

"Ho ho aah," Jeff repeats.

"That's mean good," Avi says.

Xu offers brandy to the three *gweilohs*. Jeff follows Moishe and Avi's lead and politely refuses. The three Chinese then take their leave, along with the brandy bottle. Jeff follows them toward the door before Avi calls him back. "There's some dessert still, unless you have to go back to work like them. Relax a bit." Avi pours him another cup of tea, and Jeff drums his finger on the table. "You tell us what you want, and we'll get Xu to make it. Work here is very good, and Moishe here is the best QC man in southern China." Moishe smiles and raises his teacup in a mock toast.

"I thought we'd need permits, contracts. . . ." Jeff says.

"This is China, *boychick,*" Avi says. "More simple you make things, the better. Contracts is for lawyers, and what do lawyers know from *schmattes?*"

A woman in one of those long slit dresses—she looks like same one who seated them, but Jeff can't be sure—enters the room and smiles. The three men follow her back through the restaurant, now nearly empty and quiet except for the clanking of plates and laughing and coughing from the few lingering diners. She leads them behind a black lacquered screen, pushes a doorbell there and, when a buzzer sounds, pulls the door open and holds it for them. Another woman in the same style dress in green greets them and leads them to seats on a vinyl couch in what looks like the reception area of a small, tired hotel. Clerks in black vests scurry behind the counter taking money from customers. The woman brings a tray to the table and pours them tea, and Jeff remembers to tap. She then approaches the desk.

"Welcome to the JCC of Guangzhou, *boychick,*" Avi says. "We already know you like jacuzzi. Then massage. "

"Special massage," Moishe says, smiling.

The woman in the green dress returns and stands in front of the couch. She offers more tea, which the men decline. She motions for them to stand and leads them to a glass door. She pushes it open when it buzzes, and they file past her down a narrow corridor. Jeff takes a bundled towel from a male attendant seated on a stool behind a table. He follows Avi and Moishe into a locker room, sits on the low wooden bench and unfolds the towel, finding a pair of shorts inside. "Change," Avi instructs.

"I still important meeting in Zhuhai," the only other customer in the locker room says into his mobile phone. "Okay, okay. Tell them CK sorry. Tomorrow I sure meeting. Okay?" The man, Chinese, short, about 50, pockets his phone and nods at Jeff as he hangs his blue suit coat flecked with dandruff inside his locker.

Jeff undresses, slips on the shorts, piles his clothes into an open locker, pulling the rubber flip-flop sandals out of the locker and onto his feet after seeing Avi and Moishe do it, then locks the door, slips the key over his wrist, and drapes the towel over an arm. Outside the locker room, there's a tiled chamber featuring whirlpool baths side by side and showers lining the walls beside them. The whirlpools must be 25 feet long—big enough to swim laps in, Jeff thinks. "Hot left, cold right," Avi says loudly to be heard over the bubbling tubs, takes off his shorts and hangs them and his towel on a hook on the wall, then sits in the hot one. "Like the JCC, but no button." Jeff and Moishe follow. Jeff closes his eyes and lets the water warm his full stomach.

After a few minutes, an attendant appears. Jeff takes his cues from Avi and Moishe, toweling off, putting on his shorts and following the attendant to the head of three long, dim corridors painted dark red with doors lining each side. Three women in those long dresses with the slits, all tastefully made up, greet them. "Enjoy your massage," Avi tells Jeff. "Wait at the pool if you finish first. But take your time. Enjoy." Each woman leads her guest down a different corridor.

Jeff's masseuse smiles at him, then walks quickly down the corridor, tottering on her four-inch heels. She opens a door, flips on a light and walks in. Jeff follows. The room is small, with a bed—just a mattress on the floor—a small table with towels, a tissue box, and some plastic bottles next to it, a sink, hooks on the wall, and a black lacquered Chinese screen. The masseuse locks the door. "Me Mah Lin." She motions him toward the bed.

"I'm Jeff."

"You can Chinese?"

"What?"

"You," Mah Lin points to her mouth, "Chinese?"

"Oh, no. You English?"

"No." Mah Lin smiles, showing short, stained top front teeth. "Okay." She nods, points toward the bed, and goes behind the screen. Jeff sits on the bed, hears the dress unzip then sees it flop over the top of the screen. Mah Lin emerges wearing a short blue and white robe tied in the front, a fanny wrap made of acetate with a silky finish that retails back home for about $38, probably costs 38 cents to make here, Jeff thinks. She motions for Jeff to lay down on his stomach.

Mah Lin sits on the edge of the bed and pulls at his shorts. "Okay?" she says and removes them. She straddles him, and he can feel her bare skin on his. She applies oil to his back that tingles with warmth and begins to rub. As she massages with her small, strong fingers, he feels her pubic hair tickling his ass, and his penis stiffens, struggling against the bed and her weight. He hopes she doesn't notice. She moves to his neck, his arms and hands, pulling on his fingers to crack the knuckles, then moves down, giving Jeff's burgeoning erection more room to grow, to massage his lower back, his ass, thighs, calves, and feet, cracking his toes. She taps his head, and he looks up.

One of her small, pointy breasts peeking—or maybe it's Beijing, Jeff thinks—out of the robe, Mah Lin motions for him to turn over. She places a hand lightly on his erection and smiles. "Sorry," he says.

"Okay, okay," Mah says with a small smile. "You big you." She straddles him, positioning herself just below his scrotum, and begins to massage his forehead. Jeff closes his eyes, and she moves to his chest. He feels something wet on his left nipple and opens his eyes to see Mah Lin, her robe front open, kissing it.

"Wait, wait," he says, in a panic, pushing her away. What the hell is this? He wonders if Avi and Moishe are setting him up. Is this one of those clip joints he's heard about where they'll give him a bill at the end for a few hundred dollars . . . US?

"Okay, okay," Mah Lin protests. She leans down and rubs her breasts up and down on his chest.

Jeff swings his legs off the bed, knocking Mah Lin to the floor, grabs his shorts and key off the hook and opens the door. "I want my friends," he says loudly.

"Okay, okay. *Dang-dang,*" she says, flapping her arms at her sides, the universal motion to calm down. She points for him to stay in the room, ties her robe, shrugs, and walks past him out the door. Jeff fears she'll come back a couple of goons, notes that his erection has subsided, and walks down the corridor toward the locker room.

From behind him, he hears a husky, female voice call, "Hey you, mister." He turns and sees a short woman so pregnant she's more wide than tall standing in front of Mah Lin. "Is problem?"

"I just. . . ." he begins.

"Come here," the woman says, motioning for him to approach. He does.

She extends a hand. "Me Jin Xi. Speak English. You problem?"

"Sorry, I just don't understand. . . ."

"Massage okay, yah?" Jin Xi asks.

"Yes. Okay. I just didn't know. . . . I was afraid I'd have to pay. . . ."

"Friend you already paid. Full massage, extras, everyt'ing. You not pay. Okay?"

"Already paid?"

"Yah, yah. You just make fun wit' Mah Lin. She nice girl. Good massage. Good fucky-fuck. Very pretty, yah?"

"Okay. I'm sorry."

"You no like Mah Lin, you take me. Okay?" Jin Xi smiles. "Five hundred Hong Kong dollar, I give you everything."

"No, no," Jeff says. "Mah Lin is fine. It's just. . . ."

"Is problem?"

"It's just . . . I'm married," Jeff says. "I just want a massage, nothing else."

Jin Xi looks at him as if he has two heads. "Only massage? Is okay for. . . ?" She motions sideways with a loosely cupped fist, the universal symbol for hand job.

"No. Just massage."

"Sure?" Jin Xi asks, and Jeff nods. She turns and speaks in Chinese to Mah Lin, who groans "Aaaiiiyaaah," then begins talking excitedly to Mah Lin who finally manages to interrupt and calm her down. "You scare Mah Lin. Okay now. You go finish now, okay?"

"I think I'm finished," Jeff says. "I'll just go back to the jacuzzi and wait for my friends. Okay."

"Sure, sure, okay," Jin Xi says, and explains to Mah Lin, who mutters something as she goes back to the room. "I take you," Jin Xi says.

"I'm very sorry. . . ." Jeff says as they walk.

"No problem. You not understand. Besides, I know mister want Jin Xi. You come back for me and baby give you hand job inside." Jin Xi laughs, and leaves him at the entrance to the whirlpools. "I see you again, mister."

Jeff takes off his shorts, finds his towel where he left it, and soaks in the hot tub, waiting for Moishe and Avi. It would probably be bad enough if Laura found out he was in a place like this. If he'd actually done something, that would have been a lot worse. He had no problem lying to Laura about screwing Rosalinda while they were going out back home, but now that they're married, it would be different, probably. But maybe he was just being stupid.

"You must be one of those American minutemen," Avi says as he and Moishe reenter the pool area.

"Good, yeah?" Moishe says.

"Yeah," Jeff nods. "How much is that?"

"Usually about 200 yuan, 25 US," Avi shouts over the sound of the water, "but the factory pays, and must have a discount." Avi lowers his voice, "You used condom, yes?"

"I just had a massage."

Avi cups a hand over his ear to indicate he didn't hear. Jeff shrugs and makes the universal hand job sign. Avi smiles, and Moishe points at his watch. Avi says, "Listen, if you want to stay and soak, you can, but we want to take the bus at three."

"I'll go with you. If you leave me here, then I'll really be screwed."

CHAPTER 6

Just the Two or Three or Four of Us

RIDING THE ESCALATOR on rainy days always worries Laura. As on the MTR, riders ignore basic courtesies, particularly the bilingual admonition to stand to the right and walk on the left. Laura is a walker, though the first two segments above Queen's Road with slick rubber ramps pitched at 45 degrees, can be treacherous. After that, it's conventional escalators with steps, some with overpasses above traffic, some ending two steps before the curb that create human traffic jams, particularly when people stop to open umbrellas or wait for the rain to abate before crossing the street while the escalator relentlessly delivers a crowd behind them. Laura is convinced of two things: there will be an ugly accident someday, and Fiona Fok won't send an FGN Asia crew to cover it.

Based on her experience residing in both, Laura has concluded that New Yorkers are rude—they actively insult or inconvenience others—while Hong Kongers are aggressively inconsiderate—they're oblivious to others therefore unaware that anything they do could bother someone else. In fact, most Hong Kongers seem to Laura only vaguely aware of much that doesn't involve making money.

For Laura, that's the most bizarre aspects of the handover—Hong Kong people don't seem to care about it. Most of them are just a generation or two removed from escaping the Communists on the mainland, so it's not as if they could trust Beijing or welcome the handover out of ignorance. They certainly don't welcome or trust people from the mainland; illegal immigrants—IIs—are blamed for all crime and social woes. But Hong Kong people act incredibly casual about being put under Communist China's thumb in less than four months' time. Edie says it's self-selection: the ones who are afraid have already left, or, more usually, left, gotten foreign passports as insurance policies and come back, because they can't make nearly as much money any-where else on the planet. The ones still here are either not afraid, or simply resigned, since they're powerless. Resignation, surrendering to the inevitable, is another Chinese characteristic, according to Edie, but Laura can't quite buy it. The attitude about the handover goes beyond resignation to her, more like unconsciousness. Go to sleep in the British empire, wake up in the People's Republic of China—Red China, for god's sake—and pretend nothing has changed. And while Laura believes little will change for FGN Asia or expatriates, she's certain things will change dramatically for people who really live here. How can they not?

What she really wonders, as she rides up the elevator of Proper Gardens past that noise just above the eighth floor, is whether things will change for her, whether she'll ever get off this miserable shift, whether things will ever work right at the station. Or maybe this is just the way television news is—it always has to be perfect and it never is. Or like Hong Kong, she thinks, squeezing through the door of their $2000-a-month shoebox, where nothing ever turns out the way you'd expect. When FGN told her they would double her salary in Hong Kong, she couldn't believe her good fortune. Once she arrived, she realized it would take all of that fortune—including the extra thousand US dollars in monthly housing allowance she got for marrying Jeff—to be able to live a fraction as well as she did in New York. And that was New York. Being in Hong Kong at this moment may be an opportunity to witness history, but Laura finds constant reminders that history was never her favorite subject.

Jeff greets her after she works her way through the door and they kiss, her mouth always open a little too wide for Jeff's taste. He can taste her last glass of wine, white, and the salted peanuts chaser.

"How was your day?" he asks.

"Starting from the end," she recounts, walking into her bedroom to drop her bag, then to the kitchen for a glass of wine, "I had a drink with Edie and Andy, he's one of the other producers, his wife works for CNN as an anchor. He says our network is going to fold a week after the handover. Do you want a glass of wine?"

"No thanks," Jeff says. "I've got water."

She returns to the living room, clinks her wine against his water, and takes a big sip.

"I'm glad you're home," Jeff says, "because I have a surprise for you. . . ."

"I'm really glad you're home, too, sweetheart. I don't know why, but, god, am I horny. Your room?"

"A new position."

"Let's not make it too difficult. I just thought we could try a new room."

"I know, that's what I meant by new position. . . ."

"Oh, I get it. Funny, Jeff."

They step into the room, and fall onto the bed, wedged between three walls, the window at the foot looking toward the harbor and two along the side toward Central, blocked by the apartment house three feet away. Jeff begins to drop the blinds, but Laura grabs his hand. "Don't bother. Let 'em watch. Maybe they'll learn something."

They do it enthusiastically, Laura lapsing almost immediately into a series of barely audible phrases, mouth quivering. During her apparent nearly unbearable ecstasy, Jeff thinks he hears the phrase, "Roll tape." He senses someone across the way watching. Amid Laura's muttering, Jeff feels the dull spasm of ejaculation without the rapture of orgasm.

"We better get up now, before I fall asleep and stay here all night," Laura says.

"Okay." Jeff slips a quick glance to the next building but doesn't see anyone. "Like I said, I have something I want to show you. . . ."

"You showed me plenty already, mister," Laura says, smiling, lying on her side, her head raised and resting in her hand. "Do you mind if I have the first shower?"

"That's fine. I'll have a shower at the gym. I didn't have a workout today. I was tied up with. . . ."

"Would you be a dear and get me my wine?" Laura asks, stepping up into the bathroom and flipping the switch for the gas water heater. "It's been a long, lousy day—until a couple of minutes ago, I mean—and I just want to relax." She opens the window above the toilet, the required safety measure to prevent asphyxiation from the heater.

Jeff brings her glass of wine. Laura drains it and hands it back to him. "Thanks," she says and starts the water.

Jeff opens his gym bag and spreads the items across his still warm bed sheet. Then he goes to the kitchen to check the refrigerator. Leftover rice and salad fixings, but otherwise barren beyond second-string condiments and open bottles of red and white wine. Maybe he'll treat himself to a glass after the gym.

"Do you want me to run down and get something for dinner?" he calls to Laura over the running water.

"Talk to me when I'm out," she answers.

He goes back to the bedroom and holds up a pair of yellow box-cut panties to the light in the window, the very first of what he hopes will be thousands of these Golden Beauties from China. He examines the stitching on the waistband and snaps it, enjoying the crisp report of quality elastic. He examines a light blue, low-cut lacy bra, hooks it together in the back and pulls. There's slight give in the side panels, enough for comfort, none in the front, and the fabric keeps its shape under the stress.

Across the way, Jeff sees a Filipina amah at the kitchen counter, turning away, her face hidden by her shoulder length hair as she chops vegetables. She must think I'm some kind of pervert, Jeff realizes, standing here naked, playing with women's underwear. He's talked to Laura about getting an amah once a week to clean their place and do the laundry, but Laura refuses. "I can clean my own house," she protests, but he's the one who winds up doing the work. Except for ironing: Laura irons her clothes and then insists that Jeff, who never ironed before since every piece of dress clothing he owns is permanent press, iron his.

The water stops and Laura emerges from the bathroom wrapped in a towel. "Another day's sentence in Chai Wan down the drain," she says.

"Do you want me to run down and get a barbecued chicken from the window in the Chinese place? Jeff asks.

"Another chicken, geez," Laura says. "I'll start growing feathers."

"Or I can go to Wellcome. . . ."

"I'm not really hungry, to be honest. I had a couple of Edie's potato wedges. I think I just want to sleep. Midnight rolls around pretty fast."

"Okay," Jeff says. "But first take a look in my bedroom."

"Whose underwear is that?" Laura says, sounding annoyed.

"It's mine . . . yours," Jeff stammers. "It's the first set of Golden Beauties samples from the factory, and I had them made in your sizes. I hope. . . ."

"You told everyone my sizes?" Laura gasps.

"I did, but . . . but I didn't say it was for you," Jeff quickly adds.

"Good. It's very nice," Laura says, turning and walking into her bedroom.

Jeff follows her. "It's for you, the underwear. I'd like you to try it, kind of field test it. . . ."

"Okay, okay," Laura says.

"It's our set of first samples. I'll get you some from the first production run, too, and if you let me know what you want, Moishe and Wian can draw it up and we'll make up some of that, too. Just think, you'll be the inspiration that launches our entire Golden Beauties line. . . ."

"The ass that launched a thousand shorts," Laura says, putting on her own oversized tee-shirt for sleeping and pushing past Jeff through the doorway. "What an honor."

"I thought you'd be a little excited," Jeff says, trying his best to sound hurt.

"It's just underwear," Laura says, pouring herself a glass of white wine, leaving the empty bottle on the kitchen counter. "Underwear from China, no less. My grandmother gives me underwear in my Christmas stocking. . . ."

"You used to like it back in New York when I gave you underwear, and that stuff was from China, too, probably."

"I'm sorry, Jeff, I'm too tired to get excited about underwear right now," she says, flopping into the wicker chair. "It just keeps getting worse and worse," Laura replies to a question she may have imagined he'd asked. "Every day, every show, I feel like the water keeps getting deeper and deeper, like the surface keeps getting further and further away, the air keeps getting thinner, and the current keeps running faster and faster." She takes another gulp of wine. "You don't know what a relief it is to be able to rely on you. To know you'll be home and here for me. No surprises, no bad news, no disappointments." More wine. "Especially in bed, never any disappointments."

"I don't need this kind of pressure," Jeff says, standing between the kitchen and her, smiling.

"Pressure? You think what you can or can't do with your dick is pressure? Who cares about your dick besides me and you? Is a global news network with millions. . . ?"

"Laura, I was making a joke."

"Oh." She takes a deep breath. "God, you see, I'm losing perspective. It's the pressure, the hours. When you work in television, you can't be a normal person. . . ."

"It's okay, sweetheart. Things will change. You'll get better . . . better help, more support at work. It takes time to adjust. It's still only been a couple of months."

"Going on four," Laura says, shaking her head. "I hope you're right."

"Things turned around for me, they'll turn around for you."

"I hope so. I've tried, I keep trying to talk to our boss, CK, the station manager. But he's always having meetings up in Zhuhai or Shenzhen and never has time to talk to anyone. . . ."

"It's okay. . . ."

"It is not okay," she whines. "It's so unfair. . . ."

"You're right, you're right. It's not okay. That isn't what I meant. I mean that you'll find a way around it. My father always said there's three things you can do with a problem. . . ."

"Are."

"R?"

"Are. There *are* three things you can do with a problem. . . ." Laura patiently points out.

"Thanks. Right. There are three things you can do with a problem. Fix it, forget it or farm it out. If you can't farm it out to your boss or your employees, then you've got to either fix it or forget it."

"Easy for you to say. You don't know how it is there. It's like there's a two-ton weight hanging over my head every show. One false move, and it comes crashing down on my head."

"But isn't every job like that in some. . . ."

"No, it's not." Laura takes another sip of wine. "It's even worse than that. It's like the two-ton weight is already on top of my head, pushing me down, and I've got to use all of my strength just to keep it from crushing me."

"Can't your friend Eleanor help you?"

"You mean Edie . . . Edie, Edie." Laura shakes her head, disappointed that Jeff doesn't pay a little more attention to her work that pays the rent around her. "Edie does everything she can to help, but you don't understand. . . ."

"Then. . . ."

"I'm in the control room by myself. I mean, there's other people around, but I'm the producer, I'm in charge. When I make the wrong decision, or even when I do everything right and someone else screws up, which is usually the case, that weight pushes down even harder."

"Sounds awf. . . ."

"Is there more wine?" Laura asks.

Jeff walks to the kitchen, sees the empty bottle on the counter and opens the refrigerator. "There's another white. . . ."

"Open?"

"There's an open red in the door. . . ."

"That'll do," Laura says. "Thanks," she adds as he brings the bottle and fills her glass.

"Try to see the big picture, sweetheart. You came here to be a witness to history," Jeff reminds her, trying to recall the words he'd heard her repeat so often to explain to people who wondered why she'd leave not just the *Journal* but New York to move to Hong Kong. "This is all part of the learning curve so that when it comes time for the handover. . . . What's that you say there? 'It's the stupid handover'?"

"Close: 'It's the handover, stupid.' But it's not just the handover. What happens every day matters. If we keep screwing up, by the time we get to the handover, no one will be watching us. Everyday, I get the abuse whenever there's a screw-up, whether it's mine or the graphics girl or the director or the anchor. It doesn't matter. I get the blame." She sighs. "It's not just the job. The crazy sleeping, the whole routine is just beating me down. And living here just makes it worse. Yesterday, I didn't get finished until after three, Edie was already gone, and I missed the shuttle bus, so I get in a taxi and I say, 'Heng Fa Chuen MTR,' and the driver just looks at me. So I say 'Heng Fa Chuen MTR' again. He looks back at me and says 'Heng Fa Chuen?' and shrugs. I get out and wait for another cab. When I tell this driver 'Heng Fa Chuen MTR,' he wrinkles his forehead as if he's working out the theory of relativity, then says, 'MTR, Heng Fa Chuen?' I say yes and he says, 'Oh. Heng FA Chuen.' The time before, another cab driver, after we go through this same routine, says, 'Heng Fa CHUEN.' As if, there's some other MTR station I want around there that sounds the same as Heng Fa Chuen, like Chai Wan or Shau Kei Wan. They're worse language snobs that the Parisians. . . ."

"But what about the cab drivers in New York?" Jeff says.

"They might not speak English either, but at least they don't expect your Farsi to be perfect. New York," Laura mutters, shaking her head then sipping wine. "I'm not the same person I was in New York. I used to care about how I looked, used to. . . ."

"I think you look great, sweetheart."

"Thanks. But you don't see me at 12:30 when I'm rolling out of here with no makeup, a work shirt, pants from college and sneakers. In the studio, it's so cold I put on a cardigan that looks like a hand-me-down from Mister Rogers. When I was at the *Journal*. . . . You remember how I dressed then. I was on Barney's preferred customer list. But here, it's like, who the heck is going to see me anyway at two in the morning in Chai Wan?

"And it's not just the grind everyday, it's not just that. It's worrying about the handover. Edie says CK won't even discuss it with her."

"Discuss what? I mean the handover is going to happen, right? It's not going to be delayed for six months or something?"

"No, of course not." She takes a gulp of wine. "But am I going to be the handover night producer? That's what I'm worried about. If not, I came an awfully long way for nothing."

"Well, not for nothing. I mean you're learning a lot. . . ."

"The way I see it, Edie likes me, so that's in my favor," Laura says, holding up one hand and looking toward the ceiling. "I think Lamont likes me well enough, too, but we don't really work together. He knows Sara's work better—Sara Fergis, the *Market Wrap* producer—so he'd probably vote for her, but he wouldn't veto me, probably. On the other hand, CK doesn't like me, though I don't think he likes anyone except his cousin KS and the bosses whose asses he kisses and whoever it is in Zhuhai or wherever where he keeps having those meetings every day." She takes another drink of wine. "But then there's Deng, and he's a real problem."

"Deng?"

"My anchor," she says, glancing at Jeff, then fixing her gaze upward again. "He still hates me, and it's a done deal that he'll be the anchor on handover night. But maybe he'll be happy to have me, somebody he knows he can bully. . . . But it doesn't matter, because the anchor is always right." She drains her glass. "I better get to bed, or else my graphics girl won't be the only one drunk and sleepy tomorrow morning in the control room." She kisses Jeff on the cheek as she walks past him to the bathroom.

He takes her glass to the sink, puts the wine bottle back in the refrigerator, and hears her bedroom door close.

In his bedroom, Jeff packs a clean outfit in his gym bag to wear after his workout. He changes into that pair of shorts that he uses for the gym as well as the swimming pool and reminds himself to talk to the factory about making a men's and ladies' line of shorts modeled on it. Maybe call them Gym Dandies.

He checks the clock on the headboard above his bed, after seven. His mother will be up, and at least she'll be excited about the samples. He carries the phone into his bedroom, closes the door behind him and dials the number.

"Hello," his mother says, picking up on the first ring.

"Hi, Ma. How are you?"

"Who's this?"

"Who else calls you Ma?"

"Is this Jeffrey?"

"Of course it's Jeff."

"I just don't expect so early in the morning for you to call me."

"It's night time here, about seven."

"But here it's morning. I always like this time of the morning, nice and quiet. . . ."

"A good time to plot those canasta moves that make you the most dangerous woman in Mid Island. . . ."

"Don't laugh. I won 35 cents from Sadie and Esther last week."

"Don't spend it all in one place, Ma. Listen, I've got samples from the factory, and we've shipped a set to you. You should have them tomorrow or day after tomorrow."

"From China so fast? Must be expensive."

"The factory is paying, long as we give them the order."

"You've seen the samples?"

"Yes, I have a set here, in Laura's sizes, and I'm having her try them."

"How do they look?"

"They look good," he says, seeing the Filipina amah in the window across the way removing her shirt over her head. "Very good." A 34B, he estimates.

"Well, the samples, that's really your department."

"Okay, so about the payment. . . ."

"Since you already sent the samples, a look I'll take. I'll bring them to Ruthie at the Plainview store—she has a very good fashion sense—and then we can decide how much to order."

"But the payments need to be. . . ." The Filipina across the way, in a schoolgirl white bra, definitely 34B, sits on the edge of her bed and leans forward to remove her socks.

"We can talk about it all later, after I see the samples."

"When you have the numbers for the order, make sure you call me and then I can get the final prices. . . ."

"Final prices you don't have?"

"I do, but it depends on the numbers and any changes we might want on the merchandise. But yes, we've settled on prices per gross."

"Grosses? You think grosses we can take. . . ?"

"We talked about trying to do some wholesaling. You and Jerry Lewis or whoever. . . ."

"I know, I know."

"How's that going?" The Filipina finishes with her socks, and, leaning back on the bed, unsnaps her jeans.

"I have to talk to Jerry."

"All right. Talk, look, just let me know when you have it all figured out. You can call me. . . ."

"I should call you?"

"Yes." The Filipina slowly rolls down her jeans, then sits up and holds them out in front of her to smooth them. "But don't call this time. Laura's already asleep for her crazy job, and if you call you'll wake her. You can call me at the office, but you'd have to do it after ten o'clock at night your time, and I'm not always there. Sometimes I'm at the factory. . . ."

"Oy, so confusing. My time, your time. . . . Your old mother can't keep track. . . ."

"You can also fax it."

"A fax you have?"

"Send me three hundred bucks and I'll buy a fax machine." The Filipina walks away from the window showing the baggy seat of her beige panties, rayon probably, so they don't breathe, awfully warm and sweaty under the jeans. She's probably going to take a shower.

"Buy one with your own money," she tells him. "The money I pay you."

"I just spent a hundred fifty on my China visa," Jeff says. "Anyway, you can send the order to the fax machine at Avi and Moishe's office." The Filipina hangs the jeans on a hook on the back wall of the room, turns to the right and unhooks her bra as she walks out of sight. "I gave you the number, and it's on the fax I sent. . . ."

"You should watch those Israeli guys."

"Don't worry, Ma, I'm watching. Very closely," he says, in case the Filipina comes back into the picture. "You have the fax number, right?"

"Yes. All these numbers I have. Whatever I save from merchandise, I'll wind up spending on AT&T."

"Meanwhile, I am, Ma, so I should hang up. Let me know the order details, call at night or fax or whatever, and we'll get production going. Love you."

"You, too, son."

As he clicks off, he notices a sliver of light piercing the room across the way, undoubtedly from her bathroom, where the Filipina must be naked, giving herself completely to the powerful nozzle, scrubbing her tan, wiry arms with a bar of bright, white soap. Then lathering her soft, warm belly and down to her thighs, making small circles yielding rich foam bubbles. At the end of her smooth thighs, vigorously rubbing her small black crest of hair until her breathing quickens to a pant. . . . I guess she reminds me of Rosalinda, Jeff thinks, as he carries the cordless phone back to its living room cradle.

He can imagine Rosalinda back home listening to his thoughts and having one of those great laughs of hers, with her mouth wide open and showing all her teeth. She used to call him *culeador,* butt maestro, even though she never let him put it in hers, no matter how much he begged her. *Culeador* was her way of calling him heartless. He'd have her at the store but never see her outside work, never took her to a movie or the marina. He did pay for her meals at the store, but he usually did that for whoever was working (out of the register, not his pocket), and give her little presents. When he was horny, he'd ask her to come in to work, never just to come in and fool around, but ask her to come in and work and pay her for a full shift, even on days when he locked the door and put up the "Back in 5 Minutes" sign as soon as she walked in and left it there until closing time. One day, while they ate the lunch he'd bought following a particularly memorable 30-minute double, Rosalinda had seemed to read his mind. "Thanks for the san'ich, boss. I don't 'spect nuthin' from you, you know," she declared. Before he could swallow his bite of ham and swiss on rye to reply, Rosalinda added, "I like coming to work and doing that and getting paid, too. There are lots of worser jobs." She giggled. "You couldn't do that at no Burger King . . . even if they say it's the home of the whopper." She just laughed and kept coming back for more, calling him *culeador,* and pocketing the cash. Just who was heartless, Jeff wonders.

If Jeff misses Rosalinda a little, he misses Laura more. The Laura who'd caught him screwing Rosalinda that winter morning just about a year ago was the kind of smart and sassy woman he was ready to spend the rest of his life with. The problem right now is that job of hers. On that crazy schedule, she's working for the station 24 hours a day. Television really is her life. Of course, they pay her pretty nicely for it. But by the time she comes home from work, it's time to go to bed so she can get up and do it again. But it's not forever, Jeff hopes.

Jeff visited the newsroom once. What a mistake. It was a madhouse, no place for a sane person. The vast space was eerily quiet except for the hum of the fluorescent lights, fingers tapping on keyboards, and the beat of feet dashing toward the control room. Occasionally somebody would yell out a question, in tones as harsh as the lighting. That anchor-woman—when Jeff first saw her on TV, he thought, that's one of the ten most beautiful women I've seen in my life—was walking around in bedroom slippers with curlers in her hair and teabags taped under her eyes. It's all a big illusion, complete fantasy, and Laura is one of the people who make it look real. To Jeff, that seems like magic.

It's a lot different from the underwear business, which he understands inside out. With what he knows about the market in the US and what Avi and Moishe know about China, they've got a winning partnership. Sure, he needs his mother back home with the stores to get things started, but once they have merchandise moving, once people see the quality they can deliver at a big discount to what the labels offer and how they can do custom work, adapt to the market fast, have product in the stores in seven weeks—five, maybe—then Jeff will really be pulling down serious numbers.

Jeff's mother plays dumb, but he knows she's a smart cookie, too. She may not have many ideas of her own, but she knows how to pick up dollars lying around on the ground. She'll convince Jerry Lewis that it's more fun selling ladies' underwear than writing leases. Take something simple, lace-front bikinis in pale colors, the sort of garment you could promote that Filipina to from her beige baggies. Retail $3.50, maybe you offer a six-pack . . . seven-pack, panties for the week, in different colors for $20. They cost six cents a piece to make, including the cut for Avi and Moishe, a dime to ship, add a penny for Jeff. Move a hundred pieces a week at each store, that's $1665. Wholesale them to other stores for a buck-fifty and you're a hero, and you've got another $1330 per thousand for him and $1000-plus for his mom. That's real money, he realizes, enough for Ma to pick up and to give Jeff a decent living, too. From just that one simple item.

From the foundations king of Mid Island to the intimate apparel emperor of the Middle Kingdom: what a long, strange trip it's been. For now, though, Jeff's throne room is still this tiny apartment, rigged for silent running after dark, hard by the escalator, all that Laura's housing allowance can afford. When the money starts rolling in, maybe he can contribute enough to get them an adult-size place. He tiptoes out the front door, keeps the gate from slamming, rides down the fifteen flights, shushing the scrape above eight, and walks to the JCC for his workout.

After a 40-minute session on the stepper, leg lifts on the parallel bars, sit-ups on the inclined bench, and a trip around the weight stations, his light workout, Jeff hits the pool for 50 laps, then the jacuzzi. Avi and Moishe are having a soak, and he joins them.

"Lieh ho ma, boychicks," Jeff says.

"The massage girls was all asking for you," Avi says with a sly smile.

"Everybody loves the American minuteman," Jeff says.

"You ever try over here?" Avi asks.

"They have places like that in Hong Kong?"

"Plenty," Avi says. "Some very expensive, but some reasonable over in North Point. Less than a thousand Hong Kong."

"That's expensive for me," Jeff says.

"Over in Wanchai, you can get anything you want, sometimes cheaper."

"I thought it was all clip joints. . . ."

"The girly bars, yeah," Avi says.

"We go if a client pay," Moishe says.

"But you go to the places like Joe Bananas or Big Apple," Avi says, "and there's plenty of what do you call it . . . unattached?"

"You mean singles?" Jeff asks.

"No, independent. Like a writer. . . ."

"Freelancers."

"That's right. You have a drink and relax. Mostly Filipina. They're okay," Avi assures.

"Nice blow job," Moishe adds.

"Also over there in Kowloon, you know the ATMs across from the bus terminal," Avi adds. "At night over there, the girls wait for you to take out money, so they know you got money. . . ."

"That sounds like Hong Kong," Jeff says.

"Of course, all kinds business in Hong Kong is more expensive," Avi continues. "For the girl about a thousand, then another three-four hundred for a room. Sometimes you get cheaper, but it's like in *schmattes*: you pay cheap, you get cheap. For quality, you pay top dollar."

"Words to live by, partner." Jeff really is lucky he ran into these two burly Israelis, guys he would have run away from back in New York, for no other reason than that they looked too Jewish. Here, it's almost like no matter how Jewish they are, or he is, it doesn't matter. No one notices, except for that crack from their landlord about the Jewish Center, a crack that made Laura so angry but turns out to have been the most important advice he's gotten in Hong Kong.

"I talked to my mother," Jeff says. "She says she'll send the order details after she sees the samples. I told her to call me or to fax the final totals to your office."

"That's good. When everything is ready, we make a visit Mister Xu."

"He say like Mister Jew," Moishe says, laughing.

"We're gonna make good business together," Avi assures him, "the three of us. You and me and Moishe."

"The four of us," Jeff says. "Don't forget my mother."

CHAPTER 7

Motherfucked

Avi and Moishe ask Jeff to come to the factory with them, and he's glad to go. He's still waiting for the final order numbers from his mother, but there are a couple of loose threads he needs to take care of with Xu and Wian. He wants to see final color samples, especially the green and pink. He wants the pink subtle, not something that looks like electric bubble gum.

They're taking a later bus, at ten, because Avi says he has errands to do in the morning. Jeff leaves Laura a note that he may be home late, and meets Moishe and Avi at the bus stop in Kowloon. They're waiting for him at the head of the boarding line with about a dozen plastic shopping bags between them. "We saved a place for you," Avi says.

"A lot of bags. . . ." Jeff says.

"Gifts," Moishe says.

"Take a few," Avi says.

Jeff peeks inside one bag, and sees the usual tins of butter cookies. "Always the same gifts?"

"Inside is variety," Avi answers. "Like with Golden Beauties underwear."

When the door opens, Avi and Moishe lead him to a seat two rows from the front. "Do like Chinese," Moishe instructs, pushing his bags into the floor space in front of the window seat, putting a bag on the seat, then pointing for Jeff to sit in the aisle seat to discourage other passengers from taking the seat next to him. Avi does the same across the aisle, and Moishe stakes out a place behind Avi. This bus isn't as crowded as at eight o'clock so no one objects to their ploy.

At the border crossing, the mainland guards in their drab green uniforms and oversized caps that swallow their foreheads beneath short black visors seem annoyed about their bags. *"Wei shema?"* the guard asks Jeff, looking inside the bags.

"Cookies. For big party, birthday party," Avi says from the spot behind Jeff in the line, and Moishe translates. The guard nods, stamps the passport, and tells Jeff to pass with a twitch of his head.

They reboard the bus, taking the same seats. As they ride, Jeff notices that even since his last trip to the factory a week ago new construction cranes have joined the flock. At the bus stop, the driver from the factory has a uniformed policeman with him, making the VW a tighter squeeze than usual. Jeff gets squashed between Avi and the policeman in the back seat, with a least nine bags on the floor around them. By the time they reach the factory, Jeff feels as if he'll fly out the door when it opens, or shoot through the roof if it doesn't. Lugging the bags across the factory floor, amid the deafening noise, Jeff notices two sections of sewing machines producing sleepwear. Simple nightgowns in one cluster, pink baby-doll nighties with matching panties in another cluster. Look at how fast they move, Jeff thinks. With a penny a piece on our orders, I'm gonna retire.

At the office, Xu and Wian greet the trio effusively. Constable Zhao accepts a salute from the police officer who accompanied them from the bus stop, then dismisses him and pours a nip of brandy for all. A vigorous toast from Xu and all down their shots. Moishe speaks to them in Chinese while Avi unpacks the bags, stacking tins of butter cookies on Xu's desk.

"I want to check the colors on our order," Jeff says, "the pink and the green especially."

Avi speaks to Moishe in Hebrew, Moishe speaks to Xu in Mandarin, Xu speaks to Wian in Cantonese, Wian nods to Moishe, who nods to Avi, who tells Jeff, "Wian can take you out around to see what's what."

Jeff follows Wian into the clattering of the factory floor. They walk through a section where the girls are stitching gym leotards to another cluster where they're putting linings in bras. Wian approaches the forewoman pacing around the cluster, points to Jeff, and she nods. Wian hands Jeff a light pink bra. This color is good, Jeff thinks, and the fabric is fine. We should get this for our order. Wian points to the back clasp and straps and says something, but the noise drowns it out and it's Chinese anyway. Examining the bra, a knock-off of a popular Maidenform model, Jeff notices shortcuts, including nylon thread instead of cotton on the side panels. That means the thread wouldn't wear the same as the material, so eventually the stitching will get loose. That won't happen until dozens of washings, so the bra wouldn't be a suitable family heirloom, but otherwise the change won't make much difference to buyers. At another station, Wian hands him tightly-woven cotton briefs with teddy-bear designs. God, Jeff thinks, this is the kind of junk my mother would give to Laura as a Chanukah present: "Here, Darling, some nice underwear so you wouldn't be embarrassed in case you get in an accident, the way my son drives with his crazy boat." But he could never imagine his mother taking the trouble to give Laura a gift.

They pass flannel nightshirts, also suitable for his mother's gift list, and lacy polyester green and black teddies, the sort of impractical presents guys buy for girlfriends who throw out the lingerie after they break up. When guys came in to the store asking for those things—and it was always guys, women never bought this stuff for themselves—Jeff would steer them toward the sheer negligee. "Good view, easy access," he'd tell them. The green is the right color, but the artificial fabric feels rough. This stuff on the assembly line isn't great, but Jeff enjoys getting tangled up in women's underwear again. Like his pop, Jeff knows it top to bottom, and finally he can see the pot of gold at the end of the front bow.

When Jeff and Wian return to the office, Xu and Zhao are standing behind the desk, Avi and Moishe in front of it, stacks of cookie tins piled on both sides of them. Everyone glances as the door opens, then turns their attention back to the middle of the desk. Approaching the desk, Jeff sees they're counting money, bundles of stacked US$100 bills and a few bundles of Hong Kong $500s and $1000s inside open cookie tins. "We just counting up the payment," Avi says.

Jeff estimates about $50,000 US per tin and about two dozen tins. "Nice order."

Avi nods.

"I saw a pink fabric out there I like," Jeff says. "among all that *chazarei*. The green on the teddies looks right, but the texture is rough. . . ."

"We'll talk about it over lunch," Avi says. "As soon as they finish counting."

Jeff takes a seat on the couch, and Wian pours him a brandy.

The factory people can't join them for lunch, Avi explains, because of the lateness of the visit. "And they need to do things with that cash," Avi adds, as the three of them settle into a private room at the restaurant.

"How come you make payments this way?" Jeff asks.

"Because it's China," Avi says. "You can't send a check or make a wire transfer."

"No?"

"They say maybe next year the banks will accept foreign currency transfers. But even if they do, and you trust the banks, then it's harder for everybody to get something under the table."

"I see, I think," Jeff says. "Who needs to get paid off?"

"Party officials, local police, plus suppliers and shipping. They all prefer US or Hong Kong money if they can get it, and it makes it easier to do business."

Jeff nods. "So whose order is on the line now?"

"Yours," Avi says.

"Mine? All of it?"

"Your mother didn't tell you?"

"No. I thought we were still waiting for her confirmation on the numbers. . . ."

"I thought your mother told you. . . ." Avi says.

"Told me what?" Jeff realizes he's raised his voice. "Sorry," he says more quietly, "but I don't understand."

"Your mother told us go ahead."

"The colors. . . ?"

"I checked everything," Moishe says. "Strictly kosher."

"But I didn't see the goods on the list, except the M-18s. . . ."

"Your mother made changes. . . ."

"Like what. . . ?"

"She and the Jerry guy there says they found a big buyer," Avi says, "that wants different things. I think you just talk to her. . . ."

"What happened?" Jeff asks, more exasperated than interested in any possible answer. "The payment?"

"Also yours. Your mother made a transfer. . . ."

"Wait a minute. Did you bill my mother?"

"Yeah," Avi says, "of course."

"Without telling me?" Jeff says. His tone of voice leads Moishe to lean toward Avi to make sure he understands completely.

"That's what she told us to do," Avi explains. After five years in Hong Kong and China, Avi still gets a kick out of the idea that an Israeli can be the voice of calm reason among the other crazy people here. Now he's trying to be the voice of reason between a nice Jewish boy over his head in women's *gotkes,* from New York, no less, and his mother 12,000 miles away. Life is a funny thing, Avi thinks. "What did you think. . . ?"

"I thought I would get the order from my mother, then review it, and you would bill me," Jeff begins.

"You was going to make a cut on your mother?" Moishe interrupts.

"No, but. . . ."

"I thought you work together, you and your mother" Avi adds. "She said she pays you. . . ."

"She pays me enough to survive in the US, maybe," Jeff says, and have a nice sports car and a boat, assuming you live at home and have an insurance nest egg. "But for here, it's nothing. If my wife didn't pay the rent, I couldn't afford bus fare."

"So you was going to cut on your mother," Avi says. "Just like she said. . . ."

"No, I wanted to work with you and use them as our distributors to other outlets. . . . The contracts. . . ?"

"Already, with her."

"Samples. . . ?"

"Already. Xu sends FedEx, and she approve by fax."

"Designs. . . ?"

"From her specs from the customers."

"How much did she order?"

"A hundred-eighty-thousand. . . ."

"A hundred-eighty-thousand pieces?" Jeff says in astonishment.

"A hundred-eighty-thousand dozen," Ari says.

"A hundred-eighty-eight-thousand dozen," Moishe corrects. "Eight is a lucky number for Chinese."

"All the stuff in production now," Avi says. "It should start to ship next week."

"Wow. I didn't know." At a penny a piece, that would be more than $20,000 US. "She didn't tell me."

"You should talk with your mother more often, *boychick.*"

Despite his impulse to storm out, Jeff stays through the meal, allowing a feeling of Zen resignation to wash over him, aided by several bottles of beer. He remains civil with Avi and Moishe while picking at the lunch and hearing details of his mother's huge order, and, at the massage parlor afterward, recalls only being rudely awakened by rapping on the door. "Finish," his masseuse says, as Jeff rolls over onto his back. "Finish," she repeats. Back in the locker room, he checks his watch and sees it's already past eight o'clock. Too late to call Laura to say he'll be late. Moishe and Avi have already left; Jeff finds a note taped to his locker telling him there are buses in the normal spot every half-hour until eleven; for later, there's something written in Chinese to show people. When he gets home, he'll talk to his mother and find out what the hell is going on. Even if Jeff thinks he can stay calm and keep his voice down, what can he say to her? He was planning to take a cut of the shipments but instead she ran around him to these Israelis that she seems to trust more than her own son, who only wanted a small cut anyway, a lousy penny a piece.

Jeff leaves the massage parlor through the restaurant, asks for another big beer and, after checking to make sure he hasn't lost his return ticket for the bus, hands over his last HK$20 to pay for it, then goes outside to wait for the bus. The night air here is cool and crisp, the way it was in Hong Kong when they arrived before it turned cold, sodden, and gray, as if it was on the verge of raining, or even snowing, though it wasn't nearly cold enough for that. It never falls below freezing there, so they leave the water pipes on the outside of buildings, everything that belongs in the sewer out in the open, the way he feels now about business with his mother. The bus arrives nearly on time and is not crowded. Jeff finds a window seat and sleeps curled around his beer. He sleepwalks through the border crossing and has to be prodded off the bus at Kowloon, another stupid, drunk *gweiloh* back from a massage parlor across the border.

The brightly lit ATM cluster across the street reminds Jeff that he spent the last of his cash on that beer. He checks the back of his ATM card to see if the symbols there match up with any on these machines. He still doesn't have a goddamn bank account. He's still getting money from his account in New York where his mother puts his lousy $500 salary, his spending money, his allowance. It would have been a year's salary from that one order, and that was just the beginning. Them, they're making, 188,000 dozen, with shipping maybe $2 a dozen, selling for $9 a piece; even wholesale that's $30 a dozen . . . my god that's more than $5 million. On one order. Instead of cutting on his mother and that fucking Jerry Lewis—that's her real son and you can bet he's taking a cut on her, on him, on all of them, like he has ever since he drew up the papers that keep Jeff away from the fortune his father built, the fortune that he spent the past decade protecting, while protecting his mother from the realities of the world—they just cut on him again.

It's not enough how they played him for a fool, his mother and Jerry Lewis. Imagine that, being a fool to Jerry fucking Lewis. He didn't have to give up college, didn't have to spend the past ten years pushing Murray's ladies' fat asses into girdles, making himself a *maven af gotkes,* a *maven af drek,* for a lousy $500 a week. He didn't have to do it, not any of it. They could have closed the stores, probably would have made more renting them than running them. The rentals alone from those five properties would have been enough to support his mother and to pay for his college. Just from those five Golden Beauties stores, the rent would have been plenty. And it wasn't just from the five stores, it was from five goddamn shopping centers, from Waldbaum's and Chicken Delight and Buy-Rite and Stride-Rite and Thom McAn and Manufacturers Hanover and Chase Manhattan and Klassy Kleaners and Pergament Paints and AID Auto and Helene's House of Glamour and Genovese Drugs and Gymboree and Empress Travel and H&R Block and Loehmann's and Modell's and Aaronson's Army Navy and Forschmann's Gifts and Fleischmann's Bagels and Sonny's Pizza and the Chinese takeaways like Jerry Lewis' parents' place where names changed over the years from Hong Kong Palace and Chow Mein Street to Great Wall Szechuan and Portable Panda. Instead of letting him live a good life, where the property worked instead of the owner, they cut on him, cut on his life, while they had millions. Now they're making more, and paying him $500 a week to work for them. That's one one-hundredth of one percent of five million.

Without a thank you, without a single word from his mother. That's how she operates, always has. "It's not what you say that counts," she used to say in the car after a day among the cackling hens at the beach club, "it's what you don't say." She didn't say anything about their millions in property, about the irrelevance of the Golden Beauties stores in the family finances, about where things really stood after his father died. She never said a word about that, so Jeff tried to do what he thought was right based on his assumption that the family's unspectacular living from the stores was under threat from their decline, not that retailing was daycare for his father to give him something to do, the way Jeff now needs something to do in Hong Kong since he's cut out of the business he's built for Avi and Moishe and his mother and Jerry Lewis, the Gang of Four.

Jeff quit school and dove into women's underwear because he thought that was what was best for his mother, best for the family, and she just let him, probably thinking he was a good little boy, the way she did when he drank his milk or did his homework or said the Chanukah *baruchas* in front of her canasta club, probably laughing behind his back all the time. If he hadn't done what she wanted, Jeff surely would have heard about it, or not heard about in such a way as to hear about it. Like when he decided to buy the boat using the payoff from Murray's insurance that went directly to him—money he now realizes his father had arranged that way so that Jeff could continue his college education unimpeded, money that his mother must have known his father had arranged that way for just that reason, money that must have been a fraction of what his mother got, but she never said. When he told his mother that he said he wasn't going to save all his money for a rainy day but use it to enjoy the sunny days, she wished him luck with the *goyim* at the marina and said she was sure that after just four years of eternity his father was happy Jeff could take pleasure from his death in a way she never could bring herself to, as if the shows in New York and the trips to Israel and Europe with the girls had nothing to do with his father's money. She never acknowledged the boat again in any conversation after that, never asked him a question about it, and never even went to see it, deflecting every invitation to come out for a sail with an "Aah" or "Oy" until he stopped making them.

If he'd only known about the property, about his family's true circumstances, he would have sold the stores, given them away for the cost of the stock and supplies if someone wanted them, or just closed them. He could have done it all in a few months and gone back to school

the next semester to study real estate or investing or property development. He definitely would have gone back to school—maybe a school
closer to home—where women's underwear would have been nothing
more than a flimsy, high margin barrier between him and his passionate-
ly desired objective. Maybe things had wound up that way, after all.

But he shouldn't have had to move halfway around the world to find
out all that. Now, here he was, stuck in a place where he has no place,
in a new life without a life except as the errand boy—the Geisha
Boy—for his mother and Jerry Lewis and a couple of Israelis who may
or may not be screwing him and his mother and the business that he
gave his life to for almost ten years—a third of his life—for no good
reason. Here he was, all the way in Hong Kong, where he didn't speak
the language, totally dependent on his mother and his wife, now without
any way to change that, without enough money to live on, without
anything in particular to live for, without companionship because his
wife is so totally consumed with her life in TV and receiving her dose
of Vitamin J before she goes to sleep before dark, floating on a pillow
of cheap wine, pumped with the thrill of performing live, which is what
people in retailing do all the time. He always thinks he's doing something
for the women in his life, never realizes that they're really doing
something to him.

At least with Rosalinda at the store, they had things to share besides
the righteous fit of their genitals. They had common ground of the
customers, the stock, the other help, the neighbors in the shopping
center, even their differences. He loved the way on Fridays after watching
Seinfeld she'd ask questions about cultural references in the show. *"Es
verdad* that *Judeo* mothers are always *noodging?"* she asked once while
stuffing her pert little breasts back into that blue 32-B high-riser he'd
given her. "What's *noodging* anyway?" Who in Hong Kong could talk
to him like that?

Here, he doesn't even have a bank account, though Laura says when
he's ready, he can write her a check from his US account and she can
write him a check in Hong Kong money that he can use to open an
account here, now that he finally has his ID card. The ID card doesn't
fit right in his wallet: could there be any better sign that he doesn't
belong, that he should have told Laura no back in New York before they
left, stood up to her instead of getting swept up in the circumstance she'd

created with his help? But, whatever he should have done, here he is, without a bank account, paying $2.50 a pop to take his own money from the US, assuming he can get this ATM to work at all. He better take out a lot, so he doesn't have to pay a fee again until he finally gets his local account open. He'll do it this week. So how much ... it's like eight dollars Hong Kong to one US, so $200 Hong Kong is like $25 US, $2000 Hong Kong is like $250 US, so maybe he should get that, if he can get that much.

Jeff punches in the numbers, chooses "English" from the screen menu, and hears that wonderful sound of the machine shuffling through a stack of bills before spitting them out with a beep and a receipt. He takes his card and cash, as the screen politely reminds him, and turns away from the machine, one of three in a row on the wide street. He glances across to the bus terminal to get his bearings for walking toward the ferry, then realizes this must be the place that Avi was talking about, these are the ATMs where the hookers hang around. But he doesn't see any hookers ... oh, wait, across the street, that skinny Chinese girl—of course the hookers here would be Chinese, what else would they be?—with those tits making her top groan—gotta be a 34-C—between halves of her open black bomber jacket with the fur collar, hot pants, no stockings. Jeff thinks she smiled at him before starting to teeter across the street toward him on a pair of ridiculously high heels. Small hips like Rosalinda but a lot more meat on top. She's pretty, too, hardly any makeup, big eyes and full lips.

"Hi," he says casually as she approaches, and turns to walk beside her. "What's your name?"

She seems a bit startled that he's spoken to her—maybe she doesn't get many *gweiloh* customers—and answers in an unsure tone that he wouldn't have expected from a street walker. "Pussy," she says, slowing her pace. "Pussy."

Well, he likes her style, no BS. "A thousand dollars," he says. "Take me to a room."

She stops, turns her head toward him, looks him over and smiles. "Okay," she says and leads him to a guest house on a side street up three flights of stairs, where she giggles, covering her mouth with her fingertips, as he pays HK$300 for the room.

He wakes up shivering from the air conditioning and wonders how he wound up in Laura's room. He pierces the brain fog far enough to see that he's made a much more serious wrong turn, recoiling as he realizes Laura would have woken up for work with him not home. In less than 24 hours, he's blown his fortune, his marriage, and the roof over his head. He's got to get home, as soon as someone moves this bag of cement off his head.

CHAPTER 8

Bobbing for Hummus

"So THEY INSISTED we had to have a banquet to close the deal," Jeff explains, "and by the time it was over, we'd missed the last bus and it was too late to call, so we. . . ."

"All I ask is that you don't come home roaring drunk and make a lot of noise and disturb my sleep or get in my way while I'm getting ready for work," Laura says. Her husband gets banquets in China while she gets a midnight alarm for Chai Wan. That's so unfair.

"My day went well for a change," Laura says, trying her best to be cheerful instead of resentful. "My graphics girl, the one who messes up every day and makes my life miserable, today she looked like she got a little sleep and wasn't drunk and didn't screw up once. I told her to keep doing whatever she did last night every night."

Jeff, however, knows he can't do what he did last night every night. He was drunk, he was pissed off, and he made a mistake that he's not going to repeat. Making alibis with Laura wouldn't be much of a challenge if he ever changed his mind, but he can't afford forking out HK$1000 for hookers. Funny, he could swear he only took $2000 out of his account last night. After paying for a pair of salmon steaks that set him back more than HK$200 and a bottle of New Zealand white that broke his $10 rule for the apology dinner that Laura had had too many wines and chicken fingers with Edie to eat, he still has $1600 left. But he remembers handing a pair of $500s to that hooker. At least he thinks he remembers that. He certainly remembers her incredible body, which appeared genuine—he's fitted enough women with implants to know— and her passion, which she also made appear real, and his flashback is pushing this session with Laura well beyond the usual grind. Jeff can tell he's going at it with atypical enthusiasm, and she can tell, too, he surmises, from her squirming and squealing what sounds to him like, "Camera turn, camera turn."

When Laura's tucked in for the night, Jeff returns to his real dilemma, getting his fair share of his mother's latest millions. He's afraid, if he asks now, she'll just say, and not without good reason, "Jeffrey, you want I should keep you in thousand-dollar-a-night hookers? Stick to pussy you can afford."

Still, he has to ask, maybe just for expenses, to offset the bus fare to the mainland and the phone bills, so he can at least call her more often to keep up with whatever the hell she's doing, and still have the whole lousy $500 a week for himself, for shopping at the Wellcome and maybe occasionally going out for a beer. She'll be up by now—she wakes up early the way his wife goes to bed early—so he calls.

"Hi, Ma."

"Who's this?"

"Who else calls you Ma? It's Jeff."

"Oh, Jeffrey. What's wrong?"

"Nothing's wrong. The shipment that you. . . ."

"You know, I paid six thousand dollars for a bond on those Israelis. Do you think I can trust them?"

"Instead of taking a bond on them, you could have sent the money to me. I could have. . . ."

"Oy, so complicated. You don't have a bank account. . . ."

"I could have opened one if you told me. . . ."

"Then, which is your money and which. . . ?"

"So you're saying you trust them more than you trust me?"

"Of course not. But you don't understand. . . ."

"Ma, I understand that you made a deal that's worth millions of dollars behind my back, and that. . . ."

"Behind your back? What are you, crazy?"

Jeff wonders how the conversation reached this stage so quickly. "That's not what I mean."

"It's what you said."

"I mean. . . ."

"And it's right," his mother says.

"What?"

"I mean, you're right, son. I need partners who know the business and can. . . ."

"Who ran the stores for nine years!?! You think I. . . ."

"That's the business here, it's not the business over there. People who know China, who know production there, who. . . ."

"I know product, I know the market. . . ."

"You take the clothes off *schvartzedik* girls who work in the stores and you think this makes you an expert?"

"Maaa. . . ."

"You know I don't care about what you did with those little teenagers, as long as you were careful, and I'm glad you married that *shikse* Lois Lane and moved to China. But for this kind of business, it's better, for all of us, and, after all, this business is not for me anymore. For me, I could retire tomorrow and never worry about a cent. So it's not for me. For us, for you, better a real expert we get to make sure. . . ."

"So what am I supposed to do. . . ?"

"What you already did is enough. How would me and Jerry Lewis do this if you didn't find these Israelis? That's why I'll keep paying you a salary, and the Israeli boys will let you keep using their office. You got us to here, and now we can do fine. . . ."

"Without me. . . ."

"I'm paying you, so every so often you'll take a look at some samples. . . ."

"You're going to make millions, thanks to. . . ."

"And when the time comes, whose millions will they be? Before you know it, your old mother will get planted in the ground . . ."

"Maaa. . . ."

". . . and maybe by then you won't care so much about teenagers and their underwear."

"How else was I supposed to modernize pop's stores, bring them into the 1990s? More girdles?"

"Don't yell at your mother, Jeffrey. I'm not hard of hearing yet. Soon enough."

"Ma, you should live to be a hundred twenty."

"Oh please. But whenever the time comes. . . . Ever since your father went, I've been ready. It's only for you that I stay, so I can help, so you'll be ready. . . ."

"So help me, Ma. Make me a partner in this deal. . . ."

"A partner?" She snorts a laugh. "You are a partner. In the end, every cent, plus interest. . . ."

"But what about now? I know you can't believe it—I can't believe it—but 500 dollars a week doesn't go very far here."

"So you want more money?"

"Yes."

"For what?"

"How about for expenses like this call?"

"God forbid, you should pay for a call to your mother. . . ."

"For business phone calls, for my costs visiting the factory. . . ."

"You don't need to go to the factory so much. . . ."

"You just cut me out, after everything. . . ."

"I'm still paying you. You should thank me. . . ."

"It's not enough."

"Not enough for what? For rent?"

"You know Laura's company pays the rent. . . ."

"For food?"

"We share that, but things here are very. . . ."

"I know: it's not enough for a boat."

"What?"

"For a boat, it's not enough."

"Is that what. . . ?"

"The beach club, a swim, that wasn't good enough for my big shot son, Mister Ivy League, even if you never did manage to make your diploma. . . ."

"Because I stopped to manage pop's stores for you. . . ."

"Like a hole in the head I needed you then, too, Mister Too-Good-For-the-Beach-Club. So you spent what, fifty thousand dollars, sixty thousand dollars . . ."

Actually $112,000, Ma.

". . . for a lousy boat. Not even a nice boat, but a wood boat with no motor. What kind of a *yutz* spends so much money for a boat and doesn't get a motor?"

"Ma, it had a motor, but the idea was to use the sail. . . ."

"With this kind of sail, you're an expert. But selling foundation garments the way your father and your grandfather did to make a good life for us, that you complain about. So off you go in your boat. What did you think, you'd meet a Jewish mermaid? Now you need money for what, a new boat?"

"Ma, I just want to...."

"You can use those Israeli boys' office, and you'll get money from me every week. If you don't want it, don't take it."

"Gee, that's mighty white...."

"So, we'll leave it like that, and you'll be a little patient and grow up a little and learn not to raise your voice with your mother. Just remember, Jeffrey, nobody else is ever going to treat you like your mother."

"I'll never forget it." He hangs up the phone, goes into his bedroom, lays down in the dark, and, for the first time since his father died, has a good cry. Then he changes into his workout clothes, packs a salmon steak in Laura's lunch container, and heads for the gym. Maybe he can't get the money or respect he deserves from his mother, but at least he can get in shape.

Outside Robinson Place, a small woman in a long coat with an oversized blue knit beret on her head and a backpack slung over one shoulder follows Jeff through the front gate and catches him halfway up the building's circular driveway. "Excuse me," she says, coming to Jeff's side and looking up at him. "I hope you will help me."

Her face seems familiar to Jeff but he can't place it. "I hope so," he replies with a smile.

"I am Yogi from Japan," she says in a soft voice, her words clipped to emphasize the spaces between them.

"I am Jeffrey from Long Island. You are Yogi? Like Yogi Berra?"

"This is baseball player, yes?"

"Right. And like Yogi Bear. You know the cartoon...?"

"Yes, yes," she beams, lighting up her beautiful, familiar face. "For me, favorite is not picnic basket, is Jew food. I love Jew food. Please may you bring me to JCC restaurant to eat hummus and pita bread? I will pay your dinner also."

"I can, I guess," Jeff answers, "But I was planning to have a swim first."

"Good," Yogi says brightly. "I like to pool and jacuzzi before dinner. May go?"

"Okay." Jeff swipes his card across the sensor to open the bulletproof glass front door of the JCC. After the guard searches their bags and he signs her in as his guest, Yogi and Jeff ride the elevator down to the indoor pool. He signs them in again at the towel desk. "I meet you in pool," Yogi says before the tall, blond wooden door to the women's locker room rattles shut behind her.

Jeff puts his bag in the locker and checks the jacuzzi—thankfully, Avi and Moishe aren't there: he doesn't know what he should say to them yet, doesn't know if they're his enemies or potential allies against his mother. Then he walks out to the pool where Yogi wades in tepid water just below her small bust, wearing a modestly cut bikini. Except for the two Chinese lifeguards, a teenage boy and girl seated at the corner of the L-shaped pool and paying attention mainly to each other, Jeff and Yogi are the only two people there. Without her hat, Jeff sees Yogi's pageboy haircut and a face he now realizes looks like the one on those porcelain dolls sold in every souvenir shop. "Come. Show me how to float," Yogi suggests.

Jeff walks down the steps of the pool and asks, "Do you want to float on your front or your back?"

"Which one is easier?"

"It depends."

"I do not have big chest," she points out, cupping her hands under her breasts. "Does that more easy or more difficult?"

"I'm not sure, but start with your back."

"Okay. What must I do?"

"Lie back. . . ."

". . . and think of Emperor. . . ."

"What?"

"You say, lie back, yes? But I will sink and drown?" She pronounces the last word "duh-loan."

"Maybe." Jeff smiles. "No, you won't. That's why they call it floating, not duh-lowning." Jeff holds out his hand just under the level of the water. "Go ahead and lie back on my hand."

Yogi leans back, resting the back of her bikini top on his hand. "Don't snap it," she says and keeps her feet resting on the floor of the pool.

"Now lift your feet off the bottom," Jeff says.

She makes several attempts to lift her feet, but they keep slipping back before she can float. "Help me," she pleads.

Jeff puts his other hand under her knees, but she buckles at the waist. Yogi shifts his hand upward to support her bottom and she finally lifts off the pool floor. "I am floating," she declares.

"Well, on my hands anyway. If I take them away. . . ."

"Keep there, please," she says, clasping the hand on her bottom. Jeff doesn't have big hands, but he palms Yogi's bottom comfortably. Though it's small and more firm than cushiony, it has a nice curve to it. In fact, looking at Yogi, floating there in his hands, he sees a host of splendid curves: her China doll (or is it china doll? Jeff doesn't know) cheeks curl into a teardrop chin; her neck slopes to an intricately patterned collarbone; from the modest swell of her breasts to the sweep of her rib cage around her flat stomach flowing into the knots of her hip bones and that knoll under her bikini bottom; her hips thinning into her thighs; the circles around her knees welling into her calves, shaved down to the turn of her ankles, the arches of her feet, the round mounds of her cheery toes. With all those curves, Jeff wonders if Yogi has an angle beyond hummus?

"Do you want to try floating on your front?" Jeff asks.

"I think so," she says, "but perhaps I must know you better first." She giggles but Jeff doesn't get the joke. "I enjoy this. Quite restful. For you is okay?"

"Having my hand on your behind is quite pleasant, though it's not exactly the kind of exercise I had in mind." Holding her like this, it's difficult for Jeff to avoid imagining her cartoon namesake, Yogi bare.

"Do you want to stop?"

"Not really," Jeff says. "And I think your front would be more difficult. Can you try this by yourself while I do some laps?"

"Can," she replies. "But is better with you helping."

After Jeff swims and Yogi tries solo floating with mixed results, they budget 25 minutes for a soak in the jacuzzi in their respective locker rooms and a shower, meeting at the towel desk just before nine, then riding the elevator to the kosher restaurant on the second floor. Jeff has never been up here. The place has potential, with a high ceiling and full-length windows overlooking the synagogue's domes and the greenery behind it (there's a *mikvah* somewhere back there, Jeff's heard), but the lighting is too bright, the square, bleached wood tables and chairs too institutional, the orange plastic cushions on the chair backs and bottoms too loud, the volume increased by matching paper placemats on the tables.

Jeff and Yogi seat themselves across from each other at a table by the windows. Maybe a half-dozen of 30 tables are occupied: a female gym regular pushing 50 Jeff recognizes, reading a magazine and picking at a salad; a pair of bearded businessmen in black nattering in Hebrew, a more orthodox version of Avi and Moishe; three mothers with a total of eight kids (cumulative age under 30) and a lot of excess ketchup on their plates; an apparent committee meeting or study session featuring four people with note pads at a table littered with coffee cups, water glasses and nearly empty plates of finger foods; and two other mixed couples, one Jewish man and Asian woman, one Jewish woman and Asian man.

"Do you like baba ganoush and mutabak?" Yogi asks, taking a laminated menu from between the salt and pepper shakers and vase with a single flower.

"What?"

"Do you like baba ganoush and mutabak?"

"What is it?"

"Sure you are Jew?" Yogi asks. "Mother does not prepare this for you at home?"

"My mother's favorite thing to make for dinner is reservations."

"What is this?"

"Reservations," Jeff explains. "At a restaurant. To go out to eat there."

"Oh, I see. Like booking," Yogi says. "Is joke."

"Yes."

"Oh," she says, smiling politely. "Mutabak. . . ?"

"Sorry, I've never tried it."

"You will try now." Yogi studies each page of the menu carefully, while Jeff can't help studying her doll face. "I will order for both to eat, yes?"

"Sure."

She flips more pages with her small fingers. "What is franken?"

"Franken? I don't know. Can I see?" She turns the menu around toward him and points. "Oh, flanken. Flanken is boiled beef. Beef in soup. . . ."

"Like *shabu-shabu.*"

"What?"

"*Shabu-shabu.* Kobe beef, slice very thin and boil with vegetable. What type is beef for franken?"

"I don't know, but it's not sliced thin. It's usually in a big chunk, kind of tough, at least the way my mother cooked it." Jeff chuckles. "*Shabu-shabu,* that sounds dirty."

"No, it is very fresh and. . . ."

"No, no. I mean sexual dirty. Like, 'Let's go back to my place for *shabu-shabu.*' But I'm sure it doesn't sound that way to you. Sorry, stupid thing to say." Jeff opens his menu as an excuse to stop talking.

"You drink sampain?"

"Sampain?"

"Here." She flips the menu again and points under wines to "Champagne."

"Oh. Sure, I'll have a glass." Jeff adds, "You're paying, right?"

"Here they sell best one-hundred-dollar bottle of sampain in Hong Kong. . . ."

"For a hundred bucks it better be good. . . ."

"Not so expensive . . . one thousand three hundred yen . . . about thirteen US dollar. Is good price for sampain."

"Oh right. I still get all confused with the money here."

"You have how long here?"

"About three months."

"This is not long. I am banker, so take money serious." Yogi catches a waiter's eye to order. "Please bring one hummus, one mutabak, one pickle herring, one gefilte fish, one bottle Aviva sampain, and extra pita bread." The waiter keeps writing long after she's finished talking before walking away.

"Impressive," Jeff says.

"You have not eaten here?"

"Never."

"Sure?" Yogi says with astonishment.

"Maybe I would have tried it if I knew they have pickled herring."

"Can buy in Wellcome supermarket also." She smiles at him sweetly. "You enjoy Jew food or prefer Cantonese?"

"I like Chinese barbecued meats," Jeff says, "and the vegetarian food we get at this place when I go to the factory in China. . . ."

"You are in what business?"

"You'll laugh."

"I hope so. I enjoy to laugh. Your business is funny? More funny than bookings joke? Maybe you are Seinfeld?"

"How do you know about Seinfeld?"

"Have Seinfeld in Japan. Also in Hong Kong, but do not understand. He is also Jew, yes? Or you are clone?"

"Seinfeld's clone?"

"No, no, clone. Like circus." Yogi giggles, "You have big nose and white face. . . ."

"Oh, a clown."

"You are clo . . . clown?"

"I feel like a clown sometimes," Jeff admits. "But no. I'm in ladies' underwear."

"Excuse. . . ."

"I work for a company that sells ladies' underwear in America. It's kind of complicated."

The waiter brings the champagne, pulls out its plastic cork with a struggle—ignoring Yogi's advice to turn the bottle, not the cork—and puts it on the table. He returns with a pair of filled water glasses that he places at the edges of their placemats, then comes back again with a white plastic bucket with water and ice and two wine glasses rather than champagne flutes. He puts the bucket on the table, pours champagne into the glasses and drops the bottle into the bucket with a splash.

Yogi lifts her glass and clinks it against Jeff's. *"Ra-hayim,"* she says.

"L'chayim," Jeff replies and sips the champagne. It's tangy and the bubbles tickle his nose, better than the cheap stuff he stocked for brunches on the boat. "That's good."

"I say so." They exchange smiles, breaking their eye lock with another sip. "So what is your difficulty with ladies' underwear?"

"Well, you know, it just doesn't fit me right, especially the brassieres," Jeff says.

Yogi giggles.

"Good. Some of my jokes you do understand."

"Yes." She nods and refills both of their glasses. Jeff taps on the table as she pours, and she responds, *"Ho-aah, ho-aah."*

"My problem is with the business situation. My mother has stores in the US and now has begun wholesaling. . . ."

"You work in ladies' underwear with mother?" Yogi giggles.

"Yes."

"Excuse, please." She puts her tiny hands over her face and continues to giggle. "Sorry, sorry. I think is quite funny for man to work in underwear for lady with mother. Sorry to laughing."

"It's okay. Don't worry." Jeff sips more champagne. "Maybe it's ha-ha funny, but now it's also become strange funny. My mother wants to get rid of me."

"Mother does not want you in her underwear?"

"Something like that," Jeff says.

"You do not think is funny?" Yogi wipes her face with a paper napkin, then places in on her lap. "You should drink more sampain perhaps."

"How about you? What do you do?"

"My work is in bank."

"Oh, right . . . you said. Maybe you can help me," Jeff begins. "I have an account at Emigrant Savings in New York, at the Syosset branch, but I want to open an account here in Hong Kong. . . ."

"Excuse. . . ."

"I'm trying to open a bank account here. Transfer it from Long Island if I can. . . ."

"Oh. Oh." Yogi laughs. "Not this type of bank." She tries to stifle her laughing with her napkin. "Sorry, sorry."

"Then what type?" Jeff asks. "A blood bank? A river bank?" He sips his champagne and giggles as the wine tickles his nose. "A sperm bank?"

"Investment bank."

"What does an investment bank do?"

"We make investment."

"Investments in what?"

"In project and in market."

"What kind of project?"

"Many project. Power plant, corporate finance for expansion, trade credit, telecom . . . telecom is quite popular. . . ."

"I still don't understand."

The waiter brings their food on a tray, mystified about how to distribute the plates. "We're sharing," Jeff tries to explain. "Just put everything in the middle." But the table doesn't have much of a middle, particularly with their water and wine glasses and the bucket already there. After assessing the situation for a couple of seconds, the waiter starts placing plates randomly on the tabletop. Yogi pulls out a chair and moves the champagne bucket to the seat. "Please two more small plate," she tells the waiter as she rearranges the items to make everything fit while Jeff watches. "I study engineering," she says.

"And Jew food," Jeff adds, surveying the selection.

"You know all?"

"Sorry."

"This one mutabak," she says, pointing to a gray paste, "this one hummus, best in Hong Kong. Here, try." She picks up a wedge of pita, spoons a dollop of the beige paste onto it and holds it in front of Jeff's mouth.

Jeff accepts the pita and takes a cautious bite. "That's good. It's very light."

"You never try before? Sure?"

Jeff shakes his head and tries the mutabak on the rest of his pita. "Good also."

"You know fish?"

"I haven't had gefilte fish in years, except at Passover."

"This is Jew Easter. . . ?"

"Not exactly. . . ."

"Like fishball and good wasabi." She breaks off a hunk of small white loaf with a fork and dips it in the purple horseradish.

"I was never brave enough to try it with horseradish," Jeff confesses. He doesn't mention that, although he likes gefilte fish, the shape and texture always remind him of a turd.

"Then you try now," Yogi says, diverting the fork from its path toward her mouth to his. "Try."

Jeff winces then opens his mouth. It's hot, he thinks, but nice. "This is just too weird," he thinks aloud. "Learning about horseradish and hummus from a Japanese girl at the Jewish Community Center of Hong Kong. . . ."

"Woman, please."

"Sorry."

"I always too much say sorry. Is bad habit. You must not."

"Sorry."

As they work through the dishes, Yogi explains how she spent a semester of high school in Mexico living with a Jewish family. "In Japan, people do not know what is Jew," she explained. "I find out Jew is nice people eating delicious food. In Hong Kong, I learn every Jew is not speak Spanish. I also learn Jewish Center have lovely swimming pool and also tennis court. Can play tennis?"

"I used to hack around when I was a kid," Jeff says, "but it's been years. . . ."

"So we must play," she says, reaching across the table to wipe some horseradish from above Jeff's lip with her napkin. She pulls out her mobile phone, punches in numbers, and asks for the booking desk.

"Monday night at seven can?" she asks. Jeff nods. "Yes. Jeffrey Golden, M34595."

After the call, Jeff asks, "How did you know my last name?"

"I see on JCC card. Also JCC number." Yogi scoops hummus onto a wedge of pita. "I have good mind with number. I win math medal in high school. This is time I also have interest in women's underwear. Wear on outside in style of Mah-do-nah."

"Mah-do-nah?"

"In high school, all Harajuku girl wear underwear outside because Mah-do-nah do this."

"Ah, yes, Madonna. That was the first time I ever saw any fancy underwear. In my father's store, there was only white underwear. Or black underwear. All for old ladies. Like suits of armor from the middle ages."

"Father also is in underwear business with mother?"

"Well, he was. It's complicated. Before, it was my father's business and my mother helped. I took over his job when he died."

"Sorry."

"It was a long time ago," Jeff assures her, adding, "Thanks."

"Did you study underwear?"

"I worked some in my father's store when I was a student. But mainly I studied how to get underwear off female students." He smiles, and Yogi smiles back.

"Now you want them to wearing more."

"Maybe that's because my mother is boss." He smiles again. "But back when I saw the stuff Madonna wore, I realized that there was a lot more we could sell in the stores besides extra stiff white girdles."

"She was hero for Harajuku girl also."

"Is that your hometown?"

"I am come from Tokyo."

"But Halajugu. . . ?"

"Harajuku is place cool young people in Tokyo go for latest fad. Now fad is American cowboy clothing and blond hair. So wearing underwear on outside is not so bad perhaps."

"Better for my business, anyway."

"And for mother. Also for my mother."

"Your mother? Why?"

Yogi fills his glass then hers and shoves the empty champagne bottle neck down into the plastic bucket. "In this fad my mother say, 'At least you are wearing underwear.'"

"And now. . . ?"

Yogi drains her champagne glass and smiles. "Now, I do not say."

CHAPTER 9

The F in FGN Asia

"T HAT'S A WRAP FOR *AM ASIA* this Wednesday, March 26th, 1997, 97 days before Hong Kong's return to Chinese sovereignty. Thanking you for your time this time until next time, I'm Deng Jiang Mao in Hong Kong, saying, 'Buy low, sell high,' and have a profitable day."

"Clear," Quickie announces.

"Good work, everybody," Deng says as he pushes back his anchor chair and leaves the set.

"Good show, everybody," Laura says as she pushes back her chair and leaves the control room. She means it. No glitches. Quickie is her savior in there, keeping all the Cantos on board, even Pussy. Helios is beginning to get the hang of writing scripts. Deng decided to run the interview long, but asked her if it was okay before he did, and the guest was thrilled to get more global network television face time. With things going this well, Laura can only imagine what disaster looms.

She's on the phone to tomorrow morning's guest, a telecoms analyst from NGI Berman to discuss the mobile-phone industry when CK walks by and nods pleasantly. She's even been getting along with CK better since the flap over the name of her show and the memo. That is to say, they haven't had any interaction, except for the occasional nod and small talk while passing each other in the newsroom. His memo on guidelines for revising show opens, inspired by her reckless behavior creating *AM Asia,* has not yet emerged. Edie tells her the matter has never come up in senior meetings with CK, and that, although CK doesn't say much, he doesn't seem averse to using Laura as the handover-night producer. According to Edie, CK keeps muttering about wanting a Chinese perspective, but there are no Chinese producers, unless you count Lamont, and putting him in charge of a live broadcast would be a disaster. Even CK seems to understand that, Edie assures her. Laura's improved relationship with Deng has to work in her favor, given that he's the only available Chinese on-air talent. Still, she worries. Every show remains a minefield, a single step away from calamity, but everyone knows their jobs better, including Laura, and she now believes that no one wants to provoke a catastrophe simply to make her look bad.

With a few minutes to kill before the meeting, she drifts across the newsroom to the mailboxes. Since she didn't know what her address would be when she moved to Hong Kong, she had her mail forwarded to the office. Today's haul includes a brokerage statement from her account back in New York—which she really ought to pay some attention to; at the *Journal,* she made some nice stock picks, nothing that violated newsroom trading rules, just keeping her ears open and being smart—and a newsletter from her high-school alumni association. There's also a letter that doesn't belong, addressed to Lincoln Washington Lee. She scans the mailboxes to confirm that there's no one by that name in the newsroom. But the address is correct.

"Hey, Edie," she yells across the newsroom, "do you know who Lincoln Washington Lee is?"

"Sounds like some bloody Yank history class," Edie answers.

"Yeah, you're right," Laura says, walking toward the slot with the letter. "Somebody's parents had a sense of history, not to mention humor, to stick their kid with a name like that. Lincoln Washington Lee."

"Born on the fifth of July," Edie laughs.

"Fourth," Laura corrects.

"But with a name like that, you'd want a fifth, to drown your sorrows."

"Maybe his father was a Minuteman. He was very patriotic. . . ."

"And his mother was quite frustrated."

"What's the joke?" Deng says, making a detour on his way to the conference room.

"We've got a letter here for Lincoln Washington Lee," Laura explains. "We figure his father was a Minuteman, and his mother was frustrated."

"Where'd you find it?"

"It was in my mailbox."

"Geez, this network can't even get the mail right," Deng says, shaking his head. "It's a miracle that we put television out there every day, such as we do. . . . Listen, I'm going up to the 28th floor after the meeting. I can drop it off at HR and let them figure it out." He takes the envelope from Laura and puts it in the inside pocket of his jacket. "Now if you ladies care to join me. . . ." he says, walking toward the conference room.

Staff are already spilling out of the door. But Deng, Edie and Laura find chairs for them at the conference table, three in a row.

"I saved those for you," Lamont says and stands to begin the meeting. A new face, chewing gum briskly, with short, curly brown hair, an expensive-looking gray suit, white-on-white shirt open at the neck, no tie, is seated next to Lamont.

"First," Lamont opens, "CK wants you all to know how disappointed he is that he can't be here today. He said there was an unforeseen and urgent change in his schedule that required him to leave immediately. But he wanted me to make sure to tell you he thinks the shows have looked great this week.

"For a long time, you've heard me talk about how vital our operation is to putting the global in Franklin Global Network, and how it's a key component in bringing FGN into the forefront of 21st century communications technology. I know some of you have snickered when I've said it; I've seen you. But it's right there in our draft mission statement, which we'll be sending to New York corporate in the coming weeks after final reviews here. I know some of you think the people in New York don't know and don't care what goes on here, except when it comes to budget, of course. If you were dialed into the conference calls that I am, you'd know that that's just not true, and today we have further evidence of just how crucial the brass in New York believes our shop is to the future of the network as a whole.

"It is my great pleasure to introduce FGN Asia's new chief executive officer, Mister Peter Franklin."

As in the 28-year-old, only son of Maurice Franklin, founder of Franklin Global Networks, previously the network news vice president in New York. Lamont sits down next to Franklin, who makes a move toward standing, then pushes his chair closer to the conference table. He turns toward Lamont. "Thanks for the introduction, Lamont. You're fired."

Lamont sniffles his schoolboy laugh as Franklin reaches into the pocket of his coat and pulls out an envelope. "That's an example of the incredible sense of humor Peter is renowned for in New York and around the world," Lamont says, grinning.

"Yeah, right," Franklin says, looking at the envelope. "Lamont, here's the back half of my round trip ticket, New York-Hong Kong-New York. It's only valid for another. . . ." Franklin takes the ticket out of the envelope and scans it, "26 days, so you may want to get busy. Sorry but not refundable, though you can change it to a different destination city in the US. Certain restrictions apply."

Franklin hands the ticket to Lamont, whose face has gone blank. Murmurs of disbelief in Cantonese come from the back of the room and beyond in response to Quickie's simultaneous translation.

"And Lamont, this is a staff meeting, restricted to fuggin employees, so you'll have to leave. Stop by Human Resources. They should have all your papers ready by now. If you see CK or KS up there, say good-bye from all of us."

Lamont pushes back from the table and leaves.

Franklin takes a look at the group around the table, the buzz quieting as he begins. "In case you haven't figured it out, I was the unforeseen and urgent change in CK's schedule that forced him to leave immediately. I thought Lamont put that very well. He's been fired, too, CK . . . and KS Lau, also gone.

"I'm Pete Franklin. I love making television news. I hate BS. Some people think that's a contradiction; I think it's an imperative. News and BS don't mix." He takes a sip of coffee from the FGN Asia mug in front of him and clicks his gum, making a chook-koo sound. "All of you know more about Asia than I do—I've been in Hong Kong for"—he looks at his watch, a plastic digital with the FGN *US Prime News* logo—"fourteen hours now. Long enough to take a shower, let my jet lag catch up with me, and buy some of this nicotine gum without a prescription. You can't smoke on the plane, so since I had to go cold turkey, I figured I'd try to stick with it." Chook-koo.

"Anyway, all of you know more about Asia than me, and some of you even know more about TV news than me, like my old pal Mike Hartman." Franklin nods at Old Hartman, who nods back, grinning broadly. "I need you to tell me what you know. I've got KS's old office on the 28th floor, but I'll mainly work in CK's former space down here, and my door's always open. As for BS, these meetings are done, as of today. People need to meet, meet. But you can get more done talking to each other than meeting. Anybody feel differently about this suggestion?" Franklin pauses for three counts and looks toward Quickie in the back. "The Chinese delegation is okay with that?" Franklin waits three counts more. Chook-koo. "Okay, then you're all still working here. That's fortunate, because I don't have any more fuggin plane tickets to hand out."

Edie laughs out loud, and Laura kicks her.

"By the way, while we're all meeting, who's minding the store?"

"We're taking FGN Europe live," Richard Yakamoto chimes, "Mister Franklin."

"Call me Pete. Geez, the only thing more boring than business news is European business news. With that anchor who can't even say his own name—Jean-Claude Berrach-ch-chuch. You're Yamamoto?"

"That's right, sir, Richard Yakamoto."

"Well then it's not right if it's Yakamoto. But thanks anyway, Richard. Like I said, it's going to take me a few days to get up to speed on things here. Contrary to what you may have heard, nobody in New York knows anything about fuggin Asia, except that it spends way too much money and doesn't make enough. As of this morning, we're saving almost a million a year. That may sound like a lot of money, but it's not even three weeks of fuggin Asia's variable expenses. I'll need a little time to see what's going on, what's good, what's bad. I'll also need to figure out what to do about an afternoon supervising producer now that Lamont's no longer with us. . . . What time does the last fuggin Asia show air?"

"Market Wrap runs six to eight," Sara Fergis says. "I produce it—I'm Sara Fergis—with Jimmy Lee as AP."

"Who's March?"

"That's me," Edie says.

"Oh, the hyena. Is she good, this Fergis?"

"Very good."

"And she comes in now to produce two hours at six?" Chook-koo.

"Yes," Sara and Edie both reply.

"Congratulations, Sara, you're the new fuggin Asia PM supervising producer, in addition to your show duties. No extra pay, not much extra work, I hope—mornings does the heavy lifting, right?—and my undying gratitude, naturally."

"Thank you," Sara says.

"At least until you mess up. Okay, that's settled." Franklin claps his hands.

"Not every fuggin Asia problem is going to be that easy to solve, I'm afraid. I didn't come here with some magic formula from the fuggin brass in New York or the scriptures. That's because, since I've been in this business, I've learned there's no magic formula for good TV news. It's like they say about pornography: you can't define it but you know it when you see it. And, also like pornography, it depends on community standards—it's different in different places. So we're all going to try to find a fuggin Asia way to do it right, right for us and right for our audience. Any questions?"

"Pete, first I want to say that it's reeeeally greeeeat to have you here in Hong Kong," Old Hartman booms in his on-air voice. "It's a genuine indication that the network cares about us. You know, being out here, halfway around the world from New York in the wilds of Hong Kong, it's easy to think that we've been forgotten, lost in the shuffle.

"Pete, like you, I came to Asia without knowing very much about what was going on here. In my years in this business, I've had the privilege of seeing a lot of history made—a man on the moon, Nixon's resignation, the fall of the Berlin Wall that marked the triumph not only of freedom, but of free enterprise, the meat and potatoes of this network. I came here because I thought the Hong Kong handover, the first instance I know of, at least going back to the betrayal of Yalta, of free people peacefully subjugated to the forces of totalitarianism, presents a great historical moment, the kind of moment that anyone with a drop of newsman's—or newswoman's—blood their veins wants to witness firsthand. .

"But, Pete, when I got here, since I've been here, I've witnessed something far more remarkable, far more compelling. These Asian tiger economies are the greatest creators and distributors of wealth the world has ever seen. Over the past decade, tens of millions of people have been lifted out of poverty and into the middle class, or beyond even. People whose fathers—and mothers—drove water buffalo now drive Toyotas, or even Mercedes. History is being made every day here, and with every passing day, the center of the financial universe moves eastward.

"So, Pete, I think what all of us want to know, all of us caught in this vortex of history unfolding all around us—we want to know how we can best integrate these historic times into our network's global coverage, not just for Asia but for the world. At FGN Asia we're uniquely placed, as witnesses to history every day, to bring this story to audiences around the globe. As someone who's been a witness to so much history, for more decades than I care to count, I appreciate what a rare opportunity we have, and, Pete, I think I'm speaking for everyone in this room, when I say, we're dedicated to bringing this story to the world."

"Mike and I go back a long way," Franklin says, "and he goes back even further with my father, who sends you his best. I don't think anyone doubts you know history, Mike. Some of you may remember that afternoon in Philadelphia back in 1776, when all the other networks were lining up to interview Thomas Jefferson. But Mike, our Mike, got a fuggin exclusive with John Adams." Old Hartman beams at the joke and a few of the Americans giggle. Quickie shrugs as he translates for the bewildered Chinese speakers. "And, Mike, you are probably the only network anchor who knows the spread on five-year Treasuries on the day Reagan was shot."

"One-hundred-seventy-one basis points," Old Hartman spouts with a grin.

"So, Mike, because of our relationship," Franklin continues, "I think I can speak frankly to you, and you won't be offended. What you're talking about is exactly the kind of nonsense I just sent out the door, exactly what we don't need around here." Chook-koo.

"We're not in the history business," Franklin says. "We're in the news business. Yes, sometimes news is historic, and they'll replay your coverage on the year-in-review or decade- or century-in-review show. But news is really everyday stuff, and, to paraphrase Tip O'Neill, all news is local. Either it's local or it's sensational pictures, and you don't get a lot of those for business news. People care about *my* stocks, *my* company, *my* economy, *my* job, and what happened to it today."

"That's right, Pete," Deng says. "As you. . . ."

"I know you. You're. . . ."

"Deng Jiang Mao. Call me Deng."

"Okay, Deng. I'll cue you when I'm finished talking. If that's all right." Franklin looks straight at Deng, who blinks. "To succeed in any news operation, the first step is to recognize what the audience wants. Sitting here with our Ivy League diplomas and—that's okay, I don't have one either—it's easy to think we know what the real news is, the news that people should want to hear. And, when you do that, you know what you usually get? The sound of one hand clapping. They say that in Asia, right? The other hand, the one that's missing, is your audience. Television news that doesn't connect to its audience is a waste of everyone's time and energy. Starting from today, fuggin Asia rule one is to connect to our audience, to those millions of people out there, who, as Mike pointed out, now have cable TV and access to a lot of other world news, and most of it is probably as relevant to them as fuggin Europe business news, for instance. We need to relate to those people, to our audience, to make our broadcasts meaningful to them in some way that matters to them, to touch them. . . . Deng, you wanted to say something?"

"No, Pete. You made the point better than I could have. Thank you."

"Okay, any other questions, comments. Anchors? Producers? By the way, I know Yakamoto here, March, Fergis, who else?"

"I'm Sylvia Barrett from Canada. I produce *Money-Go-Round,* ten and four."

"And she's single," Deng adds, prompting giggles. "Like Edie."

"Andrew Steiner, eleven and five *Money-Go-Round.*"

"Robert Ching, *Money-Go-Round,* nine and three. Also single. . . ."

"Laura Wellesley, *AM Asia,* six to eight."

"And she's not," Deng says.

"That it?" Franklin says. "I know what I said sounds like a lot to swallow, but it's not brain surgery. You live here, you know what's on people's minds. That's where these fuggin Asia shows need to be. Get them there. Simple. Who's graphics?"

Shirley Hung raises her hand.

"Name, please?"

"Shirley Hung."

Franklin smiles. "You and me both, sister. Tapes?"

Fiona Fok and Nancy Black each say their names.

"Fiona is the news editor," Edie explains, pointing, "in charge of assignments. Nancy runs the editing functions and feeds. And over here, Pang May Pau is our reporter."

"Great, thanks. What I want to stress to you producers and editors is that you have plenty of tools to try to get fuggin Asia into people's heads. Use them creatively. Creative failure makes much better television than routine mediocrity. If any of you are taking notes, write that down. Fuggin Asia rule one."

"Put it in the next *Rabbit Ears,* Mike," Deng says.

"Other questions, comments, anything?" Franklin says, watching Quickie translate. "If not. . . ."

From just outside the door, a strong voice asks, "Why you no Chinese?"

"Whoever said that please step inside," Franklin says. Quickie whispers, chairs part, and Pussy steps up to the table.

Franklin looks her over and asks, "What's your name?"

"She doesn't speak English," Quickie says.

"I Pussy," Pussy replies.

"You're kidding." Franklin shakes his head. "You, translator—what's your name?"

"I am Quin-qui, but everyone call me Quickie."

"Well, you guys are quite a pair, along with Shirley Hung over there. Listen, tell Pussy that she has the most expensive name in America. People could be sued for millions of dollars just for saying it to her." Quickie translates. Pussy responds with a sophisticated smile while several other Chinese titter. "Now what was your question?"

"July one Chinese in charge," Pussy says. "Why you no Chinese?"

"That's a good question." Franklin nods to Quickie, who translates. "To tell the truth, nobody in New York thought about that. What we did think about was that fuggin Asia loses more money than there is tea in China, and we had to do something about it. Until you mentioned it, I didn't even realize that KS, Lamont and CK, all overpaid and underperforming, are Chinese, and they're the highest ranking fuggin Asia Chinese executives. Or at least they were." He pauses for Quickie to catch up. "I don't have a good answer, but it's a very good question. Quickie, tell Pussy I want to talk to her after the meeting. You come along, too, to translate."

"Okay, okay," Pussy says, in response to Quickie's explanation, smiling wide to reveal front teeth nearly as profound as her bust.

"All right," Franklin says, "enough of this meeting. Let's all get to work for fuggin Asia's success." Franklin stands, then pauses. "Hyena March and Fergis, come to my office here. Quickie, you and Pussy wait for me upstairs on 28," he says, and walks out the door toward CK's old office.

Edie, standing to follow, turns to Laura and says, "Well, he's certainly different."

"Not to mention profane," Laura answers.

"Disappointingly American to use the f-word as punctuation," Edie says.

Deng shakes his head. "Don't you get it?"

"Get what?" Laura asks.

"That's the name of the network. FGN Asia—Fuggin Asia."

CHAPTER 10

Where There's Smoke. . . .

"**D**ID YOU KNOW?" Laura asks as the door to the fire stairway slams behind Edie and the heat and humidity hit her. A bulldozer rumbles as it dismantles a dilapidated dock below.

"If I knew, don't you imagine I'd have told you, *mei-mei?*" Edie replies. "All I can say is Fuggin Asia."

Laura climbs up a couple of steps and sits down, leaning against the railing. She's learned it's better to sit higher than Edie, beyond the range of her ashes and above the papers, butts and cups littering the concrete floor. "What did he say to you and Sara?"

Edie brushes her hand over the concrete step at the bottom of the landing then sits, leaning against the wall and looking up at Laura. "He wants us to spend less money and get more viewers," she shrugs. "Only that."

"Do you know anything about him?"

"I know he was smart enough to get born to a billionaire father and that he's single, 28, and cute even if he wasn't so bloody wealthy. . . ."

"He looks a bit like Jeff, my husband, only richer," Laura says, smiling. "But I mean about his work, his TV experience, what he's going to do. . . ?"

"I know Maurice Franklin didn't become a billionaire by running stations that lose money hand over fist. Like father like son, I reckon."

"So you think he's here to shut us down?"

"Not before the handover . . ."

". . . stupid," they chant in unison. Edie lights a cigarette. "But I do think he'll find ways to stop the hemorrhaging or at least limit it. And did you see who was waiting outside the bowling alley when I came out?"

"Who?"

"Andy, of course."

"Brownnosing?"

"Precisely. . . . Do you realize Andy is the reason you're here?"

"Did he recommend me or. . . ?"

"No, recruited you would be more accurate. You should know." Edie ashes her cigarette. "We began with a couple fewer hours of programming a day, but the plan was to get another producer, eventually, and build up the hours. One of the rules was that everyone had to take the morning show for a month. Sara started out with it, and actually did it for two months to get the format sorted. Then Richard with his cologne. But when Andy's turn came, he said he wouldn't do it. He said it was because of their four-year-old daughter. But everybody knows it was due to Patricia. . . ."

"His daughter?"

"No, his wife. Patricia Yao, the CNN anchor. . . ."

"Right. Of course."

"And, knowing our man Andy, it should come as no surprise that Patricia fucks anything with a pair of trousers and five minutes to spare."

"That ice queen?"

"Bet your bollocks, *mei-mei*. The reason they're here is that she was bamping the CBC bureau chief in Vancouver—you do know they're Canadian, don't you?—and Missus Bureau Chief got all huffy about it, threatening to cut off their funding—among other things—through some connection in Ottawa. So the bloke in Vancouver called Johnson Thomas at CNN, because he knew they were looking for a Chinese face here. Patricia got a big package to relocate, but she insisted that Andy had to get a job, too. After all, without your husband there to suffer the humiliation, what fun is cheating? It's as if you're single and that's no fun at all, take my word. Andy worked in radio, in sports, no TV experience, but Johnson Thomas called KS Lau—they're old pals—and, *voilà,* we got Andy. And that's why CK didn't fire him when he refused to take the morning shift.

"Andy also managed to convince the other producers that the morning shift was unfair duty somehow, so they all refused it. Poor Sara, who really deserves the bouquet she got today, volunteered to fill in until we found someone. But, of course, we couldn't find anyone in Hong Kong. CK wouldn't poach someone from KS's pal Johnson at CNN, and the people at the local stations are all dolts—the Chinese ones are as disagreeable as Fiona and not as smart, the expats are drunken sots, pure FILTH, and the returnees are. . . ."

"Returnees?"

"Born here, got degrees and passports in Canada or Australia, came back—they're all bi-illiterates, English and Chinese both not up to snuff. Besides, anyone here with a scintilla of sense is in either banking or property. Journalism is something girls willing to show a bit of leg do until they can land a job in corporate PR."

"So when you couldn't find someone here, you got me."

"More or less. Lamont asked Human Resources to talk to corporate in New York, and here you are. So when you're napping in your taxi on your way here before dawn, dream about throttling Andy."

"So with KS gone. . . ."

"With KS gone, Andrew has lost his rabbi. So he's eagerly chumming up to the new boss. At least he's not a rival for Franklin's affections. . . ."

"What do you mean?"

"The way he looked at Pussy. Once he got his tongue back in his mouth, the first thing he said was 'Come to my office after the meeting. . . .'"

"Oh, come on. He told her to bring Quickie."

"I'd say quickie is precisely the plan. But young Master Franklin will learn about these Hong Kong girls."

"Are they all like Patricia?"

"Oh, *mei-mei*, Patricia is not a Hong Kong girl. She's a Canadian with a Chinese face, and I suspect she's a lot like you and me, with smaller tits, of course. . . ."

"That they all dress like hookers, but none of them mean it?"

"Actually, that statement isn't as simple as it sounds," Edie says. "Hong Kong girls are from Hong Kong, and like everyone else in Hong Kong, all they care about is money. So Pussy won't bonk anyone without the proper quota of presents. That famous mobile phone of hers that you tried to drown. . . ?"

Laura nods, wondering when people will ever stop talking about that.

"A gift from an admirer, no doubt. Where's she going to find two thousand Hongkies for a mobile phone when she only makes fourteen a month? Anyway, you pay the toll and the gate will swing open—somehow in all that dog's breakfast of Chinese religion they seem to have left out any restrictions on sex. The only thing that keeps AIDS and pregnancy from becoming an epidemic here is that nobody can afford a flat of their own to do it in. They're like little rabbits, except that I gather rabbits enjoy it more than Chinese girls. Of course, with Chinese men the way they are. . . ." Both women giggle.

"Have you. . . ?" Laura asks.

"Have I what?" Edie says, exhaling smoke.

"You know, been with a Chinese guy?"

"I've been around the block a few times."

"That's a British answer."

"Well," Edie admits, ashing her cigarette. "I dated one Chinese fellow a bit. We got a little slap and tickle going one night in Hong Kong Park after a movie. I gave a little grope, looking for something to hold on to, but, to paraphrase Gertrude Stein, there was barely there there. I didn't return his calls. Poor bugger's probably in therapy, or using one of those suction machines."

"What about here? Franklin?"

"Well, I reckon he's big enough. . . ."

"I mean what did he say about changes here. . . ?"

"He asked me and Sara to gin up some cost reductions. I told him it would be nice if we could increase revenues instead. . . ." Edie takes another drag on her cigarette. "Off the top of my head, it's hard to imagine how we can do anything but air fewer hours. We've only got the two crews, one reporter, so what can we cut? Bonny Prince Peter didn't seem keen on taking more hours from Europe. . . ."

"Where there's smoke, there's someone I can fire," booms a voice from above on the stairway, echoing off the bare concrete walls. They look up and see Franklin looking down from two stories above. "Don't move, I'll be right down," he says, quickly descending the stairs. "They told me I'd find the smoking lounge here. Very classy for the world's most popular media company." Chook-koo. "Do you mind if I join you?" he asks, hops down to the step above Laura, then sits, leaning against the railing opposite her. His two top shirt buttons are undone. "What's that racket?" he asks, glancing toward the construction.

"Building a brighter future for Hong Kong," Edie says.

"It never stops," Laura says.

"When the last factory is gone, they'll still make plenty of noise here," Edie says, crushing her cigarette underfoot.

"Hong Kong is the jack hammer capital of the universe," Laura adds.

"How did your meeting with Pussy go?" Edie asks.

"She knows a lot about Hong Kong," Franklin says. "Man, doesn't the custodian clean here?" he adds, surveying the mess on the landing.

"Well, I believe she grew up here," Edie says. "To whatever extent she has, that is."

"They need to hose this place down." Chook-koo. "March, make sure you get the custodial crew in here, everyday."

"I'll talk to building management," Edie says.

"I thought I saw a budget line for our own cleaning staff," Franklin says.

"Well, yes, but they only do the offices," Edie says. "The building crew does. . . ."

"Tell them to do our smoking lounge," Franklin says, "unless that will make trouble with some union."

"One of the few British bad habits that didn't take root here," Edie says. "I'll ask."

"But even with sweeping," Laura says, "these stairs won't do wonders for that gorgeous suit. It is. . . ?"

"That's why they have dry cleaners. They do have dry cleaners here, right? And what do they call the Chinese laundry here?" Franklin takes a deep breath. "Aaah, the stench of tobacco."

Edie holds out her cigarette pack toward him.

"No," he says. "I really do want to stop, and I've got my gum. But I wouldn't mind if you do."

"Fuggin Asia," Edie says. She lights a cigarette and blows the smoke upward.

"Quickie said he didn't understand that I was talking about the network when I said Fuggin Asia. I can't believe you don't call this place Fuggin Asia." Chook-koo.

"Fuggin Asia is what we say about the price of a flat," Edie says.

"Flat?"

"Apartment," Laura says. "They speak British here. And telephone numbers when it comes to rents."

"Fuggin Asia," Franklin says, shaking his head.

"On the subject, I was asking Edie what changes you're planning. . . ."

"No smoking policy," he says, smiling broadly. "Gimme a break. I've been here twenty hours, fired the three top people, told March to pick a fight with our janitors, and you're asking what changes I'll make?"

"You talked about saving money," Laura reminds him.

"I talked about making the network viable," he says. "That's not only about money. It's about creating a property that fits our company's agenda and its interests."

"That sounds quite a bit like the recent, unlamented Lamont...." Edie says.

"How do we do that?" Laura asks.

"You're the ones who've been here more than twenty hours, so you tell me. Laura, what would you do to make the morning show better, besides assaulting Pussy's mobile phone?"

"She broke the rule," Laura replies, astounded that Pussy brought that up during her first, and likely last, face time with the boss, "although I know it was for the right reason. And I've apologized to her."

"She didn't mention any apology. But she did say you're a very good producer, even if you're a little uptight." Chook-koo.

"The way a producer should be, of course," Edie adds.

"You'd be uptight, too," Laura says, "if Deng Jiang Mao, who turned down network millions to come to Hong Kong and has never made a mistake in his life, was your anchor, and you had to work with no tapes, a Chinese-speaking writer...."

"I know the problems," Franklin says. "I'm looking for solutions."

"Mister Franklin...." Laura says.

"It's Pete. Mister Franklin is my pop, and you wouldn't find Big Mo ruining his Armani original on these stairs." Franklin smiles at Laura.

"Peter," Laura says, because Pete sounds too informal to her ear, "I think we need to get deeper into the stories, play up the idea that we're financial experts, the way the *Journal* does back in the US...."

"Spoken like a loyal *Journal* alumnus." Franklin nods. "I don't disagree with you, and I'm not just trying to pull your chain. But what stories are the ones we need to get deeper into?"

"That's a key point, Pete," Edie says, because Peter means penis to her ear. "We haven't done proper research to find out...."

"And we don't have budget for any, so that's not the answer," Franklin says. "I think the real answer is that we need to get closer to our audience—maybe actually talk to some of them—to get inside their heads, to know what's on their minds, what they want to watch. Maybe it's not a business news network—that idea came from New York. Maybe it's the wrong idea, though we thought it was pretty clever. Hong Kong is the center of the universe, at least until the handover. . . ."

Edie and Laura silently add "stupid."

"When is that, by the way?" Chook-koo.

"Midnight, June 30th," Laura replies.

Franklin shakes his head. "Geez, three months. We've got a lot of work to do. Who's the SP for the handover coverage?"

"CK and I had discussed that," Edie says, "but he hasn't—he didn't appoint the supervising producer, anchors. . . ."

"You have some ideas. . . ."

"Certainly."

"Good. We'll need to discuss them. I think we should bring in Christina Volpecello for handover night. . . ."

"That prima donna?" Edie says.

"She's actually known as the Broad Bottomed Wolf," Franklin says. "Just wait until the messages from her and her producer Benny Wilson start. . . . But point taken. Still, she is the network's leading foreign correspondent, and this is a leading foreign story. . . ."

"I thought this network didn't use the term 'foreign,'" Laura says.

"Excuse me. You'll find I'm political-correctness challenged. That's why I need you guys to help me, to make sure I don't come in and start making a zillion mistakes." Franklin takes a deep breath of Edie's exhaled smoke. "When we meet, should Sara be there? Do you want to discuss that together with her or without?"

"Together would be fine." Edie calculates that having the plain and sexually dormant Sarah at the meeting as a contrast to her own vibrant womanliness outweighs the benefit of being alone with Franklin, at least for the time being.

"Okay. Tomorrow, 12:30. Tell Sara."

"Fine. You can buy us *dim sum.*"

"Maybe, if someone tells me what *dim sum* is."

"It's Chinese hors d'oeuvres," Edie says, "served as breakfast or lunch."

"What's in it?"

"There are all kinds," Edie says, "some are fried, some steamed. . . ."

"Never mind. I'll ask Pussy to take care of it." Chook-koo.

"I moved from the *Journal* to here because I was really interested in the handover," Laura says, eager to regain Franklin's attention. "I think it's one of the most fascinating moments in modern history."

"Why?" Chook-koo.

"Like Mike Hartman said. . . ."

"A good reporter would have already realized that quoting Mike back to me is no way to score points."

"Mind your audience," Edie adds.

"Okay, okay," Laura says. "But it is amazing that the freest economy in the world is about to be run by Communists. . . ."

"Is that really so?" Franklin says. "Don't they call it something different these days—'Capitalism with a Chinese face'?"

" 'Socialism with Chinese characteristics,' " Edie corrects. "The brain-child of the recently late Mister Deng, not to be confused with our own quite lively Mister Deng. The term communism may not apply, but dictatorship certainly does."

"Back in the US we hear a lot of talk about how fast China's changing, about elections for village leaders, competing factions in the Polit-buro. . . ."

"You'll find that the dragon may change its skin, but it's still a dragon," Edie says. "Especially when you live in its shadow. Or its belly."

"Chinese proverb?" Chook-koo.

"I reckon I've been here long enough to gin up a proverb or two."

"Fantastic. That's what we need to tap into here. If you give people what they want to watch, then the rest—ad revenue, distribution, resources—that all falls into place. If you don't, then you're just wasting everyone's time, and truckloads of money. Which happens to be my pop's money, and I know how much he hates throwing it away."

Edie and Laura glance at each other. "You're right, of course," Edie says, "in the long run. But in the short run, you can't operate effectively without resources. . . ."

"We have resources. I've reviewed the staffing. It's not like there aren't enough people for an operation this size. Now, some of them may not be the right people, or maybe they're doing the wrong jobs. If you want to mention any names, now or anytime, you can, and I guarantee it will be strictly between us. Same if you want to tell me which sections aren't pulling their weight. But meanwhile, we've got a job to do, and we need to do it better."

"I'll talk to Sara about the afternoon situation," Edie says, "and then we can name a few names. . . ."

"Fine," Franklin says. "That's on the agenda for tomorrow, along with the *dim sum.* I need to hear it all from you guys, because if you don't tell me, then I go with my best judgment and the input I do get. We're not talking about a five-year plan here. More like a five-minute plan."

"But," Laura says, "one of the great things about the *Journal* is that we took the time and resources to develop. . . ."

"This whole network is the time and the resources, Laura. It's a blank slate, still, and I'm asking all of you to decide how we should fill it." Chook-koo.

Edie shakes her head. "Pete, I can't imagine you came out here simply to ask us. . . ."

"Guilty as charged. Oversimplification. I do have some ideas. We have a great story, the handover. Pussy and Quickie tell me you already say 'it's the handover, stupid'—now that goes double. If it wasn't for the handover, and the fact that—like Mike said," Franklin smiles at Laura, "these economies are worth skaddillions of dollars now and the stock markets are out of control, Fuggin Asia wouldn't exist. I see you're almost done with that butt, and I'm not going to ask you to light another. But look at those stories and figure out the best way we can cover them to make them come alive for our audience. Now I'm going back to wrestle with the bureaucracy upstairs, but starting tomorrow, I'll try to stay down in the newsroom as much as possible, and my door will always be open. Pussy will be manning the executive suite as my assistant, trying to get Chinese people to tell us what they want from Fuggin Asia. Like it or not, they're the ones closest to our audience, and the ones we need to be programming to. Anyway, that's today's five-minute plan. Ciao."

Franklin gets up and, with a parting "chook-koo" and good byes from Edie and Laura, bounds up the stairs two at a time for three flights. They lose sight of him, but wait until they hear the fire door slam to speak.

"Pussy. . . ." they squeal.

"He'll be bonking her in no time," Edie says. "If he isn't already. Bollocks. . . ."

"You really think so?"

"You don't?" Edie takes a last puff and grinds out her cigarette.

"I don't know," Laura says. "That would be awfully irresponsible. . . ."

"But typical. He is, after all, a man."

"Maybe. But what he says makes sense, doesn't it? I mean, we have no idea what our viewers want to watch."

"That's nonsense, Laura. You know what they want as well as I do."

"Which is. . . ?"

"A literate, fast-paced look at the day's business news. What Franklin says is true only to the extent that people care about what impacts them directly. . . ."

"That's exactly what he's saying. . . ."

"But it doesn't work, because 50 people care about 50 different things. If you take that approach, you wind up with that wretched 'news you can use' in the States. Television is a mass medium, not a bloody support group."

"I'm not saying you're wrong, but Franklin seems to know TV news. . . ."

"Bollocks, Laura. He's where he is because his name is Franklin and his papa owns the place. It would be an enormous mistake to assume he knows anything. . . ."

"Maybe. But wouldn't it possibly be just as much of a mistake to assume he doesn't?"

"Touché. But I think Franklin's simply looking for clever ways to cut the costs here and keep Pussy close enough to get into her knickers. Overall, I'd rate that disappointing."

"Particularly since he's so cute, rich and single, no?"

"Laura, dear, true wealth remains long after looks fade. And I'm shocked that a married woman. . . ."

"Jeff and I let each other look, we just don't touch. Except each other, of course. Besides, his eyes are bigger than his. . . ."

"That's quite enough." Edie sighs, "Oh well, look at the bright side, *mei-mei,* if Pussy's upstairs, you'll get a new graphics operator. Maybe even one who reads English."

"Without a mobile phone?"

"Impossible. This is, after all, Hong Kong."

"The heart of Fuggin Asia."

Franken Queen

ALL LAURA CAN TALK ABOUT IS HER STATION and the new boss, and all Jeff can think about is what the hell to do all day. He can't bring himself to go to Avi and Moishe's office and see the junk his mother is putting his Golden Beauties label on. At least she keeps sending money, now transferred to his Hong Kong account through Avi and Moishe, so he doesn't have to pay a fee to get it out of the ATM.

There's not even any TV on during the day, at least not in English, and they're demolishing the building across the street, floor by floor, making it too noisy to think in the apartment until five o'clock, except during lunch hour. So he goes to the gym and works out for a couple of hours and reads the newspapers and the magazines Laura brings home and soaks in the jacuzzi. Then he visits the Chinese market that runs down the hill toward Central a couple of blocks west of the escalator. Those dead pigs that go straight from the floor of a truck onto the bare back of a little guy in shorts and flip-flops, the hooves on hooks, and the sidewalk butchery have put him off meat. He jostles the *tai-tais* with their umbrellas, rain or shine, and Filipina maids, to check the produce prices, but usually winds up buying onions and cucumbers and carrots (which he used to eat right out the bag at home, but here are too huge and must be sliced into strips and stored in water) and greens at the vegetable stall run by a youngish woman with short hair and yellow rubber gloves. Cheaper than the supermarket and better choices. She speaks a little English, which helps, and he's picked up a little Cantonese, at least for prices—*gay do cheen-aaah?* how much? *yi sap man,* twenty Hong Kong dollars, *aaaiii-yaaah,* seems kind of high (much like the Yiddish *eh?* for "Excuse me, I didn't understand you, would be so kind as to repeat that, please?"). Tomatoes and fruit are hit and miss with several of vendors along the street, especially with tangerine season nearly over. Laura likes apples, and they're always abundant, Washington State delicious, and relatively cheap, but sometimes mealy if they've lost their stems. He always finishes up at the green wooden stall on the corner by the escalator with the skinny old women with leathery skin and long, gray hair in a braid wearing a traditional outfit like pajamas with baggy sleeves and, sometimes, a conical straw hat. She sells the little bananas he likes—*wong dai zui,* emperor bananas—and, occasionally, ballpark-size unsalted roasted peanuts in their shells. The carrot lady with the gloves says the banana lady is a Hakka. At the Hakka's neighboring stall, Jeff sometimes finds miniature mangos, a little bigger than a golf ball with a relatively small pit, for a reasonable price. After Chinese new year, when the markets reopened, she featured tiny, sweet tangerines he adored that he thought might be kumquats, a word he'd only heard as a joke before. Jeff's taken to calling himself the king of small fruit.

After shopping, he hauls his bags up the escalator, slices his carrots, cooks dinner for Laura, listens to her talk about the station not the news, until finally, she goes to bed. Now he's heading back to the JCC for a swim and another soak. Tonight's the night he's supposed to try tennis with this Yogi, if she shows up. He doesn't even have her number in case she doesn't. She seemed really funny at dinner, and she's sure nice to look at. Maybe she'll have a little tennis outfit that shows off that cute tush of hers. He'll see how she plays. Maybe they can make it a regular thing, tennis and Jew food, as long as she pays. He could try tennis again. They've got lessons at the JCC, but they're like HK$200 an hour. He's already spending enough on the cooking. Anyhow, he's getting in shape, and if reading the paper and magazines is worth anything, maybe he'll learn how to get in on this Asian economic miracle that's making everyone else rich.

Yogi is waiting for him outside the JCC, not in a tennis outfit, but a man's dress shirt and, it appears, nothing underneath, until she bends to pick up a tennis bag nearly as big as she is, revealing a pair of box cut shorts, like hot pants in the 1970s. At the gym desk, she hands over the fee, which she knows is HK$60—"You provide court, so I pay"—and after waiting for the previous hour's players to finish, they enter the room, higher than it is long, buried beneath the apartment towers. She opens the bag, looks at Jeff's steel racquet, state of the art ten years ago when he made the third round at the beach-club tournament, and hands him a purple model with a much bigger head. "Try this. Is more modern," she says, pulling out a matching weapon of her own.

"It's huge," he says, taking it, "and light."

"Titanium."

"What's one like this cost?"

"You may use for free," Yogi says, smiling.

"Yes, but. . . ."

"About twenty thousand yen. Maybe here one thousand five hundred Hong Kong dollar."

"Wow, that's expensive."

"Is good racquet. Must pay."

"Same with *schmattes.*"

"Schmothers?"

"I assumed you're fluent in Yiddish," Jeff says. "*Schmattes* means garments or cloth, but literally it's rags."

"*Schmattes.* I like this word. It has funny sound."

"Like *shabu-shabu* to me."

"Sometimes *shabu-shabu* is funny. But not if properly done." She lifts her shirt off over her head and wears only a gray sports bra underneath. "Mah-do-nah and your mother has tell me to wear this."

They both confess it has been a while since they've played, so they just hit the ball back and forth for an hour. Yogi plays tennis better than Jeff expects, very quick around the court, smooth strokes, surprising power. The racquet she gave Jeff is small for his hand, but the huge head increases the margin for error, and it adds a lot of zip. The whoosh of the air conditioning and high ceiling swallow up their words, so they just keep hitting, working up good sweats and occasionally running into the padded walls. "Shows you have to be crazy to play here, I guess," Jeff says.

"Excuse?" Yogi answers, so he hits her another ball.

After the hour, they make a booking to play again the following Monday night and head for the swimming pool. Again, thankfully, Avi and Moishe aren't in the jacuzzi. Alone except for that same pair of lifeguards, Jeff swims a couple of laps, wishing the pool was cooler, while waiting for Yogi. She emerges from the locker room in a different bikini, green, also modestly cut, and wades into the shallow end of the pool.

"Let's see you float," Jeff says.

Yogi tries to lie down on her back, but founders as she lifts her legs, splashing her arms wildly as her head goes under. "Help me, please," she pleads.

Jeff slides one hand under her shoulders and gives her butt a gentle lift with the other, positioning it so that his palm samples a slice of bare flesh on one thigh.

"Thank you," she says.

"No, thank you," he replies, with a smile. Her ass has the feel of a ripe tomato. "I still don't understand what you do."

"I learn to float, and you keep bottom from sinking."

"No, I mean about your work." Jeff loosens his grip on her shoulders, and she begins to spin clockwise, very slowly and gently in the pool's prevailing current.

"Is quite boring. I am one of many thousand of banker in Hong Kong."

"But you told me it's not like the bank at home. . . ."

"Actually, many investment bank on Wall Street. But bank is same everywhere. In Tokyo, Hong Kong, New York, London, all same. Take money from one people and give it to different people. And keep some for bank. This part is most important."

"That sounds simple enough."

"It is. But money can be tricky also."

"So what do you do, exactly?"

"I follow stock markets and make recommendation to management about client money."

"So," Jeff looks into her eyes because this discussion seems serious to him, "you decide which stocks are good to buy for the people who put their money in your bank?"

"I do not look at individual equities. I take macro view, at market level, country level. Other people do same with currency. Sometimes we make different conclusion about same country."

"You've lost me."

"You must understand about currency since you are selling underwear from China to America."

"Not really."

"Sure?" She gazes at Jeff.

"Sure? Oh, yes, I'm sure."

"Currencies are traded, like equities and bonds are traded, and price fluctuates depending on underlying economic factors. . . ."

"And when the price goes down, people say, 'Flucked again.'"

"That is joke?"

"Well, is try."

"This is funny. I wish I know this joke when I am work on currency desk."

"Why didn't you laugh then?"

"I did. Must pay attention."

"I guess I'll have to watch you more closely." Jeff smiles and feels her soft flesh on the heel of his hand. "But how does it work, how does the price reflect those economic factors?"

"Sometimes does not." Yogi sighs. "You see, price of equity or bond or currency is determined by what buyer will pay. Should be related to underlying economic factors, profits, balance sheet and other, but maybe is not. Depends." Yogi giggles.

"Caught you this time. What's so funny?"

"Is funny that I am explain about money to Jew."

"See, not every stereotype is true." Jeff sighs. "You know, you are very beautiful when you smile."

"Only when I am smile?"

"No, no. You are very beautiful all of the time, but especially when you smile."

"Thank you. Banker does not smile so often. Must serious. We are take other people's money, so they expect we very serious. Bank is serious, and money is serious. Bank make very serious money."

"And you?" Jeff asks, mainly to see if she understands the idiom. "Do you make serious money?"

"I make serious money, yes. But I only plan this job for five more year."

"Then back to Japan. . . ?"

"Oh, no. Japan also too serious. In Japan is society pressure to work, but do not think woman is serious, so cannot good job. Supposed to be office lady, get drunk"—she pronounces it "duh-lunk" as in "duh-loan"—"then get marry, no more drunk, have baby, and husband always work. I do not think this is fun for me. In Hong Kong can have good job, serious money, and people do not expect me with husband and baby. Here, I can make fun for me and not thinking about society pressure."

"So you plan to stay here?"

"Five year only. Then I shall retire to Bali, and surfer boys must worship me," Yogi says. "So it is quite important that I know to float."

"I think you could get all the surfer boys you want to hold your bottom. . . ."

"Excuse, please. I do not permit everyone to hold bottom. Am quite selective about who is hold."

"Excuse me. I didn't mean to insult you."

"I am try not to insult," Yogi says with a smile.

"Thank you." Jeff sighs. It's been fun, but now it's time to inject a dose of unpleasant reality. "I have a confession to make. You're permitting a married man hold your bottom. Should I move my hand?"

"Please keep," Yogi says, giggling. "Did you think was secret?"

"Well, I didn't tell you. . . ."

"You are wear wedding ring."

Jeff glances at his left hand to confirm her observation. "Oh. You're right. I wasn't sure whether you knew. . . ." he stammers. He was confident the revelation would extract him from this ticklish situation immediately, by her choice, and hadn't given a thought about what to say if it didn't. "In Japan, do you use wedding rings?"

"Is not traditional, but people now wear. Have see enough American movie to know this. But I never see your wife."

"I do have one. But I don't see her much either. . . ."

"She never to JCC?"

"Have you been watching?"

"No. But I see you, never see her when I to JCC with boyfriend."

"You have a boyfriend?"

"Before I have boyfriend. But he has back to England."

"Your boyfriend was Jewish?"

"Yes."

"Do you only date Jewish men?"

"Perhaps."

Jeff laughs. "That's funny. I know some Jewish men who only date Asian women—they call them Rice Kings—but I never met an Asian woman who specializes in Jewish men."

"Maybe I am Franken Queen." Yogi smiles. "Where is your wife? Why is I never see her?"

"She's at home, already asleep. She goes to work at midnight."

"I see. She is Tsim Sha Tsui prostitute?"

"No. Television news producer."

"Perhaps is different," Yogi giggles. "That is my joke."

"Funny." But there's nothing funny about this dalliance. Jeff can't take any more chances, not with Laura holding the roof over his head, for another woman, no matter how gorgeous and clever and funny she seems to be. There's no way to justify the risk. "But I don't want to take advantage of you and your bottom. . . ."

"Before I have many married boyfriend. For me, it is not problem. . . ."

"Married boyfriend? You mean married men who were your friends. . . ?" Jeff says.

"Yes, yes. Important now is that we tennis and pool and Jew food. In American baseball Yogi is catcher, but this Yogi not always ask for fast ball."

While Jeff tries to process that, Yogi smiles and adds, "I have secret also. Do you want to know?"

"Yes," Jeff nods. She's right: it's just tennis and the pool and dinner, nothing more. There's nothing wrong with being friends and playing a little tennis.

"Sure?"

"Yes."

"In high school, I say I win mathematics medal. . . ."

"Yes."

"Also win swimming medal," Yogi announces, bolting from her back float into a forward tuck and doing a speedy crawl across the shallow section of the pool. "You cannot catch me," she calls over her shoulder before diving under the rope into the lap area, "unless I permit you."

CHAPTER 12

The Time Is Always Now

Laura walks out of Franklin's newsroom office and directly to Edie in the high slot, who is saying "Six hundred fucking dollars. . . ." in a stage whisper.

"Before, you would have said, 'six hundred bloody dollars,' big sister," Laura says. "You're turning American."

"In any case, it's six hundred bloody dollars a case for this fucking water the Broad Bottomed Wolf demands. . . ."

"What are you talking about?"

"Christina Volpecello, the Broad Bottomed Wolf, says she has to have this Aburzzi water. And if we can't get it here, she'll have it flown in and bill us. One case per day for every day she's here."

"Can't we get it here?"

"I'm asking Fiona to check on it locally . . . and on her bloody dog food. . . . That's 400 dollars, but she only needs one case of that. And of course, Fiona won't bother, so I might as well just budget it. Six hundred fucking dollars. . . ."

"Why not just. . . ?"

"Pete says this Broad Bottomed Wolf is one of his father's favorites— I'm not sure exactly what kind of favorite that might be—reckon, like father like son—so she must be accommodated. Six hundred. . . ."

"Listen, big sister, call off Fiona. I can try. . . ."

"Don't you have enough to do. . . ?"

"Peter says this is important, right?"

"Well, yes. . . ."

"And it's . . ."

Edie joins in with Laura, ". . . the handover, stupid."

"And if you can do something important to assist the handover coverage," Edie says, "that can't hurt one's qualifications for being studio producer on handover night." Laura smiles. "Time for a fag, *mei-mei?*"

"I thought you'd never ask."

Edie dismounts from the high slot, and yells across the newsroom, "Sara, watch the monitors while I drag a fag."

They sit side by side on the fire stairway, swept clean, and Laura asks, "Has Franklin said anything to you about a supervising producer for the handover?"

"Do you know who it is?"

"No."

"Oh, well." Edie lights up a cigarette.

"But he said that maybe there won't be one."

"No SP," Edie shakes her head. "Interesting."

"I went in to ask him about producing on handover night, and he said that he'd pick the SP and then the SP would pick the show producer. But then he said there's no one here. . . ."

"Ideally, they'd be Chinese . . . CK maybe, if he wasn't in a brothel in Guangzhou every afternoon. . . ."

"Geez, that's what Franklin said. The CK part, not the brothel. . . ."

"Speaking of which," Edie says, "I heard a rumor about why Pete got sent here."

"Which is. . . ?"

"Which is to hush up a sexual harassment lawsuit back in the US." Edie exhales broadly. "I heard from the news director in LA that he was boffing some reporter and it got nasty. So they paid her off and bundled him off here. Just wait until Pussy gets a lawyer. . . ."

"Stop saying that, Edie, please."

"What?"

"About Franklin and Pussy."

"Why?" Edie stops looking at her cigarette and fixes on Laura's eyes.

"It's just," Laura averts Edie's gaze, "so disgusting. I can't believe that people believe. . . ."

"Just a joke, though I'm sure Pete wishes it weren't. He does spend a lot of time up on twenty-eight. . . ."

"And," Laura reports, "he says we should be damned glad that he does."

"Better him than me."

"Better who than you?" Franklin asks, swinging open the fire door. "We pay you to smoke?" He notices only Edie is smoking. "Actively and. . . ." looking at Laura, "passively. I just came for my fix, but you're almost done. Light another and I'll tell you huge network secrets. Grant Prebo wears a toupee. . . ."

Laura nods, "I knew that hair couldn't. . . ."

"But he doesn't wear it on his head," Franklin adds.

"Sorry, Pete, but I have to go back and finish up," Edie says, grinding out her cigarette.

"Finish up? What time do you leave?"

"About now."

"Geez, it's not even two o'clock. . . ."

"She got here at five, Peter," Laura says, thinking how good a workout at the gym and a dip in the JCC jacuzzi will feel. "And I've been here since one a.m."

"So you have," Franklin nods. "Now what? Go home, pick up the dry cleaning. . . ." He swings the door open and the two women rise to exit.

"We've been known to have the occasional after-work cocktail in Lan Kwai Fong," Edie says.

"I've heard about that place and been wanting to see it," Franklin says.

"Perhaps some evening we can arrange. . . ." Edie says.

"How about now? I'm the boss. If you're going now, I can go, too. I'll get my jacket." He bolts toward his office, nearly letting the fire door slam into Laura and Edie as they follow.

Ten minutes later, the three of them are making small talk squeezed into the back seat of their Toyota Crown taxi, Franklin seated in the middle, during the 25-minute, HK$98 cab ride from Chai Wan to Lan Kwai Fong. "How about we go to the FCC?" Edie suggests. "I can put it on my tab and charge it to the company."

"No." Franklin says. "I'll put it on my tab."

"I'm ashamed to say," Laura lies, "I've been to the Foreign Correspondents Club in New York dozens of times, but never here."

"You're not missing much," Edie says. "They still think it's bloody 1975 in there, swapping stories about the fall of Saigon. . . ."

"Listen," Franklin says, "let's go somewhere divey."

"Pete, darling," Edie says, "Every bar is divey at 2:30."

"Afternoon or morning?" Laura chimes in.

"Yes," Franklin responds.

They settle for a table in the back of a bar called The Time Is Always Now, next to the darkened stage for live music later than evening. They are the only people in the place besides the staff. Edie orders a white wine and Franklin suggests a bottle of a New Zealand Marlborough sauvignon blanc at HK$420.

"Impressive," Edie says.

"I learn fast," Franklin says. When the wine arrives, he lifts his glass for a toast. "Pussy and Quickie told me your joke: to the handover, stupid."

"The handover, stupid," Laura and Edie repeat, clinking their glasses. The wine could be colder, Laura thinks but it goes down smoothly.

"Later, maybe a valpollicello for Christina Volpecello."

"Laura says she's going to stay on top of things for Christina, starting with the water and dog food. . . ."

"Oh, god, she's bringing the mutt," Franklin says. "Thank you, Laura, that's the spirit." Chook-koo. "Listen, Edie, what do you think about an SP for handover night? Anybody you like?"

"Besides Laura or me?" Edie says, taking a sip of wine. No one else speaks so she fills the silence. "I also said CK would have been the best. . . ."

"What do you mean, 'you also said'?"

"I told Edie about us talking. . . ." Laura confesses.

Chook-koo. "That's good." Sip, chook-koo. "People should talk, share information. No secrets in the newsroom. You can't keep them if you try, anyway, so don't bother. We put our heads together and that's the best thing for the network." Chook-koo. "I'm thinking that maybe we're better off without an SP, unless there's someone who's really outstanding."

"Outstanding not," Edie says. "Outrageous certainly."

"Speaking of which, what is up with the chick with the hair?"

"You mean Nancy in tapes," Edie says.

"Woman, not chick," Laura says.

"In my book, anyone who comes to work with purple hair is a chick," Franklin sips his wine. "Don't file a lawsuit, okay?"

"Pete, speaking of lawsuits," Edie begins, ignoring Laura's kick her under the table, "I heard that you left the US because due to litigation."

"That's not true, exactly."

"You Americans," Edie shrugs. "So what is *exactly* true?"

"It'll probably take another bottle of wine," Franklin says.

"You're paying," Laura says.

"And we're listening," Edie adds.

"Okay listen," Franklin says, taking a big gulp of wine, topping off everyone's glass with the dregs of the bottle, whistling to catch the barman's attention and holding up the bottle, turned upside down. "There was an anchor. . . ."

"Diana Smythe in New York?" Laura asks. "I know her. Actually. . . ."

"No names," Franklin scolds. "Man, America is sooo ridiculous with all these lawsuits and political correctness." Chook-koo. "Nah. I'm not telling you this story. Not today. I've only been here a week, I have to save some material for. . . ."

"Oh, come on, Pete," Edie says brightly. "You can tell us." She pulls out a cigarette.

"Of course I can tell you. But I won't." Chook-koo. "Listen, let me have one of those." Edie holds out her cigarette pack to Franklin. "No, no, I won't. Just smoke in this direction." Chook-koo.

"Tell us, Peter," Laura implores, as Edie lights up and kicks her.

"I love you reporters. You think you have a right to know everything in the world." Franklin takes a slug of wine. "God bless you for that. But I don't have to tell you anything. Nobody does. I've never understood that: Why does anyone tell reporters anything?"

"Some people have a need to tell," Edie says.

"Well I don't. Let's drop it."

"What about Old Hartman?" Edie says. "Do you believe that he wants us to send him to Tokyo next week to interview Madonna?"

"He got tired of pestering me about the handover," Franklin says. "Stupid."

"What about it?" Laura asks.

"He wants to know what his assignment will be. After all," Franklin says, switching to his Old Hartman imitation, "it's the biggest story of the decade. . . ."

"Have you thought about who. . . ?"

"Like I told you, Laura, that's for the SP to decide."

"Bloody cop out," Edie says.

"Correct." Chook-koo.

"But if it was up to you. . . ." Laura says.

"It is up to me," Franklin says, smiling at Laura. "What if it was up to you, March?"

"If it were up to me, I'd anchor Old Hartman with Deng."

"Both Americans and need a girl," Franklin says, swilling wine in his glass.

"We've got Anna and Kathy."

"Both airheads," Laura says.

"I think of them as empty vessels, *mei-mei*. They're as good as what you pour inside."

"Brains in an anchor are generally a waste of time anyway," Franklin says. "If they think they know something, they want to be the producer, the director. . . ."

"Like Deng," Laura blurts.

"Like Deng. All you newspaper people think you're too smart for TV. So, Edie, would you take Deng as the male anchor for handover night?"

"It would break Mike's heart, but I'm afraid so. You need to have a Chinese face, even if he's a bloody Yank."

"A banana," Laura says, brightly. "You know, yellow on the outside, white on the inside."

"I get it." Chook-koo. "It would kill Mike. And if it did, we'd get out from under that ridiculous contract. Geez, I was with Old Hartman when he interviewed Jack Welch. He spoke at one of our sales conventions—my pop spoke at one of his—and Mike drones on so long with his questions that they have to change the tape in the camera. This is right before Mike came here, and while they're changing the tape, Mike's telling Welch about how great it is to be going to Hong Kong for the big story. And Welch is completely tuned out until the red light goes on again." Chook-koo, sip, chook-koo. "And Old Hartman, Mike senses how miserably he's failing to impress Welch—after all these years of interviewing these guys, Old Hartman thinks he's one of them, whereas the CEOs think he's just another phoof and would prefer one with a short skirt who's free for dinner—anyway, Mike's dying to impress Welch, so in that grave tone he gets when he wants you to believe he's letting you in on the whole truth as only Old Hartman can see it, he says, 'Yes, Jack, I'm going to Hong Kong, because that's where the next big story is. And, you know, Jack,' he says, 'I've been there for all the big stories. Kennedy, Tranquility Base, Watergate, the fall of the Berlin Wall. . . .' "

"Oh god," Edie chuckles, blowing smoke through her nose.

"And I'm thinking, yeah, Mike, you were there for all of them, writing Treasury bond reports."

Edie's laugh mixes with smoke and becomes a deep cough.

"Now, Peter," Laura giggles. "Be fair. Remember back in 1776, when Old Hartman got the interview with John Adams, that's where he got the stock tip for General Electric."

"No," Edie says. "The tip came from Pete's great-great-great-great grandfather, Benjamin."

"In fact, ol' Ben was the one who suggested we hire Old Hartman. That's my clever great-great-grandpop."

"You're kidding," Laura says. "I mean about Benjamin Franklin, your grandfather, great grandfather."

"Afraid not, *mei-mei.*"

"Wow," Laura says, but the information is more than she can parse.

"Geez, a guy can't have any secrets around here."

"What really happened with Wallace Michaels?" Laura asks, seeking more familiar footing.

"Who?" Edie says.

"He was an FGN network . . . a Fuggin network anchor on the US evening news for years, and then one day, he was just gone," Laura says. "About ten years ago, one of the great mysteries in the history of American television. And he was my mother's favorite. . . ."

"His mother's, too." Chook-koo.

"But what. . . ?" Laura says, topping off everyone's glass.

"I've never told anyone, but. . . . Between us, right?"

Laura and Edie nod.

"Okay, we're having a network production meeting and my pop is sitting in, and they're brainstorming special report ideas for the next ratings sweeps. My pop wants them to do a follow-up on Chernobyl, five years after or whatever, and what's happened since.

"So Wally, who's a wise guy like our Deng, he says, 'Chernobyl? Let's make a music video.' You remember those McDonald's ads with that great tune, 'Glasses to go'? You wouldn't, March. . . ."

"Sure," Laura says, and starts singing. "Glasses to go, glasses to go, McDonald's has McDonaldland glasses to go. . . ."

"That's the one," Franklin says. "Anyway, Wally starts singing. . . ." Franklin sings loudly, so that the bar staff turn to watch:

> *"Asses that glow,*
> *Asses that glow,*
> *People from Chernobyl have asses that glow.*
> *Radioactive gas has really fucked 'em.*
> *The Soviet leadership's totally chucked 'em. . . ."*

Laura collapses into hysterical laughter.

"That's brilliant," Edie says.

"Well, from a strictly creative point of view, perhaps," Franklin says. "Are you okay?" he asks Laura.

She gasps for air and nods.

"Okay. Don't die. You've got a show tomorrow." Chook-koo. "Now, my pop has a terrific sense of humor, except for a couple of things. One is that he hates cursing—profanity is the crutch of small minds, he says. The other thing is that there are only two things in life that my pop takes seriously, money and the environment, especially nukes. He's like Turner on that—I tell you, those two guys hate each other because they're so alike. Anyway, my pop hears Wally's little ditty, turns completely red and walks out of the meeting without saying a word. Fifteen minutes later, two lawyers and a security guard are walking Wally out of the building, handing him papers to sign. He got a seriously huge settlement on his contract, but agreed never to discuss his tenure at Fuggin News and never to work in broadcasting again. I'm sure that's what killed him. He's like Old Hartman, living for that red light. . . ."

"That is the funniest story I've ever heard," Laura says, still chuckling.

"Is it true?" Edie asks, refilling everyone's glasses.

"It might be," Franklin says. Chook-koo.

"Think of who the competition is in New York or LA," Franklin says, a couple of hours and three bottles later. "You've got all-news radio, all-sports radio, all-business radio. Here, you haven't got anything like that."

"But Peter, we're a news network. . . ." Laura protests.

"And this format gives people news. And we've got the crawls for people who have to know what the Nikkei is doing right now." Chook-koo.

"You'd keep the ticker," Edie says.

"Yeah, of course, and the bug with the indexes," Franklin says. "Couldn't live without them. Smoke this way, March."

"Peter, this is the news business," Laura says.

"It's the news business," Franklin says, refilling his glass. "Yes, it's the news business, but it's also show business. Do the news—do the motherlovin' heck out it—but don't forget the show." Chook-koo.

"Tell that to our anchors," Edie says.

"This format will give viewers more variety. The *Money-Go-Round* shows are all the same now. No variety. And that Kathy Trang. . . ."

"Crocodile Cup-D," Edie says.

"Right," Franklin says. "When we run the ticker under her neck, there's goes half the reason for watching her."

"I'm still trying to figure out a role that suits her," Edie says.

"Unemployment, maybe," Franklin says. Edie giggles, and Franklin smiles appreciatively. "That's a joke, don't repeat it. But we're just not giving people anything by reading the same news from different faces. We need more interviews, live stuff. If our people don't know what they're talking about, then let's hear from people who do. Things need to move, feel more dynamic. It's the news business. . . ."

"All in fifteen minutes?" Laura says.

"Twelve," Franklin says. "Don't forget the breaks."

"You know how long twelve minutes can be, *mei-mei,*" Edie says, pulling her pad toward her and twirling her pen. "Let me sort through this. You have fifteen-minute news blocks, then fifteen minutes of features. . . ." She begins to jot. "So you're really only producing a half hour of news. . . ."

"So the show producers can cover three hours, instead of two," Franklin says, "and they'd still have less air time to fill than they do now."

"Interesting," Edie says, writing. "But the anchors would still need to be on set for the full hour. . . ."

"Not if you put the feature blocks on tape," Franklin says.

"A news show on tape?" Laura gasps.

"Why not?" Edie says. "Think of it as a long package."

"That's ridiculous."

"No, it's not, *mei-mei.*" Edie jots, asking Franklin, "When would you put down the feature blocks?"

"We could do them in Laura's show, live and then replay them. Deng would love it. More face time."

"So, I'm supposed to. . . ."

"You'd be producing the same two hours," Edie says. "One full hour, six to seven, then two halves with the taped blocks. Or maybe run *AM Asia* until nine. . . ."

"You'd know your show format every day, half the battle." Chook-koo.

"Who'd make sure the packages were cut. . . ?"

"Nancy, Fiona, the same people. . . ."

"Oh, god. Just kill me now." Laura takes a big slug of wine. "Those two G-Spots. . . ."

"G-Spots?"

"We call them G-Spots, Pete," Edie explains. "Difficult to find."

"Cute. But sad, girls, very sad."

"Laura gave them the name," Edie adds and resumes jotting. "You could get by, Pete, I reckon, with at least one less anchor and one less producer. . . ."

"And you, dear, could have the pleasure of choosing which ones."

"Possibly two producers."

Laura shakes her head. "You're both crazy. New York would never. . . ."

"I am New York," Franklin says, smiling. "They sent me here to fix things. They got sick of all of the nonsense from Lamont. Nobody in New York can do what needs doing for Fuggin Asia. It's up to all of us, not New York."

"But I think a major change like this needs to be thoroughly. . . ."

"Three bottles of wine isn't thorough enough?" Chook-koo.

"Four," Edie says, "if you're counting."

"I think we need. . . ." Laura says, knowing this idea is so wrong yet finding the way Franklin is putting it together on the fly so impressive.

Just because he's the boss' son doesn't mean he can't know his stuff. After all, Jeff knows underwear, maybe, Franklin knows news.

"You think too much, Laura," Franklin says. "When I played baseball, the coach always said, 'Don't be thinking on me out there.' Know the objective, eyes on the prize, and get it done. Rule one for a producer is to make a decision. You can be wrong, but never in doubt." Chook-koo.

Edie looks up from jotting. "Definitely, two less producers. That is, if we decide to go ahead. . . ."

"We've already decided," Franklin says, draining his glass.

"Shouldn't we have a meeting?" Laura implores. "Hear other people's. . . ."

"We've already had a meeting. What do you call this? Three-hour discussion with my two best people in the newsroom. . . ." Franklin reaches for the bottle in the bucket and finds it empty. "Write the memo tomorrow morning, March. Everybody want to go for five?" Chook-koo.

"Peter, you can't. . . . Half news, half tape?" Laura protests. "What . . . what kind of journalism is that?"

"Journalism? That's an awfully strong word for what we do."

CHAPTER 13

Reformat Rolls

"THAT'S A DENG-DONG," Laura says into the control room microphone. "You owe the kitty ten Hongkies."

"What'd I do, boss?" Deng protests from the set.

"It's Bel-a-roos, not Bel-ar-us. You made it rhyme with Toys 'R' Us."

"Oh, you're wrong, Laura," Deng says, shuffling pages to find the scripts for the D feature block. "Bel-ar-us is the star that has guided eastern European mariners since time immemorial. . . ."

"Just pay up so we can have donuts Friday," Laura says.

"Frosted," Quickie the cross-eyed director adds.

"Finished," Nancy Black with her violet hair growing out to its black roots announces, entering the control room. She squats between Laura and Ashrami, who has replaced Pussy at the graphics station. Honest Ho has replaced Ashrami as Laura's PA. "Your D-block packages are cut and fonted. There's no sign-off on one, riverboat gambling, so I added a tag. All those scripts are printed."

"Thanks." Laura clicks the microphone switch and tells Deng, "Nancy's here. Are you okay with the package leads all in D block?"

"Read 'em all during B, loved 'em all."

"No sig-out. . . ."

"On the sidewheeler, D-4. Got the tag."

"Then I'll tell Nancy she can go."

"Tell her to have a drink for me at Chinese Godown. . . ." Deng says.

"That's so not-the-handover-stupid, stupid," Nancy says leaning into the mike. "I'm strictly a G-Spot girl."

"Hard to find," Deng says.

"Maybe for you," Nancy replies before releasing the mike lever.

"You know," Laura says, "I came up with that—G-Spot, hard to find—and somehow they stole it for the name of that bar."

"Two minutes," Quickie announces.

"Things get around fast in this town," Nancy says. "Do you ever go there?"

"I'm in bed by dark every night," Laura says. "My husband is scripted for the G-Spots."

"Quality programming, I hope."

"You bet. Man, when he comes home from China. . . . I don't know what's in the water up there but I hope we'll be getting some of it come July first."

"I just hope I'll be getting some, full stop."

"You've lost some weight. . . ."

"Little bit. These days, I do some health clubbing, too, since Pete and Edie made sense out of the schedule."

"And no more meeting," Quickie says.

"New blouse?" Nancy asks.

"It's from New York, but I haven't worn it here."

"It looks fab. And Laura dear, your face, is that . . . makeup?"

"I guess I've regained some of my will to live since we changed the format," Laura says. "How are the handover packages coming?"

"May is still hopelessly sentimental but they're coming. We're cutting tape every night, she's got a crew out every day. . . ."

"Every day? What about breaking news? How do we. . . ?"

"Fiona has her crew. . . ."

"Who would have thought we'd ever get her out of the newsroom?" Laura shakes her head. "But aren't they also taping on 28. . . ?"

"Promos."

"Who's shooting them?"

"That's a feature crew from the US. Like a Hollywood set up there. Do their own editing, too, so you won't hear me complain."

Both women turn their heads toward the sound of screeching tires as the official luxury sport sedan of FGN Asia hugs an alpine curve. "These Audi spots are great," Nancy says.

"I just wonder what happens if we get a fifteen-car pileup on the Guangzhou toll road, our luck, all Audis, the official luxury sport sedan of Fuggin Asia. . . ."

"I think Fuggin Asia's luck has changed, dear." Nancy says. "I'm off. Good night, good morning, whatever."

After their hour of tennis, laps in the pool where, instead of Jeff holding Yogi's bottom, now she kicks his ass, a soak in the jacuzzi and a shower, they meet at the towel desk. "So what's for dinner tonight?" Jeff asks, as Yogi emerges from the locker room. "I saw kasha varnishkes on the menu and I've been thinking. . . ."

"Tonight is change menu," Yogi says.

They leave the JCC and walk to the escalator. "My apartment is here," Jeff says at the stairway down from Robinson Road.

"We go up," Yogi says, turning toward the escalator.

"I've never gone up above Robinson Road."

"Sure?"

"Do you promise I won't fall off the edge of the world?"

"You may fall into Stanley Market and be purchase by expatriate *tai-tai* as bedcovering."

"Or maybe I'll find 30,000 Golden Beauties bikini sets that fell off a truck. . . ."

"Or maybe is counterfeit. For Jew with padding for bra that can wear for *kippah.*"

"Golden Jewties," Jeff says, as they come to the end of the flight up and cross the overpass above Robinson Road. Instead of continuing upward, Yogi leads him to a building entrance. "Wow, this place? I can see this building from my living room. We're on the fifteenth floor, but I can't see over it or around it."

"Is rooftop restaurant," Yogi says, punching a code to buzz them through the doors to a set of elevators they ride to the 32nd floor, the top. "Because of hill and very high building is excellent view."

The door opens and he follows her onto the landing with fresh flowers on a table and a mirror between two doors. The walls are white, the moldings glossy black. "This looks like the entrance to someone's apartment," Jeff says.

"Yes. Is to my apartment," Yogi says. "I make dinner tonight, not booking."

"Oh, that's very thoughtful," Jeff says, telling himself it's still just tennis and pool and dinner.

"I am in mood for something different," Yogi says, opening the apartment door.

Jeff nearly gasps when he sees the view of the harbor and Central. In the water, there so many ships so close together, they look like strings of Christmas lights. But it's the view to the east—the right half of the panorama—looking down over the tops of the city's skyscrapers that's most impressive. He steps, mesmerized toward the window, but Yogi brings him back to earth saying, "Please take shoes off. Is Japanese home."

"It's magnificent," Jeff says, unlacing his sneakers and stripping to bare feet in the front hall, larger than the Proper Gardens living room, with a tall, narrow Chinese style landscape painting in black and white on the side wall.

"Thank you." She leads him into the living room, larger than his Golden Beauties stores back home, with a terrace beyond the windows. More paintings and pieces of elaborately carved wooden furniture line the walls.

"This place is unbelievable," Jeff says. "Is it all your furniture?"

"Painting and antique from bank. Wives of boss become Chinese art dealer and sell painting and antique to bank. Is good business for them. A few things from me." Yogi hands Jeff a book from the coffee table: *The Kama Jewtra, Torrid Sex from the Torah.* "Maybe you know this book?"

"A girlfriend once gave it to me, but she made me practice by myself."

"Wife does not know this book?"

"She's not Jewish. . . ."

"You are marry *shiska?*"

"*Shikse,* yes."

"Maybe this is why she never to JCC. She is afraid of bite from gefilte fish. . . ."

"I think she's more afraid of exercise. . . ."

"*Komban-wa,*" comes from a voice from the other end of the room. The woman making a quick bow in a white maid's outfit looks Filipina but speaks Japanese to Yogi.

"Are you hungry?" Yogi asks Jeff, as the Filipina opens the doors to the terrace, larger than the entire Proper Gardens apartment.

"Sure," Jeff says, and follows Yogi. She leads him to a raised platform along the side wall, enabling them to enjoy view even though they sit on mats and pillows at a low table. There's a tall silver urn with flame underneath in the middle of the table set for two with an elaborate array of plates and bowls plus silver chopsticks. "Welcome to Chez Yogi," she says, pouring him clear liquid from a ceramic pot into a small matching cup. She pours one for herself, lifts it, says, *"Gan bei,"* and they both drink.

"That's good," Jeff says. "A flaming Homer?"

"Is sake. You have never try?"

"No. Is it always served warm?"

"Is very soothing for digestion."

"It goes down quite smoothly," Jeff says as Yogi refills his cup. The amah comes out with a platter in each hand, bows, and places them on the table. "What is all this?" Jeff asks.

"I think you are want to try," Yogi says. She picks up a platter and pushes ingredients into the water in the urn with chopsticks. "You can also," Yogi says, handing Jeff a platter. He copies what she's doing until both platters are empty. "Is *shabu-shabu*. I hope you will like."

"I'm sure," Jeff says. "I appreciate you're taking the trouble. . . ."

"Is trouble for Georgia, not for me."

"Georgia?"

"Amah."

"And she speaks Japanese."

"Yes," Yogi says, then lowers her voice, "but like *gaijin*. She have name of British king and American state, so is not surprise."

"This place is just spectacular," Jeff says. "How big is it?"

"Is about 2,000 square feet. Five bedroom."

"All for you?"

"Yes. Amah is also stay, but her room more far away than Wellcome supermarket. Is supposed to be flat for managing director, but his wife not happy because does not receive sunset view. So they are move to Tai Tam. Is empty, so I have."

"How much does it cost?"

"Is in package. I do not pay. But I think is about 20,000 dollar per month."

"That's crazy," Jeff says. "Our little dollhouse costs 15,000."

"Hong Kong dollar?"

"Yes."

"This 20,000 US, I believe."

"No shit."

"I believe I am worth this." Yogi sips sake and refills their cups, Jeff tapping on the table. "More important: bank is think so."

"I'll say this: It's nice to be somewhere that's adult sized. We live in a shoe box. All our furniture seems like it's made for a dollhouse. In fact," Jeff says, looking down, "the shoe box right there, next to the escalator. You can see our window from here. In a few hours, Laura will be waking up, and stepping into her Golden Beauties samples. . . ."

"How is your business?"

"Same. They've stepped in and I'm out."

"I have speak to friend at bank who is work with joint venture teams," Yogi says, stirring the mix, her face reflected in the side of the urn. "They have factory which can also produce lingerie for quite low price if you are. . . ."

"Oh, Yogi, that's very sweet of you," Jeff says, shocked that she took the trouble. "Thank you very much."

"Maybe Jeffrey can make good business with bank and Chinese customer. . . ."

"It's too bad I didn't meet you a couple of months ago," Jeff says, "when I was still looking for a partner to help me get started in China. Now I'm afraid it's too late. . . ."

"Sure? I think you are still know underwear. . . ."

"That's true. If I could get goods made to my specs, I could probably kick their ass . . . no pun intended. . . ."

"I think you would enjoy this. . . ."

"I would. After all, it's all my idea, from the start, when I first thought about coming over here," Jeff says, taking a sip of sake. "I did the legwork, I connected my mother, the canasta queen who didn't know anything about China except you can get it with a discount at Fortunoff, to the factory. I did everything I was supposed to do, and wound up with nothing. . . ."

"This is story your mother has write," Yogi says. "Jeffery can write story for himself."

Jeff sighs. "Yes, maybe I can. But not on this subject. To really make it work, whatever it is, you really need to have a passion. But I'm afraid I'm not passionate enough about this, about ladies' underwear. . . ."

"You are lose interest in lady underwear?"

"As a business at least. . . ."

"I am disappoint that I cannot see Jeffrey working in ladies' underwear."

"I can still model some for you later."

"My brassiere probably too small for you," Yogi says, holding a palm over her face to hide her giggling.

"It's not just passion, though," Jeff says, "it's distribution. Without people in the US to find customers there and deal with them, it's too much trouble."

"Perhaps it will not be trouble. Is not American say if build better birdhouse world will fly to you. . . ?"

"Close enough for me," Jeff laughs. "But I had enough trouble trying to work with my mother and the Israelis, I don't even want to think about working against them as competitors."

"Tonight we are work together for *shabu-shabu*." Yogi guides Jeff through the meal, starting with meat and vegetables, then the soup, keeping their sake cups full. "Really delicious," he tells her several times. For dessert, Yogi says, "Taste this," and gives Jeff a kiss. He's surprised at how unsurprised he is.

Following all the rules, Jeff thinks, doing what I think is right, that let me waste ten years managing underwear stores when I could have been handling a multimillion dollar property portfolio; moving to Hong Kong for the Chinese takeaway when I should have stayed on Long Island to take away what belongs to me from the Chinese lawyer; getting cut out of another multimillion dollar deal, this time one that I conceived and executed, gift wrapping it to be taken away from me; living with a wife who goes to bed before dark and seems much more concerned with her job, her drinking buddy—I'd drink with her if she'd invite me (and pick up the tab)—her boss, her archenemies, Anchorman and Graphics Girl, than she is about me. That's where following the rules got me, Jeff thinks, and the one time I did mess up, it wasn't warmly buzzed on a penthouse terrace with banker but sloppy drunk in a flophouse with a hooker. Maybe it's worth breaking the rules on purpose at least this once to see what happens.

As they drop clothes on the mat and he touches more of Yogi's bare skin, Jeff realizes how much he's wanted to do this since that first floating lesson in the swimming pool. The ecstasy at climax makes him feel like he's floating over the skyscrapers, the harbor, the Golden Beauties fiascos past and present, that he's above it all, beyond it all, that it can't touch him. Still thrilled but exhausted, he hugs Yogi as hard as he can, kisses her, then pulls his head back to look her in the eyes and try to tell her everything he's feeling, all thanks to her. He takes a deep breath, and still quivering, declares, "That was fantastic *shabu-shabu.*"

Yogi smiles and says, "Sorry, but this was only *shabu.*"

"It's really improved with Peter's new system," Laura says, over her plate of squid in black-bean sauce with mushrooms and carrots with rice, Jeff's latest experiment in the kitchen. She takes a sip of white wine. "This is good. A little hot maybe."

"The sauce is from a jar," Jeff says. "I can water it down, or add a little. . . ."

"I have a meeting with Nancy and Edie around five to choose the packages, and in fifteen minutes, half the show is done. Sometimes we have to tweak a lead-in to give it an Asian angle or whatever, but that's easy."

"Good for you."

"So it's three hours, but, like Peter says, it's really only two, two in the morning, which is really an hour and a half, and then another hour at ten, that's really only fifteen minutes twice. And we've got the New York package, the markets—Deng's a pain in the ass, but when you put up that market board or roll out a guest, he knows what to say. Never at a loss for words, that boy. And since I got my old PA Ashrami on the graphics instead of that stupid Chinese teenager who couldn't speak English, that works, too. My new PA, Honest Ho—can you believe that name?—she's very good. Never says a word unless you talk to her. She's like I thought Hong Kong people would be—you know, like Chinese back home: quiet, hard-working, smart, don't make trouble. . . ."

"It sounds like things are. . . ."

"I mean, it's still live TV, and there's still all kinds of issues, and I still don't understand all of it, but it's manageable. After the first hour, I have fifteen minutes between blocks to get myself organized, and that really helps."

"Good," Jeff says, pushing food around his plate. He'll eat after tennis with Yogi, and probably stay at her place for *shabu-shabu,* so he just pretends here, and will pack up his portion as Laura's lunch for tomorrow before he goes.

"And we've even got sponsors now, ads. It's amazing. I don't know how Peter did it. He fired all the old ad staff—they were all KS and CK's cousins and I don't know what they did up on 28, but it sure wasn't selling any ads. Peter cleaned them all out, and he's been out there himself selling ads. We've gotten the Peninsula, Singapore Air, Audi . . . big accounts. It must be impressive to companies when the boss of Fuggin Asia—and the son of Big Mo in New York—comes to your office and sits down to talk to you personally about the network and about building a lasting partnership. . . ."

"Sure beats the son of Murray the Golden *Gotke* King. . . ."

"Peter really is a genius. I had my doubts about him and about this new format and all, but it's really working," She nods her head as she drinks more wine. "You figure, the guy's the heir to the empire, our age, what does he know? But he's really smart. He's been around TV all his life, so he really gets it." She takes another bite. "Grows on you, this stuff."

"Good. I can try. . . ."

"Peter says what needs to be done, and he lets people do it. None of the bullshit we had with CK and Lamont. Before we were never clear about what was expected, so people were unsure about what to do. Edie says that's a very Chinese thing: give vague instructions so you can criticize whatever goes wrong and blame someone else. Now, people are motivated, challenged, not worrying about nonsense. Peter says, if you make a mistake, know why it happened and don't do it again. So, people just think about doing the job, take responsibility for it, and that's all Peter's doing."

"When I ran the stores, I had my managers. . . ."

"Well, a TV network is a little different from running a lingerie store. . . ."

"Five lingerie stores. . . ."

"Okay, five. . . ."

"Dealing with people, employees and customers. . . ."

"Peter says knowing people is the most important part of being an executive, and that's what I am when you bottom line it. A TV producer is an executive: my job is to get people to do their jobs the way we want them to. A good executive finds out what makes them tick and figures out how to reach them so that they're sold on doing the job. If I can do that—Peter says it's all about finding the right buttons to push—if I can push the right buttons with the people who work for me, then I don't have to micromanage them. I can be confident they'll do their jobs and I can concentrate on doing mine. I give Peter credit, he knows his stuff."

"I'll say. . . ."

"A guy like that, the crown prince of the empire, I thought he'd be stuck up or in outer space or whatever, but he's a normal guy. He comes and hangs out with me and Edie on the stairway to breathe in her smoke—he's trying to quit—and we get more done there on the stairs, or sometimes at a bar in Lan Kwai Fong in the afternoon, than we ever did in all of CK and Lamont's meetings put together. No, things are working out."

For everyone, Jeff thinks. "That's good."

"You know, I never thought I'd say it, but some days, I don't dread going to work. And when I'm there, sometimes I actually kind of enjoy it."

"Forgiving me for not firing Andy is not the same as thanking me for not firing you," Edie says swinging open the fire door to the stairway smoking terrace. A sign on the outside of the door, in oddly childish handwriting in marker reads, "It's the handover, stupid." One on the inside of the same door reads, "Get fired up!" The "up" has been repeatedly crossed out until the tops of the letters are level but the bottom of the "p" extends below the "u" sufficiently. Other signs in similar writing with different catch phrases—"Decide, then execute" on one, "Take responsibility" on another—are posted throughout the newsroom.

"I said I almost forgive you," Laura corrects. "Jesus, you can feel that," she says of the pile driving thud at the construction site along the waterfront.

"Now we know our studio soundproofing works," Edie says. "I've heard it'll be flats, thirty-eight stories, kill this view if they take up the option for the second phase. Best time to smoke is during their lunch break at noon."

"How long is this going to go on?" Laura asks.

"When this project's done expect another," Edie says with resignation. "At least you can't blame me for this."

"Well, I'm not thanking you for it either. . . . What about the signs? Do you. . . ."

"No idea," Edie says. "But I see you noticed 'Check your makeup'. . . ."

"Since we changed the format, I just feel a little better about things here, about myself, about being professional, looking the part," Laura says. "It feels closer to back in the old days in New York, when I turned heads, like John-John Kennedy's before. . . ."

"You did?"

"Don't sound so shocked. But it should make you even more ashamed that you considered firing me. . . ."

"Laura, it had to make sense financially, so I wasn't going to fire someone who wasn't on an expat package."

"That explains Andy, but it doesn't express regret that you actually thought about firing me."

"I wasn't going to do it, darl'," Edie insists, "but I had to consider it."

"But how could. . . ."

"I didn't, but to get the full impact of the cuts we had to choose people on packages. It freed up nearly a million dollars."

"What about this promo?"

"Strikes me as awfully late, *mei-mei*. The kind of thing we should have done months ago. . . ."

"But what is a promo?"

"It's something to introduce the station to potential sponsors. The network's ad agency from New York is doing it."

"Wow, that must cost. . . ."

"Half million US. That's where half of the savings went." Edie laughs. "It's lovely playing with the other half, though."

"How much did you save dumping Sylvia and Iggy?"

"We saved about three quarters of a million sending Iggy back to the Philippines, the rest from Sylvia."

"Do I really cost a quarter million dollars a year?"

"You aren't our highest paid producer . . . just our most valuable one." Edie looks at the tip of her cigarette. "I told that to Pete."

"Thanks, *jie-jie.*"

"Before you ask, he still hasn't said anything to me about the handover yet."

"You really think he won't have a supervising producer?"

"It's the lean and mean Fuggin Asia handover team . . ."

". . . stupid," they say in unison.

"What would you do, if you were me?"

"I'd ask him."

"I can't do that. Not again."

"Then you'll find out soon enough."

"If I don't get it, I still want to do. . . ."

"Stop worrying."

"We need more people, more expats on the story, not less."

"I'd tend to agree. But only the right ones."

"The latest on Christina Volpecello. . . ."

"The Broad Bottomed Wolf of the FCC circuit. . . ."

"Now it's the hotel," Laura says. "She wants someone to measure the Peninsula's executive suite mattress for her. . . . But we do need more westerners. . . ."

"Dream on," Edie says, adding, "And you should recall that Pete favors sourcing locally . . . for all manner of things."

"I wish you wouldn't say that."

"You really hate it about him and Pussy."

"I don't hate it. I just don't believe it. I mean she's, what, seventeen years old. . . ."

"Wouldn't you?"

"That's disgusting. . . ."

"And it's his pattern. . . ."

"One rumor," Laura says.

". . . is worth a thousand facts in this business," Franklin says, bounding down the stairs, with a chook-koo snap of his nicotine gum. "Good morning, ladies. . . ."

"Peter. . . ." Laura smiles brightly.

"Pete," Edie says more purposefully. "I heard that Vern Rivers was in town last weekend. . . ."

"Who's Vern Rivers?" Laura chirps.

"He's the network's anchor guru," Edie grumbles. "So Pete, was he. . . ?"

"He was just passing through on his way to . . . between fires."

"It seems odd that you wouldn't get him together with Anna or Kathy. . . ."

"He was just stopping over."

"I've been trying to get Vern to come here since last year. . . ."

"It was the man's closest thing to a day off in a month, and we had dinner together." Chook-koo.

"Even if you'd gotten him together with them over dinner. . . ."

"I only come here for the smoke," Franklin tells Edie, "and it looks like you're about to put that one out."

"I was about to light one," Laura says, fishing a three-day-old pack of Marlboros from her pocket.

"And I was about to check on Fiona's shoot at LegCo," Edie says, grinding out her cigarette butt. *"Bai-bai,"* she says, exiting through the fire door.

Laura lights a cigarette, her hand shaking as the pile driver wallops again. She does her best not to inhale and extends the lit end toward Franklin, admiring the smear of lipstick—Sun Spark today—on the filter. "BB Wolf says she needs to know the precise measurements of the Peninsula suite bed."

"For her BB, and that damned dog of hers," Franklin says. "But she's worth the trouble, I promise. When Christina Volpecello reports a story, viewers howl. . . ."

"Her broad bottom could cost us 5,000 Hongkies, if she needs an upgrade. . . ."

"Add another zero before you bother me about her expenses, please. Christina Volpecello wants a super-king bed, she gets a super-king bed. If we don't want to give her a super-king bed, designer water, a gold-plated fire hydrant for her mutt, then we don't beg the assignment desk in New York to send her to cover our little Fuggin Asia story. You're going to love working with her. . . ."

"You mean I'll be producing handover night. . . ."

"Everybody will work with her wherever they are. She's a force of nature. You can't avoid working with her any more than you can avoid a hurricane. What do they call it here . . . typhoon?" Chook-koo. "How are you coming with her stuff?"

"I found her water at Oliver's and put a hold on six cases for delivery to her hotel when she arrives. The dog food needs to be special ordered from the US. I put in the purchase order upstairs, also for delivery direct to the hotel...."

"That's good," Franklin says. "What about her on air stuff?"

"On air?"

"Yes, the interviews, shots and locations for her...." Chook-koo.

"I thought the desk, Edie, Fiona, were handling that...."

Franklin shakes his head. "I heard you were going to handle things for Christina. The most important part of it is getting the tape she wants shot and logged and cut...."

"Then exactly what does she do?"

"She shoots standups and reaction shots. If we get a really big interview, like Prince Charles, maybe she'll sit for that...."

"What about the new chief executive here?"

"Too local. I'd have Deng or Anna do that, maybe Old Hartman.... But this stuff for Christina needs to get done. Top priority."

"What does that mean? That I'm supposed to do it?"

"You said you'd take care of the Broad Bottomed Wolf." Chook-koo. "Well, this is what really needs taking care of."

"So I'll need to get a crew...."

"You'll need to get a list of locations, shots and interviews, from her and from Benny, and talk them over with Fiona and Edie and maybe May to see if they have any suggestions, additions or alternatives. Then set up itineraries and appointments before you even think about taking a crew."

"When am I supposed to...?"

"Your shows practically produce themselves nowadays, right? That gives you plenty of time, all during the working day, when you can get people in their offices, shoot vox pops in daylight...."

"So I need to script it out...?"

"You're going to have to work with Christina and Benny and the folks here to plan the stories and the shots. Then you're going to have to work with Fiona and Nancy on crews and tapes. Maybe you can find an intern to do logging, or maybe you'll need to do it yourself." Chook-koo. "It's great experience for you, to get out there and field produce, learn what it takes to make all those packages that you slap on the air without thinking. . . ."

"That's a lot of work."

"And that's a lot of different people you need to work with."

"I can work with anybody." Laura takes a puff on the cigarette and blows the smoke toward Franklin. "I want you to know that. I can work with all the senior staff, with the anchors, with Deng. Since the new format, things are really good between us. I think we just had to get over the initial . . . whatever. But don't worry, I can work with him. I can work with anybody."

"That's a given, Laura."

"What do you mean?"

"I mean of course you can work with anybody. That's your job. If you can't do your job, then find one you can do. . . . That's pretty good, maybe sign material. . . ."

"What is it with the signs?"

"Just reminders." Chook-koo.

"Who does. . . ?"

"Let me finish," Franklin says. "Being able to work with everybody on staff is a minimum requirement. The real question is: can everybody work with you?"

"I don't have a problem with anyone as far as I know."

"You're missing the point: does anybody have a problem with you?"

"I don't think so."

"Not even Pussy?"

"Without her, my shows go a lot smoother," Laura says.

"You didn't answer the question."

"I couldn't take it seriously." Silence. A puff. "Bad timing. Bad luck. I'm sure we'd both handle things better in the future."

"I'm asking about you. So that I know that you know that you need to handle things better sometimes. It's not always what happens that matters, it's how we handle what happens."

"Sign material, too?" Laura shrugs. Franklin keeps looking at her with his deep brown eyes. "Okay, yes. I realize I'm not perfect. I wish I'd handled things better with Pussy . . . and sometimes even with some of my other colleagues."

"And in the future. . . ?"

"Yes. I will try to handle things better with the people I work with." Laura puffs. "Should I write that a thousand times. . . ?"

"That's the hardest part of being a producer, handling the people," Franklin says. "But it's the most important part, whatever you do in life."

Somehow Laura feels at once stroked and insulted, glad about the part that pleases Franklin, grateful for his approval and his advice, and anxious to take on the extra responsibility of field producing—something she really wants to learn—for the Broad Bottomed Wolf, for the handover, stupid. Yet, at the same time, she's moved nearly to anger by Franklin questioning her abilities while piling this extra work on her. How dare he expect so much from her, without even noticing she's puffing this cigarette for his benefit. Peter has every right to expect a lot from her, Laura concedes, since she's not just some stupid teenager but a professional newswoman who knows the score and costs the company almost a quarter million bucks per annum, even if she only sees a fraction of that money. She sighs and desperately wants to change the subject. "I hear you're shooting a promo."

"I'm really surprised you guys didn't have one. I can't believe CK spent so much money without making one. You wouldn't believe his bills from this one restaurant in Guangzhou. . . ."

"But it's the handover, stupid."

"We're still going to have a network on July second." Chook-koo.

"Andy says we're not. . . ."

"That's what his wife's network wishes," Franklin says, shaking his head. "But even though we're focused on the handover—stupid—we've got to see past it to the long-term future of the network."

"I thought there was no long term in television. . . ."

"My pop always says, 'The long term is coming faster than you think. Don't get Mickey Mantled.' "

"Mickey Mantled?"

"Mickey Mantle, great Yankee centerfielder. . . . My pop loves baseball. . . . Mantle said on his fiftieth birthday, 'If I knew I was going to live this long, I would've taken better care of myself.' You've got to mix short-term focus with long-term planning. . . ."

"So, long term, Mister Mantle, how does spending a half-million bucks cut out of our production and newsgathering operations. . . ?"

"We didn't take a dime from station operations, we added a half million. And I could have fired two producers to save more money—and I'm not going to say whose names were on that list—but instead of doing that, I kept one more so we could get rid of that lousy European *Money-Go-Round* that no one cares about, and expand our programming to a full fifteen hours. We're not shortchanging our news or other broadcast components, we're building the equity of those operations by enhancing their value."

"Whatever that means."

"It means we're trying to get people to put their advertising dollars on Fuggin Asia. So we can have more crews and writers and programming to keep jobs for people like us." Franklin gets up. "You know what comes after 1997?"

"Nineteen ninety-eight, stupid."

"And you'll be here to see it, as long as you keep that smoking under control, young lady," he says, shaking a finger at Laura and bounding upstairs to the beat of the pile driver. Chook-koo.

CHAPTER 14

Smoothing Silk

"CALL HIM," DENG SAYS, sitting on the control room counter between Laura and Quickie. "I'll do whatever he says. Just call him."

It's 7:17 a.m., just into the replay of the B feature block that Deng taped last hour. Wire services are reporting a Silk Air jet with 150 passengers and crew has crashed into a mountain in Indonesia with heavy casualties likely. Laura wants Deng to do a live bulletin. Deng wants Laura to call Franklin.

"You just don't want to break the segment and have to put it down again next hour," Laura says.

"He don't need to put it down again," Quickie says helpfully. "Just re-run until break then. . . ."

"Or redo the rest of the block now," Laura says. "Whatever."

"You don't get it, Laura," Deng says. "This involves the official airline of Fuggin Asia. Silk is part of SIA. . . ."

"But it's news, Deng. . . ."

"What if Maurice Franklin was caught in a motel on Sunset Boulevard with a pair of seventeen-year-old strippers. . . ?"

"If it's news. . . ."

"Don't you think it would be wise to ask someone first? Like his son, who happens to be our boss. . . ?"

"We're in the news. . . ."

"But we're also human beings," Deng says. "At least some of us. If it's a sensitive matter, doesn't it make sense. . . ?"

"What makes sense," Laura says, sucking in a deep breath to address the entire control room, "is for the anchor to listen to the producer. It's my show. . . ."

"Oh, so we're back to that again." Deng puts his hands on his hips, purses his lips and speaks in a high pitched whine. "It's my show and whatever I say goes." He returns to his normal voice and posture. "Well, then you better say 'Deng,' because I'll be going."

"And I'll roll tape until we can get Kathy out of her curlers and made up, so go ahead. . . ."

Laura's hot line rings, and she picks it up. "Control room, Wellsley."

"It's Edie. I've got Pete on the line. . . ."

"What?" Laura gasps.

"When I saw the Silk Air crash, that's part of SIA, you know, our sponsor, I called him. Pussy got him out of the shower. . . ."

"Stop it. . . ."

"Put it on speaker in there, and I'll be in. . . ."

"Okay." She hits the speaker button and puts down the receiver. "This is Laura in the Control Room. . . ."

"This is Franklin. Who's there?"

"It's Laura with Quickie, Deng. . . ."

"Mornin', boss. . . ."

". . . Emmy from playback, Ashrami on graphics, Honest Ho the PA, the other techs, and Edie just came through the door." Laura clears her throat. "We're having a disagreement about this Silk Air crash. . . ."

"Right. Edie gave me the details on it."

"I want to report it. . . ."

"Well, of course," Franklin says.

"But," Deng says, "some of us are concerned about the relationship between Silk Air and SIA. . . ."

"That's not an issue. Forget it," Franklin says. "We're in the news business. Don't forget the business part, but never ever compromise the news part. That's rule one. My pop always says it's much easier to get new sponsors than a new reputation. Understood?"

"Yes, boss," Deng salutes above the mumbles.

"Then promise me you'll never call me to ask this kind of question again. It just takes one compromise to undo not just Fuggin Asia's integrity but the whole company's. . . ."

"What about breaking the feature block, Pete?" Edie asks.

"For a big story, of course, but I'm not convinced this one is big enough. . . ."

"But CNN," Laura says, "if they weren't in *Talk Back Live* and had people on set here. . . ."

"It's a big news story, but is it a big business news story?" Franklin says. "Look, we're not competing against CNN, not on breaking news every morning. They've got dozens of correspondents and hundreds of local affiliates. They'll have tape of the crash site within an hour. If we're lucky, we'll get some this week."

"But it's not just about tape. . . ." Laura whines.

"Without pictures, it's radio," Franklin says.

"Or the *Financial Journal,*" Deng adds, loud enough for the control room but not loud enough for the speaker phone to pick up.

"We can't hope to compete with CNN on this kind of breaking story," Franklin continues. "If the story turns out to be big, then I expect us to line up better interviews, do a better job of putting things in the broader context of Asian and global business, to kick CNN's butt on analysis. But on breaking news we can't do it. If people want CNN, they should watch CNN. If people want something different, they should watch us, and we should give them something different. We're not competing against CNN, we're competing against ourselves, to be better than we were yesterday and be more relevant to our viewers. We need to pick our spots when we take on CNN, and I don't see this story as one of those spots," Franklin explains. "Agreed?"

Laura leads the murmurs of agreement.

"How do we ID SIA?" Deng asks. "I mean, we say Silk Air is a subsidiary of Singapore Airlines, but then, do we say 'the official airline of FGN Asia'?"

"I think 'a sponsor of this network' will suffice," Edie says.

"Absolutely," Franklin seconds. "Good call, March. And while I've got you here, one more thing that I hope will keep you from disturbing my morning shower in the future. Instead of asking me, these are calls that the SP and show producer make. And where there's no SP, then the show producer makes the call, no questions asked. First rule of TV news: the anchor is always right. But just because the anchor is always right, that doesn't mean the anchor makes the decisions. The producer makes the decisions and we live . . ."

"Or die. . . ." Deng adds.

". . . or we die with those decisions. When it's Laura in the hot seat, it's her show, her calls. Edie might give some input, can even give her orders, but it's the producer in the control room making the final calls for air. The producer is the boss. She gets the blame when things go wrong. Of course, when things go right, the anchor and the crew and front office get the credit. . . ."A nasal cry of "Pee-ta-aah" pierces the background, clearly heard through the speaker, bringing knowing smiles to Deng and Edie's lips. "I'll see you all in the office, and we can talk more. You know my door's always open. Break a leg."

"He might have gotten something broken if he didn't hang up," Deng chuckles.

"Good job, team," Edie says.

"Honest," Laura says, "tell Helios to write up the Silk crash as Pre-C1. We'll lead with it but no change in the open. . . ."

"Hold all the airline spots," Edie says.

"Rev up the official luxury sport sedan of Fuggin Asia," Quickie says as everyone heads back to their places for C block live with a fresh lead.

Edie nearly convinced Laura that she shouldn't be mad about Franklin's intervention on the Silk Air story. He took Deng's side about not breaking the segment, but Franklin also said they should report the story and that the producer was in charge. "Maybe you gave ground, made a tactical retreat in the battle, but you won the war," Edie said. "Pete said you have the final word on the set."

But Laura still doesn't feel sure about it, doesn't feel in control. She has so many reasons that she needs to see Franklin: about the Silk Air story; about the handover producer spot; about other things that she can't quite put into words but that she knows are really important. She goes to Iris Wong's desk to ask if Franklin is in his office. Before she can say a word, Iris shakes her head and blurts, "Upstair until further notice," picks up her phone and focuses on the numbers she punches, ignoring Laura until she walks away.

Laura rides the elevator up to the 28th floor, the corporate level she's visited in the past solely to hear babbling from Fairy Yeung and Jelly Lam in HR about their latest screw-ups in the saga of her work visa application. She nods at the reception desk, flashes her company ID, walks until she reaches another reception area with a uniformed guard in a room filled with light stands, cables, a makeup table with lighted mirror, reflectors and other tools of the film production trade, along with lots of hard-sided metal cases of various sizes.

"Yaaa?" the guard, seated at a console in front of a single large door that has the same light wood paneling as the room's walls, asks. Only the knob on the door distinguishes it from the surrounding wall.

"I want to see Mister Franklin, but I must be in the wrong place," she says, looking around and realizing there's no other place for her to go.

"Who you?" the guard says.

"Laura."

He dials the phone then talks briefly. "He come."

Laura remains standing, and shortly Franklin enters as the buzzing door opens. She tries to peek, but there's a screen like in a hospital ward just beyond the doorway, obscuring what goes on inside.

"Some open door," Laura says.

"Figure of speech," Franklin replies, working his gum, facing Laura. "Since I'm exiled from my own office, why don't we visit the smoking lounge?"

"What's going on in there?" she asks, standing face to face with him, registering for the first time that she's not that much shorter than him, that he's about the same height as Jeff.

"Taping. And retaping. Cutting and recutting. These guys from New York are serious artists."

"Getting serious money. . . ."

"If their spots bring in one new title sponsor, that pays for it all, plus."

"You'd hope that the programming would do that all by itself," Laura says, smelling the makeup and sweat from the lights on him.

"We'd all hope it does, but it doesn't," Franklin says, turning and walking toward the stairway. "Besides, you'd be the first to say that our news programming should have nothing to do with selling."

Laura stops walking again, forcing Franklin to stop and face her again. "What makes you think you know anything about what I'd say?"

"Because that's part of running an organization," Franklin says, looking her in the eye and smiling, "knowing what the key players think and understanding them. Haven't you read the signs?" He holds the stairway door—with "Lead, follow or leave" outside and "Cover my back, not your ass" on the other—open for Laura.

"Edie says the weather will be like this until October or November," Laura says, feeling the heat and humidity forming a mask in front of her face, a mask shattered by the thud of the pile driving, now in its third week. She pulls out the crumbling pack of Marlboros from her skirt pocket and lights one, then sits, smoothing her skirt as she does. She looks forward to smoking for Franklin. Maybe it's the nicotine. She quickly exhales in his direction.

"Thanks," she begins, "for sticking up for me this morning, even if you didn't agree with me about breaking the feature segment."

"Next time you can, without even asking me." Franklin smiles. "What's your favorite color?"

"Blue. Why?"

"Because we're getting everyone mobile phones, and we don't want every phone in the newsroom to look alike."

"Oh, no. I can't have a mobile phone. . . ."

"Why not?"

"Jeff and I have a pact that if either of us gets a mobile phone, the other has to kill them."

Franklin laughs. "I'll get you the James Bond model with the high powered laser built in. You can melt his gun before he shoots." Chookkoo. "Who's Jeff?"

"My husband," Laura says, staring at Franklin's eyes, same color as Jeff's, then sighs and turns away. "What does Pussy do up here?"

"Pussy?" Franklin laughs. "She gives me the local perspective on things."

"Is that all she's giving you?" Laura takes a drag and coughs. "No," she sputters. "No. I didn't ask that." She catches her breath.

"I can answer it anyway."

"No," she insists, reestablishing eye contact. "The question I really want you to answer is whether I'm going to be the handover night producer?"

"That's pretty direct. . . ."

"Well?"

"We'll announce the whole lineup soon."

"Am I going to like it?"

"That," Franklin says, "is precisely the wrong question. You should be asking whether our sponsors will like it, whether our viewers will like it, whether our executives in New York will like it, whether our shareholders—my pop says the only people in the world who truly care about your health are ex-wives and shareholders—whether they will like it. Those things matter. Whether you like it or not, you'll deal with it, that's what we pay you to do, and, as hard as it may be for you to believe, things will go the way they'll go, regardless of your feelings and preferences."

"Thanks for that, Peter. Could you please twist my next words into a giraffe or stegosaurus?" Laura exhales a long plume of smoke, ending with a small cough.

Franklin sucks in a mouthful of her smoke and emits a string of smoke rings. "I used to be able to do hearts, but I'm out of practice."

Laura laughs. "This morning, when we called you, people were saying...." She stops herself. "What about what Edie said, that you left the US because there was a problem...?"

"Let's face it, Laura, nobody came here because they were considered indispensable back home." Chook-koo.

"What do you mean by that?"

"I mean that, for example, our favorite anchor, Deng, you know the story about how he turned down millions to go network in the US...."

"I read his tee-shirt."

"We gave him a lot of incentives to come here, including a promise that within five years—don't faint, it's a two year contract with a series of options—he'd have a shot at a key bureau, a top-five market anchor spot in the US, or a network desk."

"All that, and he still gets back in touch with his roots...."

"Well, I happen to know that the network that offered him millions to make him its top US anchor was ours."

"What?" Laura says. "So his roots were more important than...."

"Not exactly," Franklin says, looking around the staircase to make sure they're alone. "We put on one condition: he'd have to go back to his real name."

"You mean Deng Jiang Mao...?"

"Lincoln Washington Lee."

Laura, mouth full of smoke, laughs wildly, then coughs, gags, and nearly chokes.

"Don't die on me," Franklin says, patting her back as she reddens. "Not until Edie can redo the schedule."

"He's...." she wheezes as Franklin exits and returns in seconds with a couple of paper cups of water. She gulps one, coughs up a lot of it, then sips the second one with greater success. "He's. . . ." she begins again, now simply caught up in her hysteria, "He's the Star-Spangled Banana."

"Oh Deng you are Lee," Franklin sings. "Jiang Mao, not no how. . . ."

Laura falls forward laughing and singes a hole in the sleeve of her lacy blouse with the cigarette before flicking it away. "Yellow skin and black hair," she sings at the high end of her register, "but all white inside there."

"Lincoln Washington Lee, Chinese wan-na-be-ee."

"Oh say does that Star-Spangled Banana yet fake, Fuggin Asia's Chinese face, while disgracing his race?"

"Play ball," Franklin yells.

"Lincoln Washington Lee. . . ." Laura chuckles. "So television is Deng's lie, too."

"Listen," Franklin says, "you did not hear this from me. And please don't spread it around. Deng would kill me. Whatever you do, don't start calling him Link. . . ."

"Oh, I'd never do that. We have to get along. I see him more than my husband. . . ."

"The husband that no one has ever glimpsed. . . ."

"Well, I see him, every night, or should I say, late afternoon, except when he's in China," Laura lights another cigarette.

"Right, in ladies' underwear."

"Pulls down 50,000 a year."

"That doesn't bother you?" Chook-koo.

"No," Laura says, taking a pensive puff. "He's *my* star-spangled banana."

"That's more information than I need, Laura," Franklin says. "Way more."

She takes a quick puff on the cigarette. "Sorry. I guess it's getting close to my bedtime."

"Well, then run along. . . ." Franklin says. "Right after you nail down some interviews for Christina's packages."

"Will do," Laura says. She's about to flip away the cigarette and get up, then stops. "But before I do, tell me what you meant about the remark that we're here because we screwed up in America. What did I do?"

"You didn't win a Pulitzer."

"A lot of reporters are guilty of that, and not all of them get shipped to dawn patrol in Hong Kong. . . ."

"You asked to come here. . . ."

"Yes, I did. . . ." Laura concedes. "But I asked Dick my editor for a lot of things I didn't get. Why'd I get this one?"

"Dick your editor was never comfortable that you didn't have a journalism degree. . . ."

"I never heard that."

"As long as you were doing the job, he couldn't say anything about it. But then he thought you didn't go hard enough on the Salomon story, didn't lean on the tobacco story the way the Bloomberg guys did—I can see why you didn't warm up to that one, Smokey—and you started, in his words, daydreaming about Hong Kong. . . ."

"That is so unfair. And totally not true."

"He thought maybe you'd be better suited to TV."

"This is all such BS. . . ."

"Their loss, our gain, is how I see it." Chook-koo. "Okay, time to get back to work."

"But you. . . ." Laura realizes maybe she shouldn't ask but feels she's gone too far to stop, "What about that sexual harassment suit. . . ?"

"Geez. . . ."

"Tell me." She sucks on the cigarette and blows out a long train of smoke.

"It's just such. . . ." Franklin shakes his head. "Okay, one time, and never, ever repeat any of it. Because, whether I tell the truth, whether people believe me or they don't, whatever story goes around, I lose, and I swear, I've learned my lesson."

Laura crosses her bare legs and blows more smoke his way.

"It was in Provo, Utah, Channel Two, News Two Provo. She was a writer when I got there and I suggested that, when we got in a pinch with vacations, that we try her as an anchor. She was older than me, like 32 then. . . ."

"How old were you, Pete?"

"I'm 28 now, so 23 or 24 then. . . ."

"So we're about the same. . . ."

"I know."

"Oh, right. Of course. Know your players."

"Anyway, she anchors for a few months, takes a regular slot on the late news in a two-anchor format, and we begin messing around . . . she started it. It was Provo, Utah, out there amongst the Mormon flock, so it wasn't like there was a lot of action. I mean, the Holiday Inn was the only place to get a drink within twenty miles of the studio. Even a Diet Coke was a scandal. We had to pay a special tax to have a soda machine in the studio.

"We were the only two single people at the station who weren't locals, weren't Mormons. We were both grownups, and we lived together, more or less. I was the News Director/EP, so we both worked late, and afterward, we'd go to one of our houses, bring home a nice dinner, or have something cooked up and waiting, crack open a bottle of wine, sit by the fire. . . ."

"I get the idea. . . ."

"Anyway, Myra—that's her name, Myra, though now I think of her as the litigant; our tabloid got the other tabloid in New York to call her the whore suer," he says with the rhyming New York pronunciation as "hoo-er soo-er"—"Myra gets near the end of her contract and she lines up a job with a station in Reno, an independent. She decides it would be a good idea for us to cool things off, so she can leave Provo clean, and we do. At Myra's request, we terminate her contract early, and she goes to Reno to make arrangements to move, look for a place or whatever.

"Anyway, at the station, since she's leaving, we bring in a new anchor, a Provo kid from local radio, deep community roots, 25 and cute as a button. We do a "Two knows news" promo campaign and ratings go through the roof." Chook-koo.

"Then something happens, some kind of incident with Myra in Reno. One story I heard is that somebody said something to her about sleeping with the News Director—we didn't hide our relationship, but we didn't broadcast it either—and she made a remark about not wanting to step on the toes of the senior anchor—they were both guys and, for all I know, these guys were in the closet. Whatever the case, it didn't go over well. I heard another story that the reporter in Reno who was subbing as anchor until Myra came aboard heard how much they were planning to pay Myra and offered to work for less than that, and since their ratings had picked up with her, they decided to keep her and had their lawyer find a loophole to cancel Myra's contract. Somebody else told me that

Myra just really wanted out of Provo and our relationship, thinking the whole thing was a black mark on her career, and the Reno job was more hope than reality. I don't know the real story, and it doesn't really matter.

"Bottom line is that Myra's got no job in Reno and she comes back to Provo with a lawyer, demanding that we put her back on the air, claiming sexual harassment and wrongful dismissal, saying we let her go because I broke off our relationship. We work out a compromise where she gets her old writing job back and trains to be a producer, while we try to find her a job at another Fuggin station, on air preferably. And we keep paying her what she was making on air, even though her contract had been paid off and she was the one asked out of it. And after all this, she still keeps wanting to get back together with me, since it's so boring in Provo without someone. . . ."

"Weren't you bored, too?" Laura asks, puffing on the cigarette.

"I'm too busy to be bored. Then and now. . . . Anyway, we finally manage to slot her as a reporter with a Fuggin station in Tallahassee, where they tell me she spends all of her time making audition tapes, since her deal lets her terminate at her option while we can never get rid of her. Anyway, after a few months, the ABC affiliate in Buffalo gives her a nice deal as a reporter, and she terminates her contract with us, and we all think that's the end of it. But, we don't realize, her lawyers aren't done." Chook-koo.

"Is that when your father found out?"

"What?"

"Your father? Is that when he found out?"

"Are you nuts? My pop found out the minute Myra showed up with a lawyer in Provo. I mean he knew I was seeing her. I brought her to company functions in LA. My pop knew everything. I made sure of that. You can't keep secrets from your boss—or your parents—and expect to get away with it. Maybe it's the same thing with husbands and wives. . . ."

"You can't keep secrets from anybody in Hong Kong, that's for sure."

"Anyway, my pop sure hit the roof, and fired our lawyers, when he found out that she could still sue us after everything we'd already done to straighten things out. We got her to agree to drop all claims when we made the settlement in Provo but we didn't realize that her lawyers would have the gall to make up new claims, this time age and religious discrimination, since the replacement anchor in Provo was younger and

Mormon. So finally, we made another settlement that covers everything from wrongful termination to black plague, got the record sealed, slapped a gag order on her, so she can't get somebody to write a lousy book about it for her, and we thought maybe Hong Kong would be a good place for me to lay low for a while."

"Wait a second, you were a News Director in Provo, Utah, and now you're running Fuggin Asia...?"

"Provo was four-five years ago." Franklin sighs. "After that, I went to network management, then to *US Prime News* then to the division.... If you're hiring, I'll send you my résumé."

"Sorry. But, that's it? That's the whole story?"

"That's the whole story." Chook-koo.

"But you didn't do anything wrong, Peter."

"Damned right, I didn't, and it still cost the company millions, not just for the settlement, but the lawyer time, the waste of corporate energy and talent...."

"When you didn't do anything wrong...."

"It's not about right and wrong, Laura. That's a luxury very few of us get, being judged by right and wrong." Franklin shakes his head.

"That's so unfair."

"Life isn't fair, generally."

"But the facts...."

"It's not about the facts either. People just aren't that interested in facts. What matters is what people think. People judge us by whatever standards they choose, usually whichever ones happen to be handy at the moment and most convenient for them."

Laura smiles, takes a final puff on the cigarette and blows the smoke between them. "Okay. Thanks for that." She crushes the butt. "You say you learned your lesson from Provo?"

"Oh, absolutely," Franklin confesses, standing and pulling open the fire door.

"What's that?"

"TV news managers mate for life. Or pay big if they don't."

CHAPTER 15

Candy is Dandy

To: All Staff
From: PFranklin
Re: Reception, Friday, 3 May, 7pm, Dynasty Royale Hotel,
    Pacific Place—ATTENDANCE MANDATORY
Date: 30 April 1997

Major announcements regarding FGN Asia handover coverage
will take place at this event. We have invited network sponsors,
present and future, and need a large, impressive turnout from our
side. Family members age 12 and above welcome, including
spouses and significant others. Business attire, please.

As stated above, ATTENDANCE IS MANDATORY for all
staffers. If you don't show up Friday night, don't bother reporting
Monday.

"JEFF, I KNOW IT'S A PAIN, but all these people in the newsroom say they
want to meet my phantom husband," Laura says from her bedroom.
"I'm happy to go to a party, hon'," Jeff replies, "especially since we've
hardly ever gone out together since we've been here."

"When I get things under control, I'll take you out for a serious night
on the town, like we used to in New York. . . ." Laura sighs, and walks
into Jeff's bedroom. "Can you help me with this zipper?" She's wearing
her old reliable little black dress from the cocktail circuit in New York,
feeling a little tighter around the waist and hips than she remembers
from those days. "I need to get to the gym more often."

"You look great to me, sweetheart." Jeff, in his underwear and socks, says as he lifts and locks the zipper, punctuating his assessment with a pat on Laura's behind and a breathy dog bark.

"Thanks," she replies, fairly certain he can't be telling the truth. "You really don't have a suit?"

"Sorry. You're lucky that I've got a pair of shoes. I've got this sport coat, and I can wear these. . . ."

"Oh god," Laura erupts, "I'm not going to the mixer with Ivy League Joe in his blue blazer and khaki slacks. At least wear the dark pants. . . ."

"Okay, I will. Thanks." Jeff pulls out a white shirt and a tie featuring Daffy Duck and Porky Pig. "These okay?"

"Look, I'm not trying to be a bitch, but it's going to reflect on me. . . . Geez, that's Turner. . . ."

"No, it's Daffy and Porky. . . ."

"They're Warner Brothers, and Warner is Turner, and Turner is Peter's father's blood rival."

"How was I supposed to know?" Jeff shrugs.

Laura sighs. "Sorry, I'm just cranky after my nap. I'm usually in bed by now."

"*We're* usually in bed by now," Jeff says, kissing the back of her neck.

"C'mon, c'mon. No time for that now." Laura smiles, spins around and gives him a peck on the lips. "But it's nice to know you love me. You might think I'm crazy now, but I'd be nuts. . . ." A nasal one-note electronic version of the opening chords of Beethoven's *Fifth Symphony* sounds in the next room. As Jeff says, "What the heck. . . ?" Laura dashes to her bedroom to answer her mobile phone. "Laura Wellesley here. . . . Hi, hi. . . . Right. . . . Black. . . . Around the knee. . . . I think 'business attire' includes stockings. . . . I am. . . . Oh, yeah, you should. Franklin said he wanted the place packed. . . . Oh, no, sorry. . . . Maybe you'll get lucky on the MTR. . . . See you. . . . Bye." Laura clicks off the phone and puts it into her little black bag. "That was Sara, Sara Fergis, wondering if I was wearing stockings. She also asked me if she should bring a date, then asked me where to find one. Poor girl. . . ." Laura shakes her head.

"What was that thing?" Jeff asks, buckling his gray pants.

"I know, I know," Laura sighs. "I've been meaning to tell you. Peter made us all get phones, so he can reach us 24/7, as if he doesn't own enough of our lives already. . . ."

"Whatever. It's your problem, not mine. . . ."

"As long as you're not going to carry out your half of the death pact. . . ." Laura says. "You're not, right?"

Jeff laughs and nods.

"Well, then why don't you get one, too? That way. . . ."

"So that my mother and Chinese underwear makers can bother me whenever they feel like it? No thanks. Yours is enough mobile phone for the whole family. Unless you want me to reconsider our contract. . . ."

"Very funny," she says, slips her bag over her shoulder, and adds, "C'mon. You can tie your tie—the striped one is good—in the taxi."

Jeff clips on the Rolex copy watch he got while waiting for the bus on a visit to the factory—black face, gold band, HK$35—flings his jacket over his arm and puts his palm on the small of Laura's back. They take a step linked that way before splitting apart to weave between the living room furniture and squeeze through the door. Down the elevator past the scrape above eight, up and down the lobby stairs, through the buzzing gates, down the hill and to the corner, and since no cabs have come screeching around the turn by then, up the escalator to Robinson Road, down the block and across the street to the taxi stand. A double-decker yellow bus pulls in before a taxi comes.

"We can take this to Pacific Place," Jeff says.

"Are you sure?" Laura says.

"Positive." Jeff ushers her up the stairs, counts out HK$9.60 in silvery and coppery coins, and drops them into the fare box. "I meet buyers at their hotels there sometimes." Actually, he goes to Pacific Place with Yogi to buy Japanese produce—"Taste is different because of soil, like French wine," she claims—at the supermarket in the basement of Seibu, at prices so high Jeff thinks the stuff must fly over business class.

"Oh, that's what I'm supposed to do with the brown coins," Laura says with the mock amazement, mounting the winding stairs behind the driver to the bus' upper deck. Jeff nods and points toward the vacant front left seats, and Laura takes the cue.

"Except, of course, for the Queen's-head coins that you save in a coffee can as collectors' items, like everybody else in Hong Kong."

Laura is no longer listening, caught up in the thrill ride aspect of the bus barreling along the dips and rises of Robinson Road, navigating a narrow channel of two-way traffic between towering apartment buildings and fenced in sidewalks with barely enough space for cars, trucks, and buses, including other double-deckers coming in the opposite direction. Buses pass so close so to each other, Laura can read newspaper headlines through the windows. Their bus skids to a stop at the curb in a wide spot at the end of Robinson Road, then slithers back out into traffic and around the bend along the side of the hill above the zoo. Rounding the curve unveils an unobstructed view of the Central skyline with night newly fallen, all the way to the rocket-ship building in Wanchai and its smaller cousin in Causeway Bay. To the left, there's the harbor, with dozens of ships anchored off the container port in Kowloon, like little light bulbs, rather than candles, bobbing on the surface of a swimming pool at a big party like the one they're heading for tonight, like the one they're all speeding toward on June 30th. "That's the view from my bedroom window," Jeff notes, "if that building next door and ten others weren't there."

The bus whines past Government House, the governor's mansion, spotlighting the Union Jack and the new Hong Kong flag with the flower that reminds Laura of the *Ghostbusters* logo or maybe a gothic calligrapher's rendering of a starfish waving just below her eye level. The bus drops into a narrow cut and shoots down steep Garden Road, wheezing and grinding to a stop at the light in front of the US Consulate where concrete barriers protect sheet-metal fences concealing extensive renovations as the outpost prepares for the transition from a friendly government to a possibly hostile one headquartered in the complex of low-rise offices just across the street. Beyond that, more construction on the left, the black Citibank Tower with its two convex facades on the right, far more imposing during the day, when Laura habitually whizzes past in a cab with Edie heading toward Lan Kwai Fong; across the intersection a pair of beige concrete towers with lumps along the sides; and dead ahead, an escape route: if not for this red light, the bus could build momentum on its long downhill run and leap over Chater Garden, between the Furama Hotel and Hutchison House and land in the harbor, perhaps even fly all the way to Kowloon. Instead, when the light changes, the bus veers right onto Queensway, the compromise name for the street between Queen's Road Central, Queen's Road East—what will those names be on July first?—and Hennessey Road, past the sleek Bank of China tower with its three-step, off-center wedding cake top. Jeff touches the signal strip and taps Laura to move toward the exit. She stumbles against the side of the winding staircase to the lower level as the bus negotiates an overpass that looks as if the double-decker can't squeeze under until it does. They exit across the street from the Pacific Place mall, which serves as a four-story outer lobby for three hotels and two office towers, connecting them with the MTR interchange between the Hong Kong and Kowloon lines, trams and minibuses plus a major bus and taxi station.

"Gee, that didn't take much longer than a cab," Laura says as they dismount, "and the view's a lot better from up there." They ride the escalator up to the walkway across Queensway and into level two of Pacific Place, then up again to find the elevators to the Dynasty Royale Hotel tastefully tucked between designer retailers Azukii and Stramba.

The noise, smoke and heat at the Grand Ballroom level tell them they've arrived fashionably late enough for a crowd to have gathered. Mingling is underway between the pair of semi-circular staircases leading down from the lobby. As opposed to the more subdued wood and black marble of the hotel lobby, this lower level features vivid yellows and oppressively bright lighting. A phalanx of FGN Asia personalities greets the guests. Kathy Trang, in a blue silk cheongsam with the FGN eagle in gold thread spreading its wings across her ample chest, attracts the biggest crowd, flanked by Old Mike Hartman in a brown silk Chinese jacket and Deng in a white one, the FGN golden eagle flying across their backs, Pang May Pau in a red cheongsam, nearly a full foot shorter than Deng, using him as a shield, Anna Nissan in purple, Fiona Fok in green, and Edie in orange, who puts a foot forward to strike a pose and says, "Hot enough for you, *mei-mei?*" to Laura.

"To die for, dear," Laura replies.

"And this must be Jeffrey," Edie says, extending her hand. *"Enchanté."*

"Sorry, I don't speak Chinese," Jeff deadpans, shaking her hand.

"I like him," Edie says. "Go get a drink. Fuggin Asia's buying."

They wade into the room, Laura surveying the crowd for other staffers or people she's interviewed for Christina Volpecello's piece— gosh, maybe the Broad Bottomed Wolf herself will storm in tonight. Jeff surveys the fancy food spread. The bar, where white-gloved waiters and waitresses fill trays with wine and beer for guests, displays a full array of brand-name hard stuff for the asking. In deference to the colonial power, there are three varieties of gin, plus cognac and scotch, preferred by Chinese movers and shakers. Food tables along the curved wall include a crowded sushi bar with a trio of chefs in white headbands with big red dots wielding their long knives quickly to keep up with demand, and carving stations serving roast beef, Châteaubriand, ham, suckling pig—head and all—and *char siu,* Chinese roast pork, each table with its own chef in a tall, white hat. Laura, white wine in hand, has turned away from Jeff, chatting with a tall, cross-eyed Chinese guy. Jeff approaches and asks if she wants some food. "Just get whatever and we can share," she says, then adding, "Quickie, this is my husband Jeff." The Chinese guy says hello and nods. Jeff nods back and walks toward the food. He loads up a plate for two with raw salmon and shrimp, mixes a little trough of soy sauce and a dollop of neon-green wasabi.

"Must put more wasabi," Yogi, in a black business suit with a very short skirt, says, looking over his shoulder.

"What are you doing here?" Jeff says in a whisper.

"You do not look happy to see me," she replies.

"My wife is here."

"Finally I will see. I think you telling me *bubba mieses.*" Yogi smiles.

"Bubba what?"

"Sure you are Jew? *Bubba mieses* is stories from grandmother. Later, you will introduce?"

"What are you doing here?"

"I am friend of Edie March. She is boss of your wife. Edie and I working on currency desk at bank many years ago."

"You look so fabulous, there's no way I can introduce you to Laura," Jeff says, trying to smile.

"Must more wasabi," Yogi replies. "Here," she says, grabbing the spoon from the bowl and dropping another dollop into his trough. "You try."

"Thanks." Jeff carries the plate toward Laura, who has moved to another group including one of the guys in the matching jackets, a fresh white wine in her hand. He hovers next to Laura, waiting for her to notice him.

"Oh, Jeff. . . . Thanks," she finally says, grabbing the plate. "Oh, Deng, this is Jeff, my husband."

"Ah, the phantom of the underwear," the Chinese guy in the white silk jacket says with an American accent. "I'm the fellow she goes out to meet every night." he says, extending a hand, adding, as Jeff shakes it, "Deng Jiang Mao, *AM Asia* anchor."

"I don't see Pussy here," Laura says. "Maybe she's going to get fired."

"Oh, you'll see her," Deng says, then turns to Jeff. "This is Sara Fergis and Andy Steiner, two more of our producers. Andy's wife couldn't be here because she's anchoring for a rival network."

"The one we'll bury with our handover coverage," Sara says. "Glad to meet you."

"Likewise," Jeff says. Andy extends his hand and Jeff shakes it.

"Don't eat too much," Deng warns Laura. "You might have trouble keeping down during the program."

"What?"

"A word to the wise, or thereabouts," he says before showing the group the golden eagle on his back.

"The fish is good," Laura tells Jeff, "but too much wasabi. Did you get yourself any food? Better go now because I think they're about to start the show." She veers off with the plate in a different direction from Deng, while Sara and Andy continue their conversation. Jeff wanders toward the food.

"The *char siu* is delicious, but is pork, not Jew food," Yogi says, as she walks past him briskly toward Edie.

As Jeff approaches the roast beef, he hears "Bing-bang-bong," FGN's signature broadcast tone that everyone in America grew up with. He grabs a plate of pink meat, which in this setting he doesn't associate with street-market hoofs on hooks, wolfs it down, and takes another as the doors to the ballroom open and the crowd begins moving in that direction. Jeff finds a waiter and grabs a glass of red wine, takes a gulp and works on his second plate of roast beef.

"It is more tasty with mustard sauce. Quite hot," Yogi says, wafting by.

Jeff goes to the bar for a refill and to separate him from Yogi before heading toward the ballroom. There's a stage at the front of the room with styrofoam letters on the drapery at the back spelling out "Franklin Global Networks Asia: Hong Kong 1997 and Beyond" and a podium at the front left corner bearing the FGN golden eagle. Below the stage, seats in the first three rows are covered in gold cloth, occupied by members of the FGN Asia family in their matching outfits and Chinese men in blue suits, most smoking furiously, as waiters distribute drinks and ashtrays. Other well-dressed middle-aged Chinese men and women fill the rest of the VIP rows. Jeff scans the room to find Laura. He spots her near the front, seated between Sara Fergis and the cross-eyed guy. He approaches them.

"Oh, thanks," Laura says, taking the wine. "I prefer white, but this will do."

Jeff stands there stunned until Quickie says, "You sit, please," and gets up.

"Thanks," Jeff says, and sits next to Laura. "Big crowd."

"I wish I knew what was going on," Laura says. She glances at Sara, who shrugs.

Old Hartman climbs the stairs on the left of the stage and Kathy Trang comes from the right, meeting at center stage, each with a handheld microphone.

"Good evening everyone, and thank you for coming tonight. I'm Mike Hartman."

"And I'm Kathleen Trang. In case you don't recognize us, you should."

"We're news presenters for Franklin Global Networks Asia, the business news leaders in Asia."

"FGN means business in Asia. We're here tonight to introduce you to the FGN Asia team covering the Hong Kong handover, and all the news you need every day in this amazing, exciting part of the world."

"That's right, Kathy. We're part of a worldwide news-gathering team, with the reach and the resources to help you make every day productive and profitable."

"But even though we're a global network, our hearts," Trang turns to her partner on stage, "and our Hartman, belong to Asia."

"Indeed, FGN Asia means business in Asia," Old Hartman chuckles. "And now, I'd like to introduce the leader of our team in Hong Kong, Franklin Global Networks Asia's chief executive officer. . . ."

"And, something we Asians can really relate to," Trang adds, with her beauty-queen smile and Australian twang, "the big boss' son, Peter Franklin."

Old Hartman and Trang lead the applause. Franklin strides up the stairs to the podium, wearing a black silk jacket with the golden eagle on the back.

So this is that Peter guy Laura's always talking about, Jeff thinks. He's shorter than I expected, not bad looking, though.

"Thanks, Mike and Kathy, and thank you all for coming. I'm particularly pleased to welcome some of our special guests around the room: our esteemed, good friends from the mainland, the Foreign Ministry and the Hong Kong and Macau Affairs Office...."

"No friends of mine," Laura tells no one in particular.

"... members of the Hong Kong government and the Legislative Council, and our beloved sponsors: Rodney Tan from Singapore Airlines, the official airline of FGN Asia; Maureen Goh of Dynasty Royale, the official business hotel of FGN Asia and our gracious hostess for tonight's festivities; Paula Schwartz-Liu of Peninsula Group, the official luxury hotel of FGN Asia; Lily Wong of Acer, the official portable computer of FGN Asia; Gerhardt Schloss of Audi, the official luxury sport sedan of FGN Asia; and all of our other advertisers, who are still too shy to take up a category sponsorship.

"On that note, I want to introduce a new member of our team who's going to be talking to you about that in the days ahead, FGN Asia's executive vice president for sales, who I just poached from TVB, Gladys Fung. Gladys, stand up and say hello."

Gladys Fung, a chubby woman around 40 in a red suit stands up and waves. "Thanks Peter," she says, as Kathy Trang rushes over with a microphone that Fung doesn't need at all with her booming voice. Trang holds the mike for Fung, who grabs it. "Thank you, Peter. I just want to tell all of you to make sure that we exchange business cards tonight. Several of my cards have 500-dollar bills attached to them...."

"Further proof that we mean business in Asia," Franklin chuckles, then continues as Fung sits, "Tonight, we want to introduce you to the FGN Asia team that will lead our coverage of the Hong Kong handover and the upcoming era of restored Chinese rule in Hong Kong. The entire resources of our worldwide network will be drawn upon for this story, to cover it from every angle that matters—FGN international correspondents like Christina Volpecello will be here—but it's our team on the ground in Hong Kong that'll be leading the way.

"Before introducing our coverage team, first I'd like to introduce you to our network and this city, the hub of business in Asia, and the home of FGN Asia. This short video will present the real star of the show for the handover and beyond."

A screen descends at center stage and the lights dim. The video begins with an aerial shot of central Hong Kong's skyscrapers from The Peak, Victoria Harbor in the background.

"Welcome to Hong Kong, FGN Asia's hometown," an unfamiliar, resonant but friendly female voice says in slightly accented English, "and . . ." Cut to the reporter, Chinese, in a smartly tailored, turquoise suit, standing in front of the Bank of China building, the BOC logo visible, her hair falling about her shoulders, her lips delectably red and full, ". . . my hometown. I'm Candace Fang."

As she opens her mouth on screen, revealing her overbite, in a shot that also reveals the bulge of her chest, Laura and Jeff both realize that she's someone familiar. FGN Asia staffers murmur, Jeff wheezes, and Laura gasps to Sara, "Oh my god, it's Pussy," then turns to Jeff, "my graphics screw-up specialist."

"Your graphics girl she is?" Jeff mutters.

"Yes, the stupid, drunk teenager. This must be a nightmare."

"Yuh," Jeff agrees.

Pussy *cum* Fang continues, "On behalf of 135,000 employees of Franklin Global Networks, the world's largest and most comprehensive media organization, and billions of satisfied customers around the world, let me show you around."

"When did she learn English?" Laura spits.

"Or get that great voice to go with the body?" Sara adds.

"That is so unfair," Laura agrees.

"Perched at the crossroads of Asia, Hong Kong is an international Chinese city that's always on the go. . . ." Fang says over time-lapse video showing quaint green double-decker trams, yellow and blue double-decker buses, and red taxis speeding among the crowds crossing Hennessey Road in front of the Sogo Department Store and its giant video board in Causeway Bay. As day becomes night, the shot widens to the west to the brightly lit skyscrapers of Central and ships in Victoria Harbor, zooming in on a Star Ferry boat chugging from Kowloon toward Central. The shot of the grimy lower deck narrows on a crew member facing astern in the ferry's incongruous uniform: powder-blue sailor suit with red neckerchief and white hat with red pompon. The crew member turns to the camera, revealing that it's Fang, ". . . built around Victoria Harbor, the Fragrant Harbor that gives Hong Kong its name at the mouth of China's booming Pearl River delta. Since the announcement of its return to Chinese rule, Hong Kong has ridden a rising tide of prosperity. This city of nearly seven million people has the third-highest per capita income in the world," cut to the trading floor of the Hong Kong Stock Exchange, with Fang in the foreground wearing a dark blue trader's bib, with "FGN Asia" emblazoned across the front where other traders have numbers, "and the third-biggest stock market outside of Wall Street. With our reporters on the ground, around town and in the pits, FGN Asia means business in Asia."

Cut to a Chinese man at his desk, wearing a white shirt and red tie with the Hong Kong bauhinia logo on it, text below his talking head identifying him as Alec Tsui, Stock Exchange of Hong Kong Chief Executive. He speaks in Cantonese while a translation of his words runs below his name. "Hong Kong's stock market is the most dynamic in Asia," Tsui says. "It's the financial center driving the Asian economic miracle, the greatest engine of wealth creation in human history."

"Will that change with the return to Chinese sovereignty?" Fang, wearing a dark blue suit, asks in Cantonese, according to the translation.

"Hong Kong is already the financial gateway to China," Tsui says, "and our closer ties with the mainland will mean more growth, more opportunities, more direct participation in the unprecedented potential of the motherland and its 1.2 billion people."

Cut to a traditional Chinese junk with a red sail passing container ships in the harbor, Fang's disembodied voice saying, "For centuries, the Pearl River and Victoria Harbor have made Hong Kong the world's gateway to China and China's gateway to the world."

Cut to Fang wearing a blue hard hat and gray coveralls in a busy port area, shot from below, so it looks as if the cranes are moving shipping containers directly over her head. "Today, that link makes Hong Kong the world's busiest port, moving thousands of containers of goods to and from the mainland, a role set to expand under Chinese rule."

Cut to a bald Chinese man with age spots on his face, identified as Li Ka-shing, Hutchison Holdings Chairman.

"Hong Kong's richest man," Laura tells Jeff.

"Who never gives interviews," Sara adds.

In Cantonese, Li says, "Hong Kong's economy has never been better. Opportunities have never been greater."

Fang, in a pink suit, asks in Cantonese, "Will the transition to Chinese rule change that?"

"Things will change for the better," Li replies. "The combination of Hong Kong people's entrepreneurial traditions, our free market with a minimum of government regulation, and our closer ties to the vast opportunities of the motherland will lead to even greater growth in the years ahead."

Cut to Fang, walking through a bustling street market in designer jeans, dark pullover top, pearl choker around her neck and sunglasses on top of her head, the casual uniform for a well-off *tai-tai,* a kept wife. "Indeed, business is booming all over Hong Kong. Still, some people worry what will happen when this center of free market commerce, returns . . ." Dissolve to Fang in a khaki shorts, and a tight, white tee-shirt, camera hanging below the FGN Asia eagle logo across her bust, and a black FGN Asia baseball cap, strolling in front of the portrait of Mao at Beijing's Gate of Heavenly Peace in Tiananmen Square. ". . . to the embrace of Chinese rule. Who will lead the new Hong Kong?"

Cut to a middle-aged Chinese woman, wearing a frilly white top and a pearl choker, identified as Patricia Pang, Legislative Council Chairwoman. "Hong Kong people will finally rule Hong Kong," she says in English.

"That's 'Provisional Legislative Council Chairwoman,' please," Laura growls.

"And Pang May Pau's mother," Sara adds.

"No way," Laura gasps.

"Way," Sara replies.

On camera, Fang asks, in English, "What will change?"

"Fortunately, the British leave us with strong institutions that we can build on," Pang says. "Our traditions of entrepreneurship, our business-friendly environment, and our tremendous spirit will only be enhanced by closer ties to the motherland."

Cut to Fang in a Chinese silk jacket and pants in jade green, walking along the Bund in Shanghai, the Asia-Pacific Tower with its silver ball at the top gleaming across the river. "China is in the midst of a transformation into the world's largest and most vibrant market economy, improving the lives of hundreds of millions of people. But what of Hong Kong's transition? What about its traditions?"

Cut to Fang in a policewoman's summer green uniform, skirt several inches shorter than officially sanctioned, triangular hat perched on her head at a jaunty, non-regulation angle. ". . . the rule of law, protections for property and free expression, that have been instrumental to Hong Kong's success?"

Cut to a Chinese man in a blue suit with bushy eyebrows and a receding hairline, identified as Lin Ma, Chief, Chinese Foreign Ministry Office of Hong Kong and Macau Affairs. In Mandarin, he says, "The Basic Law promises the people of Hong Kong 50 years without changes in their normal way of life. It's a promise that the Chinese government intends to honor."

"What about freedom of the press and freedom of information?" Fang asks in Mandarin.

"The Chinese Central Government has pledged to protect these rights as part of the Basic Law and the Joint Declaration of 1984 under Deng Xiaoping's cherished principle of one country, two systems. Moreover, we recognize that these freedoms are vital to Hong Kong's continuing role as an international center of commerce and finance to benefit not just itself but to assist in the development of the mainland. We also recognize that these freedoms are important to our friends in the media, like Franklin Global Networks . . ."

"They're no friends of mine," Laura snorts.

". . . and you have the Central Government's solemn pledge that these rights will be scrupulously protected and nurtured."

Cut to a wide shot of a rice field with water buffalo plows, men and women in conical hats, dark blue cotton pants reaching just below the knee and light blue shirts with loose sleeves, ankle deep in mud. The camera zooms in on one conical hat with braids looping out of both sides. The farmer looks up. It's Fang, who says, "As any Hakka rice farmer in Hong Kong's New Territories can tell you, protection and nurturing lead to bumper crops of growth and prosperity. Today's global business people need the care and nurturing of timely information and insights that . . ."

Cut to FGN studio, Fang in a blue blazer with the FGN golden eagle on the left breast pocket, ". . . only a global network focused on comprehensive business news can deliver. When we say, 'FGN Asia means business in Asia,' it's much more than just a slogan."

Cut to Franklin, labeled Peter Franklin, Chief Executive Officer, FGN Asia, in an office overlooking the Bank of China tower and the Hongkong Bank building. "'FGN Asia means business in Asia' embodies the spirit of our network. Not just about giving business leaders and investors the tools they need for success but offering them a direct channel to access a nexus of economic growth unmatched in human history. In Hong Kong, in China and throughout Asia, three billion people are sampling the fruits of unprecedented prosperity. Communities, countries, the entire region is moving from poverty and despair to affluence and hope at breathtaking speed. FGN Asia is about more than simply reporting this amazing transformation. Working with our network, your business can be part of this revolution as three billion people build not just wealth but buying habits that will last for generations."

On a steel girder overlooking Central Hong Kong, a welder with a sparking torch looks up from work and lifts the helmet's shield, revealing Fang's face. "FGN Asia is pitching in to build the future of this dynamic region, and to help businesses and investors build their futures. For FGN Asia and our partners, the sky is the limit."

Cut to Fang in the courtyard of a Chinese temple, red paper lanterns hanging between its thick, green columns, wearing a golden cheongsam with the FGN eagle, embroidered in a richer shade of gold, spread across her chest. "The handover marks a great beginning for Hong Kong and the 1.2 billion people of mainland China. Take it from one of them who knows: the party has only just begun." Fireworks explode above the courtyard. The shot moves toward the fireworks that morph into the FGN eagle in the skies over Central Hong Kong and hovering above Tiananmen. Fang says over the shot, "Let FGN Asia make you a part of the bright future of Hong Kong and China, part of this special place we call home." The first few bars of *March of the Volunteers,* China's national anthem, play as the FGN golden eagle materializes in the foreground with the Hong Kong skyline and Tiananmen with Mao's portrait in the background.

The lights in the ballroom come up, and the men at the front in the blue suits lead rousing applause. Franklin at the podium says, "I'd like to introduce you to FGN Asia's newest presenter, Candace Fang." The woman formerly known as Pussy emerges from the wings to applause and a few wolf whistles, dressed in the same golden cheongsam she wore in the last shot of the video. She politely smiles, bows her head, then lifts it, beaming a smile around the room.

"Candace will co-host FGN Asia's handover night coverage. Her partner on our special 'one handover, two anchors' coverage will FGN Asia's veteran journalist from the US who'll lend the proceedings an international business perspective—Deng Jiang Mao. C'mon up here, Deng."

"One handover, two anchors," Laura says. "God help us."

"I'm delighted to be working with you on the deeply meaningful night of Hong Kong's reunification with the motherland, Candace."

"Good morning, Deng, yes," Fang replies.

"Together, Candy and I will bring unrivaled perspective and un-matched coverage to what is sure to be the biggest news event of 1997, and one of the most significant moments of our lifetime, a great milestone in the history of the Chinese people."

"Thanks, Deng," Franklin says. "Couldn't have said it better myself. Let me just ask you two to stay up here a minute and have the rest of the team join you. Everybody, c'mon up. Mike, Kathy, presenter Anna Nissan in purple, reporter Pang May Pau in red, news editor and reporter Fiona Fok in green, our executive producer Edie March in orange—she's not hard to spot—and our executive VP for sales Gladys Fung, who's out of uniform, but has those 500-dollar bills to hand out.

"Now that you've had some introductions, let's have a bite to eat, get to know each other, and talk about how our network and your organiza-tion can work together for the continued success and growth of Hong Kong and China, and the rest of Asia. That's something that we can all drink to."

The doors in the back of the room open, revealing a phalanx of waiters armed with trays of drinks.

"Please," Franklin says, "have a drink and a bite to eat, and put your cards in the bowl for the lucky draw of two business-class tickets to Beijing from Singapore Airlines, the official airline of FGN Asia. Thanks for coming." Franklin leads the cast from the stage and into the crowd, which begins moving toward the doors.

As he walks past Laura, Deng arches his eyebrows and says, "It's the post-handover . . . stupid."

Ninety minutes later, the lucky draw over, the guests have left. Franklin is seated on the stage, his legs dangling over the edge, with Deng on one side of him, bottles of Johnny Walker Black, white and red wine on the other, Edie, Yogi, Laura, Jeff and Old Hartman on chairs around him, everyone with a glass.

"Now she's talking to Chinese TV," Franklin says, proudly. "Nothing personal," he says, looking at Hartman and then Deng, "but that's something we didn't have before. I could never image Fiona or Pang May Pau out there as the face of the network."

"Speaking of faces, Pete," Old Hartman says, "do you think it's right to have—nothing personal, Deng—two Chinese faces out there on handover night?"

"I love you, too, Mike," Deng says.

"No, listen," Hartman says. "We're talking about a global audience for a global event, one with a British flavor. . . ."

"We don't have any British talent," Deng says.

"Excuse me," Edie says.

"I meant that strictly in the on-air sense," Deng says. "You're the most talented Brit I know."

"And you don't know the half of it," Edie teases.

Hartman continues, "Do you think our global audience will accept two Chinese anchors, Pete?"

"It's a Chinese story," Franklin says. "So they better get used to it."

"It's a Chinese century dawning," Deng adds.

"Save that rot for the promos," Edie says. "Do you all know my former banking colleague, Yogi? She's an actual viewer."

"Yes," Yogi says. "We keep your station in my office."

"What's your favorite part of the shows?" Laura asks.

"We only look for picture and market prices."

"See, I tell you you worry too much about content," Franklin says. "Good visuals, the ticker and the bug. . . ."

"Do we know who's anchoring for CNN on handover night?" Old Hartman asks.

"Do we know who's producing for us?" Laura growls.

"Good question," Edie says.

"I heard CNN will use Andy's wife. . . ." Deng says.

"A pity, too," Edie says, "since our man Andy—insatiable newshound that he is—wanted to take holiday during handover week. 'My daughter's off school,' he explained to me. 'Take three days leave and get nine days off.' Always thinking, our Andy, but then he withdrew the request because he said Patricia had to work. During a major international news event, imagine that. . . ." Edie shakes her head and sips her scotch.

Deng continues, "It'll probably be Patricia and one of their big swinging dicks from the US, like Tony Lord. . . ."

"CNN doesn't have any big swinging dicks," Franklin says dismissively. "The news is the star. And here's our star," he says, gesturing toward the entrance as Fang approaches the circle. "Join the party, Candy."

Deng applauds as he scoots over to make room for Fang to sit on the stage next to Franklin. "You were dandy, Candy."

Laura and Jeff squirm uncomfortably. Jeff tries to avoid Fang's eyes by draining his wine glass and staring at the bottom of it.

"Thank you."

"Where did you learn English?" Laura asks.

"I learn in school when I girl, but forget."

"Why didn't you ever use it when you were doing graphics for me?"

"What for-aah? Then you expect me more work." Fang laughs. "Better you think I stupid Pussy."

"Television is her lie, too," Edie says with a smile.

"I practice writing stupid signs that Peter put in newsroom," Fang continues. "Still lesson. . . ."

"But no more signs," Laura says, "thank god."

"We can bring them back," Franklin says.

"How about the name?" Old Hartman asks. "Candace Fang?"

"I like Candace Bergen. Murphy Brown good newslady," Fang says. "First, I say Regina. . . ."

"Rhymes with vageena," Edie says.

"But there's already that local phoof called Regina," Franklin says. "Candy is dandy."

"Liquor is quicker," Deng adds. "Care for a drink after all that traveling?" he asks Fang.

"Yeah," Laura says, "When did you do all those shoots, Beijing, Shanghai. . . ?"

"See, I told you," Franklin says as Fang and Deng laugh. "It was all up on the 28th floor with chromakey."

"Chroma-what?" Laura asks.

"Video backgrounds projected on blue screen behind her," Franklin explains. "How'd you like my harbor-view office?"

"God, what's not a gimmick here now?" Laura grumbles, shaking her head and gulping wine. "Can't we ever. . . ."

"Someday you'll grasp the magic of television, Laura, dear," Deng says. "The whole video was super, Pete."

"How'd the interviews go?" Franklin asks Fang.

"They all want to know my family and why I in Hong Kong."

"Your family?" Laura says.

"Yah. . . ."

"Yes," Franklin says sternly to Fang.

"Yes," Fang sighs. "English hard."

"Yah," Yogi says, smiling at Fang. "I am Yogi from Japan. Also still have difficulty with English."

"Hello. Very good to meeting me," Fang replies.

"They say the best way to learn a language is in bed," Old Hartman says, glancing at Franklin and Fang, then eyeing Yogi.

"You will find I am very diligent student," Yogi says, returning the look until he turns away.

"Your family. . . ?" Laura asks Fang, winning a silent thank you from Jeff, who doesn't dare look at Yogi either.

"Yes. My family send me Hong Kong 1989 to finish university. . . ."

"University?" Laura says. "But you're seventeen or eighteen. . . ."

Fang laughs, her fingertips covering her mouth in a gesture of geisha-like shyness. "Ha. That Pussy. Candace Fang 29-year-old, same-same Laura." She pronounces the name RO-ra.

"Oh my god," Laura says. "You look like a teenager."

"Thank you," Fang says. She looks at Jeff and smiles. He smiles back uneasily. "Is your family?" Fang asks Laura.

"Oh, yes, this is my husband, Jeff."

"Pleased to meeting me . . . you," Fang says, turning up her chin as she smiles. Jeff can't be sure but hopes the gesture means that she knows that he knows that she knows and that she's happy to keep it between them. He hopes that Laura and Yogi haven't noticed. "You man in ladies' pant?"

"Not every lady's," Jeff says, wondering how guilty he looks.

"That's not what I've heard," Edie says. Laura snarls and shakes a fist at her, Yogi laughs, and Fang smiles, covering her mouth with her fingertips again.

"Do you source your products in the mainland?" Old Hartman asks Jeff.

"Right."

"There could be a story for us there," Old Hartman says. "Your personal account of the difficulties of doing business in China. . . ."

"And the advantages," Deng adds. "It's the post-handover, stupid. Didn't you watch the video, Mike?"

"That was an interesting perspective, Pete," Old Hartman says, nodding and cutting the air with his left hand, as he does when he thinks he's being insightful. "Of all the countries of the so-called Asia miracle, China is the one country that hasn't taken off, the one that hasn't experienced the kind of transformation that you've seen in, say, Thailand or Indonesia, or even here in Hong Kong."

"And this isn't China?" Deng says.

"You know what I mean," Old Hartman says. "I for one don't believe that any country can undergo that kind of profound economic change without political reform. You can't have economic freedom alone, without all the freedoms that go with it. It's not as if it's a Chinese menu with one from Column A. . . ."

"Name me another place in the world were you see fistfights among investors lining up for IPOs," Deng says.

"The real headline there was that people queued at all," Edie says.

"That's just crazy Hong Kong people," Old Hartman says. "And those shares are nothing more than a gamble, and we all know how much Hong Kong people love to gamble."

"I think you're letting your American perspective blind you, Mike," Deng says. "It's nothing less than miraculous what's happened in the mainland since 1979, and especially the past five years, what Zhu Rongji is doing. . . ."

"And look at where they are now," Old Hartman says. "Engineering a recession to cure inflation. . . ."

"As if Alan Greenspan doesn't do precisely that in the US?" Edie says. "Or the Bank of England for that matter?"

"Point taken," Hartman says. "But you'll never see China boom the way Malaysia or Korea have as long as the government remains in the driving seat. I think you're going to see something more like Japan's decade of stagnation in China, without the nearly 50 years of transformational growth that preceded it."

"I think we're in the midst of precisely that kind of transformational growth, and we're ignoring it, missing it because we don't understand it," Deng says. "It's hard for westerners to understand Chinese society...."

"Like you do?" Laura swipes.

"Look at the equity markets," Old Hartman says. "In the tiger economies, you've got vibrant equity markets, but Chinese stocks keep treading water. Mainlanders who have no where else to put their money, even they won't buy them."

"Yogi analyzes markets for Bank International," Edie says. "So let's...."

"I should have you as a guest," Laura says, as Jeff looks away. "We'd have a lot to talk about."

"Pre-interview," Edie says. "What's your analysis of China's stock markets, Yogi?"

"I do not follow Chinese equities. They are not suitable for investment for our bank."

"See?" Old Hartman says.

"Mike, you've followed stock markets long enough to know how little they have to do with the real economy," Deng says. "The real story in China is companies like GM pouring in billions...."

"That's true," Edie says, "When I was with the lawyers in the eighties, even then we were seeing seven-figure deals every week that never got in the papers. Heaps of money has been going in there...."

"But has any come out?" Old Hartman says. "Is any foreign investor making money there?"

"Fuggin Asia will," Franklin says, patting Fang on the knee. "Or we'll all be looking for new jobs. *Gan-bei,*" he toasts in Mandarin, draining his glass.

"Gan-bei," all reply, Deng adding, "To the post-handover ... stupid."

"Well, that was the most bizarre night of my life," Laura tells Jeff in the taxi on their way home.

"Uh-huh," he agrees.

"Pussy turning into Candy, the dandy handover anchor. It's like Cinderella. Or maybe like *Pretty Woman.*"

"What do you mean?"

"They say Franklin's screwing her. Personally, I don't believe it, though Hong Kong's like a small town, you can't hide stuff like that. So if he was, I'd know it, but that's beside the point. The point is, one day she's a stupid graphics girl who can't speak English, and now she's our hand-over-night anchor. Television is everybody's lie. But her English. . . ."

"It was very good in the movie."

"But we're not doing movies, we're doing live TV. It's so unfair," Laura says, shaking her head. "And can you believe that promo? One big, wet kiss for the butchers of Beijing and their pals. . . ."

"But after the handover, they will be running the show."

"Not my show, mister. Not my Fuggin show."

CHAPTER 16

Chicken and Horse

"I TRIED TO GET LAMONT BACK HERE to preside over this noon meeting revival, but the Dell Computer sales office in Houston wouldn't give him the day off," Franklin says, the Monday after the promo video premiere. Chook-koo. "You know I hate meetings, and Anna and Andy are back live in fifteen minutes so let's get through this." The show producers are all gathered around the conference table with Edie, plus the news and production managers and on-air talent, except the former Pussy, Candace Fang.

"Basically, we're here to lay out the handover night plan. We're live for the network global feed from ten to two. Then we go to tape and New York covers live, with one studio anchor on call here for live pops, maybe a reporter, maybe nobody. . . . We'll see how many bodies we need where. That's why we're having this meeting.

"Like we announced on Friday night, Deng and Candy are going to anchor ten to two in the studio. In honor of the principle of one country, two systems, we've got one show, two anchors . . . Chook-koo."

"Pete," Old Hartman says.

"In a minute, Mike, let me finish what I have to say. . . . Where was I?"

"Anchor and reporter assignments," Edie says.

"Right. So, Deng and Candy in the studio, ten to two, we'll have Christina Volpecello on the floor of the Convention Center or thereabouts with Benny Wilson, her producer, and her crew. By the way, all those notes you get from Christina, they're really from Benny. May, you're going to be on the day stories with your crew, then after that I want you on the street. . . . We don't have the complete tick-tock yet, do we?"

"Not yet," Edie says. "Later this week."

"I'd also like you to be at LegCo, May and Bobby, he'll produce at night for you. LegCo isn't going to go into session until after all the ceremonies end, so it might be better for you to be on the street near there."

"There's supposed to be a demonstration there by the deposed legislators," Fiona says. "That's what I'm hearing from Martin Lee's office."

"That sounds like a news event," Laura says.

"But is it an event we want to cover?" Deng says.

"If it's news. . . ." Laura says.

"Hang on," Franklin says. "Edie is the SP for our handover coverage." Chook-koo.

"Congratulations," Deng says to Edie.

"It's a news event," Edie says. "We're covering handover news events." Franklin asks Edie, "Then, how do you like it?"

"I like May and Bobby on the street looking for vox pops from Hong Kong people, maybe in Causeway Bay, then at night in Lan Kwai Fong for handover revelry. So we put her and Bobby there, and we put Fiona and Andy at LegCo."

"What time is that?" Andy Steiner asks.

"Everyone will need to be ready for air at ten. . . ."

"You know, I've got a daughter, and my wife will be working that night. It would be better if I swapped with Sara and. . . ."

"This isn't a negotiation," Franklin says. Chook-koo.

"But my daughter. . . ." Andy protests.

"Andy," Edie says. "Your amah will have to work, too, that's all. And little Paulette will sleep as peacefully under Chinese rule as she does under the Union Jack."

"I think this is going to be a problem," Andy says.

"No, it's not," Franklin responds. Chook-koo. "You go where Edie tells you or you go work someplace else. Decide now."

"Do you mean. . . ?" Andy whines.

"Done," Franklin says. "They'll have a crew at LegCo. That's three crews, two of ours and Christina's."

"I've got three crews scheduled," Fiona says. "Also, one standby."

"The pool will shoot the hall, with three shots," Edie says. "They'll also shoot the afternoon events at Government House, the LegCo floor, the border, and of course, the royal yacht and the fireworks in the harbor."

"These pools are how they handle the presidential inaugurations," Old Hartman says, "in the US."

"I'll get the tick-tock this week with exact times," Edie says. "But we already know enough to know where people need to be."

"And we've still got one of our crews, right?" Franklin asks.

"Yes," Edie and Fiona both say.

"Right," Franklin says. "Mike, we've saved the best for last. You'll be at the border crossing."

"What will be happening there?" Old Hartman asks.

Edie responds, "Thousands of school children will wave Hong Kong and PRC flags as the brave members of the People's Liberation Army arrive to protect Hong Kong's new freedom."

"Andy, you can send your daughter there to toss flowers, and Mike can bring her home," Franklin smirks. "Seriously, Mike, it's the best story out there for a guy who's done everything in television."

"They'll likely have a pool crew out there," Edie says, "but you'll have your own shooter, and Richard will produce."

Old Hartman begins to speak but Franklin holds up his hand and continues, "So that leaves Kathy and Anna. Anna and Sara will be doing *Market Wrap* and they'll stay on set with their show crew for live pops to the US for the morning shows until Deng and Pussy. . . . I mean, Candace come on."

"Are we going to be working here?" Deng asks. "Or are we going to set up at the Convention Center?"

Franklin says, "I looked into a truck, and it's just too expensive. It's also silly. I mean, instead of being on set here, you're locked up on set in a truck outside the Convention Center. The anchors still aren't on the scene in any meaningful way. . . ."

"That's the first thing I've ever heard from anyone in TV that makes sense," Laura says.

"Of course, we're going to build you a special handover set in this studio. I've got the design up in my office," Franklin says. "The logo's got the Chinese and British flags and the Fuggin eagle, and we'll have the blue screen behind you for chromakey of the Convention Center and the harbor beauty shot from the robot cam and lots of other great stuff. You're going to love it, and it's going to be a lot more simple for everybody.

"Let me just wrap our tick-tock. When Deng and Candy come on, Anna and Sara go home to get some sleep." A couple of people giggle. "Don't laugh. Everybody on set or in the booths is going to be sleeping here. We'll have beds on 28 and some food up there, and down here we'll have pizza and stuff."

"And donuts, because at six, we roll *AM Asia,*" Edie says, "special handover edition. Candy and Deng until eight, then Kathy, Mike, Deng, as usual. A few markets will be open, but mostly, we'll be showing off our brilliant packages from the handover. Nancy. . . ?"

"We work all night, every night, anyway, so no difference on our end," Nancy Black says, her black hair now cut short, all traces of pastels gone.

"Maybe a little more volume than usual," Edie says. "Shirley, dear, graphics?"

Shirley Hung nods.

"You feed us the tape," Nancy says, "you'll get your packages. No worries."

"Kathy, you'll be the designated voicer for whatever needs it, until you're back on air. But I expect field people to do their own standups and feed tracks. You can do it on location or come back here, but you'll need to schedule everything with Nancy."

"I'll post sign-up sheets for the booths, and keep a master," Nancy says. "Screw up, you deal with me," she warns, shaking a fist.

"Watch out," Franklin says.

"I'll be here all night, too," Edie continues, "so double trouble if there's any mishap. Each team—producer and field reporter—needs to give me a preliminary list of what you think you'll be packaging. I've got my own list, but I want your ideas. This week, please."

"Any questions about the assignments?" Franklin asks.

"So," Laura asks, "who's the handover studio producer?"

"Oh, that," Franklin shrugs. "You are, Laura."

"Congratulations," Deng says.

"You'll also be packaging," Edie says, "with help from me and Nancy, and we'll decide on the night whether we want Deng or Candy or Kathy to voice for you. But I doubt you'll package anything before you get off the air. Just think about rough bites and VO. We'll try to have loggers, so you shouldn't need more than a few notes."

"How are you doing with the Volpecello tapes?" Franklin asks Laura.

"Coming along, but I can use help."

"Fiona?"

"Give me a shot list, though I can't promise anything. We're all running around out there every day, but if we can get your shots, we will."

"Same here," Pang May Pau says.

"My big problem is logging the interviews," Laura says. "Volpecello insists that to cut all the packages in two days she needs complete transcripts. God forbid she could show up a day or two earlier. . . ."

"Do you really want to deal with her dog food and designer water here any longer than necessary?" Edie says.

"Whatever the Broad Bottomed Wolf wants, she gets," Franklin says. "Thank god, we only have a handover once a lifetime or so." Chook-koo. "Any more questions about the assignments?" No one at the table speaks.

"Okay. One last item to discuss." Chook-koo. "You may have noticed that there's one anchor who's not here." Franklin takes a deep breath. "On Friday night in the promo you all saw what Candace can do. Gladys says the phone's ringing off the hook, sponsors who want to know about Candy. . . ."

"The flowers in the hallway," Edie says. "All for her, most accompanied by wedding proposals. I've already sent two batches to hospitals. . . ."

"She's got potential, as an anchor," Franklin says, "but she's very green. So she needs help from all of you." Chook-koo. "We're going to start working her into the daily schedule, solo in the feature segments and live in double anchor formats with all of you, because I want her to see how different anchors and producers work, but mostly with Deng . . . and Laura. I want notes on her from you, anchors and producers. She knows about it, and she wants our help, so be frank. Give me your notes, and I'll give them to her. You can discuss things with her, but I want to know. . . ."

"Pete," Old Hartman says, leaning back in his chair. "As I said on Friday night, I want to make sure we've thought this through completely. . . ."

"We have, Mike." Chook-koo.

"Do you really think that a raw, inexperienced anchor is the right choice for a historic four-hour live global feed. . . ?"

"Mike, you saw her Friday night. . . ."

"But that was a promo video, not a live broadcast. . . ."

Chook-koo. "That's why we're asking you to help her."

"I'll be more blunt, Pete," Old Hartman says, chopping the air with his left hand. "Her English. . . ."

"Flawless in the promo," Deng says.

"Yes, but that's not live. . . ."

"When she has a script, she reads it perfectly," Franklin says. Chook-koo. "Better than some of you. Yes, she needs to be prepped. She'll need help, there's no question about that, but we've got six-seven weeks. . . ."

"Pete, this is a showcase for our shop, a crucial moment for FGN Asia, for the whole network. I've known your father since before you were born and. . . ."

"Mike, he's totally on board. Everybody in New York is on board."

"May I ask why?"

"You saw why on Friday night. You're seeing why with the Tournament of Roses out in the hallway." Chook-koo. "The camera loves Candy. She's Chinese. . . ."

"Pete, I think that's an added negative. I'll be blunt again. Having two Chinese anchors may not be the most acceptable way to present this story to the world."

"Well," Deng says, "obviously not the most acceptable way to you, Mike. . . ."

"Please," Old Hartman says. "This is not a joke."

"So, you want me to go with you instead of Deng?" Chook-koo.

"I can wave a flag with the schoolgirls at the border," Deng says.

"Seriously," Old Hartman says, chopping with his left hand as he speaks. "I don't believe that we should be presenting the handover as a completely Chinese story, and I recognize that Deng brings an international perspective and a business perspective. . . ."

"And Candy brings a local perspective." Chook-koo. "It's my turn to be blunt, Mike. I think we do want two Chinese faces, particularly if one of them is drop dead gorgeous . . ."

"Thanks, Peter," Deng says, flickering his eyelids.

". . . and so does New York. But that's a very superficial view and not what drove this decision."

"Then what did?" Old Hartman asks.

"Who can cover this story best, Mike. Deng has the business chops, he's got the global perspective, he's got all of the stuff I'm looking for, and he's got absolutely fabulous US Q ratings. Maybe you've heard: he gave up US network millions to get back to his roots. . . ."

"Which, fortunately, left more on the table for you, Mike," Deng says.

"And this story," Franklin continues, "is Candy's roots. It's her story, more than anyone else in this room. Born in the mainland, lives in Hong Kong . . . she's not just the future of this network, figuratively if not literally, but she's the future of Hong Kong. This is her story, and we'd be idiots not to take advantage of that.

"Could we run into a few rough edges because she's not our most experienced anchor, because her nouns and verbs might not always agree? We all recognize that, in this room, in New York. But, as much as I may love the chromakey and effects and production values, at the end of the day, great television is about heart, about emotion, about caring. And nobody here cares about this story the way Candy does, and we should give her a chance to tell it. Because she cares, because it's her story, she wants to tell it, to tell it right. And with the help of everybody in this room, Fuggin Asia can let her tell it to the whole world. And it's gonna be great television. Television no other network can match." Chook-koo. "So help her."

"So help us all," Deng says. "Amen."

"I didn't fire him because he's not on a package," Edie explains to Franklin in the stairway a few minutes after the meeting.

"Because of his wife?" Franklin says. Chook-koo. "Sleeping with the enemy?"

"I hear she sleeps with just about anything, but yes, that's why he's not on a package," Edie replies. "And that's why I didn't fire him. Not because I think he's the least bit worthwhile. Just relatively economical."

"The most jerk for the money," Franklin shrugs. "Smoke that thing this way."

"I thought you handled him and Old Hartman very well," Laura tells Franklin.

"It was all I could do to not say, 'Mike, if you think some other network will give you 450 grand a year, two round trips to the US business class, plus a twenty grand a month place on The Peak, a car and a driver, and listen to you bitch about not being able to park your ass on set and get max US face time on handover night, then go work for them.' I can't believe his gall," Franklin shrugs.

"But don't you think he has a point," Laura says, "about Pussy's English."

"Candy's English?" Franklin answers. "She reads copy better than any of our other anchors."

"But what about what's not scripted? It's live TV. . . ."

"Use Deng for the ad libs, and I'll be there to help you get things scripted," Edie promises, grinding out her cigarette. "Be happy about having her, darl, someone who won't run off at the mouth. You've finally found an anchor guaranteed to follow your script."

"I really didn't like being teased like that," Jeff complains.

"Sorry, sorry. I could not stop myself," Yogi says, cuddling with him on her couch looking onto the terrace and the window with the million dollar view of the harbor and Central skyline and Laura's bedroom. "I date married man, but I never see wife. Wife always still in Japan or she is asleep on Caine Road. For me, wife is not real. At this party, I finally see wife so I want to make some fun, have adventure like you have adventure when you are with Yogi. . . ."

"You thought it was fun, that this is a big game?"

"For me, party is quite amusing."

"For me, it was torture."

"Maybe is fun for me because I have less risk."

"Thanks."

"Why do you say 'thanks'?"

"Because you're saying that you don't care very much about me."

"For you was torture because you care for your wife, not care for me." Yogi takes a sip of the large Sapporo beer she and Jeff are sharing straight from the bottle.

"But I do care for you. Very much. . . ."

"Is not problem for me that you care for wife. I enjoy that we have Jew food and swimming and tennis. I do not want you leave your wife. I never expect this from a married man."

"Did your other Jewish boyfriend have a wife?"

"Which other Jewish boyfriend?" Yogi smiles.

"The one in Hong Kong. The one who taught you more about the JCC than I knew."

"No. This boyfriend have no wife. He goes back to London to marry his fiancée."

"He must have been crazy," Jeff says.

"No, he is very smart."

"I'd never be stupid enough to leave you for somebody else."

"No. Do not say like this. You sound too serious," Yogi says with a mix of real and simulated anger. "Also, this is lie, because you leave me every day for wife."

"That's different."

She takes another sip of beer. "I tell you something serious. Perhaps you know. Your wife in love with boss."

"Boss?"

"Her boss Peter."

"No way."

"Sure?"

"She always talks about how much he makes her work."

"See, she always talk about him. Woman can see when is in love. Husband is last to know."

"Well, you should see when we're in bed. . . ."

"You invite me to watch? I will buy telescope. . . ."

"You know what I mean," Jeff sighs. "She's absolutely wild. . . ."

"Is like man to think in bed and in love is same."

"Well. . . ."

"In bed we are also wild, yes?"

Jeff nods.

"So, when she is wild, it prove she is love you, but when we are wild, does this prove we are also in love?"

"Maybe."

"No," Yogi pounding her palms into her lap, but smiling. "Is different organ to make love and fall in love."

"I understand that, but I also understand that the best love making happens between two people who are in love."

"Sure?"

"I think so."

"You think so because the man's brain is inside penis." Yogi shakes her head. "This is not problem."

"No?"

"Problem is man's brain very small and mushy."

"That's not what you were saying half an hour ago," Jeff says, kissing the bridge of her tiny nose.

"Yes, but maybe I am think it." Yogi smiles and drinks again. "I have question about English I must ask you."

"Okay. I hope I know the answer."

"What is difference between chicken shit and horseshit?"

"That's pretty simple. Chicken shit is really insignificant, something small that doesn't matter. Somebody who's more worried about paper-work and procedures than performance, you say they worry about chicken shit."

"This is chicken shit."

"Yes," Jeff says, taking a drink of beer. "You should ignore chicken shit because it doesn't matter. Horseshit, on the other hand, is too big to ignore. It's ugly, it's in your face, and it stinks. . . ."

"I think I understand. I am chicken shit," Yogi says, taking the beer from him and draining it. "And you are horseshit."

"Repeat it," Laura says into the control room microphone, into the ear of Candace Fang, in her third week on air, doing feature block package lead-ins.

"Vi-o-lins."

"Thirty," Quickie says."

"Not quite. VI-a-lins. Emphasis on the first syllable, the second very quickly and not so much like an 'o' than just a short 'a' or 'e', then the third stretched out a little. Try again."

"VI-a-lins."

"Very good." Laura nods to Quickie, still pressing the anchor lever to Fang's ear. "Okay, let's put it to tape. When Quickie comes in with the cue. . . ."

Fang and Laura await the countdown. "In three, two, one," Quickie says, "cue."

On set, Fang reads, "All around the world, law enforcement agencies are confronting new criminal threats that often take unusual forms. From Paris, FGN's Monique LeClaire reports on how French police are coping with a rising tide of VI-a-lins."

"Rolling tape," Quickie says. "Three minute eight."

"Perfect," Laura says. "That was great, Candy."

"Thank you," she says. "Please explain."

"Explain what?"

"Explain package toss. It is not correct to say, 'vi-o-lins'?"

"Yes, it is 'vi-o-lins' for the musical instrument, but what you said was perfect."

"I do not understand. What is meaning?"

"Ah, the lead-in is a joke. It's a package about police in Paris finding many violins, the musical instruments. But we are making a pun about violence. Violins, violence. Get it?"

"I see," Fang says, "It is funny?"

"To me it is," Laura says.

"Then I must laugh," Fang says. "Ha-ha."

"No," Laura says with mock annoyance. "You must just read the way I tell you and look beautiful. Only the audience must laugh."

"Thank you," Fang says. "I still learning TV."

"You're a good student," Laura says.

"Thank you."

"Two minute," Quickie says. To Laura, he says, "In magazine, they say Pussy was Beijing student in 1989 and she go to Tiananmen, then when troop come, family send her to auntie in Hong Kong to avoid embarrassing. Because of family." He punches his microphone button to speak to Candace on the set, "One-thirty."

"Wow," Laura says. "Who's her family?"

"Her mother is a professor of chemistry at Beida, very high prestigious university. Her father is department head at Ministry of Foreign Affair." He hits the button again, "One minute."

"Foreign Affairs," Laura nods. "That sounds appropriate." She punches her button to Fang's ear. "Okay on the tag and good bye?"

"Yes," Fang says.

"Thirty."

"We put it to tape and then bring back our pal Deng for another block of fun and games."

"Is better making your show in this chair than in graphics chair."

"I agree with that," Laura says.

"Ten," Quickie says.

"Okay-aaah," Fang says.

"Five . . . in three, two, one . . . cue."

"Sorry if you think I was stringing you along on with that report. I've tried not to hit any wrong notes during this quarter hour. I'll be back with more business features from around Asia and the world in fifteen minutes. Until then, I hope the latest business news after the break will be music to your ears. I'm Candace Fang from Hong Kong for FGN Asia: we mean business in Asia."

"Keep smiling and making love to the camera," Laura says in Fang's ear. "Keep rolling," she tells Quickie, "and pull back."

"Already," Quickie says, adjusting the robot camera. "Okay, out."

"You were terrific, Candy."

"Thank you," she says, arranging her pile of scripts for the seven o'clock hour as Deng enters the set.

As the anchors settle in, Quickie says to Laura, "They was worry about her uncle."

"Her uncle?" Laura says, "Candy's uncle?"

"Her uncle Li Peng." The premier of China. Or prime minister.

After the show, Laura throws her scripts in the recycle bin and strides across the newsroom perfumed with roses and lilies from the continuing stream of bouquets for Fang. Lamont's former chair in the slot has become the home for teddy bears, Snoopys, Hello Kittys, Minnies with and without Mickeys, and other stuffed toys accompanying the flowers between pickups from local orphanages. There's an open box of chocolates—sweets for Candy—on the slot and more placed around the newsroom. At Franklin's office, as promised, the door is open. Laura nods at his secretary Iris Wong and closes the door of the bowling lane behind her. Franklin, with the phone to his ear, holds up a hand to her and smiles.

"Soft drink is too broad. . . . I understand who they are. I have heard of Coca-Cola. Headquarters in Atlanta like some second rate news network. . . . Yes, I know they also own the hotels, but where were they when that was up for grabs? Now that we're hot, he thinks we owe him?.... Offer official diet drink and title sponsorship of *Market Wrap* and we'll see how serious he really is.... You're doing great, Gladys. You've got him hooked, now reel him in. Bye." Franklin puts down the phone and shakes his head. "It's the old story: when you're struggling and need help, no one knows you, but once you get your feet on the ground, everybody thinks they deserve a piece of the action...."

"I thought maybe you did it because you were screwing her like everybody said," Laura says. "But, no, you really did it because you want to suck up to the butcher of Beijing, to make us all part of the massacre...."

"Laura, please re-rack this tape and roll it from the top...."

"Pussy, Candace, whoever.... She's Li Peng's niece."

Franklin doesn't respond.

"You're putting her on the air because she's Li Peng's niece...."

"Careful when you object to nepotism at this network," Franklin says, smiling. "Some people here have connections pretty high up in the company."

"You know what I mean. You're here because your father trusts you and because you know more about running a TV station than just about anyone on earth since you grew up doing it. That's different from getting a job because of family connections that have nothing to do with your competence or ability...."

"You're free to think whatever you want about Candy, and I realize that you guys didn't get along very well at all from the start. So I give you a lot of credit for doing the job you're doing with her, and she does, too. I mean today, that bit with the violins, that was sensational and really makes her look like a million bucks, an extra million bucks to go along with the million bucks she looks like when she's just sitting there on camera. I appreciate your professionalism and your dedication to the network."

"Thank you, but she's Li Peng's niece."

"Laura, that's really none of your business."

"You made it my business when you made her my anchor and didn't tell me she's Li Peng's niece."

"Laura, I didn't know it either until it came out in the Chinese magazines. It's not tattooed on her forehead and she doesn't talk about it. Now I admit that I'm happy about the *guanxi* we might get from Candy," Franklin says, holding up his hand to stop Laura from responding, "in Beijing, even though a lot of it is offset by reactions like yours from people here. But, first, Li Peng has a lot of nieces, and, second, that's absolutely not why she's got the job any more than any personal considerations had anything to do with it." Chook-koo. "Fuggin Asia is promoting Candy and making her a focus of coverage—and people are responding—because of what she brings to the programming. Period. She's got the potential to be the best anchor in Asia, the best this network has ever had."

"Emphasis on the 'had'," Laura snarls. "But I don't care about that. I care about Fuggin Asia's integrity. . . ."

"Are you saying that Candy shouldn't be an anchor because of some family connection to the Chinese leadership? Where's the integrity in saying that since one of your relatives did something that we don't like, or belongs to the wrong political party, or goes to the wrong church, you have to suffer?"

"No, I'm saying that. . . . But it's different when you put them on air as a representative of our network and our values—not to mention taking chances because she can't speak the language and doesn't know TV. . . ."

"You didn't know TV when we put you in the control room, Laura. But you learned. We're doing the same thing with Candy. . . ."

"But why? Why her?"

"I said why: because she's a natural. Haven't you noticed the flowers?"

"That's just horny bankers with too much money. . . ."

"Prime demographic," Franklin says, smiling again. "She's going to be the biggest newscaster in China in a couple of years, the first superstar of Chinese news. . . ."

"You think they'll let you show news in China? Real news?"

"Whatever they'll let us show, they're much more likely to let us show it with Candy on it."

"Deng was right: it is the post-handover . . ."

". . . stupid," they say in unison.

CHAPTER 17

Weekend to Howl

"So which handover parties will you be attending, Deng?" Fang asks in a two-shot out of Fiona Fok's package on June 30th galas. Laura has to admit that Franklin is right: the two of them look brilliant on screen together, Deng in a dark blue jacket and Fang in the FGN eagle gold that's fast becoming her signature color.

"You know very well that I'll be right here with you, Candy, throughout that glorious night, anchoring FGN Asia's special coverage of Hong Kong's return to China."

"That's right, Deng. Our live coverage from the Convention Center and all over my hometown begins. . . ."

The full screen graphic with the broadcast times appears as scripted, to Laura's relief.

". . . at ten p.m. Hong Kong time Monday night and goes on all night."

"Then Candy and I will be right back here Tuesday morning at six with a special edition of *AM Asia* offering a hearty *'Ni hao'* from Chinese-ruled Hong Kong."

The graphic dissolves to show the anchors in a two-shot again.

"For now, that's all from us for this Friday, June 27, three days before the Hong Kong handover. I'm Candace Fang in Hong Kong, thanking you for waking up with us."

"You get a good rest over the weekend, Candy, for our big night ahead on Monday. Thanking you for your time this time until next time, I'm Deng Jiang Mao, saying, 'Buy low, sell high,' and have a profitable day. Remember, FGN Asia means business in Asia."

"Three, two, one, finish," Quickie says.

"Beautiful show, everyone," Laura says to the crew in the control room and the anchors. "Like Deng says, rest up for the big day Monday."

"After more show," Quickie adds.

"Just one more," Laura says, clearing out for Richard Yakamoto, his cologne preceding him. "Break a leg, Rich," she says as he drops into her seat. He grunts, she sneezes.

Laura stops at Helios' desk to brief him for the ten a.m. show. "Just dupe everything," she tells him, "and add the new market boards. I'll be in tapes. Call me on my mobile if Richard's show breaks any news."

Helios says, "Okay," without looking up from his screen.

Laura takes the clipboard from her desk drawer along with two apples and a few of those funny little bananas Jeff keeps buying. She reaches into the plastic shopping bag under the desk for the last three tapes for Christina Volpecello's packages. I can finish and go home tonight, she thinks, finally. There was something too weird about using Peter's shower up on 28, especially after that joke he made about the camera in there. She walks to the tapes area, nods to Nancy, who's shut behind the sliding glass door of an editing booth, and takes a seat in front of a tape machine and monitor in the row outside the editing bays, leaving a seat between herself and a translator creating Chinese subtitles for her just-completed show and an intern transcribing for Fiona and May. Laura wonders why she hasn't gotten an intern, then she realizes she'd need one who knows English. These days, people who know English are investment bankers and TV personalities earning six figures a month, not interns. Laura puts on her headphones and starts transcribing her interview with the chairman of the American Chamber of Commerce.

After an hour of logging, then a smooth hour, half on tape, on the air with Deng and Fang, and another 45 minutes of logging, she heads for what Peter has promised will be the last noon meeting (moved to 11:45 while they're in tape and limited to fifteen minutes) "at least until the next handover" to make final preparations for handover day and night. So much had gone wrong over the past eight months, it had been such a struggle, yet as the big moment approaches Laura concedes that things are working out all right after all. She's gotten what she wants: she is the handover night producer. She isn't completely comfortable with Pussy as an anchor—and she can't stop thinking of her as Pussy, even though she's trained herself to call her Candy, especially after she said, "You call me anything except not too late for cue." But, Laura has seen she is brilliant on air and great with Deng. Laura feels surprisingly calm about the historic night ahead, quietly confident that it's all going to work. She trusts Edie and Peter, though, god knows, she doesn't always agree with them. But they know what they're doing, she knows what she's doing, and that's the best you can hope for going into a four-hour live-event broadcast. At least that's how it seems to a producer who's never done it before.

Schedules labeled "Final" for handover day and night are stacked in the middle of the conference table, where the anchors, reporters, news managers and producers filter in. Franklin is waiting and nods when Richard and Kathleen arrive from their eleven o'clock show.

"Here we go," Edie says. "Everybody take a schedule. Chop-chop."

Old Hartman picks up the stack, and passes it to Fiona, who divides it in two and passes one stack to the other side of the table.

"Everything is also entered in the system," Edie says, "but I want all of us to review it now, together, and to speak up if there are any problems. Read it through please. May, you should be ready for live pops from six p.m. on. Bobby, you need to be there with her. Everybody else in the field, we'll use your location packages as previews for our afternoon and the US morning shows until ten p.m. From our air time at ten, you all need to be on stand-by to go live. Tech assures me that even if we have rain like today, we'll have signal. So bring your brollies." Edie pauses for people to review the schedules.

"Everybody's set-up pieces are very solid," Franklin says while they're reading.

"If no one's in LegCo until after the ceremony, then why do we need to be ready at ten?" Andy asks.

"For the demo," Edie says.

"Won't be much of a demo in weather like this," Andy says. "Can't we. . . ?"

"Maybe Mother Nature votes Democrat," Franklin says.

"Be there," Edie says. "Anything else?" The table is quiet. "Laura and I will make the calls on who we're going to live and when. The plan is in her preliminary rundown."

"But it's just preliminary," Laura says. "We're gonna rock 'n' roll all night."

"I'm just wondering," Deng says, "why go to Christina at the Convention Center so quickly. . . ."

"She's a star," Franklin says, adding, "too." Chook-koo.

"It's a live event, so we want a live shot from the event. I'm hoping that she'll snag someone from inside the hall," Laura says. "Otherwise, she'll donut her package about the origins. . . ."

"Fine," Deng says. "You know what you're doing."

"I never thought I'd live to hear that," Laura says. "Thank you, sir."

"Anything else?" Edie asks. No one speaks. "All right, then. Fiona, is everyone done shooting?"

"All of our people are. Christina will be using her own crew, right?"

"Yes, but. . . ." Edie begins.

"She's scheduled to arrive tomorrow morning," Franklin says. "Knowing her, she'll want to walk her dog and then start shooting, but her crew might not. So please have the backup crew on standby. I authorize the overtime. They'll have plenty of time to relax starting come Tuesday."

"Done," Fiona says.

"Thank you," Edie says. "Tapes will be staffed all weekend. Nancy, please tell. . . ."

"I've got editors on duty, packaging evergreens so we don't get caught short for the rest of the week, when they'll get a few well deserved days off like everyone else in town," Nancy says. "But they will be on hand to cut current packages for you whenever you need them, right through Tuesday night at least."

"Christina has priority, though," Edie says.

"She'll take it whether we say so or not," Old Hartman says.

"The newsroom and production facilities will be open all weekend," Edie says, "and the beds for 28 are coming in tonight. Sara has volunteered to be on call until Sunday morning in case there are issues that need to be resolved, and her numbers are on the schedule."

"I have no life," Sara says, "so call, for a chat even."

"I'll be on call from Sunday noon on," Edie says, "and I'll likely stay straightaway until we're finished Tuesday. I used to have a life, but then came Fuggin Asia." She smiles. "If you need crews, if you need more editors, whatever, you must call us for authorization. The only exception is Pizza Express, the official handover night pizza of Fuggin Asia. Just call them, say Fuggin Asia, and, like that man I've yet to find, they'll deliver."

"And like all the ones Edie has found," Deng says, "they'll put it on her bill."

"Pete," Old Hartman says, "will you also be here for the big event?"

"I wish, Mike," Franklin says. "But Gladys and I and two dozen or so major sponsors and their significant others—and couldn't that get interesting?—will be on the temporarily christened Fuggin Asia One Country, Two Executives junk in the harbor to watch the fireworks. . . ."

". . . and the broadcast, of course," Edie says.

"Of course." Franklin smiles. Chook-koo.

"The official Fuggin Asia contribution to water pollution," Deng says.

Franklin continues, "Let me tell all of you, you're doing great work. I've been involved in a lot of major event coverage, with a lot bigger budgets, a lot more experienced hands, at stations with a lot more practice producing this kind of coverage." Chook-koo. "I've never seen a group that's worked as hard and as well—and that's the key, because anybody can work hard, that's not what matters: what matters is how well you work, what you produce. 'It's the outputs, not the inputs,' as one of those signs we used to put around the newsroom said." He glances at Fang, who smiles and raises her fingers in front of her mouth to hide it. "Your output has been sensational so far. Go home this weekend and take a rest, but keep your focus. That's the difference between good and great. Great television happens when everything and everyone is in focus. It's a great story, and with our focus, we are going to nail it. So, thanks, and stay focused."

"Rah," Deng says as the meeting breaks up.

"Thanks," Laura says to Deng. "You guys are going to be great Monday night."

"You're right, kiddo," he says. "Go team."

"Time for a fag?" Edie asks Laura. She nods. The stairs are wet from the driving rain, and a cloud seems to envelope the landing above and the landscape beyond.

"You seem very relaxed," Edie says, fumbling with her clipboard as she lights up.

"Maybe I'm just anesthetized from logging the Wolf Woman's tapes. But I feel good about things. They're terrific."

"The tapes?"

"Deng and Pussy."

"Yes, they are. There is some chemistry between them."

"And I feel like all the other parts are ready, or as ready as they can be. I'm going to spend the weekend with Jeff, just us, a little quiet time, and maybe, for once, do it after dark."

"You will finish them this afternoon?" Edie asks, looking up from her clipboard.

"What?"

"Christina's tapes, darl'. You will have the logging finished this afternoon?"

"Absolutely. Just a couple of hours to go."

"Fabulous," Edie says.

"That's my middle name," Franklin says, banging the door open, then pausing. "I thought rain was supposed to make things fresh and cool."

"What's this rot about the Fuggin Asia junk?" Edie asks.

"I didn't tell you?"

"You didn't."

"Can't you handle things without me?" Chook-koo.

"Of course," Edie says. "I just question how you were selected for this assignment."

"It was Gladys's idea," Franklin says. "I didn't know about this whole junk thing. I just hope the weather isn't. . . ."

"What whole junk thing?" Laura asks.

"Oh, it's the only thing that people do here that's the least bit of fun," Edie says.

"That would explain why I've never heard of it," Laura says.

"You're married," Franklin says. "To the king of women's underwear, no less. How much more fun could you possibly handle?"

"Is it a junk like we saw in the pictures of China in our third-grade geography books?" Laura asks, "With the big sail. . . ."

"The Tourist Board has one of them, with a gorgeous red sail," Edie says.

"The one we used in the promo," Franklin reminds them. "Maybe you can use that shot Monday night. We own all that footage. . . ."

"Yes, perhaps, *mei-mei,*" Edie says, making a note on her clipboard.

"Okay," Laura says. "But that's not the kind of junk you're taking. . . ?"

"Oh, no," Edie says, with a laugh. "Corporate junks are these grubby old wooden cruisers, with a cabin and a covered area in back, a few seats in the bow and, on top of the cabin, a sun deck where English girls take off their bikini tops after they've had a few."

"Especially at night," Franklin adds. "It's actually not after they've had a few, but how they manage to get a few. . . ."

"At the bank, I received my best evaluations after our junk trips," Edie says with a smirk. "Every company here worth its salt has a junk that they use for booze cruises with clients in the harbor or staff trips to the beach or to seafood restaurants in Lamma. It's the one setting where everyone loosens their ties and gets pissed. Even the Chinese. It's brilliant."

"So when is Fuggin Asia getting a junk?" Laura asks.

"First, we need enough food on the table," Franklin says. "Then we'll add salt."

"You are afraid of wife," Yogi says. "But wife not afraid of you."

"Why do you say that?" Jeff asks.

"If wife afraid of you, she is not in love with boss."

"But that's nothing. I mean they say he's doing that anchor woman, and he'd never look at Laura."

"Sure?"

"Look, I'm a man. I know. If I had a choice between that Candace Fang—that her name?—and Laura, I know who I'd choose."

"What is American saying? 'Cannot select a bed from its covers'?"

Jeff smiles. "That's 'you cannot judge a book by its cover.' But your version is more interesting."

"Is not joke. If wife afraid of you, she is not in love with boss."

"I don't think she is, but. . . ." Jeff sighs. "Yogi, this is stupid."

"Man always think that is stupid to talk about relationship," which she pronounces "re-ray-son-sip," and continues, "But relationship is very important. It is what we have."

"And I like our re-ray-son-sip very much," Jeff smirks, reaching to hug her.

"Do not teasing me. I am serious."

"I am, too," Jeff says, slipping his arm around her. "You are very important to me."

"This is thought. This is feeling. This is not what matters. Action is what matters."

"I'm here, aren't I?"

"But is chickenshit," Yogi says, pushing his arm away. "Feeling that matter most to you is that you are afraid of wife. You afraid of her, so she does not afraid of you. Only you worry about her. End of day, you always go back to her."

"Well, yes. But I don't understand. . . ."

"You see? You are afraid of wife."

Jeff sighs. "I'm not afraid of my wife, sweetheart. I'm afraid of what could happen, if I wind up here in Hong Kong without Laura's roof over my head, with no money, no business prospects. . . ."

"Then you go home and sell underwear to American ladies and wait for mother to die and you become rich. This is normal for Jew. . . ."

"But I don't want to go home, sweetheart."

"Why not? Life for you is better. . . ."

"But I wouldn't have you." He tries to slip his arm around her again but she squirms away.

"You say like this, but then you will not go with me to cocktail parties for handover. . . ."

"They conflict with Laura's dinner."

"Will not come to junk trip Saturday to swim at beach in Sai Kung. Is beautiful."

"It's a Saturday, Laura's home. . . ."

"You must trip to China," Yogi says. "Big brassiere emergency. . . ."

"I told you. I promised to spend this weekend with Laura. We promised each other that we'd spend some quality time together before her crazy handover night. She thinks she may not survive, that Hong Kong will never be the same. . . ."

"When you will with me?"

"Handover night I will be with you. Laura will be working all night and into the next morning, so I can play house with you on your morning off. We can have a nice *shabu-shabu* and then I can cook you a cheese omelet. . . ."

"This is not enough."

"I'm with you almost every night, after your cocktail parties. I should move clothes here. Why is this junk trip so important?"

"It is what people in Hong Kong do. If I go alone, it is not fun for me."

"I wish I could go with you. I want to go with you. But I can't."

"Because you are afraid of wife."

"I'm afraid I didn't have time to make dinner tonight," Jeff says.

"That's okay," Laura says, seated on the single chair in the living room, sipping a glass of red wine. "I'm so burned out from the day, I can't think about food right now. Monday, I'm going to come home early, and you're in charge of dinner then."

"How early?"

"I need to be at the station by six, I'll be home around noon, take a nap and we can eat around four, if that's okay. They'll have pizza at the station, but let's wok up some veggies. No wine, though."

"Is there anything I can do to help?"

"Get some of those little *bok choy.* I like them better than the *choi sum.* Or that spinach stuff. . . ."

"I mean about the handover." Jeff sighs. "I mean are there any temp jobs over there for drivers or porters or whatever?"

"You mean work. . . ?"

"Maybe pick up a little extra cash." Jeff realizes he's blown his cover and scrambles. "Our payments on the shipments have big lags, so I could use. . . . I mean it wouldn't hurt us. . . ."

"Don't worry about that. You stick to ladies' underwear. . . ."

"That sounds painful, sweetheart."

Laura chuckles. "Don't I know it? But don't worry. Money's the least of our problems. I'd trade a million—US, if I had it—for a couple of extra hours in the day. Or a couple less hours live on handover night." Laura takes another sip of red wine. "Come here, you," she says, extending her arms. Jeff gets off the loveseat, and she embraces him. "Let's get started with that quality time."

They go to the bedroom, undress and make love. Amid Laura's moaning—it sounds to Jeff like "Take Pang. . . . Take Pang now. . . . Pang now . . . now"—her mobile phone rings. "Oh god, I have to get that," she says, pushing Jeff away and rummaging for her phone.

"Laura Wellesley here. . . . Well, Jeff and I were. . . . Because I thought it might be important. . . . It was my second one, so it's okay. . . . Well, no, not always. Sometimes, three, four. . . . Oh, god, no. . . . Of course I should come, too. . . . I'll catch a cab. . . . What does Peter say?. . . Okay, okay. . . . See you soon." Laura clicks off the phone and turns to Jeff, her cheeks redder than they were in bed. "We've got a crisis. This Wolf Lady reporter from overseas who's been driving me nuts the past three months, now she's not showing up. So we have to package all of her tapes ourselves and figure out the coverage without her. I'm going to the studio, and I'll be late."

"Are you okay?"

"I'm fine, but I've got to go," she says, stepping into the bathroom for a shower. "Just stay out of my way so I can get out of here. I'll call you later."

"Congratulate me," Edie says as Laura, fresh from a taxi ride to Chai Wan, joins her and Franklin in his newsroom office.

"Edie passed her screen test," Franklin says. "Meet the new Christina Volpecello, Fuggin Asia style."

"I don't quite have the bottom for it, but I'm sure in time. . . ."

"What are you talking about?" Laura says, exasperated.

"Instead of parachuting in someone else," Franklin explains, "and there's nobody available who's good, Edie will package the Broad Bottomed Wolf's reports and take her place at the Convention Center."

"Rearranging everyone else is just too hard," Edie adds.

"What happened with Christina?"

Franklin shakes his head. "She was in Somalia, and a sniper shot her. . . ."

"Dead?" Laura asks.

"No, but critical. Medevaced to Paris," Franklin says.

"Where they get her?"

"Around the block from the hotel," Franklin says.

"No, physically, on her body. . . ."

"Oh. Right leg and the bottom. . . ."

"Big target," Laura says, nodding. "Is she going to be okay?"

"They say it's touch and go. . . ."

"At least, it wasn't her face or anything," Laura says. "If she recovers, she can still report and. . . ."

Franklin and Edie laugh.

"What's so funny? I mean we've got a crisis here and Christina got shot. . . ."

"Christina didn't get shot," Franklin says.

"It was her bloody dog," Edie says.

"And she's not coming because of that?"

"You should have heard on the phone," Franklin says. "Completely hysterical. She would have been calmer if it was her."

"She won't leave Honey's bedside," Edie says. "Some veterinary hospital in Paris will have two howling bitches on its hands. . . ."

"Have you told. . . ?" Laura asks.

"The changes are on a need-to-know basis right now," Franklin says.

"I've gotten the backup crew with Lok Kin-ming," Edie adds. "He's quite good. I can be my own producer at the Convention Center on handover night, and I'll drag along a PA to hold my clipboard. . . ."

"You're not taking Honest," Laura says.

"Wouldn't dream of it. . . ."

"Meanwhile," Franklin says, "there's a lot of tape to cut, standups to shoot. . . ."

"We'll start shooting tomorrow," Edie says, "and Laura will be my producer for those. Right?" she adds, looking at Laura.

Laura nods, still stunned. "Okay."

"Tonight, take me through BB Wolf's plans and your tapes. . . ." Edie says, then notices Laura's terrified, vacant look. "It will be great fun, *mei-mei.*"

"So get started," Franklin says, smiling. Chook-koo. "I'll order pizza."

"Is this going to be okay?" Laura asks.

"Haven't you ever seen *A Star is Born?*" Franklin says. "We play it twice a month on Franklin Classic Movies back home. My pop loves. . . ."

"No," Laura says. "I mean, I've seen the movie. I mean, I'm sure Edie will be fine. . . ."

"Fine?" Edie says, feigning anger. "Weather is fine. I'll be magnif. . . ."

"You'll be great, Edie," Laura says. "Absolutely fabulous. But what about here in the studio?"

"I'd be here watching you do things right," Edie says, "eating too much bloody pizza, and trying to find ways to throw my weight around. It's much better that I'm out of your way, throwing my weight around where it may possibly do some good. . . ."

"But what about a supervising producer?"

"You don't need one, Laura," Franklin says. "We trust you. And I'll just be a phone call away."

"I've also talked to Sara. She's agreed to sit in the slot to support you in the newsroom. She has no life, you know. . . ."

"But you'll be in charge," Franklin says. "It's a producer's dream. Huge story, all your baby. . . ."

"I don' know nuthin' 'bout birthin' no baby," Laura squawks, quoting from another Franklin Classic Movies favorite. "Peter, do you call that movie network Fukum?"

All three of them laugh.

"So tonight. . . ?" Chook-koo.

"Tonight," Edie says, "we'll go through Laura's tape logs and Christina's package outlines. . . ."

"Such as they are," Laura says.

"Indeed. And we'll suss out what's worthwhile to package."

"We'll need to have five or six packages, at least," Laura says, looking at the preliminary rundown in Edie's hand. "And they'll all need to be donut-able."

"Piece of cake," Edie says. "Then we'll come up with a shot list for tomorrow and Sunday. So much for your relaxing weekend with the husband."

"Don't worry about him," Laura says. "He'll understand. I mean, it's the handover . . ."

"Stupid," they all say.

"Hello," Jeff says, answering the phone while watching the Filipina in the window, her back turned, a towel wrapped around her waist, shaving her armpits. He'd been expecting a call from Laura for a couple of hours already.

"*Moshi-moshi,*" Yogi says barely audible over the noise in the background.

"You should never call. . . ."

"I know you alone, so do not angry with me."

"How do you know?"

"Because Edie tell me your wife is in TV station with her."

"That's right. . . ."

"She also tell me that you can come to junk trip with me tomorrow because they are busy all day making television program."

"Where are you? It sounds like you're in the middle of rock concert."

"Lan Kwai Fong. First UrBank cocktail party. You should come. Quite fun. Many famous people. Many party. I drunk. . . ."

"You sound duh-lunk," Jeff says, imitating her pronunciation. "But no, I'll stay here and wait to hear from Laura. She'll be calling soon."

"Sure?"

"Positive."

"You are afraid of wife. If you drunk, you not afraid of anything."

"I'm afraid of you, sweetheart." But mainly afraid he can't afford to spend what it would take to get drunk in Lan Kwai Fong.

"This is better. I will give you reason to afraid tonight. Many men here, maybe some Jew. . . ."

"Enjoy yourself. Good night."

Her armpits done, the Filipina moves closer to the window, her back still turned. Jeff sees the ends of towel part. She lowers her eyes and moves her hands to her groin, making short strokes with the razor.

"There's some really spectacular stuff from Professor Chang," Edie says.

Laura looks away from her tape of the head of the British Law Society and peels the earphone closest to Edie away from her ear. "What?"

"Sorry, darl'. This bite from Professor Chang about reverse engineering free markets is really terrific. I'm not sure how we can use it, though. . . ."

Laura hits the pause button on her machine and drops her headphones on the table. "I think we can work it into the package on mainland businesses in Hong Kong."

"I was thinking maybe we could do something about China becoming more like Hong Kong. Maybe what things will look like in 2047, the 50 years. . . ."

"That's not on Christina's list."

"I know. But I'm not the Broad Bottomed Wolf. We can use that bite, a couple of bits from May's interview with the governor and one from Deng's with the CE Mister Tung."

"The better to lick Beijing's ass, my dear."

"The bit about how China is changing. . . . I could do a standup in front of the Hongkong Bank building. Start with how the lion that dates to 1867 or whatever and then a shot of the building, about how the past mixes with the future every day in Hong Kong. What do you think, *mei-mei?*"

"You'd need to script it. Or at least sketch it out more."

Edie sighs. "I can't wait to get out there tomorrow. I hope we get a little sunshine. The forecast says fine. . . ."

"What time does the crew report?"

"Seven."

"Oh shit." Laura looks at her watch. It reads 1:34 a.m. "I was supposed to call Jeff. . . ."

"I'm sure he's out getting pissed. Everyone in town is out getting pissed tonight. This is the biggest weekend of drinking in human history. I'm invited to nineteen cocktails, picnics and junks this weekend alone, and I'm not even popular. Yogi, my cute little Japanese friend you met at the promo screening, she said she saw Grace bloody Jones in Lan Kwai Fong."

"Wow."

"She also said that Roger Moore bought her drink."

"Geez. Double-oh-seven-point-two."

"He's no Sean Connery, but he'll do in a pinch. If you go to the Forbidden City in Beijing, he narrates the tour on tape, and it's brilliant. . . ."

"We'll have our own Forbidden City when the Chinese take over."

"You can't really believe that. . . ."

"You're not worried?" Laura asks. "These are Communist dictators coming in here."

"They're politicians, and, to me, one brand is hardly different from another."

"These guys are from a different league. . . ."

"Perhaps, but they all play the same game."

"Maybe." Laura sighs. "I hope you're right."

"I think so, *mei-mei.*"

"Are you going to stay here tonight?"

"I thought I would. I brought some clean pants for the morning, but I'll need outfits for shooting. We can swing by my place, shoot some VO en route. I can pick up clothes for you, too, if you want. The beds on 28 aren't so bad."

"You think we're going to sleep tonight?" Laura smiles. Edie nods, and they both put their headphones back on.

"No, I figured you got tied up," Jeff says, standing naked in the doorway of his bedroom, looking for the alarm clock. "What time is it?"

"It's about nine," Laura says. "We're in the van with a crew, shooting around town."

"Okay." Jeff sees the Filipina washing dishes at the kitchen sink wearing comically large, pink rubber gloves, pretending not to look at his wakeup erection.

"We'll be shooting all day, and then going back to the studio to cut tape and put the packages together, and we'll probably have to shoot again tomorrow. I borrowed some clothes from Edie, so I might not be home until tomorrow night. Or maybe after the show on Monday. But don't worry. We'll be fine."

"Okay."

"I'll call you again later."

"Okay."

"Thanks for being so understanding. Love you."

"Love you, too."

"Bye."

"Bye."

Jeff hangs up the phone, lets the Filipina have one more good look at his pecker, slips on a pair of shorts, goes to the kitchen to start the coffee machine and dials the phone.

"Hello."

"Moshi-moshi," he says. "It's Jeff. Good morning, sweetheart."

"Is what time?"

"Do you have a hangover this morning?"

"I have headache. This is hangover?"

"Could be, but Doctor Jeffrey can't be certain without a thorough examination. Am I still invited to your junk trip today?"

"What happen to your wife?"

"She's with Edie, like you said she would be."

"Today also?"

"Yes, you told me so last night. Don't you remember?"

"No. Too much drunk. . . ."

"My wife will be with Edie all weekend. . . ."

"Maybe they are lovers."

"Maybe. It would be fair, wouldn't it?"

"For me, you are better lover than Edie."

"I think you are still duh-lunk. What time is the junk?"

"Come here ten o'clock. Bring orange juice, please."

"Okay." That fresh squeezed from the fruit store she likes is $20 for a little bottle. It's not worth it, but she is.

"You are not afraid?"

"Today I won't be afraid of anything."

"More so than in the boardrooms of international companies and corner offices of local tycoons, you can read the pulse of Hong Kong business in street markets like this one across the harbor from the gleaming towers of the Central skyline. And at least for now, the pushing and shoving and bargaining for the best price indicate that, handover or not, it's still business as usual. From the back alleys of Mongkok, I'm Edie March, FGN Asia in Hong Kong."

Laura motions for Edie to keep walking and unplugs her microphone cord from the camera. "Zoom out," she whispers to the shooter, then, squatting in front of him, holds up fingers, three, two, one. "Okay, we're out. Thanks."

"How'd it look?" Edie asks.

"Terrific. We got a serious haggle in the background, and some good nat sound," Laura answers. "Kin-ming, shoot us a little VO from around the corner and some Nathan Road traffic, 30 seconds, with sound, while we break down. Thanks."

"We're having some good luck with the weather," Edie says.

"We deserve it."

"I've told you that in New York I had a sail boat, 26 feet long."

"For American, size always matter," Yogi says, lifting the brim on the white Bank International baseball cap given to each passenger as they boarded the junk. They are occupying the bench seat at the bow on the lower deck, high-rise public housing of eastern Hong Kong Island on their right, and, beyond the airport on their left, green rolling hills of the New Territories, occasionally slashed by more high-rise towers or the white powdery mounds and steel frames of new construction. As they leave the harbor area, the water becomes bluer.

"I used to be out there every Sunday, at least, eight months a year," Jeff says. "During the summer, when the days are really long, even during the week, I'd leave the store at three or four, just sail out somewhere, by myself usually, drop anchor, drink beer, eat a sandwich, listen to the ballgame and fall asleep on the deck, under the stars."

"It is good to be boss."

"Captain," Jeff corrects her. "And, even without a boat, it's good to have a mate like you."

Yogi makes a sour face. "For not big ship, you have many mate."

Jeff changes the subject. "These people are your bosses?"

"This is my bosses and colleagues." Yogi takes a sip of her beer from the bottle with a foam rubber Bank International holder around it. "There are also many visitors from US, from headquarters. Tomorrow night we have big company dinner at Hyton Hotel. I hope I do not fall asleep in middle of chairman speech."

"They all came for the handover?"

"They come every year. Quite disappointed Edie is not here."

"Edie?"

"Lover of your wife."

"Why?"

"Because on sundeck, she always remove her top. Is four years ago, but everyone remember. Is good career move."

"Then why don't you try it?" Jeff asks.

"I do try. But nobody remember." They both laugh. "But handover, they think is big thing. . . ."

"You don't?"

"Chinese are very reasonable," Yogi says.

"Yes. . . ."

"Not like Japanese. . . ."

"I have some experience with unreasonable Japanese. . . ."

"This because Japanese are so passionate." She pronounces the last word without the "sh" sound—pass-on-it.

"Ah," Jeff says, sipping his foam-jacketed beer.

Yogi pushes the beer away from his mouth, turns the visor on his cap to the side, and locks his mouth in a long kiss.

"That's okay in front of your bosses?"

"Is okay. They don't see. Too busy making small conversation."

"Passionate is good," he says, pronouncing the word as she did.

"It is quite good some time. Japanese men harder."

Jeff looks at her quizzically.

"Is true."

"What do you mean?"

"Western men bigger. But Japanese harder."

"Really?"

"I think so."

"Which one is better?"

"Is like handover: when change happen, must adapt."

"That's not an answer," Jeff says, sipping his beer. "It seems to me that it would be very difficult to make it bigger, but it's possible to make it harder."

"Sure?"

"I will try." He takes another sip of his beer. "But if I fail. . . ."

"I will hold it against you." Yogi says, repeating the joke Jeff taught her.

"I want to put down the whole track up to the first bite here, so keep rolling for the sound and we'll put in the VO over it in edit," Edie explains, standing in the shadow of the statue of Queen Victoria in the park bearing her name.

"Got it?" Laura asks the shooter, Kin-ming. He nods. "Okay. Let's do it. You ready?" she asks Edie, who steps from the shadow into the light on the other side of the statue on an eight-foot pedestal. "Take a level."

"Check." Edie says. "Check, check."

Kin-ming nods. His assistant holds a sheet of white paper in front of the camera to reset the visual levels. "Okay," Kin-ming says.

"All right," Laura says, moving into position in front of Kin-ming to the right of Edie and out of the shot. "In three, two, one, roll."

"In Hong Kong's Victoria Park, Queen Victoria regally oversees the last bastion of her empire in Asia. Even with Beijing replacing Britain as sovereign of Hong Kong, the old Queen will remain on this throne, and this vast expanse of open space among the towers of Causeway Bay will still be known as Victoria Park. Queen's Roads Central, East and West will remain Queen's Roads, and the street that runs alongside Hong Kong's Central Market and the headquarters of Hang Seng Bank will still be known as *Vigdoria Wong Hou Gai,* Queen Victoria Street. The deepwater port that is Hong Kong's reason for being and the key link between mainland China and the rest of world will still be called Victoria Harbor. Sometimes, things change in name only. But with the transition to Chinese sovereignty, many things in Hong Kong will change in all but name."

Laura looks at Edie, who nods, then holds up five fingers, counting them down. "Okay. That's a wrap. Absolutely fabulous, Edie."

"Thank you, darl'. You don't think this blue suit looks too dodgy. It's a leftover from my banking days."

"You look terrific."

"In those old banking days, I'd be on the deck of a junk right now, with my top down, making believe it's perfectly normal to be bare breasted, ensuring a favorable annual review. Much wiser that way than in private, where they wouldn't be satisfied with only a look. . . ."

"We can't do that here, *jie-jie,*" Laura says. "You'd embarrass Kin-ming."

"I think Fuggin Asia's ready for topless presenters."

"That would be Pussy's job," Laura says.

"Already is, I reckon."

Laura giggles. "Okay, let's shoot the close, with clothes, and get moving."

"Yes, sir." Edie salutes.

"Do you want to walk?"

"Oh, yes. I think that's good. Is that all right with you, Kin-ming?"

"Fine, fine."

"Good," Laura says. "Levels still okay?"

Kin-ming nods.

"All set then," Laura positions herself. "In three, two, one, go. . . ."

"So, despite all the changes taking place around her, this old girl isn't losing her seat of honor just yet. But someday soon she may visit one of Hong Kong's legendary tailors, to trade her royal robes for a Chinese cheongsam. From Victoria Park, I'm Edie March, FGN Asia in Hong Kong."

Laura holds up five fingers and counts them down silently. "Okay. That's a wrap here. Kin-ming, get some VO of the skyline from here, and try some park footage. Kids playing, Filipina picnics, Chinese lovers . . . nothing more than a hug, though."

Kin-ming giggles.

"How about the swimming pool?" Edie asks.

"We have time?" Laura says, looking at her watch. "Sure. You never know when it might come in handy."

"Taking the plunge . . . struggling to keep their heads above water. . . ." Edie murmurs. "Definitely useful."

"Drown," Kin-ming adds. "No problem." He scampers off, letting his assistant carry the camera.

"You really think this blue is all right?" Edie says.

"It's gorgeous," Laura says. "Now you sound like a TV star. . . ."

"A Fuggin Asia TV star, *mei-mei.*"

"I never thought you could actually swim in the water in Hong Kong," Jeff says.

"Is like tropical fantasy island," Yogi says, gripping the other end of the donut life preserver dragging behind the junk's stern, enjoying the view of the palm-fringed beach. Other guests are taking a motor launch to the white sand, about 100 yards away.

"It is like a dream. Why isn't anyone else here?"

"There is no road. To get here, must take MTRoo, then bus for one hour, then hiking three hours over mountains. Hong Kong people too lazy to come here. Besides, is no shopping."

"And no food."

"Did you enjoy lunch?"

"I wish the British could have taught someone here to make a decent sandwich. That butter or whatever it is on the bread. . . . And white bread."

"British keep only place in Asia with bad food and bad weather."

"At least the chicken was good."

"It was American, KFC. Is why you like it." Yogi smiles.

"What's that smell?"

"Is from boat motor."

"Awful."

"We can swim." Yogi points to a hidden cove. "Over here. Is even more beautiful."

"You're sure they won't leave without us?"

"We stay here for at least three hour."

"Sure you're not too duh-lunk to swim?"

Yogi dunks Jeff's head in the water and takes off toward the point. Jeff recovers, clears his nose and paddles behind her. The mounds of her bottom break the surface as Yogi swims powerfully toward the cove through the calm, clear water. Around the bend, Yogi awaits him in water just covering her bust, placid waves lapping the white sand beach, palms swaying gently. He stands next to her, and she wraps her arms around his neck and legs around his hips. She has taken off her bikini bottom and tucked it into the back of her top.

"You're right," Jeff says. "It is beautiful."

Yogi kisses his neck and then licks his ear.

"Not too salty?" he asks.

"Delicious," she answers. "Taste." She puts her lips on his, and they share a long kiss. The surf pushes them closer together.

Yogi reaches inside his bathing suit, and they kiss again. She pushes down his suit using her hand and feet.

"Are you sure it's okay?" Jeff says.

"No one can see us," she assures him.

"No, I mean, is it safe? For you?"

"Do not be afraid," she says, rubbing her wiry pubic hair against him and guiding him with her hand. "Oh," she gasps, holding his cock.

"What?"

"Is like song. . . ."

"What song?"

"I think you turning Japanese."

"I think I like it better with the bite spliced in," Laura says. "Willie, play it back again please," she asks the editor.

The tape squeakily rewinds then rolls. "We have an excellent relationship with the Chinese government in Beijing. And we have an excellent relationship with the Hong Kong government. But we don't know about the Chinese government in Hong Kong and that unknown makes people somewhat nervous."

"I think that says it all," Laura says. "And he's the managing director of TexCal, so. . . ."

"It's just a whinge," Edie says. "There's nothing to support it."

"Just like assurances from your average government officials. . . ."

"Touché," Edie says. "Point taken."

"The bite captures the uncertainty that people are feeling, despite their hopes for the best. And we could add a shot of that building that's been airbrushed out of the skyline on the new stamps because the company reincorporated in the Bahamas, the one with the portholes, you know, the round windows. . . ."

"The house of a thousand assholes," Edie says. "Yes. . . ."

"I shot that footage for BB Wolf. . . ."

"Okay, Willie, splice it in," Edie says. "Where will that put the time?"

"About two-fifty," the editor says.

"And that's perfect," Laura says. "I'll find that building footage. The sheet is. . . ." She glances at her watch, which reads 1:17 a.m. "Shit, too late. Remind me first thing tomorrow to call Jeff before we start shooting."

"Or we'll call it the house of a thousand and one assholes."

CHAPTER 18

'Twas the Day Before the Night Before

"SINCE ANDY CALLED IN SICK," Franklin tells Laura in his office, "I'll need you on the border with Old Hartman."

"But. . . ."

"That's what I need you to do, Laura. I really need you, desperately."

"But what about my show?"

"I really need someone for the show," Franklin says, "desperately."

"I can do it after the live shot, Peter," Pussy says, adjusting her breasts inside her tube top. She then bends from the waist, exposing cavernous cleavage while running her hands down the bare leg below her short-shorts to adjust a strap on her open toed, five-inch black heels. "Is this a good show, Peter?"

"Back in thirty," Quickie says.

Laura shakes her head. That's at least three times she's dozed off during her show, she realizes. She barely slept last night, finishing the packages with Edie, then logging and entering those scripts into the system for the other producers, here and in New York. She paws through her *AM Asia* scripts to find the right page. "Back to Candy for the promo, then the board, then to a two-shot for the goodbye," she says into the microphone to the set. She glances at the clock. "We're long, so keep it short, under thirty."

"Okay," Fang and Deng say simultaneously, then smile at each other.

"Three, two, one . . . cue," Quickie says.

"Our special handover coverage begins tonight at ten Hong Kong time. That's ten in Singapore, eleven in Tokyo, and 7:30 in New Delhi. Deng and I will be right back here for that. For now, that's all from us this hour in Hong Kong, June 30, 1997. I'm Candace Fang saying thanks for watching."

"Thanking you for your time this time until next time, I'm Deng Jiang Mao, reminding you to 'Buy low, sell high' and have a profitable day on this final day of colonial rule in Hong Kong. Stay with FGN Asia all day and all night for complete coverage of the historic events. Remember, FGN Asia means business in Asia. Candy and I will see you again tonight."

"Three, two, one, finish," Quickie says.

"That was tight, folks," Laura says.

"We don't miss time cues about here," Deng says, "any more."

"Good job, everybody. Save some energy for tonight," Laura says.

She gathers her scripts and rushes out of the control room, meeting Deng and Fang as they come off the set.

"Man, I wish we could go home now," Laura says.

"This is one day it's worth having our ten o'clock," Deng says. "Do we have someone coming in to talk about the Hong Kong market?"

Laura realizes that logging the Volpecello/Edie tapes had preoccupied her last week and she hadn't booked a guest. "I'll check. I'll try."

"That's important," Deng says. "We can't just mail this in. It's part of the handover . . ."

"Stupid," the three of them say.

Laura drags herself to Edie's slot overlooking the newsroom and helps herself to a chocolate-covered cherry from the open box on the counter. As usual, Edie has a phone to her ear. She smiles at Laura. "Yes, we have the permits. . . . No, we're not the BBC. . . . That's correct. . . . Good. . . . Thank you." She hangs up the phone. "Bloody bureaucrats are worried about our truck at LegCo. How are you feeling today, darl'?"

"Exhausted," Laura says.

"A tad gamey, as well, I'll wager."

"I turned your underwear inside out, so it'll be good for another few hours."

"It's come to that for the wife of the king of ladies' pants."

"Don't remind me," Laura says. "Listen, I screwed up and didn't book a guest for ten. Deng wants. . . ."

"I saw there was no booking slip, so I called Alan Ong from Perpetual. Sara uses him often for *Market Wrap*. He's quite clever, and a real dear who also has to work today. He'll be here for C block, and pre-interview is in."

"Thank you, thank you, thank you."

"I got it done Friday. Before we were all in a state. . . ."

"Now I'm feeling better. I feel like it will all be under control, once I get a little sleep."

"A bit busy for sleeping up on 28 right now. . . ."

"I'll try my desk and pray no one commits news until ten."

"Make it eleven," Edie says.

Laura inserts the guest into her ten o'clock rundown, messages Deng to tell him, and lays her head down on the desk. Shouts through Franklin's open office door wake her.

"That's unacceptable, Pete. No. I could accept it with Christina. But this . . . this I cannot accept."

"So Mike, what are you going to do?" Franklin says in a normal voice.

Silence throughout the newsroom.

"You walk," Franklin continues, "you know what you walk away from. It's up to you."

"I expect to be on air plenty out there. When those Chinese troops come goose-stepping over the border, you have that camera. . . ."

"Talk to the producer. . . ."

"I'm talking to you, Pete."

"And I've stopped listening, Mike."

Laura pretends she's asleep as Old Hartman stomps to her desk and then stomps away.

She lifts her head when she feels a tap on her shoulder. It's Franklin. "Smoke?" he says calmly. She gets up, and Franklin motions for Edie to follow them to the stairway. As the fire door slams behind him, Franklin says, "I just want you to understand about Mike."

"I've been trying since I've been here," Edie says, lighting a cigarette.

"He thought he'd be the star of the handover coverage." Chook-koo. "He's got this whole idea about it being history and him being a historic figure." Franklin imitates Old Hartman, " 'It's the reason I came to Hong Kong, Pete, because I've always been there when history has been made. You remember, I reported live from inside the Trojan Horse. . . .' "

"A legend in his own mind," Edie says.

"I just wish he was history already," Franklin says. "I stuck him as far from the Convention Center as possible. I figure he can't do much damage out at the border. Who's he going to overwhelm with his pomposity there?"

"Those Hakka rice farmers can get rather testy," Edie says.

"I'm worried about him trying to buttonhole a Chinese general and winding up in a gulag." Chook-koo.

"That sounds like a plan," Edie muses.

"I almost put Andy out there with him, but if you have two grumps together, they convince each other that they're right and that's an accident waiting to happen."

"Richard will keep him in line," Edie says.

"You, too, Laura," Franklin says. "Don't let him walk all over you. When it's time to take him, take him, but don't let him hog the broadcast. He's dying for US face time."

"All right," Laura says.

"And Edie, have a PA try your lunch, just in case. We can replace PAs."

"This market has been ramped up like a roller coaster," says Alan Ong, a dapper Malaysian-Chinese in his forties with slicked-down hair, a subtle pinstripe in his elegant brown suit, and a slight British lilt to his voice. "And you know what happens when the roller coast reaches the top of the hill."

"So you think Hong Kong investors are in for a wild ride," Deng says.

"That's an optimistic view. I see the market heading for a precipitous drop, followed by a lot of twists and turns and further dips."

"But surely there are solid, fundamental reasons behind the Hang Seng's record high. . . ."

"It's not polite to say this, but I think political factors are behind the market's rise. Tycoons here want to show their confidence about the handover . . ."

"Six minutes, go long as you want," Laura whispers into Deng's ear. "Great stuff."

". . . so they've been pouring liquidity into the market."

"But people like Li Ka-shing and Lee Shau Kee—and I'm not suggesting that either of them are doing what you've said—these people haven't become Hong Kong's richest men by losing money in the stock market."

"Of course not . . ."

"Font the guest again," Laura tells Quickie. "Single shot."

"Okay," Quickie says, and, with a couple of jingles of her bracelets, Ashrami makes "Alan Ong, Chief Equity Strategist, Perpetual Holdings" appear on screen.

". . . but the stock market is just a minor component of their overall interests in Hong Kong. The tycoons want to protect their property interests, their utility interests, their retailing interests, all of their other holdings. Keeping the stock market high at this time, while the whole world is watching, serves as an insurance policy for their entire basket of Hong Kong enterprises. And when you look at property prices, which have climbed at an even faster rate than the stock index, you can see that their strategy is working. The record Hang Seng also signals confidence that China will keep its promises in Hong Kong, and that public show of confidence—giving face to Beijing—is likely to win these tycoons favor for their mainland business ventures."

"Ah, but isn't that the real fundamental factor driving the Hong Kong market higher," Deng says, "the enormous potential of mainland China and the dawn of a new era of cooperation between Hong Kong and Beijing?"

"At the concept level, I agree with you that China fever is one of the things driving the market higher. But at the practical level, I don't see many attractive investments. . . ."

"We need to get out in about two and a half," Laura tells Deng. "Maybe one more question." Quickie nods. She releases the lever to his IFB and tells Quickie, "I know we've got nearly four minutes, but these boys are pretty chatty."

"The infrastructure plays are, in reality, cash calls for risky projects," Ong says. "H-shares and so-called red chips present enormously complex, virtually opaque structural and governance issues, and the newly issued red chips are priced for the most favorable injection scenarios, basically gambling that the government will give away assets for the benefit of private investors."

"So Perpetual didn't bid for hot new issue stocks such as Guangdong Holdings or Beijing Enterprises. . . ?"

"We passed on those."

"But, as you know, investors . . ."

"Roll the queue VO," Laura says, asking for the tape of the brawl among people waiting on line to submit their applications for shares.

"Rolling," Quickie says.

". . . were fighting to get those shares, literally," Deng says. "Doesn't that indicate widespread investor enthusiasm that will drive prices higher?"

"Nice. You've got about a minute and a half," Laura tells Deng. "And, yes, we're rolling the VO."

Deng checks the monitor, sees the VO and gives a thumbs-up.

"It signals enthusiasm, but it's unfounded enthusiasm," Ong says. "It's not finance but fashion, a fad, and Hong Kong people love fads. . . ."

"Lose the VO," Laura says. "Two-shot."

"The mania for China shares is more similar to the interest in McDonald's Snoopy dolls, which also caused fistfights on queues, than it is an indicator of rational analysis by serious investors."

"Let's take a look at where the Hong Kong market index stands right now."

"Gimme that board," Laura says.

"In early trading on this eve of Chinese sovereignty, the Hang Seng Index is off twelve points, that's less than a tenth of a percent, virtually unchanged, hovering near Friday's record high."

"Lose the board," Laura says, then pushes the button. "Last question and wrap it up. Two-shot."

"That doesn't look like the start of a precipitous dive, Alan," Deng says.

"One of the hazards of my profession is that you don't simply have to be right, but you have to be right at the right time."

"Where do you see the Hang Seng a year from now?"

"Out," Laura tells Deng.

"At Perpetual, we project the Hang Seng at the 10,500 level in twelve months. . . ."

"That's a 25 percent drop."

"That's a level that more closely reflects the fundamental value of the market."

"We'll have you back in a year to check that prediction. But we'll have to leave it there for now. . . ."

"After Deng, Candy," Laura says, holding down the A-2 lever, "one-shot, no goodbye, fifteen seconds."

"Our guest has been Alan Ong, chief equity strategist at Perpetual Holdings in Hong Kong. Thank you, Alan."

"Thank you, Deng," Fang says. "That's all for this segment of *Money-Go-Round.* After the break, we'll be back with a comprehensive look at tonight's Hong Kong handover. . . ."

"Promo board," Laura says.

". . . Our special handover coverage begins tonight at ten Hong Kong time, ten in Singapore, eleven in Tokyo, and nine in Bangkok. Deng and I will be hosting that report all night . . ."

"Lose the board," Laura says, "and be ready to cut audio."

". . . so stay right here for more on the handover."

"Stop," Laura says. "Get us out."

The robot camera pulls back from the anchors. "Clear," Quickie announces.

"Okay," Laura tells the anchors, "five seconds to spare. Nice, Candy. Great interview, Deng."

Deng nods and turns to shake hands with the guest. He and Fang unplug their IFBs. Deng continues talking to the guest, who lingers over his handshake with Fang. Deng sidles alongside and keeps talking as Ong walks toward the door with Fang.

Laura says, "Back in a minute" to Quickie and rushes to the door to thank the guest. She exits the control room as the trio leaves the studio.

"I'm just surprised to hear that view," Deng is saying, "coming from a fellow Chinese."

"Money is colorblind," Ong says.

"But. . . ." Deng continues.

"Alan," Laura says, "I have to get back in the control room, but I just wanted to thank you for coming. That was a heck of an interview, gentlemen." She smiles at Ong and at Deng.

"I always enjoy coming here," Ong says, "And meeting Candace Fang is a special treat, a lovely excuse to send more flowers. . . ."

Fang smiles shyly and says, *"Xie-xie,"* placing her fingers to her nose to cover her mouth.

"We'll cut some sound bites from there, so you'll probably be seeing yourself throughout the day and night," Laura says.

"The voice of doom," Deng says smiling.

"I just hope nothing I said comes back to haunt me," Ong says.

"The desk will arrange your ride back," Laura says. "Thanks again for coming, and I hope you'll be a guest with us again, a lot sooner than next June 30th." Laura extends her hand.

Ong shakes it. "My pleasure. I enjoy your programs. Which way to the desk?"

"Candy can show you," Laura says, smiling at Fang. "Gotta go, but thanks, and see you both tonight." Laura turns and goes through the door to the control room.

"Honest, get that interview tape and cut three bites. The one about the roller coaster. The one about Li Ka-shing and Lee Shau Kee. And the one . . . it starts with talking about 'the concept is right.'"

Honest nods as she gets out of her seat.

"Quickie, roll that feature block tape and wake me up when it's over," Laura says, laying her head on her scripts. "Or if a nuclear bomb hits."

Minutes later, Franklin enters the room and nudges Laura's shoulder, leaving his hand there. "Go home," he says softly. "Get a decent sleep and be back here, fired up. Both of you," he adds, looking at Quickie. "I'll watch the tape. Go."

They leave the control room. Quickie heads for the elevators. "See you tonight," Laura says, as she heads to the slot.

"What brings you here?" Edie asks with mock surprise. "You have a show to re-run."

"Peter ordered me to go home. Do you have everything. . . ?"

"Obey the man. We'll survive without you for eight hours."

"I'll be back by six."

"Seven is early enough."

"Six. I don't want anyone committing history without me."

Laura sleeps in the cab until it takes the big turn at the top of the hill onto Robinson Road, dozes on her feet in the elevator until the scrape above eight, slides through the door into the apartment, and sets her alarm for 4:30. Jeff is at the office, so she leaves him a note to wake her up at 4:30 and have dinner ready by 5:00. Then she dives into bed face first, asleep before hitting the pillow.

Jeff wakes her with a kiss just as her alarm goes off. She pulls him into bed with her for an overdue lovemaking session. He's slow to warm to the task, but eventually gives Laura a lengthy ride. "Wow. That sure made up for those missed classes," Laura says afterward as he lays on the bed exhausted. "I get the first shower." She bounds to the bathroom while he wonders how long he can keep up the pace with Laura and Yogi. Then he smiles, wonders what he's complaining about, puts on his tee-shirt and shorts, and heads for the kitchen. He calls into the bathroom, "No wine, right?"

"I'm already drunk," Laura replies. "But I need to be sober for tonight. Thanks."

He checks the wok of baby *bok choy* with carrots, tree ears, garlic, green onions and ginger, briefly stir fried in sesame oil and light soy sauce, then steamed with an added splash of vinegar. Yogi was kind to share the recipe, Jeff thinks. Laura gets something out of this re-ray-son-sip, too.

When he hears the shower stop, he brings plates, utensils, then glasses and water to the coffee table, scoops the veggies into one bowl and rice from the rice cooker into another, and carries them the five steps across the apartment as Laura sits on the loveseat wrapped in a towel. She fills her plate as Jeff pours her a glass of water.

"When I was a little girl, I remember seeing people on TV eating breakfast in their bathrobes, which I thought were towels, and I thought that was so cool," Laura says with a smile. "For a while, I even did it myself, ate in a towel. I must have been three or four. But I never realized I could do this." She opens her robe and flashes Jeff.

"Yummy," he says.

"So's this," she says with her mouth full. "If you ever get tired of ladies' underwear, you could have a future in cooking."

"Thanks. Ready for your big night?"

"After all those nights sleeping in the office, I better be ready, right?" She pauses to chew.

"I missed you, but I understand. After all, sometimes I need to be in China. . . ."

"Tonight feels like prom night. After all that gossip, the scrambling for dates and the catfights, here we are. We had our disaster with the Wolf Woman, so that should mean smooth sailing, knock wood." She raps the table. "We're all dressed up, we'll be out past dawn, and. . . ." Laura's mobile phone rings. "Oh god. Let's hope nobody else's date has canceled."

She goes to the bedroom for her phone and carries it back to the love seat. "I can't really hear you. . . . Yes, that's better. . . . Oh, Brian, yes, how are you?. . . Edie is probably busy prepping for tonight. She'll be reporting, you know. . . . Yes, on the air. . . . I'm sure. . . ." Laura takes a forkful of food and chews as she listens. "Okay, okay, slow down. What's your source?. . . No, I haven't, but I'll take your word. What about the bank?. . . But officially?. . . Okay. Now back up for me. What's it mean if they float the boat?. . . Okay, the baht, what's it mean if Thailand floats the baht?" She takes another forkful of food, and hasn't quite finished chewing when she says, "But there's no way, not now, with the handover. The peg is solid." She swallows. "Do people really care? I mean, we don't even have boards for those currencies. . . . The stock markets? All of them?. . . I believe you. . . . I understand. . . . I understand it could be huge. But we have a saying around here, 'It's the handover, stupid.' We're focused on that right now. Did you try Sara? She's filling in for Edie. . . . Did you message?. . . When do you think you'll get back to the office?. . . Listen, I think we need something harder than what you've got—I mean it's really only a rumor. . . . No, I understand that, but should we be reporting rumors? Especially if you think it could have the impact you say it would. . . . I'll talk to Peter and Edie and see what they say. . . . Yeah, if you get something firm, call me or Sara, she's on the desk. . . . Yeah, I know, 'the handover, stupid.' But I really appreciate the heads up. Keep digging. . . . Thanks. . . . Okay. Will do. . . . Cheers."

She switches off the phone and takes another forkful of food. "Our reporter in Bangkok. He's got a rumor about a currency devaluation, claims it's really important. But tonight, it's the handover, stupid, and nothing but the stupid handover." She cleans her plate and clicks for the time on her phone. "Geez, late. I better get going." She gets up from the loveseat, flashes Jeff again, and trots to her bedroom. She returns dressed and made up—since when does she wear make up to the station, Jeff wonders—as he's clearing the table, holding their stacked plates in one hand and the bowl of veggies in the other, gives him a peck on the cheek, and says, "Wish me luck. And if you go to a bar, go to one with cable so you can watch us."

"Good luck, sweetheart. Break a leg."

He carries the plates to the kitchen, puts away the leftovers, hears the elevator scrape on its way up and its way down, then dials the phone. Laura's story sounds like the story Moishe told about the shekel: "If I was an expert in money," he said, "I could be rich." No answer at Yogi's house, so he calls her mobile.

"Hello," Yogi answers in a noisy background.

"*Moshi-moshi*. It's Jeff. I need to ask you about something, now. . . ."

"I cannot hear you. Come to Lan Kwai Fong. Chinese Godown. You are very expensive to me."

"What. . . ?" he asks, but she's already clicked off her phone.

Jeff showers quickly, puts on good clothes, khaki pants and a blue button-down shirt. The sun may not have set on this last corner of the British Empire in Asia yet, but it rained all afternoon and is threatening again now. Still Jeff decides against lugging an umbrella and heads down the hill. He walks alongside the escalator, jammed with tourists and unlucky people heading home from their offices, the one who didn't get a holiday today to make a four-day weekend. At intersections, along with property agents handing out bilingual flyers, he passes vendors selling handover tee-shirts. One model shows a worker in a conical straw hat painting over the British Union Jack with China's red flag with the yellow stars in the corner. Another has Hong Kong Island between a pair of chopsticks with the caption, "The Great Chinese Take-Away."

"Excuse me," a woman with an American accent dripping with honeysuckle asks, "where's the down escalator?"

"One escalator, two directions," Jeff replies. "But only one at a time. All up now. Walk down."

At Lan Kwai Fong, a horseshoe of streets lined with bars that Hong Kong's expats frequent, Jeff gets waved through the police barrier—a precaution for big events after celebrants got crushed to death a few New Year's Eves ago, Yogi said—and begins searching for Chinese Godown. The street is already busy with revelers, warming up for the big night and holiday ahead. By the time he finds the bar, halfway up the second leg of the horseshoe, Jeff's sweated through the back of his shirt and gets a chill from the blast of the air conditioning, highly effective despite the bar's open front to the street. He slips through the crowd at the bar and finds Yogi in the back with her friends gathered around two round cocktail tables pushed together.

"Hello," he says to Yogi, standing beside her at the table.

"Hi, Jeff," she says, not yet drunk but happy. "You need chair."

He gets one from another table and pushes into the circle next to her. The table is filled with drinks, ashtrays, cigarette boxes and mobile phones.

"This is Jeff," Yogi says over her glass of white wine. "He is not banker, but still friend."

The others, four men and two woman, introduce themselves: Mike, American by his accent; Tom, British, wearing a terrycloth Union Jack top hat; Raj, Indian; Gilbert, Chinese; Winnie, also Chinese; and Sophie, British. All are dressed in business suits, and none appears over 30.

"I couldn't find this place," Jeff says.

"Yes, you don't see Chinese go down often," Mike says, "I'm still looking. . . ."

"Keep talking that way, and you never will see it," Winnie says.

"If you're going to join us, then you must expose your phone, sir," Tom, drinking beer from a fluted glass beside an oversized can, tells Jeff.

"It's a game we play," Mike explains, seated behind a scotch on the rocks. "You put your phone on the table. Whoever's rings first has to pay for the next round of drinks."

"You call me, I have to pay," Yogi whines with a smile.

"Mike is our telecoms expert," Raj explains, seated behind a beer stein. "He carries with him always his emergency number."

"But a number which you can't call, which only he can call upon," Sophie says, drinking an apparent gin and tonic, with a smirk.

"And I reckon you call it often," Tom says, with a bigger smirk.

"Gimme a break," Mike says, then, in an aside to Jeff, adds, "If you ever need something—smoke, blow, whatever—get in touch. I can hook you up."

"They have that stuff here?" Jeff asks.

"Crossroads of Asia, pal," Mike says. "Yogi's got my number."

"Haven't we all?" Sophie chuckles.

"So, James, was it. . . ?" Tom begins.

"Jeff. . . ."

"Jeff," Tom continues, "place your phone on the table please."

"I don't have a mobile phone," Jeff confesses.

"No shit," Mike says.

"Then this calls for a ruling," Sophie says. "As the British queen of this table. . . ."

"I thought that was Tom," Mike says, swirling his glass.

"I'm the sovereign here," Sophie insists.

"Only for another five hours, 28 minutes," Raj interjects, consulting his plump watch.

"I rule that Jeff will pay for the next round," Sophie declares, "if no phones ring."

"Splendid decision," Tom applauds.

"There's an element of unfairness in it, however" Raj reasons. "Whether we pay or not is dependent on our popularity, so there is an element of control for us in it. Whereas for Jeff here, there is no element of control. He is simply a pawn, completely at the mercy of our sparkling personalities."

"Sounds like the stock market," Sophie says.

"Very unlikely for him to pay," Gilbert, holding a tall glass of what appears to be orange juice, says. "If we each receive fifteen personal calls a day, approximately one per waking hour, the chances are only one in 360, approximately, that Jeff will pay."

"Then we'd better drink quickly, just to make it sporting," Tom says, topping off his glass from the can and taking a gulp.

"Gilbert is a quant, in case you didn't guess," Mike says.

"Do you all work with Yogi?" Jeff asks.

"We are all in banking and investments," Raj says, "but we spread ourselves amongst a number of institutions. I work at Morley, fund management."

"I wanted to ask about something I heard, about floating currency," Jeff begins.

"Oh, no, another speculator against the Hongkie," Sophie squeals.

"Queue forms to the rear," Tom says, adjusting his hat.

"No, about the Thai dollar, the baht," Jeff says. "I heard a rumor that they're going to . . . what is it? . . . float the baht."

"That rumor has come and gone for weeks," Mike shrugs. "I trade currencies for Stagan. Here," he says, fishing into his coat pocket. "Here's my card," he says, presenting it to Jeff with both hands, thumbs peeking over the upper edge.

"Thanks. So does that mean there's something to it?" Jeff asks.

"It means it's a popular rumor," Mike shrugs.

"It is quite obvious, though, that the Central Bank of Thailand has been extremely active in the market," Raj says.

"Every central bank is active in currency markets," Mike replies, "especially when it has a managed float. . . ."

"A mismanaged float or slippery peg might be more accurate," Raj says. "If you look at the volumes, though, you must wonder where CBT is obtaining the hard currency necessary for this level of intervention."

"If it's even CBT money," Mike says. "We don't know. . . ."

"But you think it's possible that it's true?" Jeff asks.

"Anything is possible," Mike says. "A meteor could crash through the ceiling of this place right now. The handover might not happen. . . ."

"God save the Queen," Tom says.

"But it's not very likely," Mike continues. "You have to make decisions based on what's likely to happen, not on some rumor you catch in a tip sheet."

"But have we considered what would happen if the baht were to float?" Sophie asks.

"Thailand would sink, of course," Tom says.

"Actually, that's a very interesting proposition," Gilbert says. "If the baht cannot sustain its peg, I don't believe it would be possible for other regional currencies without massive reserves to sustain their pegs."

"The rupiah would collapse," Winnie says. "Move to 5,000, at least."

"The rupiah in India?" Jeff asks.

"Rupiah is Indonesia," Yogi tells him. "Winnie trades bonds at Commercial."

"Yes," Winnie says. "Bond prices would fall, and so would stock prices."

"A perfect storm," Raj says.

"Impossible," Tom says.

"Usually if bonds go down, then stocks go up," Yogi explains to Jeff.

"But here," Winnie says, "the fundamental value of the unit is under attack, the money itself, so internationally the money is worth less. That would create a blood bath."

"And, after suitable triage, all of us would be dispatched to our home countries forthwith," Raj adds.

"How could the banks possibly function without us?" Sophie says.

"It's nonsense," Mike insists. "It can't happen. Besides, all of us masters of the universe are locked away from our screens until Friday. Even if they wanted to sell, who would they find to trade with?"

"That would make the timing positively exquisite," Raj says wistfully. "But I must agree: it is highly unlikely."

A phone rings. Everyone looks expectantly at the middle of the table.

"Go on, Tom," Sophie says.

Tom reluctantly plucks his phone from the clutch, gets up and walks away from the table.

"Everyone drink up," Mike says. "Anybody hear this Chinese guy on FGN Asia today?"

"Malaysian, actually," Raj says.

"He makes a good bit of sense," Gilbert says.

"So is your family selling its flat?" Sophie asks.

"The difficulty is that we'd still need somewhere to live," Gilbert says.

"Just rent one from Winnie's family," Sophie suggests.

"My father is selling our place in Causeway Bay," Winnie says. "I am quite sad because I grew up there."

"No room for sentimentality in a boom," Raj says.

"So your father thinks there's a bubble?" Mike asks.

Tom returns to the table. "Bubble? Did you hear that fellow on FGN Asia. . . ?"

"We were talking about that," Mike says.

"I thought his head was stuck up his own fragrant harbor," Tom says.

"So you believe the gains of the Hang Seng are sustainable?" Raj says.

"I have never seen so many 200-day breakouts," Gilbert says. "It is phenomenal."

"But this place is phenomenal," Mike says.

"I agree," Sophie says. "Drink up to phenomenal Hong Kong and the phenomenal people here, like us."

"Cheers," the crowd says and drinks.

"But is it sustainable?" Raj asks.

"Historically, it is not," Gilbert says.

"History, I've heard, has come to an end," Tom says.

"And so has my drink," Sophie says. "Another flagon, my good man."

"I'll get the waitress," Mike says. "And Tom gets the check, with another mouth to feed. What're you drinking, Joe?"

"Jeff. But I think I need to go," he says and turns to Yogi. "Can I talk to you for a second? Outside?"

"Jeff is kidnap me," Yogi says. "I will escape and have another chardonnay, please."

They get up and walk out of the bar into the noisy street. "Is there anywhere quiet around here?" Jeff asks.

"In Hong Kong?" Yogi smiles then points downhill to a small public sitting area, standard Hong Kong concrete benches with hedges in planters next to a public restroom. They stand by the planters.

"I heard something from the Israeli guys, but you know more about this foreign currency stuff than I do," Jeff says. "What do you think of this rumor about the baht?"

"You must pay for this kind of advice."

"Pay?"

Yogi puckers her lips.

"Here?"

"Your wife and her friends all busy now," she says, initiating a passionate kiss. "Much better," she says. "You hear this baht rumor from Israeli *schmatte* seller. . . ?"

"No, no," Jeff says, "It was a phone conversation between my wife and a reporter in Thailand."

"Then I think rumor is possible. I am not following Thai economy closely but is imbalance in money flows. This could lead to devaluation. . . ."

"The Israelis said there's some way to make money when the currency devaluates. So how do you do it? How would you try to make money?"

"You are serious," Yogi says, looking into Jeff's eyes.

"Yes."

"Why?"

"Because I want to make money. Like everybody else here is, except me. Look at all your pals in there with their fancy suits and their watches and the way they think they run the world. I want to be like that."

"Sure?"

"Why not? Why not me? Why can't I? Because of my mother? Fuck my mother."

Yogi hugs Jeff. "Please do not stop to be like you."

"I'd like to try being like me, only richer. A me that doesn't have to rely on my mother for my allowance and my wife to pay the rent. A me who can afford to take you out for dinner or buy you a nice present once in a while. . . ."

"So sweet."

"So what would you do about the baht?"

"Trading currency, I would join speculator. They may not be correct, but downside risk is neg . . . negli . . . not great."

"Why?"

"Maybe baht will not fall, but is quite unlikely to appreciate."

"So how would you do it? How do you make money from it?"

"You must take forward position in currency."

"What's that?"

"You make contract to deliver baht in 30 day or 60 day or 90 day, and you receive present value of baht in dollar."

"I don't understand. I don't have baht."

"If baht is now 25 to one US dollar, you make contract to deliver 25 million baht and you get one million dollar, minus commissions and spread. In 60 day, you must give 25 million baht. If rate is 30 baht per dollar, then baht is cost 850,000 dollar and profit is 150,000 dollar. But if rate change to 20 baht per dollar, then baht cost 1.2 million dollar, so is 200,000 dollar loss."

"I see," Jeff nods. "Can you make smaller contracts?"

"You must ask to broker."

"Do you know a broker?"

"There are many. But they all close now. In US or London can try. They will also make contract for baht."

"Do you think that 30 baht is realistic?"

"Is quite large movement, but possible. People take large contracts in order to profit from small movement. Also is depend on length of contract."

"So how long. . . ?"

"I would not take less than 60 day and would ladder."

"Radder?"

"Build ladder, some for 60 day," Yogi explains, putting one hand out flat, palm down, "some 90 day," placing the other palm above it, "some 120. . . ." moving the lower palm above the other one. "But I would not use baht. I would use Indonesian rupiah."

"Why?"

"Raj is correct," Yogi says. "If Thai baht is float, then rupiah and other currency also float, and rupiah is most vulnerable. Indonesia quite corrupt and have many debt must pay in dollar. So if currency is floating, rupiah will sink most far, I believe." Yogi sighs. "But this is only my opinion. You will not angry with me if you lose money?"

"Of course not, this is my idea."

"Sure?"

"Positive," Jeff says. As far as he's concerned he's got nothing to lose. "Would you do it now, or would you wait?"

"Markets will react to announcement, and Raj is correct also that holiday is good time for announcement. If wait, opportunity may vanish."

"I see." Jeff sighs again. "You would do this?"

"If trading currency, yes."

"You're not duh-lunk?"

Yogi wrinkles her nose. "I would try. But is risky."

"Well, I'm already taking some big risks." Jeff initiates a long kiss, then says, "Thank you. I should try to call my friend in New York. He's a broker or something." He pats Yogi's back and they wade uphill into the thickened crowd of drinkers on the street, holding cocktails and conversations in clusters.

"You will watch handover with me?" Yogi asks in front of the bar. "I will to LegCo later to see democrats' speech."

"I'll call you."

"No, I will call you. I do not want to pay more drink."

Jeff gives Yogi a kiss on the cheek, picks his way through the crowd and rides the escalator back home. He resists the temptation to buy handover tee-shirts from vendors, thinking that, one way or the other, he'll find them more affordable in a few weeks.

Back at the apartment, he heats up a plate of rice and veggies in the microwave, waits until after eight o'clock, and dials his friend Tim's office in Manhattan.

"Stafford here."

"Yo, Timmy boy, it's Jeff. . . ."

"Jeff, my man. Still in Hong Kong?"

"If I wasn't, I'd take the *Golden Beauty* back."

"How's it going over there?"

"You got my letter?"

"Yeah. What is up with that Japanese chick?"

"Oh, she's okay."

"But you, fucking around with little foreign women with dark hair?" Tim laughs.

"You can take the bear out the woods, but he still shits. You?"

"I'm okay. Working too hard, living in a place on 31st Street, an old garment loft. They probably used to make girdles in there for your old man."

"Hey, that's great."

"Out with the bras, in with the brokers."

"How is the *Golden Beauty?*"

"Still afloat. I might move in there when my lease is up. If you're not back by then, I mean. I put in an application for a berth at the 79th Street Boat Basin. That boat's the greatest pussy magnet on wheels."

"Glad to hear it. Don't let your meat loaf."

"Right. Hey, over there, it's the big changeover tonight, right?"

"Yeah. And over here it's already tonight. Laura's excited about it, working all the time. Maybe things will get back to normal when the Communists finally do take over."

"So, you calling to request political asylum?"

"I want to ask about currency trading."

"I don't do that, but the firm does. I can tell you what I know, then connect you to someone. You're looking to protect yourself on payments for shipments?"

"Sort of. I want to know about—what do they call it?—I agree to deliver the foreign currency by a certain date in the future. . . ."

"Forwards. You want to play the exchange rate, hedge in case the local counter drops?"

"Something like that."

"What's the currency over there? Hong Kong dollars?"

"Well, yeah, but I'm interested in the Indonesian rupiah."

"Whoa. Geez. . . ."

"You can't do it?"

"I'm sure our desk does it, but I don't know shit about it. I do know that with an exotic currency like that you're looking at big spreads, probably five-six percent, plus whatever the projected movement might be. Here, listen, I can take a look for you. Let me just punch it up on the screen."

"I hear those fingers dancing on the keyboard."

"The new capitalist's piano. Remember when we failed typing together. . . ."

"General Sherman. F-f-f space, j-j-j space. . . ."

"Okay, INDR. What's your time frame?"

"I want to do it today."

"No, I mean the contract. Thirty days, 60, 90?"

"Start with 60."

"Geez, these are telephone numbers. The rate's 2,675. The forward for 60 is 2,873."

"So what's that mean?"

"Basically, it means that if you contract for 10,000 US, you'll get 260,750,000 rupiah, but need to deliver 280,730,000—and I could be off a zero there, one way or another. With commissions and everything, that's about 900 bucks."

"What do mean 900 bucks?"

"It means it's costing about 900 bucks you to protect yourself on 10,000 dollars, like nine percent."

"I don't get what you mean about protecting. . . ."

"I'm talking about using the forward as a hedge against movement in the rupiah."

"What about if it's purely speculation?"

"Whatever."

"But what would it mean then?"

"No difference. Whatever you're doing it for, the numbers don't change. You'd need the rupiah to fall nine percent just to break even."

"And nine percent is a lot?"

"Here, lemme have a look," Tim says. "Vegas don't take nine percent at the crap table, I know that," he adds, punching more numbers. "In the past year, the range has been 2.3 percent. . . . In other words, from high to its low in the past year, the rupiah has only moved 2.3 percent. So, yeah, nine percent is pretty big. What you're insuring yourself against—or what you're betting on if you're speculating—is a complete collapse. I have no idea whether that could happen, but you're over there and you know a lot more about it than me."

"Well, maybe," Jeff says, trying to make it sound like a joke. "If I want to do this, what do I need to do?"

"You just write the contracts, or buy them at market."

"And how do I do that?"

"The usual way, with money. How much money you got?"

"I need to pay first?"

"Not the whole thing," Tim says. "You just need to front the commission and spreads."

"So how much, about?"

"Okay, if you're writing a hundred grand of rupiah, you'd need eight for the spread plus another in fees and interest, about $9,000."

"Geez, I haven't got that kind of money. I blew my dad's insurance on the *Golden Beauty.*"

"Well, listen, to make it simple, I can cover you on this stuff up to the value of the boat, like a hundred grand. So you can write like a million dollars of contracts. If you make money, you pay me back at settlement. If you don't, then I keep the boat."

"If I make money, I'll give you the boat."

"Deal. Now what about collateral?"

"Collateral?"

"For the balance. You need to cover the balance, just in case."

"Well, my mother is sitting on a few million in property. . . ."

"No good. And even if it was, that shack in SplitLevelTown ain't worth a million. We'd need the title, too, and it's not in your name anyway, right?"

"Right."

"Maybe your mother can guarantee it with. . . ."

"Let's leave my mother out of this."

"Okay, no mothers. How about bank accounts, stocks, bonds?"

"I don't have anything like a million bucks."

"What about your wife?"

"What about my wife?"

"Has she got stocks, bonds, bank accounts?"

"I can do that? Use her money?"

"You're married," Tim says. "What's hers is yours, at least as far as our underwriters are concerned. . . ."

"So I need to send you her money? That wouldn't work. . . ."

"As long as you make the right bet, or can cover the losses if you're wrong, we don't touch the collateral. But we need to have the account numbers, just in case, to open your account."

"I don't know about that. . . ."

"Talk to her and see what's she got, what she says. . . ."

"I want to do this today," Jeff says, trying not to sound too anxious.

"It's early. I can get you set up with an account, and I'll talk to our guys on the currency desk. We can probably write the contracts through London, use your Hong Kong address, and save you the taxes, but we're gonna need collateral. *Capiche?*"

"Okay."

"Call me back in fifteen, twenty minutes. If it's okay on your end, I'm sure we can get you rolling."

"All right. Thanks, Tim."

"Hey, no problem, pal. Later."

Jeff hangs up and goes to Laura's room, then turns back and dials her mobile phone number.

"This is Laura."

"Hi, sweetheart. It's me, Jeff."

"Jeff. . . ."

"I need to talk to you about getting some money. . . ."

"Look, there's about 500 Hongkies in my closet on the shelf. Just take it. Can't talk. My boss is on the other phone. Bye." She clicks the phone off.

Jeff shakes his head, goes back to her room and opens her closet. He looks past the HK$500 and finds a Hong Kong bankbook. It shows more than HK$250,000, but that's only about $30,000 US. He finds a US bankbook, but that's only got a couple thousand dollars. Then he finds a stack of envelopes from a New York stockbroker held together with a rubber band. Each envelope is neatly slit open at the top, with each statement tucked inside. The May 1997 statement is on top and he can't believe it when he reads the balance of $818,374.08. Lots of eight—a good omen in Chinese, according to Moishe. Where'd she get all this money? Jeff wonders. He figures that maybe she learned enough working as a financial journalist to make some smart moves, and, besides, that house her family had down in Maryland wasn't no SplitLevelTown special. Just what he needs, another rich woman in his life. Maybe this time it will work in his favor.

With his few thousand in the bank and hers, and the Hongkies plus the stocks, he's got over $850,000 he can write contracts on, $850,000 that he can lose. But he's not going to think about that. Yogi says she'd do it, and she's a pro. He'd like to check with her, make sure he understands what she told him to do, but she told him not to call again. So Jeff's just going to have to trust his own judgment. He's got to do it now, tonight, or never. He's got the rest of his life to worry about it if he craps out. All his life, he's been doing things for other people; tonight he can try to do something for himself. With a little help from his friends.

He calls Tim again.

"Stafford on the line."

"Timmy, it's me again, Jeff."

"Hey, how you doin'? Man this connection sounds like you're just next door. You talk to your wife?"

"And my girlfriend. I've got about 850,000 in collateral."

"Good. Now, I talked to the currency trading desk, and they're okay with the Hong Kong thing and going through London, and we figured out how I can do it all for you live on the London market from my screen here. How's that for service?"

"Sounds great."

"Now, I'm going to have to sign you name to our brokerage agreements, just to make things kosher," Tim says. "Otherwise, we have to send you the form and you have to send it back, and you said you want to do it today. You're okay with that, with me signing?"

"Yes." Jeff sighs. "Tim, thanks for your help."

"No problem. Now, I need some info." Jeff answers Tim's questions for the application, giving him his details and Laura's and the various account numbers. He follows Yogi's advice about laddering and writes $100,000 in contracts for 60 days, $300,000 for 90 days and $450,000 for 120 days, all on the rupiah, a currency he'd never heard of until about an hour ago, in a country he (and Tim) couldn't find on a map.

"All in," Tim says, as the orders hit. "I'll have the desk work up the final figures and send a statement, but it looks like you're into me for about 80 grand. You're betting the ranch here, pal, the floating ranch."

"I've got a dumb question, Tim."

"Shoot."

"What do I do now?"

"Well, you watch the rupiah and see what it's doing, and if it starts going the wrong way, you think about bailing out."

"What do you mean?"

"You sell the contracts, shortest ones first, to cover the losses so we don't need to touch the collateral. Your Japanese girlfriend's a banker, right?"

"Yeah."

"Then she can probably explain it to you. Make sure you hang on to her for the next 120 days or so."

"I will. But I want to hear it from you, what I should do."

"Understood," Tim assures him. "You can always sell the contracts. There's a market in them."

"And how much will I get?"

"How ever much the market will pay. Here, for example," Tim says, tapping some keys, "the 60 day rupiah for July 15, is selling at 102 now."

"What's that mean?"

"It means that because the rupiah's gone down some, lost some value, the guy who took a 60 day contact a few weeks ago has to pay less for his rupiah, and there's less interest, than a guy who writes a contract today, so his contract is worth more money."

"How much more?"

"Two percent. Cost is 100, so 102 means you win—though that doesn't include commissions and all that—but 96 means you lose."

"And why would I sell?"

"Well, if you're ahead, you get your winnings off the table. But if you hold it to the end for settlement that's okay, too. But if you sell, you'll save the waiting and some interest."

"Interest?"

"Yeah. See, technically, we're loaning you the money for this, and you're paying us prime plus 250 basis points, about three-quarter points a month."

"You didn't tell me."

"I didn't? Sorry. I figured you knew, but it's no big deal, really. There's other stuff to worry about. Like if your wife's stock portfolio takes a dive, then you'd have to come up with more collateral."

"Geez."

"But I say you burn that bridge when you come to it. Listen, I'll keep an eye on this for you. If it starts to turn sour for any reason, I'll call you right away. Your little banker friend can help you, too. Maybe you can send me some underwear?"

"You need underwear?"

"Some of hers. I hear guys in Japan. . . ."

"Fuck you, Tim. And thanks for all the help."

"Hey, what're friends for?"

"Nah, I really mean it. I wouldn't do any of this if you weren't with me on the other end."

"Thanks. And, I almost forgot. One other thing you gotta do, Jeff, if I were you. Very important," Tim advises.

"What's that?"

"Pray, motherfucker, pray hard."

CHAPTER 19

Handover Night

"LAURA, IT JUST CAME UP yesterday afternoon. . . ."

"I shouldn't find out from the delivery man. You should have told me, Peter."

"Actually, it's was Candy's idea."

"And that makes it a good idea?"

"For what those outfits cost, we ought to get more than one show out of them."

"But it's just so. . . ."

"Yes, it's a little bit of show business. But it doesn't take anything away from the news business. Listen, Old Hartman's out there at Lo Wu, not exactly the jungles of Borneo, and I bet he'll be wearing his official foreign correspondent safari suit. The only safari you can make out there is to Shenzhen Seibu. Should we tell him to change?"

"But that stuff looks like Halloween."

"Maybe to you, Laura. Other people, who've never seen these outfits before, will think they look great. It's a special night, so our anchors have special outfits."

"It's my mobile, Peter. Hang on a second." Laura turns the mouthpiece of the desk phone away from her mouth and answers her mobile. "This is Laura."

"Hi, sweetheart. It's me, Jeff."

"Jeff. . . ."

"I need to talk to you about getting some money. . . ."

"Look, there's about 500 Hongkies in my closet on the shelf. Just take it. Can't talk. My boss is on the other phone. Bye." She clicks the phone off, puts it back on her desk, and talks into the mouthpiece of the desk phone. "Peter, it just seems so silly. . . ."

"Laura, what's silly is that among all the important things tonight, we're discussing this nonsense."

"I agree completely. . . ."

"They're wearing what they're wearing, and everyone's going to love it. Everyone else, anyway. Okay?"

"I'm still not happy about this, Peter."

"But you'll do it, and that's what matters. There are bigger issues tonight."

"Right. . . ."

"Focus on those, Laura. Channel your energy there. Okay?"

"All right, Peter. But I don't agree with. . . ."

"You don't have to. Just do it. For the handover, stupid."

"Right."

"Gladys swears they've got a dish on the boat, so I'll be watching."

"Okay."

"And Laura. . . ."

"Yeah?"

"Thanks for caring so much."

"Just doing my job."

"Doing it right, and I appreciate that."

"Thanks."

"No, thank you. Bye." Franklin clicks off.

Laura sighs. Peter's right there's a lot more important stuff tonight than the anchors' wardrobe.

The newsroom, perfumed in lilies and roses from the bouquets congratulating the network—and particularly Fang—on the upcoming historic day, is nearly empty, except for the buzz of fluorescent lights overhead and the occasional ring of telephones at the desk, where a PA is taking messages, or at the rows of vacant desks. Anna Nissan and Sara Fergis and her *Market Wrap* crew are still on set, doing US live pops. Helios is banging out package leads, tosses and teases. The anchors will arrive around 8:30, along with Quickie and the techs. She hears the clatter of cassettes and boxes from tapes, while the interns sit at the other end of the newsroom, wondering when the pizzas will arrive.

She takes another look at her rundown in the computer, checks the clock—8:17—takes a deep breath. She gets back to work on her rundown for the historic night. She remembers the song: It doesn't matter what you wear, just as long as you are there. And Laura is here, just like she wanted, with a show that, she reminds herself as she resumes typing, isn't going to produce itself.

At 9:54 p.m. Hong Kong time, when the last live pop for the west-coast edition of FGN's *Morning in America* show is done, Sara and crew vacate the control room. Laura, Quickie and their crew scramble in. Deng in Peter's black silk jacket—white wouldn't work on TV—and Candy in her golden cheongsam sit at the new set, a plywood desk covered with a red cloth two feet to the right of the usual anchor table. At the front of the desk, the words "FGN Asia" with the FGN Eagle logo flying above the new Hong Kong bauhinia flag. Behind the desk, a chromakey screen. As the anchors mike up, Deng complains, "Hey, I thought we were getting a Chinese flag on this logo."

"You've got your Chinese costume party," Laura says. "That's enough. Besides, the Hong Kong flag is a Chinese flag."

"Good point," Deng admits.

"Scripts okay?"

"They look fine," Deng says.

"Candy?"

"Ya . . . yes, okay."

Laura surveys the remote shots on the console along the wall in front of her. All those small screens, their purpose unclear until now, display pictures from the set, the broadcast feed, pool feeds from the Convention Center interior, harbor, LegCo floor and border crossing, plus shots from FGN Asia crews at their locations, with masking tape labels indicating their numbers, and more masking tape on the levers showing which microphone connects to which location. She pushes R-1 for Edie. "Test."

"I'm here, *mei-mei*. Everything all right there? See me on your monitor?"

"We're coming to you first, around seven after."

"We've set up here in the vestibule. How do you like our set?" Edie asks, pointing to a mural of the Convention Center and Central skyline behind her.

"Looks great," Laura says.

"Kin-ming found it in Mongkok for ten Hongkies, and I taped it to a sheet."

"Well done."

"I can't go live from inside the hall, but I can try to haul people out here. These charming fellows with me have set up the pool feed on my monitors, so I can give you play by play from inside when you don't take the feed."

"Perfect."

"Have you seen May's package? It's brilliant."

"It rolls ahead of you. Stand by for seven after. We'll do your harbor package, donut version, and use the scripted tag unless there's some news to report."

"I might take that shot outside, for a little variety, if this rain stops bucketing."

"Okay," Laura says, moving to the next lever. "R-2, check."

"Hi Laura," Pang May Pau says, clutching an umbrella adorned with the FGN Asia logo just inside the police barrier at the top of Lan Kwai Fong.

"You've got the rundown, right?"

"Yes."

"Okay, we come to you around thirteen after. At least that's the plan. Stand by." Laura releases the lever. "R-3 check."

"Fiona here."

"Where are you?" Laura asks, since she can't see her in the shot.

"We're set up on the balcony. We can stay dry, get shots of the speakers and can pan down on the crowd. They can turn the camera to shoot me in the wings."

"Sounds good."

"Andy's not here yet, but I'm fine without him."

"Don't tell him that. Try to call him. I've slotted you in for about twenty after, but who knows. Stand by." Laura pushes the next lever. "R-4 check."

"All present and accounted for, ma'am," Old Hartman says, holding his FGN umbrella to keep his safari suit dry. "I'm just worried that we might float way. The last story I covered in rain like this featured animals boarding two-by-two. . . ."

"Stay on dry land until we come to you, probably after the bottom of the hour. Stand by." She releases the lever, and pushes R-1. "Edie."

"Yes?"

"Stay inside. We've got enough people out in the rain. It's a handover, not a hurricane."

"Don't want to overexpose those Fuggin Asia brollies, do we? Understood."

"Thanks." Laura releases the lever and turns to Quickie. "Okay with the rundown?"

"Okay."

"Everybody," she says to the control room at large, "this rundown is a plan, the event's live, so we're gonna rock and roll our way through these next four hours." She punches the A-1 and A-2 levers for the anchors. "If you guys get tired out there, if you need a break, let me know and we'll put in a package or do a live shot without you. Pace yourselves."

Deng and Fang nod, and Laura releases the levers.

"Okay, now remember," she tells Quickie, "we roll the VO and freeze it in the chromakey for the two-shot," then pushes the microphone to the set. "Open in a two-shot."

"Three, two, one. . . ." Quickie says.

Blast off, Laura thinks.

Video rolls of the sun setting behind the concrete canyons of Central, shot on a clear day weeks ago as insurance against today's clouds and rain, as Deng says, "The sun finally sets on the British Empire in Asia, with a new era of Chinese rule on the horizon for Hong Kong." The camera seems to pull back from the video to reveal Deng and Fang in front of the setting sun.

"Good evening from Hong Kong and welcome to FGN Asia's special live coverage of Hong Kong's return to Chinese sovereignty. I'm Deng Jiang Mao."

Laura sighs. She's sure Deng has changed every "handover" in his scripts to "return to Chinese sovereignty" or thereabouts. Well, at least, he's paying attention.

"And I'm Candace Fang. At midnight local time, less than two hours from now, the British Union Jack will be struck for the final time here in Hong Kong, and the colors of the People's Republic of China will unfurl over this city of nearly seven million people."

"At the Convention Center on Victoria Harbor, dignities are assembling for the formal change of sovereignty ceremony," Deng continues. "China's president Jiang Zemin is here, Prime Minister Li Peng will address the celebrants, and Britain's Prince Charles will surrender the colors and leave Britain's colony of more than 150 years via the Royal Yacht *Britannia* as the era of Chinese rule in Hong Kong begins."

Fang continues, "That historic moment is less than two hours away, Deng. But, FGN Asia's Pang May Pau reports, it's already been a busy, emotional day for the retreating British."

"Rolling package," Quickie announces, as the taped report about the day's activities appears.

"Great cut on the open, Quickie."

"Thanks. Chromakey is easy."

"Good work," Laura tells A-1 Deng and A-2 Fang. "Edie says this package is fantastic." She releases the levers and begins watching May's report, the video cutting to people in a formal room.

"After his breakfast, the governor made a final visit to the Legislative Council chamber, posing for pictures with lawmakers, including this group shot with the so-called 'Dirty Dozen,' twelve pro-democracy legislators who, like Patten, are due to lose their jobs when the clock strikes midnight."

"Beijing promised Hong Kong people a 'through train' for our democratically elected legislators," a Chinese man labeled "Martin Lee, Democratic Party Chairman," says. "It is disappointing that this through train has gone off the track so disastrously."

"But many," May continues, "say Governor Patten derailed the train. In last year's election, the governor defied Beijing by opening more legislative seats to election by all Hong Kong voters instead of a small circle of professionals and businesspeople."

"It is clear," a Chinese woman labeled "Margaret Ng, Outgoing Legislator," says, "that Beijing will give Hong Kong only as much democracy it must, and not one iota more."

"I'm disappointed, of course," a sandy-haired western man labeled "Christopher Patten, Hong Kong Governor," says. "Living up to its commitment to democracy would be the best way for Beijing to create a climate of confidence in Hong Kong and in the international community about the future of this great city, this city that my wife Lavender and I have grown to love dearly during our five years here."

The video cuts to the garden of Government House in the rain.

"That those years were fast drawing to a close hit home with Governor Patten at the flag-lowering ceremony at dusk in the garden of Government House. As the honor guard struck the Union Jack and the colonial flag for the last time, tear drops mixed with rain drops on the governor's ruddy cheeks. And he wasn't the only one choking with emotion as these symbols of 156 years of British rule sank into Hong Kong's final imperial sunset."

"Thirty," Quickie announces.

Video cuts to the flag-lowering scene on the giant video screen at Times Square Mall in Causeway Bay with a crowd gathered below in the rain, zooming to a close up of a fortyish Chinese woman crying under an umbrella. An FGN Asia microphone appears in the shot. The woman dabs her eyes with her hand and speaks in Cantonese; the voice of Anna Nissan translates her words.

"I don't love the British but I love Hong Kong, and the British have been good to Hong Kong for so many years. This moment is like the death of a friend. I don't know if Hong Kong people will ever have such a good friend again."

"Ten," Quickie says. "You take Pussy next?" he asks Laura.

"Yes," she says, eyes riveted to the package.

The video cuts back to the teary governor receiving the flags from a policeman in a white dress uniform, then turning to shake hands with a sixtyish Chinese woman, Anson Chan, the top civil servant in Hong Kong, and then embracing her. May narrates: "History teaches that not even the mightiest empires can survive the shifting sands of time. But history also teaches that true friendships can last forever.

"Pang May Pau, FGN Asia, Hong Kong."

"Cue."

Laura looks up at the studio monitor and sees Fang, due to read the next item, in tears. She pushes both anchor levers. "Two-shot. Deng, talk, ask her something."

"That was a very emotional report," Deng says stonefaced. "Candy. . . ."

"I . . . I . . . I cry, too, when I see flag go down," Fang stammers.

"Help her English, Deng. Keep ad libbing," Laura says into the microphone.

"Why did you cry, Candy, when the Union Jack was struck? Were they tears of joy for Hong Kong's return to the loving embrace of the motherland?"

"China is motherland," Fang sniffles. "But British auntie who take care of child while mother away."

"You'll toss to Edie, A-6, out of here, Deng," Laura tells A-1.

"Child love mother, yes," Fang continues, "but also love auntie. Hong Kong people have, have, very close. . . ."

"Bond," Laura tells A-1 and A-2.

"Bond," Deng suggests.

Laura hits the R-1 lever. "We're coming to you, toot sweet, Edie. You okay?"

"Fine. You? What's. . . ?"

"May's package nearly killed us," Laura says, and turns to Quickie as she releases the lever. "Stand by Convention Center double box."

"Hong Kong very close bond with British," Fang continues, "but still not bond with China."

"I understand, Candy," Deng says, "But isn't that twinge of sadness overcome by the joy of ending a century and a half of colonial oppression, the ecstasy of Chinese people at last taking their rightful place as the rulers of Hong Kong?"

"I Chinese lady, I happy Chinese people ruler Hong Kong. I feeling in my heart that something over. . . . Nobody know what is come next."

"Beautiful," Laura tells the anchors. "Deng, A-6, single."

"But I know what's coming next," Deng says. "We're going live to Edie March at the Convention Center, the site of the formal sovereignty ceremonies. Are you there, Edie?"

"Split screen box," Laura orders.

"Thank you, Deng," Edie says.

"Lose the box. Edie solo," Laura barks.

"It's appropriate that Britain will formally surrender Hong Kong tonight at this Convention Center overlooking Victoria Harbor. This body of water, the strategic confluence of the Pearl River and the South China Sea, made Hong Kong a jewel among British crown colonies.

And Hong Kong's future will also rise and fall on the tides of Victoria Harbor."

"Roll the donut," Laura orders.

"Rolling," Quickie says, "two-thirty." He turns to Laura. "If you no change rundown, don't have to yell for every part. Four hour. Save your voice."

"Okay, Quickie. Thanks. Sorry."

"Okay. I worry you cannot talk later." Quickie smiles, "Maybe later you really need to scream."

"Right," she says, giving Quickie an appreciative smile. He pushes the levers for the anchors. "That was sensational, P—Candy. Good work, too, Deng, rocking and rolling."

"Oh, my English no good," Fang protests, still sniffling.

"Your English is fine."

"Many mistake."

The phone rings at the producer slot. "I've got to get the phone." She releases the levers and picks up. "Control room."

"Laura, it's Peter. I just want to tell you that was some of the greatest television I've ever seen. There wasn't a dry eye on deck here during May's report. Run it every hour. And, Candy. . . . That's why she's out there, for moments like that. Fantastic."

"I'll tell them."

"We want more of that. Cut the whole segment and feed it to the US, and tell them, 'Here, this is the handover, stupid, this is Fuggin Asia.' Just great."

"I'll get it cut."

"Thanks. I'm not going to be able to watch every minute, but I'll watch the air check later. Keep it up."

"Thank you, Peter."

"One minute," Quickie says.

"Honest," Laura calls, and Honest Ho appears at her side. "Hi, Honest. I'm really glad I've got a PA who knows what she's doing tonight."

"Maybe you get me promotion?"

"Maybe after the handover," Laura replies.

"July one, Chinese in charge."

"Yes, but until then ... please ask tapes to feed May's package, A-5, along with all the chat-chit on set after it, as a package to the US. And enter that tape here for us to use later with a note in the system for morning shows."

"Okay-lah."

"Thanks." Honest Ho scurries off.

Laura presses the anchor levers. "That was Peter calling. He said that was great television, the package and your reactions. Keep it up."

"Thanks," Deng says.

"I so embarrass. English so bad."

"Candy, when you speak from the heart like that," Laura says, "it's easy to understand, even if the English isn't perfect. If there's something you want to say, say it. Both of you. Peter's orders." She holds the anchor levers down, and pushes R-1, "Edie, tag the donut as scripted, and then Deng will ask about the tick-tock for tonight. That good?

"Good," Edie says.

"Got it, Deng?"

"I'll try to make it come from the heart."

"Thirty," Quickie says.

"It's in the split. Go as long as you need, we've got four minutes. If we have time, Candy reads A-9, then to break. Animation, if there's time. Okay?" The talent and Quickie nod. Laura pushes R-3, "Fiona, we'll come to you after the break, about three minutes, just for the set up. How's the demo?"

"Good crowd. The rain seems to have stopped, at least for the moment."

"All right. After your donut, chit-chat with Candy. She's got your three questions scripted, you should have them. . . ."

"Right."

Laura releases the lever. "Ten," Quickie declares.

"If there's something good from the floor feed, we'll roll that as live VO during the Q and A," Laura tells Quickie.

"Regardless of who rules in Government House," Edie's package ends, "Hong Kong's economy rises and falls on the shifting currents of Victoria Harbor."

"Cue," Quickie says.

"But tonight at the Convention Center, the story is of the shifting tides of sovereignty," Edie says. Deng appears in a split screen to the left.

"Tell us about that, Edie. What's the schedule for the night's formal activities? Are the. . . ?

"At the moment, the crowd is still settling in. They're expecting 3,500 people, including China's President Jiang Zemin and Premier Li Peng, and Britain's Prince Charles."

"Who are the rest of the people?" Deng asks.

"Stick to the tick-tock," Laura tells Deng in A-1, then tells Quickie "Lose her font in the split."

"Good question, Deng. The rest are the cream of Hong Kong's business community and local supporters of the Beijing government, including the 400 members of the Election Committee that chose Hong Kong's incoming Chief Executive Tung Chee-hwa. Mister Tung is a shipping magnate whose company got bailed out by Beijing in the 1980s. . . ."

"Edie," Deng interrupts, "that's a vicious rumor spread by enemies of China. . . ."

"Tick-tock, please," Laura says.

"Actually, Deng," Edie replies, "vicious or not, it's a fact. Mister Tung is also seen as 'hand-picked' by Jiang Zemin, since the Chinese President singled out Tung for a handshake when he greeted a visiting delegation of Hong Kong tycoons last year. And even though they talk about 'Hong Kong people ruling Hong Kong,' Tung was born in Shanghai, educated in the US and UK . . ."

"Tick-tock," Laura tells A-1 and R-1.

". . . and, of course, he's scheduled to address the crowd tonight after his formal swearing in. The program will start with an address from Hong Kong's Chief Secretary Anson Chan, the extremely popular number-two official in the local government who will continue to serve under Mister Tung. Beijing officials vetoed a speech by Britain's outgoing Hong Kong Governor Chris Patten. Prince Charles is the sole British representative scheduled to speak, and he'll follow Missus Chan. Then Premier Li Peng will. . . ."

"Prime Minister Li Peng," Deng interjects.

"Call him what you will," Edie replies. "Along with the late paramount leader Deng Xiaoping, Li Peng is known as the driving force behind the 1989 Tiananmen Square massacre. . . ."

"Crackdown," Deng says.

"Premier Li's speech," Edie continues, ignoring Deng, "should take us to a minute before midnight, when a military honor guard led by Lieutenant Colonel Rodney Whitbred will lower the Union Jack, while the Hong Kong Symphony Orchestra, which is entertaining the audience at this moment, plays *God Save the Queen.* Then a Chinese People's Liberation Army honor guard will raise the Chinese flag and Hong Kong's new flag featuring the bauhinia, a local flower. . . ."

"That's a variety of lily. . . ." Deng adds.

"Right, Deng. After the flags go up, President Jiang will swear in Mister Tung as Chief Executive while Prince Charles and Governor Patten board the Royal Yacht *Britannia,* docked here at the Convention Center, and sail away beneath a small fireworks display from the British government. A much larger fireworks display by the Chinese government will take place tomorrow night."

"Keep going," Laura tells R-1 and A-1. "More tick-tock."

"Tonight's formalities won't end when the *Britannia* sails. . . ." Deng says.

"No, they won't, Deng. There's still a great deal on the agenda once China takes formal control. After he's sworn, Chief Executive Tung will deliver his inaugural address . . ."

Laura presses A-1 to Deng, "Next question about the languages for the speeches."

". . . and then he will swear in the members of the reconstituted Legislative Council. Patricia Pang, Beijing's choice to head the Legislative Council, will then speak. That will conclude the program here at the Convention Center, but the lawmakers will then proceed to the Legislative Council building, about two kilometers from here, and go into session to enact several laws regarding the change in sovereignty that they've previously debated while meeting across the border in Shenzhen. So it's a busy night all over town, Deng."

"Indeed, Edie. One question that I think many people have, particularly our viewers watching on Franklin Global Networks in Europe and North America, is what language the speakers will use tonight? After midnight, Hong Kong will have three official languages: Mandarin Chinese, the language of the People's Republic of China; Cantonese, the dialect spoken in Hong Kong; and English, the language of the colonial oppressors. Which will the speakers be using, Edie?"

"Keep it to a minute," Laura tells Deng and Edie. She pushes the two anchor buttons and tells Quickie, "A-9 floats. Candy toss to break if there's time."

Fang shakes her head no.

Laura pushes the A-2 lever only. "Candy, just say 'Thank you, Deng. We'll have more live from the Hong Kong handover after the break.'"

Fang begins writing what Laura has said on the back of a used script page.

"Okay?" Laura asks.

Fang nods yes as she writes.

". . . news if the Prince of Wales speaks Chinese," Edie continues in reply to Deng. "The Chinese leadership will use Mandarin, of course, and I expect the Hong Kong speakers will as well. Nearly everyone is at least bilingual. Mister Tung could also warm President Jiang's heart by speaking in Shanghainese, since they're both natives of that city which some see as a rising rival to Hong Kong as the international gateway to China. Tung is also fluent in English and Cantonese. I'm not sure whether Patricia Pang speaks Mandarin, so she may speak in Cantonese, and the oaths to the legislators will also be in Cantonese. Deng?"

"All right, Edie, thank you. We'll be checking back with you throughout the night."

"Two-shot, Candy, toss, go," Laura says.

"Cue," Quickie says.

"Thank you, Deng. We'll have more live from the Hong Kong handover after the break."

"Roll animation," Laura says.

"Roll," Quickie says, "set clear. Three minute."

The animation shows the Union Jack with *God Save the Queen* playing. From the right, the Chinese five-star flag covers the Union Jack and *March of the Volunteers* drowns out the British anthem. The graphic dissolves into the new Hong Kong bauhinia flag as the music continues.

"Nice work, everybody," Laura says with the levers open. "Man, that animation is cheesy."

"Can set still hear me?" Edie asks.

"Yes," Deng says.

"Slow down, Deng. Give the reporters some space."

"But viewers need context," Deng protests. "Can she hear me?" he asks.

"Yes, Deng, I hear you. Just keep it brief."

"I thought it was fine," Laura says. "But Edie's right, just relax a bit, everyone. Thanks. Toss was good, Candy." She releases those levers, then pushes R-3. "We're coming to you in about four minutes, Fiona."

"Fine. I'll set up my donut. You have the roll cue."

Quickie nods, and speaks in Cantonese to tape playback.

"Right," Laura says, then pushes the anchor levers. "Here, Candy, Deng, here's Fiona, listen up."

"After the donut, we'll talk about the demo. How long can you give me?"

"Two minutes or so with Candy. You're okay with the questions, both of you?"

"Okay," Fang says. "Script okay. I just afraid when no script."

"You're doing great, Candy," Laura says.

"Ho-ho-aaah," Fiona adds, Cantonese for "good, good."

"Exactly," Laura says. "Don't worry." She leaves the levers open and addresses the control room, as well. "Okay, B-block. B-1 hello in a two-shot out of animation, Deng on B-2 with the VO, Candy B-3 to B-4 Fiona in the screen then the split, then B-5 and -6, back to split for B-7, go big box-little box when Fiona takes the crowd, then back to split. We'll try to keep it to seven minutes, then B-8 Deng tosses to the package, and rest as scripted. Okay."

"Got it," Quickie says. "Thirty."

"Okay," Fiona says. "By the way, Andy just got here."

"Make him stand in the rain," Laura says.

"It's stopped," Fiona says.

"Then throw him off the balcony," Laura suggests, releasing that lever then hitting R-4. "How you doing there, Mike?"

"Fine. Construction of our ark is progressing quite well. We should be afloat by midnight. Technically, I believe, the craft will be registered to the Red Army. . . ."

"We plan to get to you in the D-block," Laura says. "Hang in there."

"Ten," Quickie says.

"Animation, then as scripted," Laura tells the anchors and Fiona.

The animation rolls and winds up in the chromakey screen behind the anchors.

"God, that's awful," Laura says of the animation. "We'll have to come up with something better," she tells Quickie.

"Cue," Quickie says.

"Welcome back to FGN Asia's live coverage of the Hong Kong handover. I'm Candace Fang in Hong Kong."

"And I'm Deng Jiang Mao. Hong Kong's transfer of sovereignty to the People's Republic of China is just over 100 minutes away. Dignitaries from China and its British colonial oppressors have gathered . . ."

"Geez, that's not the script. Gimme the floor feed," Laura tells Quickie and the picture shifts from Deng to the Convention Center stage, where Anson Chan is addressing the audience with three tiers of VIPs seated on stage behind her, mainly Chinese in military uniforms.

". . . for the ceremonies to cleanse Hong Kong of its British colonial stain once and for all. President Jiang Zemin and Prime Minister Li Peng are leading the delegation from Beijing. It's already been a busy day for the imperial puppeteers who've held Hong Kong on a string for more than 150 years."

"Wipe to VO," Laura yells.

Over video cut from May's package, Deng continues, "At Government House this afternoon, Chris Patten, the final British tyrant governor of Hong Kong, turned on the waterworks with crocodile tears as the colors Chinese patriots loathe were lowered for the final time. At the Legislative Council, Patten met with traitorous delegates who will be stripped of their unmerited office in the new era of Hong Kong people ruling Hong Kong under the late beloved Deng Xiaoping's principle of one country, two systems."   •

"Now," Fang says, "we go live to the Legislative Council Building and FGN Asia's Fiona Fok. What's happening there now, Fiona?"

"Some people might call them traitors, but thousands of Hong Kong people have gathered here in front of the gothic dome of the Legislative Council Chamber . . ."

"Lose the split," Laura says.

". . . to protest the ouster of the so-called 'Dirty Dozen,' the twelve legislators elected by the people of Hong Kong who will be unseated in favor of Beijing's appointed lawmakers at midnight tonight."

"What was that ad lib, Deng?" Laura asks, pressing A-1.

"Just following your orders, letting it flow from the heart," he says.

"Easy on the political polemics," Laura says, "and don't go wandering to where we'll look stupid if we don't cover it with video."

"What's stupid is not showing the floor since we've got it."

"You don't know what we've got. I'm in the control room, not you."

"But it was better to show it."

"Yes, but let me be the producer. And cut that colonial oppressor crap."

"It's only the truth."

"Save it for the Q and A with Prime Minister Li Peng." Laura releases the A-1 lever, and pushes A-2. "Nice toss, Candy. Thanks."

"I nervous."

"You're doing great. We're all nervous. It's a big night. Don't worry. You look beautiful and you sound terrific. Relax . . . *mei-mei.*"

Candy breaks into a big smile. "Thank you, *jie-jie.*"

Laura releases the button and turns to Quickie. "Where are we?"

"Donut lolling, one-forty left."

"Okay." Laura pushes the anchor levers and R-3. "After the donut tag, do the question about the LegCo session, Candy, then just ask, 'Now, what about the protestors?' and Fiona, you let it rip. Get your camera to shoot the crowd. . . ."

"That pan'll look like shit," Deng says.

"Cover it with your talk, Fiona. Say, 'Let's get a shot of the crowd' or something, and afterward have the camera to swing back to you. You can do that?"

"Can do. May be a touch ragged. . . ."

"That's okay. Viewers don't mind when live TV looks live," Laura guesses.

"They also appreciate some insight and analysis instead of all this show business," Deng says.

"That from the man in the silk Shanghai Tang smoking jacket," Laura says. "Let's all lighten up and help each other make things work." Laura releases the levers and turns to Quickie. "That camera pan will be okay, right?"

"Good shooter can okay."

"Thanks."

"Coming out to remote in ten," Quickie says.

"Fiona, tag it, and then Candy's question. In the split."

"Cue," Quickie says.

"Those new lawmakers," Fiona says, "will take their oaths at the Convention Center before they get down to work tonight. Candy?"

"Fiona, how long do you expect the legislative session to run tonight?"

"They probably won't get started here until about two a.m. The laws set for immediate passage have already had all of their required readings . . ."

"When she's done," Laura tells Candy, "you ask her, 'Now what about these protests?' You're on camera, so just blink. Okay?"

Fang blinks.

". . . so there's only the matter of voting," Fiona continues, "but each item must be voted separately, according to the rules, and that will take some time. They could be finished by four or five, but they might go on past dawn. In any case, it's going to be a long night, Candy."

"What about these protests?"

"I don't think they'll last until dawn, Candy. But there are thousands of people here showing support for the pro-democracy legislators who will be ousted. . . ."

"Excuse me, Fiona, this is Deng . . ."

"Oh Jesus," Laura says. "Two-shot in the split."

". . . wouldn't it be more accurate to call them 'pro-colonial' or 'anti-Beijing' legislators. After all, they are relics of the colonial system, put in place by. . . ."

"Deng, the truth is that they were elected in what experts say was Hong Kong's most fair and open . . ."

"Take her full," Laura tells Quickie, then hits the anchor levers. "Don't do that again, Deng. You do your Q and A, Candy does hers."

". . . vote ever. Hong Kong wasn't a democracy under the British . . ."

"And," Laura tells Quickie, "cut Deng's mike when he's not doing Q and A on live shots."

". . . and won't become one tonight at midnight. But these protestors seem to think there's something wrong with representatives chosen by the voters of Hong Kong losing their jobs in favor of those appointed by Beijing. And they came out in the rain to say so. Here's, let's pan the camera over to the crowd. . . ." The camera turns away from Fok and sweeps to the crowd below the balcony. "As you can see, there are several thousand people here, and at the moment, the rain has stopped. That large banner in Chinese reads, 'Democracy: Let Hong Kong people choose their leaders' and the one in simplified Chinese characters, the script used on the mainland says, 'Motherland, trust your children.' There are also signs in English, and 'Liberté, égalité, fraternité,' the slogan of the French revolution."

"Laura," Deng says, pushing his lever to talk to the control room, not the air. "Isn't that your husband out there? With a hot little fastback, Japanese, I'd . . ."

"Shut up, Deng."

"You didn't see him?"

"Shut up." She releases the lever.

"Now here on the balcony, at the podium behind me . . ." The camera swings back toward Fok, then focuses on the podium. ". . . legislator Emily Lau is addressing the crowd in Cantonese. Democratic Party Chairman Martin Lee and longtime legislator and labor activist Szeto Wah are also scheduled to speak." The shot tightens and focuses on Fok. "One question hanging over the gathering is what will happen at midnight. Police are not expected to break up the speeches, and I'm told that group has agreed to leave the LegCo building before the new lawmakers arrive. But we'll have to wait and see."

"That's it," Laura says.

"Candy, cue," Quickie says.

"Thank you, Fiona," Candy says. "We'll be checking back with you all through the night on the demonstrators and the legislators."

"B-8, Deng," Laura says.

"Deng, cue," Quickie says.

Deng's lips move but no sound comes out. Quickie flips Deng's mike on again.

". . . the Queen will also disappear from much of Hong Kong. . . ." Deng continues, unaware of the gaffe.

"Sorry. I remember next time," Quickie promises, as Deng completes the package toss.

"Just leave his mike on," Laura tells Quickie. "If he interrupts again, I'll go out there myself and kill him."

"I take that shot live," Quickie says, smiling. "Rolling package, three minutes."

"Honest," Laura says, searching the control room. "Honest."

"Yes," Honest says, rising from her seat at the back of the control room to present herself at Laura's side.

"Get me that sound bite from the woman in May's package cut. I want it for the open next hour."

"Yes," Honest says.

"Thanks." She picks up the phone, and dials Helios. "Hi. . . . Scripts are good. I'm getting a SOT from May's package cut. . . . Right. That one. Write it for a cold open E-1, next hour, for Candy." She hangs up the phone. "Everybody," she says, pushing the anchor levers. "We're going to use a new cold open for next hour. I'm getting that vox pop SOT cut from May's package. Candy will read. Helios is putting in a new script."

"I though this was news, not a soap opera," Deng protests.

"Sorry, but I guess I'm just a daytime TV gal at heart," Laura replies. "We'll get you the script soon, Candy."

"Okay. I try. . . ."

"You'll do it. You're doing great."

"Maybe I cry again."

"That won't be scripted, but you want to ad lib a few tears, go ahead, *mei-mei.*"

Fang smiles.

"Okay, good. Out of this package, Candy does the B-10 reader with the VO, and then the break tease, with a live shot of Lan Kwai Fong. Okay?"

Quickie, Deng and Fang nod.

Laura pushes R-2. "May, we'll use a live shot of Lan Kwai Fong in the tease. Give us a good shot of the crowd."

"No problem. I'll tell Bei-loh," May says. "When are you taking me?"

"As scripted, about three minutes into the bottom of the hour."

"Fine. I'll do my donut, and after that, I'll feed some vox pops from here and this afternoon."

"Nancy knows?"

"Yes. And I gave her suggestions for SOTS to cut."

"You're a pro, May" Laura says. "Great package from this afternoon."

"Thanks. We do our best."

"Peter said there wasn't a dry eye on the junk."

"He's watching?"

"Of course. He's not CK."

May giggles.

"Get me that tease shot," Laura says, "in about two, and talk to you later." She releases the lever.

"Nat sound on tease?" Quickie asks.

"Sure," Laura says. "We've got US International shooting the Tiananmen countdown clock, right?"

"Yes. Monitor 12."

"Can you take that for the bottom open? We're not running that lousy animation again."

"Quickie pushes a lever and says a few words in Cantonese to master control. He waits, then nods, "Yes."

"All right, we'll open C-block with the clock at the bottom of the hour. No nat sound. Thanks," Laura says. She pushes the anchor buttons. "For open at the bottom of the hour, we'll take a live shot of the countdown clock in Beijing. Deng, give us a little 'the hour draws near' or 'time ticks away on Hong Kong's British rulers' or whatever, as a pre-C-1. We'll lose the animation, it sucks, and go as scripted with C-1 open."

"Fifteen," Quickie announces.

"That's good," Deng says, leafing through his scripts then scribbling.

"Okay, back in about ten," Laura says to the anchors. "Thanks."

"Use animation to close?" Quickie asks.

"No, it's Fiona in Lan Kwai Fong. . . ."

"Right, I forget, sorry," Quickie says. "Cue."

"According to Chinese tradition, rain is a good omen," Fang reads, and tape rolls showing afternoon downpour around town. "If the masters of *feng shui,* the Chinese folk science of natural harmony, are correct, then Hong Kong will enjoy a flood of good fortune under Chinese rule. Heavy showers pelted the city all day Monday. *Feng shui* teaches that rain cleanses away the old, leaving a clean slate for what's ahead." Fang reappears on screen. "The weather has cleared for the moment over Central Hong Kong, but meteorologists say it's only temporary relief. The forecast calls for rain to continue in Hong Kong for the rest of week."

"Okay, two-shot."

"Cue," Quickie tells Deng.

"For the rest of the night, stay with us for FGN Asia's exclusive live coverage of Hong Kong's return to Chinese sovereignty," Deng says on camera. "In the next half-hour, we'll hear from Hong Kong's top financial regulator on what the change to Chinese rule means for the record-setting stock market."

"And we'll go live. . . ." Candy says, and the live shot comes up in the chromakey with mainly *gweiloh* revelers mugging and screaming for the cameras, "to Hong Kong's favorite political party where revelers are defying the rain to toast the handover or drown their sorrows."

"Looks like they're high and dry at the moment," Deng adds. "We'll be right back."

For the next 85 minutes, the broadcast rolls ahead with a minimum of glitches. Laura thinks fast in her seat for new teases to substitute for the tacky animation, shuffles the rundown, and gives all the reporters live shots. She's careful to keep Quickie on board with all the changes, keep Fang on scripted pieces, and keep Deng from talking too much trash. Now they've dumped into Li Peng's speech, in translation from the pool, as the clock ticks down toward midnight, giving everyone a chance to catch their breath.

"Your hero is dull as dishwater," Laura tells Deng.

"I'm sure he'll hit his time cue, though," Deng replies.

Laura responds silently with "Screw you, Deng," then checks her revised rundown for the next hour and sends it into the computer system for all. She messages Nancy in tapes and Helios to alert them and tells Quickie, "New rundown in," and yells for Honest Ho, who's already going out the door to print it out and make copies. Laura hits the levers to speak to the reporters and anchors and the control room. "Okay, everyone, revised rundown is in for next hour. We'll get copies for everybody here. We'll break at 11:53 and be back here at 56. Let's hope this gas bag is done by then.

"Deng, you come in in the little/big split and say, 'We'll break now and be back for the historic transfer of sovereignty' or whatever. When we're back, after the hello, Candy reads 1-2; Helios is updating it now.

Starts on two-shot, then VOs, then big/little split, then to the live feed. If something's happening, I'll say 'stop' and you just say, 'Now let's listen in to the live ceremony.' You okay with that?"

"I try," Fang says, writing.

"You'll be fine, *mei-mei*. Okay, we'll take their sound until it's boring, and then, Deng, you'll do the I-4 toss to Mike at the border. Mike, it all depends on the ceremony, so you'll have to stand by for the toss. Mike live, I-5, under a minute, then Mike tosses to May in Lan Kwai Fong, and May, keep I-6 brief, maybe talk to one reveler, also less than a minute, and then toss to I-7, Fiona at LegCo for the demo. Everybody okay so far?"

All assent.

"Okay. After Fiona, we go to I-8, Edie, at the harbor side. You're all set up there?"

"Yes," Edie says. "Just waiting for my prince to come. Ready to sing *Fail Britannia* if he doesn't."

"Do you have an umbrella, in case. . . ."

"Kin-ming has one. All set."

"Fiona," Laura says, "I may need you to do a little chit-chat with Deng while we wait for the boarding. What's a good question?"

"I can ask about the new session. . . ." Deng suggests.

"Won't really fit with the pictures," Fiona says.

"Maybe ask what the protestors want or what the legislators want," Laura says.

"That's good," Fiona agrees. "What do the deposed legislators want?"

"Okay," Deng says, "as long as we also make the point that 48 out of 60 legislators will still be the same."

"Good point," Fiona says. "Can do. . . ."

"All right," Laura says. "Once these live shots are done, everyone in the field start feeding tape. Candy, you take the I-9 tease to the break. J-block, we'll see what's on the floor before we decide whether to go live or follow the rundown. Everybody's okay? If there's a glitch or you see that we haven't switched off you after your toss, bail out with a toss back to Deng, and I'll tell you where to go."

"You've been telling me where to go since you got here," Deng says.

"Been a two-way street, mister," Laura retorts. "Everybody got it?" She sees the reporters and anchors nod in their monitors. "Good. This is it."

Laura releases the levers for the reporters. "Candy, we'll go to break in . . ." she looks at Quickie.

"Forty."

". . . about 40 seconds. Quickie will cue you, and we'll go out on you two with the Beijing clock in the chromakey."

"You love that countdown," Deng says. "But I thought we were just. . . ."

"I'll love all of you if we get this right," Laura says. "Candy, just say, 'We'll leave the ceremonies for a moment but stay with us.' And then Deng, you say something about the countdown. Okay?"

Fang nods as she scribbles. Deng says, "Look, why don't we keep it simple? Keep the picture and little box and I'll just say. . . ."

"We don't have time to argue," Laura says. "My way. Everybody okay with that?"

"Okay," Deng sighs, "your way," as Fang mouths what she's jotted.

Laura dials Helios. "Got that script for I-2?. . . She did?. . . Okay, I'll check it." Laura hangs up, gets the script on screen that Honest Ho wrote because Helios was overloaded, corrects two typos, prints it, and sends it to the teleprompter. "Honest, get your I-2 out to Candy. Very nice job. We have that tape?"

"Yes," Honest says. "Thank you."

Then Laura dials Nancy in tapes. "Hey Nancy. . . . I know you know to cut that. Just a heads up that we've doing a live go-round in the midnight block, so around fifteen after, reporters will begin feeding. . . . Love you. Thanks."

Laura wonders what she's forgotten, and turns to Quickie, "After break, come up cold with nat sound on the stage, then we'll do I-1."

"I surprise you still have voice," Quickie says.

"Yes," Laura says, "but I've lost my mind." Actually, she thinks, it's great. I'm the brain here, and I send out all these commands and the other parts execute them for me. Before Peter arrived, I never imagined things could work so smoothly here, she admits.

"Break toss in five, four, three, two, one," Quickie tell the anchors, "Squeeze to split." The anchors appear in the left half of the screen as the ceremony pictures continue on the right. "Cue."

"We leave handover cemetery for moment," Candy says, and the picture dissolves to both anchors on set with the Beijing clock in the screen behind them in the chromakey. "But please you no stay go."

"Stay with us," Deng continues, "as we count down the final moments until China rules Hong Kong. This is FGN Asia's special coverage with Candace Fang and Deng Jiang Mao, live from Hong Kong."

"To break on the clock," Laura says.

"Out," Quickie says. "Back in three."

"Laura, that was nuts," Deng says. "Take it fuckin' easy."

"I know, I know," she says, pushing the anchor levers. "That was too much. Sorry. My fault. But you pulled it off."

" 'Handover cemetery,' " Deng says. " 'You no stay go?' for god's fucking sake. . . ."

"Shut up, Deng," Laura says. "You were fine, Candy."

"No, he right," Fang says. "I mistake, mistake. English so bad."

"But heartfelt," Deng says.

"Deng. . . ." Laura growls. "Candy, that was my fault. I got carried away and asked you to do too much. . . ."

"I sorry," Fang says. "I not. . . ."

"You have nothing to be sorry about," Laura says. "My fault. I won't do it again. If you think it's too much, just say no. Okay, *mei-mei?*"

"Okay," Fang says.

"Your I-2 script is done, copy coming. This block will be easy. The reporters will do all the work." Laura keeps the anchor levers open, and presses for the reporters. "Everybody okay out there? We're back in about two-thirty, then to the ceremony, then Deng to Mike to May to Fiona to Edie to Candy to break. Listen to each other for your cues and make them long enough for us to get the other reporter in the split. . . ."

Old Hartman interjects, "We can talk to each other, Laura. . . ."

"That could be good," Laura says, "but keep it simple."

"It's simple if they're already in the split," Old Hartman says.

"Okay, up to you, but don't step on the other reporter's story. And we want the pictures. . . ."

"May, would you mind a question from me?"

"Not at all, Mike," May says. "As long as you promise I can answer it."

"If you can't, he will," Deng says.

"Then that's settled," Old Hartman says, ignoring Deng.

"Anybody else want a question?" Laura asks.

"Play it by ear," Edie suggests. "Reporters or producers have a question or two ready and tell us first so there are no surprises on air. Then, if the tosser—and you're all such tossers—wants to ask a question, ask it. If the next reporter wants to get a question, then make the first word you say, the name of the reporter. If I want a question, I'll start by saying, 'Fiona.' Everyone follow that?"

"Good suggestion," Laura says. "If you want a question, start with the other reporter's name. Got that?"

The reporters mumble yes and nod.

"Thank you," Edie says. "I used to be a producer, you may recall. . . ."

"And will be again tomorrow," Deng says.

"It's better than turning into a pumpkin at midnight," Edie says. "Fiona, I may need to stall a little, so please be ready to talk. I'll be away from my monitor, but Laura, you'll be seeing the pictures, so you'll have a good idea of what. . . ."

"Yes," Laura says. "Everybody, if I need you to toss early, or to stretch things, I'll tell you. . . ."

"Maybe our producer should be on the phone with you during the live shot," May suggests, "instead of you talking in our ears."

"Good idea," Laura says. "Tell your producers to call me on the control room numbers—74, 75, 76, 77, 78—when you're up next." Laura turns away from the microphone and says, "Honest, you get the phones," then turns back to the mike. "Candy, you have the I-2?"

"Yes," Fang says, "but I not sure. . . ."

"You'll be fine, Candy, *mei-mei,*" Laura assures her. "Relax."

"I try."

"You read scripts beautifully. Just read this one and take the rest of the block off until the toss."

Fang smiles. "I can do this."

"Twenty to cold open," Quickie warns.

Laura pushes the anchor buttons. "Okay, Deng, you're in the little box for the first sentence, then two-shot with the feed in chromakey until I-2, then Candy. We'll squeeze her. . . ."

"I'll tell Franklin. . . ." Deng says.

"Shut up. Then we'll take the floor feed. Deng, you take us out of that. . . ."

"My permission to speak has been restored?" Deng says.

"Please, Deng," Laura pleads. "Let's just do this nice and easy and we'll all live happily ever after under Chinese rule."

"Amen," Deng says.

Laura takes a deep breath. I came here for this, she reminds herself, and it is so much more work—and later, she's sure she'll admit, so much more fun—and even more exciting than she expected. She's beginning to understand Old Hartman's thirst for the red light. Once you've done this, it's hard to go back to something ordinary. Writing earnings stories at the *Journal* can't make your pulse race like this.

Laura checks the pool feed from the Convention Center and sees the British honor guard entering. It's time to make the moment happen, for her, for Fuggin Asia, for history. "Hold Deng's cue for three seconds for nat sound on the open."

"Okay," Quickie says. "Take Pool-1," and only the sound of the honor guard's boots on the polished stage floor is heard. "Five, four three, two, one, cue."

Deng's head pops into the picture in a box at the right bottom of the screen. "These are live pictures from the Hong Kong Convention Center, where the transfer to Chinese sovereignty is just minutes away." The ceremony shot squeezes into the chromakey, and the two anchors are on set. "Thank you for watching these last gasps of imperial oppression on FGN Asia's exclusive coverage of Hong Kong's transition to Chinese rule. I'm Deng Jiang Mao live in Hong Kong."

"And I'm Candace Fang." The camera switches to a single shot of Fang. "It's already been a busy day as the sun sets on British rule in Hong Kong." Video of flag ceremony at Government House covers her. "The British colors came down at Government House for the last time this afternoon as a teary Governor Chris Patten looked on." Video shifts to Li Peng's speech. "In a speech at the Hong Kong Convention Center moments ago, China's Premier Li Peng called on Hong Kong people to love China and use their high degree of autonomy to develop the city and the mainland under Deng Xiaoping's principle of one country, two systems." Video shifts to demonstrations outside LegCo. "At the Legislative Council, thousands of protestors are listening to speeches by the twelve elected legislators who will be ousted at midnight as Beijing installs its own appointed lawmakers. The new Legislative Council will go into session later tonight to pass a number of laws related to China's sovereignty over the territory." Now Fang's in a small box in the bottom left corner and the live feed of the ceremony fills the rest of the screen in a big box labeled: Hong Kong Convention Center, Live. "As midnight approaches," Fang continues, "let's watch and listen to live pictures of the handover ceremony at the Convention Center."

"Perfect," Laura tells Fang. "Go with script," and releases the button. "Honest, nice write on I-2."

"Thank you," Honest says from the back of the control room.

"Where'd you learn. . . ?"

"I watch you."

"Smart girl," Laura says.

British flag bearers in kilts march toward the center of the stage, their boots and occasional commands the only sounds. They form a line on one side of the stage, in front of the three-tier podium of dignitaries.

"Mikes dead?" Laura asks Quickie.

"Dead," he replies.

Laura pushes A-2. "Great, Candy. Perfect timing. Start your vacation."
Fang smiles.

Laura pushes A-1 as well. "Mikes are off, so we can talk. We'll watch the actual ceremony for a while, then Deng, you'll come in with a recap—keep it short—and toss to Mike."

"Don't you want a few words under this?" Deng asks, "So people know what they're seeing."

"Let's just watch for a bit," Laura says. "Maybe later." She releases the buttons and dials Nancy.

"Nancy, it's Laura. You've got a clean feed of the ceremony for tapes, right?. . . This handover ceremo. . . . Very funny. . . . You've got the feeds and the air check from master control, right?. . . Okay, thanks." She hangs up. "Quickie," she says, as the crunch of Chinese boots goosestepping across the stage echoes, "let's take the handover clock from Beijing in the little box."

"Okay," he says. Within seconds, the clock squeezes into a little box on the left side of the screen.

"That looks like shit," Deng says.

Laura begins to push A-1 but hits the remote levers instead. "Hi team. Mike, Deng comes to you out of the ceremony, then you toss to May, May to Fiona, Fiona to Edie, and Edie back to Candy, if there's time. Your producers should call in ahead of the shot. Mike, Richard can call in just after midnight. Everybody okay?"

"Richard will call as soon as he finishes inflating our pontoon," Mike says from under his umbrella.

"That's fine, *mei-mei,*" Edie says. "Maybe we could use a little commentary over the ceremony. Let Deng tell people what they're watching."

"He thinks so, too," Laura says.

"I'm sure," Edie says.

"Okay," Laura says. "Everybody stand by." She releases the remote levers. It's 11:58:22 on the clock.

"Deng," Laura says, pushing both anchor levers, "give us some play-by-play over the ceremony. . . ."

"Great fucking idea," Deng says.

"Candy, you, too, if there's something you want to say. We'll get you on camera while you're talking," Laura guesses, looking at Quickie, who nods. "We'll start Deng in the little box, but then we'll take the ceremony full screen and stick with that. You just talk under the pictures. Not too much, please. Quickie will cue you when we're set." Laura releases the levers.

"No clock?" Quickie asks.

"No clock," Laura agrees. Quickie hits some buttons, and the clock disappears again, back into the abyss where it rested until Laura ordered it to appear. This is the closest thing to magic I'll ever do, Laura thinks. It's not just the technical wizardry. As amazing as the video gizmos and gimmicks can seem, Laura realizes that getting cash from an ATM is probably involves more sophisticated technology than making television. No, the real thrill for Laura is being at the center of it all, of being so completely immersed in the moment that absolutely nothing else on earth that matters except the relationship between her and what she orders to appear on the screen.

Quickie says, "Three, two, one, cue," as Deng's head appears in a box at the bottom right of the live feed.

"You're watching live pictures," Deng says from the box, "from the Hong Kong Convention Center with the transfer to Chinese sovereignty less than 100 seconds away. I'm Deng Jiang Mao in Hong Kong with my colleague Candace Fang on FGN Asia's exclusive coverage of this historic moment."

"Good," Laura says, with A-1 down, as the box disappears and the feed covers the full screen.

"The Chinese and British colonial honor guards are lined up face to face at center stage for the lowering of the Union Jack, the symbol of 156 years of British imperialist oppression in Hong Kong," Deng says. "Black Watch Colonel Rodney Whitbred will execute this final act of the tyrants under the watchful eye of General Wei Xender of the People's Liberation Army."

"Enough, Deng," Laura says, A-1 lever down.

"We're about a minute away from that moment as the troops exchange salutes," Deng continues. "The dignitaries in attendance on the podium include China's President Jiang Zemin, the Prime Minister Li Peng, whose speech moments ago visibly moved the assembled . . ."

"Yeah, moved them to the exits," Laura says, then pushes the lever. "Enough, Deng. Stop."

". . . military heroes, delegates to the National People's Congress, Hong Kong's incoming Chief Executive Tung Chee-hwa, and many others. And you can be sure that somewhere in this newly completed Convention Center hovers the spirit of Deng Xiaoping, who died at age 92 in February, just 131 days short of witnessing this crowning achievement, the reunification of Hong Kong with the motherland."

"Enough, Deng," Laura repeats.

"Deng's brilliant innovation of one country–two systems forms the guiding principle to secure Hong Kong's freedom from colonial oppression and shepherd this city of nearly seven million people back into the motherland's embrace. This same principle is also guiding the rectification of another colonial anachronism, Macau, a Chinese island about 60 kilometers, or 35 miles, from Hong Kong, that has been under the boot of Portuguese imperialists for more than four centuries. So, yes, at this moment, we know that Deng Xiaoping is smiling up there."

"Deng, the ceremony," Laura says.

"On stage, you can hear the colonial invader's commandant give his final orders in Hong Kong, the last gasps of British imperialism in East Asia, as he instructs his troops—and isn't it appropriate that these British soldiers wear skirts, these agents of a faraway Queen who dares not show herself at these proceedings—to fold away the hated Union Jack, watched by that son of a Queen, Charles, and the accursed final colonial governor of Hong Kong, Chris Patten, who tried his best to prevent this moment from ever taking place. To paraphrase the American patriotic hero Paul Revere, 'The British are going. The British are going.' Their flag of repression and misery is now consigned to the dustbin of history, never again to foul the skies over liberated, reunited Hong Kong."

"Deng, enough already," Laura says.

"Now Colonel Whitbred steps up to Chinese General Wei Xender and salutes the much-decorated hero. General Xu turns to his men—real men wearing pants—and gives the order to raise the colors of the People's Republic of China and the new bauhinia flag of Hong Kong as the orchestra strikes up . . ."

"Deng, we can see and hear it," Laura says. "Hush."

"I can cut his mike," Quickie says.

"No," Laura says. "It's too much, but we can live with it."

". . . the national anthem, *March of the Volunteers.* As the Chinese flag and the bauhinia rise on stage, the moment that Chinese patriots around the globe have awaited for 156 years is . . . now . . . here. Hong Kong is now reunited with the People's Republic of China for the greater glory of the motherland. You have witnessed history here on FGN Asia with Deng Jiang Mao and Candace Fang. Thunderous applause greets the dawn of one country . . ."

Laura's phone rings. "Hello. . . Yes, Richard. . . ." She glances at R-4. "We'll come to you in about a minute. Shot looks good. Hang on."

Laura pushes R-4 and A-1, "Okay, to Mike in about a minute." Then she releases A-1.

"What was all that palaver?" Old Hartman says. "Is Deng auditioning for CCTV?"

"My fault. I asked for play-by-play. Stand by."

"I'll go about a minute," Old Hartman continues, "then May will ask me a question. Richard has already given it to her. Then I'll ask her one."

"That's fine," Laura says. Anything for more face time, she thinks. "Coming to you in about 30. Stand by."

". . . as the anthem ends, a thunderous ovation engulfs this vast hall. It is the applause of generations of oppressed souls at last unbound from their colonial chains. And it is a warm thank you to the architect of this reunification, the late Deng Xiaoping."

"Okay, swear-in then toss to Mike," Laura says, A-1 and R-4 levers down, and phone with Richard in her ear. "Get the split ready," she tells Quickie.

"This is a moment of overwhelming pride for the Chinese nation and for Chinese people all around the world," Deng says. "Symbolic of that proud destiny, we're watching President Jiang Zemin swearing in Tung Chee-hwa as Hong Kong's first Chief Executive, the realization of the dream of Hong Kong people ruling Hong Kong."

Laura looks at the remote screen and sees People's Liberation Army troops coming into Old Hartman's remote shot, then checks on air, where Jiang and Tung are shaking hands. "Toss to Mike," Laura says, levers down.

"Wherever we may live, Chinese people never forget where they came from, about the great civilization that invented the printing press, gunpowder and even pasta, while the west was fumbling through its dark ages."

"Toss to Hartman," Laura yells. "Now."

"My parents named me Deng Jiang Mao as a tribute to . . ."

"Your parents named you Lincoln Washington Lee," Laura screams into A-1. "Toss to Hartman. Now."

". . . that 4,000-year-old civilization to which all Chinese around the globe proudly trace our roots. For every Chinese, everywhere in the world, this is a moment of awesome satisfaction and joy . . ."

"Congratulations, Deng," Laura says, regaining her composure. "Now toss to Mike. Immediately."

"Maybe IFB problem," Quickie suggests.

"He has the rundown," Laura replies.

". . . that's difficult to express in words. It's a feeling of completion, a feeling that Chinese people in Hong Kong will be able to realize their true destiny, that a long-lost member of the family has finally come home."

"Toss," Laura screams into A-1.

"What the hell is going on there?" Old Hartman barks.

"He won't do the toss."

"Then have Candy do it," Old Hartman says. "Just get me on."

"Candy," Laura says into A-2. "I want you to interrupt Deng and toss to Mike. Say, 'Excuse me, Deng, but now we're going live to Mike Hartman at the border.'"

Candy doesn't write the words down.

"Are you ready?" Laura asks Candy.

"What's going there?" Richard, on the telephone in her left ear, asks. "Tanks are starting to come over the border. Great video."

"Candy," Laura pleads, "nod your head when you're ready."

Candy shakes her head "no" as Laura watches in the set monitor.

"No, you're not ready," Laura asks. "Or no, you're not going to do it."

Candy nods her head.

"Yes, you're ready?" Laura asks.

Candy shakes her head "no" again.

"Chinese tanks are entering Hong Kong," Old Hartman announces. "Communist Chinese tanks. . . . I demand that you put me on air now."

". . . a wave of false nostalgia for the colonial oppressors whose imperialist rule. . . ." Deng continues.

"Honest, make sure tapes is getting the R-4 feed and all the pool footage," Laura yells, turning her head away from the microphone. She coughs. Her voice is starting to go. "And get me some water, somebody."

"This is Tiananmen Two, for crying out loud. Communist Chinese tanks are invading Hong Kong," Old Hartman screams. "Get me on air. Now."

"Candy," she says into A-2, "are you going to do the toss? Yes or no?"

Candy shakes her head "no" again.

Laura releases the lever, repeating, "Oh god. . . ." as she buries her face in her hands.

". . . despite 156 years of exploitation by London, the creative genius of the Chinese people has flourished . . ." Deng continues.

"This is major news," Hartman says in his most authoritative anchor voice. "Get me on the air. Now."

"I'm going to cut your mike," Laura says pushing A-1. "Toss to Hartman."

". . . and now we stand on the crest of the dawn of a new century, a century that undoubtedly will be the Chinese century, in which Asia, under the leadership of China, will be in the forefront of. . . ."

Laura's mobile phone rings. "Phones OFF," someone in the back of the control room stage whispers. Several people chuckle, including Quickie. "That's still the rule," Laura croaks, as she answers in her right ear. "Hello."

"It's Peter. Who told Deng to teach Chinese Studies 101?"

"He won't toss to Mike. . . ."

"Make him."

"Candy won't interrupt. I think she's afraid to ad lib because of her English. . . ."

"You're the producer."

"Should I cut his mike?"

"Do something. At least get us the live shots from the remotes."

"I was about to. . . ."

"Now. . . ."

"Okay."

"Now." Franklin clicks off.

Honest Ho brings Laura a cup of water and she gulps it, then opens all the remote levers. "Okay, listen up. Problems here, so changes. We're going to use your shots as VO over Deng's soliloquy, until it's over. So reporters, get out of the shots, just video of whatever's happening there. We'll take it in the split or big/little, Quickie."

"So I'm out here drowning," Old Hartman roars. "Drowning in rain, drowning in news. . . ."

"We'll get to everyone in the next segment," Laura says. "But for now, just VO. Now. Peter's order. I'll see when you're ready. Thanks." She releases the levers. "Got that, Richard?" she says into the phone. "Do your best to keep Mike calm. I'm sorry. Thanks." She hangs up.

". . . a high degree of autonomy as provided by the Basic Law . . ." Deng continues.

"Okay, give me R-4 in the split, then squeeze the stage feed down to the small box," Laura tells Quickie. She pushes A-1 and A-2. "We're going to be putting up video from the remotes, and squeezing the stage. Talk to it."

". . . Tung has taken a solemn oath to uphold that Basic Law," Deng continues. "Under that law, the People's Republic of China, not the British queen, holds sovereignty, but Hong Kong has the right to conduct its internal affairs in a manner consist with fulfilling its own destiny. Part of that destiny is to embrace the motherland, and without that bond between Hong Kong and the Chinese nation . . ."

"Okay, take R-4 in a split with the stage," Laura says. "Lose Deng in the little box. He can say or not say whatever the hell he wants." She hits A-1, "Border in split, gonna squeeze."

". . . there can be no meaningful future for the people of Hong Kong. As you are seeing on the screen now, the forces of the People's Liberation Army . . ."

The screen shows the Convention Center stage on the left, on the right, brown tanks with yellow stars on their turrets rolling past crowds waving flags.

"Thank god," Laura says, then tells Quickie, "Squeeze to big/little. Put up the border font."

". . . entering Hong Kong to ensure its freedom and prevent the return of foreign tyranny ever again. Those flag-waving schoolchildren may be staying up past their bed times, but in the years to come, they will look back with pride on their role in welcoming their liberators from British imperialist colonial despotism. For them, the yoke of British oppression lasted only a few years, but their parents and grandparents and their great-grandparents wore the chains of slavery for their entire lives. Only now, only with the historic arrival of the People's Liberation Army, an army of their own people, not a band of brutal occupiers in skirts, and the swearing in of a government loyal to the Chinese nation, not some distant royal throne, can the nearly seven million people of Hong Kong truly breathe free."

"Okay, let's go to R-2," Laura tells Quickie. "Split with R-4. Can we keep the little box with the stage in a split?"

"Can." Quickie says.

"Can we get the fonts in the frame instead of over the video?"

"Graphic."

"Font frames?" Ashrami asks.

"Yes, for all three," Laura says.

"Composing," Ashrami says, bracelets jingling.

"We'll take that when it's ready, then push out R-4 to a big/little," Laura says, then hits R-2. "May, heading your way, VO only." She hits R-3, "Fiona, we'll come to your shot in less than a minute, VO only." She releases the levers. "Ashrami, get three-way graphics ready for R-2, R-3, and R-3, R-1, all with the Convention Center for the little box. Call R-1 here Victoria Harbor, for the yacht."

"Loading," Ashrami says. "Write it down, please."

"Honest, help her," Laura yells. "Lan Kwai Fong/Legislative Council Building plus Hong Kong Convention Center, Legislative Council Building/Victoria Harbor, plus. . . ."

"Understand," Honest Ho says, bringing her pad over to Ashrami's console, and writing out the locators for the split graphics.

"Graphic ready," Quickie says.

"Okay, put R-3 in the split," Laura says.

"New remote in split," she says into A-1, "Lan Kwai Fong." On screen, the tanks are rolling on the left, a mix of Chinese and westerners are partying on the right, and at the bottom, Chinese men are shaking hands with each other.

". . . to know they are the lords of their own house, not slaves to a foreign House of Lords. Their elation is completely understandable, the joy of freedom. . . . And now we see that celebrations are also going on in Central Hong Kong, in the Lan Kwai Fong area. Even in this bastion of expatriate . . ."

"Squeeze the R-4," Laura orders.

"R-2 to R-3 loaded," Ashrami says.

"Thanks," Laura replies. "Honest, when you're done there, get me more water, please, and maybe a couple of aspirins."

". . . drunkenness and debauchery," Deng continues, "westerners and Chinese alike recognize that this is a glorious moment for Hong Kong, for China, for Chinese people all around the world, and for enemies of imperialism everywhere. So let them raise a glass, as, at the Convention Center, the Chairwoman of the incoming Legislative Council . . ."

Laura's phone rings. She barks, "Take Convention Center and Lan Kwai Fong in the split. Lose little box," then picks up the phone. "Control Room. . . . Yes, Richard. Oh Jesus, I'm sorry. . . . Yes, Mike should do his standup before the tanks go. Bye."

". . . Patricia Pang is approaching Chief Executive Tung to take her oath of office. Pang and the rest of incoming legislators have suffered the humiliation of having to meet across the border . . ."

"Okay, Lan Kwai Fong out. Put LegCo in the split with the floor feed," Laura says. "We have that split, right?"

"Yes," Ashrami says.

". . . under the threat of arrest under archaic colonial sedition laws. And now, at the Legislative Council building, we are seeing the real traitors, the illegally chosen legislators, raising their arms in a false victory in front of their mainly foreign supporters. After this final act of colonial bootlicking, they will slink off into the night, likely never to be heard from again. In their place, later this evening, or I should say this morning, for it's not only after midnight here, it is truly morning in Hong Kong, the loyal legislators now swearing their oaths to Hong Kong and the Chinese nation, will take their rightful place, and go into session to approve a range to bills to guarantee that the stains of colonialism will be washed out of the fabric of Hong Kong forever . . ."

"Okay, there they are, Chris and Chuck" Laura says, looking at R-1. She pushes that lever and A-1, "Coming for R-1."

"What the fuck is going. . . ?" Edie asks.

"Later," Laura says. "Split ready?"

"Loaded," Ashrami says.

"Take it," Laura tells Quickie, "Squeeze stage, then go full on R-1 when the fireworks begin."

". . . the biggest criminal of the occupation of Hong Kong," Deng continues, "boards the royal yacht to sail into a past that will be looked back on with disgust . . ."

Laura looks at Ashrami. "Why didn't you tell me the split was ready?"

"We have this one made," Ashrami replies.

"Sorry. Forgot. Thanks." Laura hits the A-1 lever, "Harbor up, going full with floor in little box." She releases the lever. "Quickie, how long to break?"

"Schedule in two minute."

"Okay, we'll take the break and go out on the fireworks. Then I'll have a little talk with Mister Deng." Laura hits A-2. "Candy, write Deng a note: break at fifteen. Nod if you've got it."

Fang nods.

". . . cursed for a thousand years," Deng says, "Patten may sail out of Hong Kong on a royal yacht, but this colonial handmaiden will never escape the eternal loathing of the Chinese nation . . ."

Laura hits the remote levers. "Okay, everybody, we'll go out on the harbor shot with the fireworks. Everyone else stand down. Do your standups, feed your tapes. I'll get back to you in the break about what's next. Thanks, everybody." She releases those levers, and presses A-1. "About one-thirty to break at fifteen, Deng. Out on the fireworks."

". . . leaving behind a legacy of racism, collusion, and families divided just as they heartlessly divided the Chinese nation," Deng says. "But now, the colonial devils are in retreat, fleeing in their regal splendor, and leaving the Chinese nation to fulfill our destiny in freedom, without interference from imperialists in London or anywhere else, ever again.

"As we see these fireworks over Victoria Harbor—you know, of course, that the Chinese invented fireworks, as well as the printing press and pasta—these fireworks remind all Chinese patriots that for their great nation with 4,000 years of glorious history, the sky is the limit, the horizon is unlimited, as long as Chinese people remain united."

"Lose the little box," Laura says to Quickie and A-1. "Fireworks full."

"Tonight, after a century and a half of colonial occupation, Hong Kong is reunited with the motherland, and for Chinese everywhere, we are more complete. Our brothers and sisters in Hong Kong have returned to the Chinese nation. For the first time in more than 150 years, China has sovereignty over Hong Kong. You have been a witness to history, a magnificent moment in the history of the Chinese nation. Hong Kong is again part of China, but Hong Kong has always been and will always be part of China. Brutal colonists may be able to temporarily change the maps and raise their flags, but they can never change the hearts and minds of the Chinese nation. Hong Kong and China are one. This is Deng Jiang Mao in Hong Kong, People's Republic of China, proud to be Chinese and proud that you've chosen to share this historic moment with FGN Asia. Candace Fang and I will be back with more live coverage of Hong Kong's return to Chinese sovereignty after the break. Stay with us."

"Break in ten," Quickie says. "Studio clear."

"Take it to break on the fireworks, full screen" Laura says, getting out of her chair, as Deng says, "What the fuck is going on in there?"

Laura walks out of the control room and pushes open the studio door, and replies, "What the hell is going on in here?"

"Nobody gave me any fucking cues, nothing," Deng says.

"What are you talking about?" Laura says.

"I didn't hear. . . ." Deng begins, then reaches under the desk and shakes his head. "New set, same electricians. My IFB got loose. . . ."

"That again?" Laura says. "That's not going to fly this time. . . ."

"I didn't hear you," Deng says. "What was I supposed to do?"

"You had a rundown, you should have followed it. . . ."

"Laura, come on. The way you've been changing things around all night, how was I supposed to. . . ?"

"Follow the rundown."

"I'm not going to take chances out there," Deng says. "I'm in the hot seat, I'm driving the bus, and I've. . . ."

"I'm driving the bus. . . ."

"We're starting that again?" Deng says.

"One minute," Quickie announces.

"J-block as scripted," Laura says to Quickie then turns back to Deng. "You are not the producer. . . ."

"Look, you were driving the bus off a fucking cliff," Deng says. "You admitted you were having trouble, you were trying to do too much. You were making Candy and me look terrible with all your jerking around. So when I thought the bus was going to crash—again—because nobody was telling me what the fuck to do, I took the wheel."

"That is not your job," Laura says.

"Well somebody had to start doing yours."

"Thirty," Quickie says.

"For god's sake, you're out there spewing bullshit. . . . 'When my parents named me Deng Jiang Mao. . . .' Your parents named you Lincoln Washington Lee. . . ."

"Shut up," Deng barks. "You want to get personal? You've never been able to do your fucking job. Get off my fucking set, or I will."

"We're not finished," Laura says as she walks out the studio door. "And don't lose your IFB again." She reenters the control room as the animation rolls. "God, I hate that," she says, taking her seat. "Playback, any VO from the ceremony yet?"

Quickie translates for the Chinese guy in the booth full of cassettes in the corner of the control room. "Yes," he says.

"Okay, we go with that in J-2," Laura says. "The exchange of salutes, then nat sound on the anthem coming up. Have we got tanks?"

Quickie translates. "Have," playback answers.

Quickie says, "Camera two in three, two, one, cue."

"Welcome back to FGN Asia's exclusive coverage of . . ."

"Candy," Laura says, pressing A-2, "we'll run VO in J-2, pause for nat sound in ceremony."

". . . Hong Kong's return to Chinese sovereignty. I'm Deng Jiang Mao, live in Hong Kong."

"And I'm Candace Fang. In the past fifteen minutes . . ."

"Have we got the yacht tape yet?" Laura asks.

Quickie translates. "No."

"Okay," Laura says. "Honest, run down to tapes and get me tape numbers on the VOs they've cut, and bring back anything that's ready."

". . . the British commander," Candy continues, under video of the ceremony, "exchanged salutes with the Chinese general who gave the signal to raise the new flags, indicating the formal change of sovereignty." Candy stops, but the anthem hasn't begun yet.

"Okay, wait," Laura tells Candy. "Straight to the tanks whenever the music starts."

Finally, the anthem begins. "Okay," Laura says.

"Cue," Quickie says.

"As that scene took place downtown," Candy says, "at the Lo Wu border crossing, People's Liberation Army troops entered Hong Kong for the first time. And, as fireworks lit the sky . . ."

"Kill VO," Laura tells Quickie.

". . . over Victoria Harbor, the Royal Yacht *Britannia* carried Prince Charles and the last British governor, Christopher Patten, out of Hong Kong."

"Deng, cue," Quickie says.

"In the hours ahead, Hong Kong's new Legislative Council will go into session. These lawmakers took their oaths tonight from Hong Kong's new Chief Executive Tung Chee-hwa. At tonight's—really this morning's—session, the new legislators are expected to pass a raft of laws designed to cleanse the stains of colonial oppression and confirm China's sovereignty over Hong Kong. Those laws will include recognition of Beijing's National People's Congress as the final legal arbiter for the territory, replacing the British Privy Council."

"Candy, cue," Quickie says.

"Tonight's handover marks the end of more than just 156 years of British rule. It also marks the end of a transition period that began in 1984. FGN's Edie March reports on what's already changed, what will change and what won't change under Chinese rule."

"Package roll," Quickie says. "Three-minute-forty."

"That was good," Laura tells the anchors.

"That nat sound was ragged...." Deng says. "And why didn't we cover with VO of the swearing in...?"

"Deng, enough," Laura says. "Let's just get through this."

"That's the right attitude for a producer on a historic night," Deng says.

"Enough," Laura says. She's decided to be Chinese about this: no more screaming; no ranting and raving; just make sure that Deng winds up with his ass in a sling when it's all over. Off her show at the very least, maybe even off the Fuggin Asia payroll. Let him go find those network millions he gave up after this. That's better than yelling and fighting.

She takes a deep breath, then depresses the four remote levers, the anchor levers, and begins, "Okay, everybody, K-block. After the open, we'll start with Edie...."

Over the next 90 minutes, there are no further casualties. Deng spars in live shots with the reporters, especially Old Hartman, who never misses a chance to call Hong Kong's new sovereign "Communist China" and mention that the Yellow Star-5 tanks that came over the border are the same model used in the "massacre" at Tiananmen Square, while Candy reads and projects beautifully on script. After the sign-off, Laura sends the anchors upstairs to nap and change clothes, and makes them bring Quickie along to rest, while she prepares a rundown for *AM Asia,* and master control rolls a tape of the four-hour show they just finished. Laura's fire to be part of history has been replaced in her by a fire to make Deng history. It's a low flame, just enough to keep her nearly boiling.

At least for Laura and *AM Asia,* the Hong Kong smart aleck answer to the question "what happens after June 30?" is absolutely right: July 1 and, with it, another edition of *AM Asia.* She and Helios, sound asleep with his head on the desk, occasionally rolling onto the keyboard and causing a beep, are, as usual at this hour, the only people in the newsroom. Honest Ho intermittently dashes in and out of the control room with an armload of tapes or a slice of pizza, including one for Laura after she asks. The rundown comes almost automatically since Laura's been at it all night and has 23 packages in the can to choose from for the feature blocks. Laura takes a quick look through the news wires before finalizing the rundown, but it's strictly the handover, stupid, across the globe. She adds the market boards, decides against putting May's package and Candy's reaction in the repeating blocks, opting instead to run it as a second handover report at the top of the hours, piecing the rest of the story together with VO, SOTs and scripts while awaiting a handover wrap package. Nancy says they've fed the script and video to the US but there's no one in-house to voice it. Laura thinks about fetching Deng or Candy but dismisses that idea. Kathy Trang can voice it; she's supposed to be around here somewhere. Laura doesn't want to give Deng an extra second of US exposure. By the time tonight's US late news runs the package, he might be an ex-employee anyway.

Edie arrives just after five, and Laura instinctively hugs her. Edie succumbs rather than reciprocates. "Let's see your rundown in the smoking lounge," Edie suggests. In the staircase, cigarette lit, rain beating on the landing above, she asks, "What happened at midnight with Deng?"

"He said his IFB was out," Laura says. "But, even if that's true, he still had the rundown, he still knew the plan, and he ignored it to mouth off that nonsense. . . ."

"Bloody awful, wasn't it?"

"And it screwed all of you reporters. That's all Old Hartman talked about for the rest of the night, through his mike, calling me on the phone. You should have heard him when the tanks came over the border. . . ."

"What about Candy?"

"She was fine. . . ."

"I mean, while Deng was going off on his own, why didn't Candy. . . ?"

"I asked her to, but she was really paranoid about her English. I kept telling her she was great. . . ."

"That's ridiculous. Just scared of Deng, I'm sure."

"Maybe, but she did have trouble with anything that wasn't scripted 100 percent," Laura says. "I told her that little mistakes didn't matter, but she was really embarrassed about it."

"She was so great with that ad lib after May's report," Edie says. "Let me see that rundown before I finish this fag." She looks it over. "Did you check the wires?"

"No one's committed news outside of this madhouse."

"All right," Edie says, handing back the rundown and dropping her cigarette. "Anything you need now, *mei-mei?*"

"Besides a hit man for Deng?"

"Perhaps Old Hartman's hired one. The triads are quite active in Lo Wu."

"Well, we've got a handover wrap to voice," Laura says. "I was going to ask Kathy. . . . Isn't she supposed to be around? Nancy's done the script and it's all cut. . . ."

"I can voice it," Edie says, handing back the rundown. "Kathy's off standby and I'm on. None of the US affiliates wanted a live shot when there wasn't any bloodshed. . . ."

"We almost had some on set," Laura says, managing a smile.

"You might get some live interest during your show," Edie continues.

"We can do it from the handover desk during feature blocks," Laura says.

"All right, I'll put down the track on the package, and maybe you can use it in C block."

"Thanks."

Edie nods and pulls the fire door open, then stops and turns back toward Laura. "Sorry if I seem out of sorts this morning. You did a good job, Laura, and I should have said so."

"Thanks."

"I'm just worried. Usually I feel like I know where the chips will fall. But last night. . . ."

"What about it?"

Edie manages to smile. "It's like the Chinese curse: may you live in interesting times. Last night was interesting enough, but I think we have more excitement ahead, thanks to Mister Deng. Maybe I'm just depressed because midnight's come and I'm back to being a news executive instead of a glamorous reporter. . . ."

"You can watch yourself on the repeat," Laura says. "And your tapes will live forever. . . ."

"All the more reason to do your package." Edie sighs. "I'll try to stop worrying. You, too, *mei-mei*. Worrying won't help, in any case."

Edie holds the door, and Laura returns to her desk to keep duping and updating overnight scripts. Then she realizes it's easier to just write new ones. She has most of them done by the time Helios wakes up from his nap 30 minutes later. He visits the bathroom and when he returns tells Laura, "Someone's on set. I see the light on."

Laura glances at the set and sees the light, visible through the covered back windows of the studio. The windows are standard in all studio construction, Edie once told her, in case the station ever wants an open newsroom look behind its anchors. "Did you see what's going on?"

"No," Helios says.

"Okay," Laura says. "I'll take a look. I've got most of the scripts done. When Quickie comes down, get him the rundowns, or find a PA or intern to do it. Look for them around the pizza and donuts. Thanks."

Helios nods as he turns to his computer screen. Laura walks across the newsroom to the set door and opens it. She hears Edie's voice, ". . . sailing off into the horizon. But after all the pomp and ceremony, the question remains whether shipping magnate Tung Chee-hwa can see to smooth sailing for Hong Kong in this post-handover era." In the chromakey, Laura sees video of the *Britannia* sailing out of the harbor, fireworks above. "As this newest city in China tries to find its sea legs, I'm Edie March, FGN Asia, in Hong Kong."

"And out," Nancy says from the control room.

"Thanks," Edie says, and pops out the videocassette out of the camera on set.

"Very nice," Laura says.

"Thought I'd tart things up a bit," Edie explains. "Nancy agreed it would look better with a standup or two. Affiliates can cut them in the event they don't want them."

"I'm sure," Laura agrees. "But isn't a standup supposed to have the reporter standing up at the actual location. . . ?"

"I was there, and now I'm simply using a little assist from technology. Time-shifting. . . ."

"But. . . ."

"The report is on tape, after all, so nothing is as it appears in any case. I'm not actually where I am when you see me on the tape. . . ."

"Oh, I see," Laura says. "So nothing we're showing is real anyway. . . ."

"Reporter or producer, television is still my lie, *mei-mei,*" Edie says, walking the tape to editing. "Ours, in fact."

"And the lies just keep getting bigger," Laura says.

"And better," Edie adds. "Compared to where we began, so much better."

CHAPTER 20

Morning After

I T ISN'T THE FIRST TIME that Jeff has woken up at Yogi's, not by a long shot, but it is by far the most settled he's ever felt there. He loves her place—it's a real apartment, with full-sized rooms and furniture, with someone who cleans things, plus that million-dollar view of Central and the harbor. Except for dinner and a tuck with Laura yesterday afternoon, he's been at Yogi's for an almost unbroken long weekend leading up to the handover. This is the last morning of playing house, but he's enjoyed the interlude. Yogi surely isn't any less smart or ambitious than Laura, but she is a lot more cuddly and seems much more interested in having fun, and more inclined to do it. And there's no denying, looking at her head on the pillow, that she is gorgeous. Those porcelain dolls are lucky they have faces like Yogi's.

Maybe it's just the novelty, like sleeping over at your grandparents when you're a kid. You had a better time there than you did on regular days at home. Maybe it was because the old folks treated you nicer, or maybe it was just because it was different, a change from the routine. If you did it everyday, then it wouldn't be different anymore and maybe it wouldn't be better. But maybe it still would.

He has to go this morning, go out in that driving rain to be back in the Proper Gardens shoebox when Laura arrives, to give her a kiss, listen to her complain about her show, and tuck her into bed, maybe even have to do her as soon as she gets home.

Even though he'll be leaving Yogi's house, Jeff realizes he needs to stay closer to her now, because of those currency contracts. She helped him decide to do it, and, like Tim said, he'll need her help to see it through. Now they have a connection beyond Jew food and *shabu-shabu*. She's not just in his head, she's in his pocket, and she's put him in Laura's pocket for 850 grand. This isn't just for fun anymore; it's serious, there's real money riding on it. No, it wasn't just Hong Kong that went through a big change last night.

They're a few minutes away from the 7:45 break and the replay of D block when Franklin enters the control room. "Good morning, Laura," he says. "In my office when you go to tape." The program is in is in Pang May Pau's package with Candy's tag. Franklin looks at the panel and asks, "A-1 and -2, right?" Laura nods. He pushes the levers and tells the talent, "Candy, Deng, it's Pete. . . ."

"Ni hao, boss," Deng says. "A gracious welcome to the People's. . . ."

". . . please come to my office after the show. Thanks," Franklin says, and releases the levers. He looks down at Laura. "I'll see you there."

"One minute," Quickie says.

"I'm glad you're. . . ." Laura says to Franklin.

"We'll talk in my office," he replies and walks out.

Laura pushes the anchor levers. "Deng tags out of the package, Candy checks the Oz and New Zealand markets. Then Deng does currencies, two-shot on the tease, and we are finished. Everybody happy?"

"Thrilled to fucking death," Deng says.

Laura releases the buttons. "Quickie, we'll go out on the VO tease of Deng's interview."

"Okay," Quickie says. "Thirty."

"All right everybody," Laura says to the tech crew whose names she doesn't know. "You've done a great job on a long and difficult night and morning, and I just want to say thanks." Quickie and others translate for the Cantonese speakers. "I hope we can do it together again for the Macau handover in 1999," Laura adds.

"I hope we promotion by then," Quickie says. "Three, two, one . . . cue."

"That was Candace Fang reacting to Pang May Pau's report last night," Deng says. "Under colonial laws still in place, traitors can be shot."

"Deng, puh-lease." Laura says.

"Cue," Quickie says.

"Markets in Hong Kong and mainland China will remain closed until Friday to celebrate the handover," Fang says. "In markets open at this hour. . . ."

"Get 'em up," Laura says to Ashrami.

"In Australia, the All Ordinaries Index is up about 32 points, or 0.18 percent. And in Wellington . . ."

"Wipe it," Laura says.

". . . New Zealand's benchmark index is up about five points, or 0.21 percent."

"Camera one, Deng, cue," Quickie says.

"Checking the currencies," Deng says on camera, before the board comes up. "The yen is trading just above 112 to one US dollar. The greenback buys a dollar-forty-four Australian. And one British pound costs a dollar-thirty-nine US."

"Camera two, cue."

"Watch FGN Asia's *Money-Go-Round* to track the markets all day, starting with Kathleen Trang at the top of this hour," Fang says. "Coming up. . . ."

"Excuse me, Candy," Deng says.

"What the hell. . . ?" Laura says, pressing A-1 and A-2 in time for the last two words, as Quickie switches to a two-shot.

"These numbers seem to show a significant strengthening of the US dollar in past hour," Deng says. "We'll be keeping an eye on that developing story all day on FGN Asia. Candy. . . ."

"Candy, cue," Quickie says.

"Coming up on *AM Asia,*" Fang resumes, "more on the Hong Kong's historic handover. We'll see where the British queen is still welcome under Chinese rule . . ."

"And after the old boss," Deng says.

"Roll the VO," Laura says.

". . . we'll meet the new boss in my exclusive interview with Hong Kong's first Chief Executive Tung Chee-hwa. That and more, just ahead, so stay with FGN Asia," Deng finishes.

"Three, two, one, out," Quickie says.

Laura hits the anchor levers. "Franklin's office." She releases them and says, "Thanks everybody."

"Something's up with the currencies," Deng says. "Laura, see if you can get me a guest for ten." He then removes his mike and walks toward the studio door with Candy.

"I feel like someone's taken a bucket of cement off my head," Laura says to Quickie as they head toward the door. "One more to go."

"I'm going to the john," Deng says, meeting Laura at the control room door, "then I'll see you in Franklin's office. Do you know what this is about, Laura?"

"I know as much as you. . . ."

"That'll be the day," Deng snorts. "But you can use this time to work on the currency guest."

"It'll be a phoner, since everyone in town except us is on holiday," Laura reminds Deng's back, "as hard as that seems to believe at this point." Stepping around a fresh batch of flower arrangements from Candy's newfound admirers around the globe, Laura says hello to Richard, scrambling for his show that starts in fifteen minutes. "Slept yet?"

"No," he says. "I missed my chance in the block after midnight."

"Fun-ny, Richard," Laura says with a smile. She stops at Helios' desk. "Take a look at currencies. Deng thinks something's up. If the wires agree, or you see a big move, ask Honest to try the list of currency experts for phoners. I'll help you when I'm out of this meeting."

"Okay," Helios says, without looking up.

"Thanks. Great work all night," she adds, walking toward Franklin's office. She opens the door and sees Deng's there already, seated in the back, saying to no one in particular, ". . . so inconsiderate, self-absorbed and irresponsible . . . finally, there you are."

Laura walks down the bowling lane, past Franklin standing at the edge of his desk farthest from the door, Edie leaning against the wall below the silent monitors, Deng and Candy seated on chairs crowded in the back of the office, one chair left for Laura, in front of the case of dog food she ordered for Christina Volpecello's visit. She sits, saying, "I was inconsiderately and irresponsibly checking that currency story and guest you want for ten. . . ."

"All right," Franklin says grimly. "I saw the midnight block, and I reviewed the tape with Edie. I want to hear what happened," chook-koo, "from each of you. Deng. . . ?"

"I'm sorry, Peter, but I think I missed the expression of deep appreciation from management for presenting six hours live overnight. . . ."

"Deng," Franklin says, "cut the crap."

"All right, Pete," Deng continues. "We showed the activities associated with the change of sovereignty with facts and analysis. . . ."

"Deng," Franklin growls, "we're all too tired. . . ."

"Why did you deviate from the rundown?" Edie asks. "Why didn't you follow the plan to toss to the reporters live. . . ?"

"Oh that," Deng says. "I'm sorry. I was looking at the big picture rather than focusing on petty nonsense. I thought the final product at a historic moment would be what mattered. But if you're intent on nitpicking. . . ."

"What happened, please?" Franklin says.

"Simply," Deng says, "I didn't get any cues or instructions—turns out my IFB had failed on our new set, but I didn't know that—so I just kept waiting for someone to tell me what to do and kept talking until I heard something. When I saw new pictures on the studio monitor, I spoke to them. . . ."

"You lost IFB and you didn't know it, so you just kept talking until somebody stopped you," Franklin says. Chook-koo. "Is that it?"

"That's right, Pete. I thought it was. . . ."

"Okay," Franklin says. "Laura, is that what happened?"

"Well, from my perspective," Laura says. "I kept giving Deng cues to toss to Old Hartman at the border, but he didn't respond."

"My IFB was out," Deng says.

"So you say," Laura replies.

"Did you try anything else?" Edie asks.

"I thought about cutting his mike, but I was afraid that would make things worse. We still had two hours on air," Laura says. "I asked Candy to interrupt him and make the toss, but she wouldn't do it. So I put up the live shots and kept giving him cues on the video and . . ."

"Which I never heard," Deng says.

". . . told him to toss to the remotes. We did that to the break. Then I went on set and asked what happened."

"After she cursed me out," Deng adds, "that's when I discovered my IFB was out."

"I didn't curse. . . ."

"Thank you. Candy?" Franklin asks. "Did you hear Laura?"

"Yes."

"So why didn't you. . . ?" Edie says.

"I nervous my English no good," Fang explains. "When I no have script, I too many mistake."

"I told you exactly what to say," Laura says.

Fang shrugs.

"You have to see the big picture here, Pete," Deng says. "Laura's a good producer, but last night she was all over the place, changing stuff on the fly, and it got to be more than Candy could handle. We already had some trouble out there. . . ."

"That was really minor. . . ." Laura snarls.

"Let him finish," Franklin says.

"Laura," Deng says, "we'd just had a situation where Candy got hung out to dry on an unscripted toss—she said, "handover cemetery, no you stay go"—and the whole thing looked like shit because of all Laura's shuffling with the rundown and going crazy with the remote shots. The block at midnight had the potential to be even worse with all these tosses and nothing scripted properly. . . ."

"They were tosses between the reporters," Laura says. "They had nothing to do with you."

"When you're the anchor, everything's got something to do with you," Deng replies. "So when something went wrong—and I didn't know what it was—I thought I better just keep talking until I got a cue. After all, I'm the most experienced hand out there and, in that situation— where I have no idea what's going on in the control room, except that the producer's been screwing up all night—I think . . ."

"How much more of this do I have to. . . ?" Laura says.

"Quiet," Franklin says.

". . . it's my duty to take charge until I'm sure things are under control. We're a team out there, and when something goes wrong, we all suffer, the whole network suffers. I did what I thought was right for the team to make sure things stayed on track."

"You done?" Laura says to Deng. "The simple fact is that you didn't follow the rundown, whatever your excuse. And instead, you spewed all kinds of crap about the glorious motherland and insulted the British and whoever else. . . ."

"When Candy, as you put it, 'spoke from the heart,' you thought it was the greatest television since Geraldo's black eye," Deng protests. "But when I did it, it was against the rules. We're supposed to speak from the heart, as long as Laura approves what's in there. . . ."

"Deng, it wasn't just politics, it was lies," Laura says. " 'When my parents named me Deng Jiang. . . .' "

"Let's leave my parents out of this," Deng warns. "I was saying what's on the minds of more than a billion. . . ."

The office door swings open and Old Hartman enters, slams the door, turns directly to Franklin's unoccupied desk and declares, "In my 44 years of award-winning broadcasting, I have never. . . ."

"Mike," Franklin says, suppressing a smile, "We're in the middle of something. Please come back later."

"Oh, excuse me," Old Hartman says, flustered, turning toward the voice. He surveys the room and regains his bearings. "Pete, may I suggest you employ Solomonic wisdom and settle this debate by slicing the offending anchor in half."

"Mike, as long as we use your rapier wit as the knife," Deng replies, "I can live with that decision."

"Dissection, I'd say," Edie snickers.

"Enough," Franklin scowls. "You can come talk to me later, Mike."

Old Hartman closes the door behind him.

As the others giggle, Franklin says, "Mike's right for once: time to settle this and get back to work." Chook-koo. "First, when in doubt, follow the rundown. The rundown is always right, until you're told otherwise. Second, if the producer tells you to do something, do it. The producer is in charge, period. It's their show." Chook-koo. "So if something like this happens again on set, everyone understands what they need to do, right?"

Deng, Laura and Fang nod.

"All right," Franklin says. "Get back to work, finish up your shows, and get some sleep. And, yes, Deng," Franklin adds, "management does appreciate your efforts above and beyond the call on the handover coverage."

"That's it?" Laura says, still seated as Fang, Deng and Edie stir to leave. "He makes up a bogus story about his IFB and presents a propaganda broadcast . . ."

"I considered it more of a promo. . . ." Deng says with a smirk.

". . . and you're letting him get away with it," Laura says. "That is so unfair."

"We can't change what happened," Franklin says. "We can only make sure it doesn't happen again." Chook-koo.

"I'll need to see your rundown for ten," Edie says approaching Laura. "Let's go."

"We'll need a currency interview," Deng says, looking back from the doorway. "Something's going on with the dollar."

Edie wraps an arm around Laura's shoulder and whispers, "Let it go. Fag after the show."

Laura walks back to her desk amid growing signs of life in the newsroom, logs back into her computer, and calls across the row of empty desks to Helios. "Anything on currencies?"

"Wires say the US dollar stronger because of the handover. . . ."

". . . stupid. . . ." Laura punctuates. "I guess that makes sense." She walks to Edie, back in the slot, and explains Deng's concern.

"You both could stand a guest," Edie says. "I'll dig up someone and put in questions. Fortunately, none of the other producers have any interest in news today." She adds, "Focus on the show, forget all the other nonsense."

"I wish I could," Laura says.

"Mei-mei, your difficulty is that you hardly focus on anything else."

With anger glowing orange inside her head—still centered on Deng but now with shares for Peter as well as Pussy—Laura revises her rundown, updates a few scripts, checks the phoner questions, and enters the control room for the last show of this marathon. For the first time in weeks, it's just her and Deng solo out there. Laura wonders how Peter will use Pussy in this brave new post-handover world. "Okay, everybody," Laura says in the control room at 9:58. "One more to go. Let's make it clean." She pushes the A-1 lever. "All set? Phoner at the bottom of the hour. Questions are in, but we're not sure about who the guest is yet. We have a package for backup in case we can't get one."

"All right," Deng says. "Listen, I'm glad we got everything straight in there with Peter. For what it's worth, I agree with his decision not to punish you."

"Thirty," Quickie says.

"Shoot me now," Laura says to herself, then tells Ashrami at the graphics board, "I'll get you the phoner fonts as soon as I have them." Then she calls, "PA, ask tapes for some generic currency trading footage for our phoner."

"Already order," Honest Ho says from the back of the control room.

"Thanks, Honest. I thought you'd be at home asleep by now."

"Hong Kong people like to sleep at office," Honest replies.

"Cold open on VO, then camera one," Laura tells Deng and Quickie.

"Five to open," Quickie says, "three, two, one, cue."

"A new dawn for Hong Kong," Deng says over the sunrise VO, "on this first day of restored Chinese sovereignty." He appears on camera. "It's 10 a.m. in Hong Kong and Beijing, 11 a.m. in Tokyo, and 7:30 in Mumbai. *Ni hao.* I'm Deng Jiang Mao live from the FGN Asia Broadcast Center in newly liberated Hong Kong bringing you this hour of *Money-Go-Round. . . .*"

Block A runs on autopilot. Everyone is too tired to make mistakes, and Laura takes a nap during the taped B block, awoken by Edie's call telling her that Michael Morris from Stagan Financial will be the phoner guest. Laura prints the guest's name for Ashrami, gives his phone number to Honest Ho, and messages Deng, who's off the set. Deng messages back, "What'll he say?" Laura replies, "I'll do a pre and ask."

Deng returns to the set at 10:28. "How do I look?" he asks.

"Fresh as a daisy," Laura says. "I like you much better in a suit than that Chinese bathrobe."

"I hope this currency guy knows his stuff."

"Edie booked him."

"Okay then," Deng says, sidling his chair up to the desk. "Fifteen minutes to go. Let's make it good."

"Amen," Laura replies.

They run a cold open of the new Hong Kong flag flying over the harbor, do the markets and then roll Fiona's fresh package on the LegCo session. "We'll do currencies out of this, as scripted," Laura says to the control room and A-1, "then take the phoner. Honest, get the guest on the line, and put him on with me for a pre."

"Ask him about the dollar," Deng says.

"No shit," Laura says after releasing A-1

Seconds later, Laura's phone rings. "Hi, this is Laura Wellesley. Thanks for doing this, Mister Morris."

"You're welcome," Morris says. "Call me Mike. Mister Morris is my father. At least that's my mother's story, and she's sticking with it."

"All right, Mike. You'll be speaking. . . ."

"You know this cost me a round of bloody Marys."

"What?"

"It's a game we play when we're out. Whoever's mobile rings has to buy a round of drinks."

"You were up early. . . ."

"Nah, out late."

"You sure you're up for doing this?" Laura asks.

"Sure, especially since I've already paid the bill."

"You'll be talking to our anchor, Deng Jiang Mao, and he'll be asking. . . ."

"The ABC. . . ."

"Excuse me?"

"American-born Chinese. You can tell by his accent. He doesn't have that British thing going like dudes from here and Singapore. Man, that chick Candy, she is suh-weet. . . ."

"You're sure you're okay for this?"

"Oh yeah. It helps to have a couple of drinks under your belt to talk currencies. We traders pass around the Absolut before logging in every morning. . . ."

"Right." Laura sighs. "You'll be talking to Deng about currencies. He wants to discuss why the dollar's up. . . ."

"People are just antsy about the handover, but it's no big deal. There's been rumors about devaluation in Thailand."

"You also heard that?" Laura asks, then reminds herself, "God, I was supposed to. . . ."

"It's a hearty perennial, that one."

"Is there any truth. . . ?"

"Not in my book. It's pure bullsh . . . nonsense."

"Thanks," Laura says. "Keep it clean on the air, please."

"No sweat, Lisa."

"Laura."

"I'll be talking to Deng, right?"

"Right."

"I'll remember that one. Deng Xiaoping. . . ."

"Deng Jiang Mao."

"I'll call him Deng, okay?"

"Fine. Just hold the line. We'll go in about a minute or so, and you'll be talking directly to Deng. That'll be live on the air."

"Okey-dokey."

Laura puts Morris on hold and punches Deng's button.

"Thirty," Quickie says.

"We've got Michael Morris from Stagan Financial," Laura tells Deng. "Call him Mike."

"What's he say. . . ?" Deng asks.

"He says the dollar's strength is no big deal, but I think he's drunk."

"Unbe-fucking-lievable. Perfect end to a perfect day . . . night, whatever."

"I think he'll be okay," Laura says. "Just keep him focused best you can, and we'll see how long we go. If you need to dump him, just do it, and go to a currency board, then we'll roll the Float-2 package, the shorter back-up. You've got the lead-in. . . ."

"Five," Quickie say.

"Jesus fucking Christ," Deng says, "deliver us a miracle."

"Three, two, one, cue."

"As we reported earlier," Deng says, "it's a quiet morning in Asia Pacific equity markets with Hong Kong on holiday celebrating its return to Chinese sovereignty. But there's been some notable action in the currency markets. . . ."

"Board," Laura says.

"The US dollar is stronger against the yen, the Deutschemark, and the British pound. It's also up against the Korean won, the Singapore dollar, the Australian and New Zealand dollars, the Thai baht, and Indonesian rupiah. . . ."

"Lose the board," Laura says, and Deng reappears on camera.

"To talk about why the greenback is rising today, we have currency analyst Michael Morris from Stagan Financial on the line with us."

"Go, Honest," Laura says.

"Mike, this is Deng Jiang Mao in Hong Kong. Tell us about the dollar's rise. . . ."

"Hey, Deng. What's up?" Morris says.

"Put up the font," Laura says. "Geez." A graphic appears across the screen reading: Voice of Michael Morris, Currency Strategist, Stagan Financial, Hong Kong.

"Well, Mike, the US dollar's up, by as much as a half-percent against some Asian currencies. Why do you think that is?"

"Man, that's a pretty big move," Morris says. "I'd be buying yen now if our office was open. . . ."

"You can get out your trading book right after we finish, Mike. But, now, tell me, what do you think is behind the move?"

"I think it's just the standard morning after jitters in the market."

"Morning after Hong Kong's change in sovereignty?" Deng asks.

"If that means the handover. . . ."

". . . stupid," Laura and Quickie say and exchange smiles.

". . . then, yeah."

"But why are markets jittery, Mike?"

"A big change like the handover introduces new elements of uncertainty," Morris says, "and markets hate uncertainty, despise it, loathe it. . . ."

"What kind of uncertainty, Mike? Chinese authorities have assured that Hong Kong's currency peg will remain in place. The Basic Law guarantees that Hong Kong's economic system will remain unchanged for 50 years. . . ."

"Well, yeah. But guarantee, schmarantee . . ."

"Phoner graphic," Laura says. A regional map with a pin in Hong Kong and Morris' name and company fills the screen.

". . . the proof is in the pudding. Traders need to see what happens. Having the markets here closed until Friday only adds to the doubts. . . ."

"So why does doubt strengthen the US dollar?" Deng asks.

"Lose the graphic," Laura says. "Font again."

"When people are uncertain, they buy the US dollar. It's like a safe haven . . ."

"Roll the VO with the phoner font," Laura says. Pictures of hyperactive traders alternate with digital readouts on a ticker.

". . .the go-to currency for traders. No one ever lost their job, and hardly ever lost their shirt, holding dead presidents."

"Dead US presidents," Deng adds.

"Yeah, although personally, I wouldn't even want to hold a living president," Morris says. "I'd rather hold that Candy chick. . . ."

"I'll tell my lovely and talented FGN Asia colleague Candace Fang," Deng says.

"Lose the VO, keep the font," Laura says, then pushes A-1. "Let's wrap this drunk, and ready with Float-2." She releases the lever and tells the control room, "Everybody, ready currency board out of the phoner, then Float-2."

"I've been hearing stuff. . . ." Morris continues.

"What have you been hearing, Mike?"

"Oh, there's always wild rumors floating out there. The market runs on rumors."

"What kinds of rumors?"

"Recue the VO," Laura says, then tells Deng, "Good. Keep him talking."

"Oh, you know," Morris says. "The usual stuff about devaluation. . . ."

"Devaluation of the Hong Kong dollar?" Deng asks.

"Give me a split," Laura says. "Deng and the phoner graphic."

"Nah. That's solid, at least near term. Beijing would lose face if Hong Kong devalued. . . ."

"Then what currencies are at the center of these rumors, Mike?"

Ashrami jingles and Quickie puts up the split.

"There've been rumors about Thailand going around for weeks."

"Devaluation of the Thai currency, the baht?"

"Yeah, that's right. The Thai baht."

"Do you put any credibility in that?" Deng asks.

"I personally don't, because, you see. . . . Here's the story: if the Thai baht goes, then that would really ream out the economy there, totally flatten it. See, when currencies go down, interest rates go up, so that's bad for business. But over there, it would be worse, a lot worse, because there's a lot of what we call three-D, dollar denominated debt. That means it would take more baht to get the dollars to pay back those debts. . . ."

"I understand, Mike. But why should that impact other currencies, like the yen or the won?"

"That's a good question, Deng, and there's a really good answer. . . ."

"Good," Laura tells Deng. "Stay with him. Roll the VO."

"You see," Morris continues, "Malaysia or Indonesia or the Philippines—a perpetual disaster area—or even say Korea, can't let the Thai baht fall in relationship to their own currencies."

"Explain that for us, Mike, please."

"See, because then Thailand would be able to undersell them, on exports, on foreign investment, on all kinds of stuff. . . ."

"So would other countries also devalue?"

"They'd have to, though people like me on the trading terminals would probably do it for them. All the Asian currencies would wind up lower to keep the countries competitive. But, of course, no one would be any better off after all that, in relation to the other countries, than they were before. But at the same time the businesses there would be totally screwed. Is it okay to say that?"

"You did, Mike. Why would businesses wind up in such dire straits?"

"Enough of the VO," Laura says. "Do we have more?"

"No," Quickie says.

"Nicely put," Morris says. "Interest rates would be higher, and, to top it off, businesses would get a double whammy, because they'd need more baht or pesos or whatever to pay back their three-D loans. . . ."

"Back to split with the phoner graphic. Drop the font."

"Okay," Quickie says.

"So you see," Morris explains, "the whole thing would be a mess, an absolute mess. And central bankers know that—bankers are not stupid— so that's why I don't think any devaluation is going to happen."

"But. . . ." Deng begins.

"Excuse me, I just wanna say that as a trader, I'd take advantage of this situation and sell US dollars and buy some of the local currencies, especially the exotics, the baht, the peso, the rupiah, to profit from this blip, 'cause I think that once things get back to normal here on Friday and the market reopens, prices will settle back down."

"So you don't think there's a chance of a devaluation in any of these countries?" Deng asks.

"Great question," Laura tell Deng. "We've still got more than three minutes to break. Keep him talking."

"I never ever say never," Morris says. "But listen, it's like the Russians and the Americans in the Cold War. If the Thais devalue, then everybody else will, they won't gain any advantage in exports, and their debtors will get killed. What did they call it with the nuclear missiles. . . ?"

"Mutually assured destruction," Deng says. "MAD."

"Yeah, that's right. And that's what it would be, mad. So, if you wanna play this game, and believe me, it's not for everybody, but if you're in trade, in the international markets, even just living overseas, then you should be protecting yourself and lowering your risks by through active trading."

"But isn't currency trading inherently risky, Mike? How can trading lower your risk?"

"Nice question," Laura tells Deng. "About two-thirty." She releases the lever and tells Quickie, "Stand down on Float-2. Deng can take him to the break. Keep the board loaded. And Honest, have you got notes on this?"

"Yes."

"Great," Laura says. "Cut a couple of bites. One from the beginning about the uncertainty in the markets because of the handover, and another about the unlikelihood of devaluation because of its impact on the local economies, the three-D thing."

"Okay."

"When he's done," Laura adds.

"Good question," Morris says, "and you're asking the right guy. First, I wouldn't play currency markets with the rent money, that's for sure. But let's say you're living in Tokyo and getting paid in yen, but you've got bills to pay back home—you're an American, right?—in US dollars. So, like it or not, you have to do some currency trading. The difference is whether you're active or passive about it. If you just wait around and fork over the yen for the dollars when your bills are due, you're at the mercy of whatever the exchange rate happens to be at that time between the dollar and the yen. And you're still paying all kinds of fees and charges to your friendly local banker for the privilege of making the exchange. On the other hand, if you work through a reputable currency broker, you'll get lower fees and better rates than at the banks and, if you watch the markets, you can buy the dollars you need at an advantageous rate, when you're getting more dollars for your yen or won or baht...."

"But you may be wrong about the rate," Deng says. "What seems like a good rate today could become a better rate tomorrow...."

"Hey, look, you lock yourself into a good rate today, then you can't kick yourself for not getting a better rate tomorrow. If you're going to do that, whether it's in currencies or stocks or bonds or oil, you're gonna drive yourself crazy. That's why I say playing the currency market isn't for everyone."

"Minute-thirty," Laura tells Deng.

"Understood, Mike," Deng says. "To sum up here, you think the rise of the dollar against Asia currencies today is just a temporary ripple."

"Good," Laura tells Deng. "We'll come out to you and do the currencies, tease, then go to break." She releases the lever. "You got that, Quickie? Wrap the interview, Deng on one, then currencies, and tease to break. We can go out on the stock boards."

"Right," Morris replies. "People just have an automatic reaction to buy dollars whenever there's the slightest uncertainty. Nothing more. . . ."

"Okay," Quickie replies.

"You don't think that there's any devaluation ahead, Mike," Deng asks, "that today's strength of the US dollar is just the effect of Hong Kong's change in sovereignty on unnecessarily nervous traders?"

"You said it."

"And so did you."

"Yup. If you've got the dollars, take advantage. Make yourself some money so you can go for a nice holiday in Boracay instead of sticking around town next time we've got a six-day weekend."

"I second that emotion. Thank you, Mike."

"Cut the phoner. Lose the split," Laura says.

"That was Michael Morris, currency trader at Stagan Financial here in Hong Kong, saying, don't worry, be happy about the rise of the US dollar in today's trading. Taking a look at the currency markets right now . . ."

"Take board," Laura says.

". . . the yen is off its low, down less than half a percent against the US dollar. The greenback is still up against the Deutschemark and the pound sterling, but looks to be easing. So, at least for the moment, it seems our guest is right, that we're just seeing a temporary spike in the dollar. But stay with us as the *Money-Go-Round* turns throughout Asia's trading day to track the latest on this developing story."

"Lose board," Laura says.

"Coming up after the break, I'll be back with Candace Fang to take an in depth look at the Hong Kong's return to Chinese sovereignty. Stay with the *Money-Go-Round* on FGN Asia for complete coverage of all the news you need to have a profitable day. Remember, FGN Asia means business in Asia."

"Take the stock boards," Laura says.

"Ten to break," Quickie says. "Set clear."

"Keep the boards coming. Toss in the currencies, too, if you can," Laura says, then pushes the A-1 lever. "Great interview, Deng. Thanks."

"Laura, you ever notice," Deng says through the studio mike, "the less you're involved with things, the better they come out?"

As Deng leaves the set, Edie opens the control room door. "Let's have that fag, *mei-mei,*" Edie says.

"But we've still got the taped segment," Laura says.

"Quickie can handle it," Edie says. "Right, Quickie?"

"Sure," he replies.

"But what if the tape breaks. . . ." Laura protests.

"Quickie, tell Laura you double-roll," Edie says.

"Right," Quickie explains. "Two tapes rolling."

"You win," Laura says, and follows Edie out of the control room to the staircase. Edie holds the fire door open for Laura, the sodden air hitting her face like a hot towel and the sheets of rain against the building drowning out their footsteps. Edie sits on the stairs and lights a cigarette while Laura paces on the landing. "Did you hear what Deng said when you were walking in?" she asks, and continues without waiting for an answer, "He says to the whole control room that the less I'm involved, the better things go."

"Charming fellow. But you've got to stop worrying about him. It's not important."

"But how can I just ignore his utter disrespect, not just for me. . . ?"

"See his good points," Edie says, "like that interview segment. No other anchor could have gotten that guy to say so much, most of it quite useful and insightful. . . . You're cutting bites, right?"

"Yes, Honest is."

"Right," Edie nods. "Deng is good, and you have to take the bad with the good, I'm afraid."

"But you know what happened out there at midnight."

"I do, and the field reporters got much worse than you did," Edie says. She takes a long drag on her cigarette, then asks, "Why didn't you just cut in a remote shot in the split and let the reporter interrupt Deng?"

Laura stops, shakes her head and sighs. "I never thought of that."

"We might've had a cat fight on air between Deng and Old Hartman, and it probably would have looked like a dog's breakfast. . . ."

"No one even suggested. . . ."

"I didn't think of it either until this morning, when I watched the tape with Pete."

"Did he. . . ?"

Edie shakes her head.

"Did you?"

"No, *mei-mei.*"

"Good. Can you believe Peter?" Laura groans. " 'Don't do it again, Deng. . . .' "

"What Deng did was wrong. That said, after watching the tape, assuming he's telling the truth about his IFB. . . ."

"Oh, yeah, right."

"Assuming he is, Laura, or even assuming he's not, seeing Deng handle the transitions between the pictures in the splits, talking about what appears on the fly giving it background and context. . . . You can't help but admire his skill on the live set."

"Granted. But what about all the drivel he was spewing. . . ?"

"Like he said, we wanted it from the heart, and that's where Deng's heart is, or at least where he wants viewers to think it is. We can't demand that his heart be in the same place as ours."

"I don't believe it," Laura sighs. "And I just can't accept that we're ready to accept what he was saying about the yoke of British imperialism, the soldiers in skirts. . . . I was offended by that. . . ."

"You'll never win this, Laura, so forget it."

"I can't forget it."

"You really must." Edie takes a puff. "He's the one who gave up network millions to return to his roots."

"Listen to your big sister," Franklin says from three landings above. "I figured you two would be here." Chook-koo.

"Peter," Laura says, as he bounds down toward their landing. "I'm still outraged about letting Deng off. . . ."

"He did a great job," Franklin says. "What went out maybe was better than what we would have gotten if he'd followed the script. . . ."

"Well," Laura says, "we'll never know. . . ."

"On the boat last night, at the end of that midnight block, people applauded."

"They did?" Laura and Edie say.

"Sponsors, who only watch for their own commercials," Franklin says, shaking his head. "I couldn't believe it. They applauded. I've never seen anything like it. Be thankful I didn't tell that to Deng."

"Tell me one thing, Peter," Laura asks. "How much of what you said in there, at the meeting, was what you really thought and how much was to protect Pussy?"

"My, my," Edie gasps and coughs.

"That's not a question I can answer objectively, of course" Franklin says. "But this is not about Candy, it's about you and Deng. And Deng made lemons into lemonade out there last night. The fit between the live pictures and his words. . . ."

"I was just telling Laura that," Edie says.

"But he planned it all," Laura protests. "He must have. How else could he prattle on for fifteen minutes straight, with all those facts and figures. . . ?"

"That's his job, Laura," Franklin says. "And it was all about the handover . . ."

". . . stupid," Edie adds.

". . . all of us probably have those same facts and figures swimming around in our heads," Franklin continues. "We've all been working the story for months. . . ."

"But it was so extreme," Laura whines. "Imperialists, colonial oppressors . . . that's not journalism. . . ."

"You've heard that's an awfully strong word for what we do," Franklin says, smiling.

"You're not going to joke your way out of this with me," Laura says angrily, turning toward the fire door.

"Wait, Laura," Franklin says. "Listen. . . ."

She turns around and leans against the door.

"Whatever happened last night—I realize it was serious and I'm not trying to make light of it—you and Deng are our best people, our best anchor and our best producer. And at the end of the block on the biggest story of the year, your audience was applauding. We need more work like that from both of you for Fuggin Asia to succeed. . . ."

"Next time Deng goes off. . . ." Laura says.

"There won't be a next time," Franklin says.

"If there is. . . ."

"Then I'll deal with it more forcefully," Franklin says. "You have my word on it."

"I guess that's the best I can hope for. Thanks." Laura walks through the fire door, trying not be angry, not to feel used and violated, wondering what it would have felt like to hear people actually applauding her show, even if it was her show as hijacked by Deng. Laura packs her things at her desk, opens the drawer, grabs the month-old, half-full pack of Marlboros and drops it into the trash, then heads for home. She surrenders to her exhaustion as the dominant emotion. As the elevator doors close her away from Fuggin Asia, a note from Brian Randolph in Bangkok hits the computer system.

> Since I talked to Laura Monday afternoon, there has been a growing buzz around town, but still no solid information regarding the persistent rumors of an imminent baht devaluation.
>
> I got my only hard information from a very prominent businessman, a well-connected telecoms tycoon, who says a Central Bank of Thailand governor asked him for his view of the impact of a devaluation. According to this tycoon, the bank is running out of foreign exchange to support the baht. (According to the last official report, end 1996, CBT had more than US$4 billion in reserves; if CBT is running out, that would mean there's already been massive market intervention.)
>
> I haven't been able to confirm any of the story with either the CBT governor or any other source, but Laura advised that the best thing to do was to put a note in the system to make sure everyone is aware of what's going on and stay alert for possible developments.
>
> As soon as I get more, I'll phone it in.
>
> BRandolph, Bangkok

CHAPTER 21

What Comes After July 1

"HOW DO YOU PRONOUNCE THIS WORD?" Deng asks from the set. "Con-tag-ee-en?"

"I can ask Honest to bring you a dictionary," Laura replies from the control room.

"How about if somebody else takes the trouble to look it up?"

"Minute," Quickie says.

"I did," Laura tells Deng, even though Honest actually did it, without Laura even asking. "It's con-tay-jun. Like in contagious."

"Con-tay-shun."

"Either way: jun or shun."

"Aren't we going overboard here on this story?" Deng says. 'The biggest international currency crisis of the past decade'?"

"That's what the wires say."

"I wish we could get a guest in. . . ."

"We've got the package and the phoner from Bangkok," Laura reminds him.

"Thirty," Quickie says.

"But that's the source of the hysteria," Deng complains. "We need someone who's got a more reasoned view, like that currency guy the other day. . . ."

"That currency guy who was totally wrong. . . ." Laura adds.

"But at least he wasn't hysterical," Deng says. "What he said made sense, more sense than the markets."

"I'll work on something for later," Laura says.

"How's this guy's English?"

"It's fine."

"Ten," Quickie says.

"Yesterday afternoon, Hartman interviewed a guy whose English was so bad, I thought Franklin would make him an anchor," Deng says with a smirk.

"Roll VO, cue."

"Asian currencies skid," Deng says under pictures of a currency trading floor, "as the Thai baht gets battered." The shot switches to Deng on set. "Good morning and welcome to *AM Asia* for Thursday, July third, 1997. I'm Deng Jiang Mao, live from the FGN Asia Broadcast Center in newly liberated Hong Kong with all the news you need to start your day profitably.

"Our top story: There's widespread fallout from the stunning devaluation of the Thai currency, the baht. On Wednesday, the governor of the Central Bank of Thailand announced that the bank would not intervene in international currency markets to support the baht's exchange rate, which had hovered around 25 baht per US dollar for more than five years. Let's look at . . ."

"Baht board," Laura calls out.

". . . the impact of that announcement on the baht. The currency is now trading at 29-point-75 baht per dollar. That's up from its low overnight in US trading. But the con-tay-jun . . ."

"Lose the board," Laura barks to the control room. "Follow script."

". . . has spread to other currencies in the region," Deng continues on camera, "as traders speculate that more Asian central banks could allow their currencies to float in response. In trading in other currencies . . ."

"Board," Laura says.

". . . the Korean won is down about three percent. That's a very big move, since currency markets generally fluctuate in fractions of percents. The Singapore dollar has slipped about two percent, while the Japanese yen has actually risen off yesterday's depressed levels."

"Camera one," Quickie says.

"Other currencies are holding steady, but many analysts are wondering for how long. As stock markets open across the region, FGN Asia will follow the impact of these exchange rate changes on stock prices," Deng continues. "Also, minutes from now, we'll talk to an economist in Thailand about what floating the baht means for the region, but first reporter Brian Randolph in Bangkok tells us more about the anatomy of the devaluation and its impact in Thailand from the boardroom to the barroom."

"Roll package."

"Rolling," Quickie says. "Three-ten."

"Nice, Deng."

"Shhh," Deng says, "I want to listen."

"Ending weeks of speculation," the package begins, with Randolph standing in front of a white, boxy building, "the Central Bank of Thailand announced Wednesday that it would stop supporting the exchange rate for Thailand's currency, the baht. Sources close to the bank said it hoped the Hong Kong handover and market closure would help ease impact from the move. But the announcement sparked a devaluation of the baht against major currencies. And when the baht falls, its impact shakes the entire Thai economy."

Shot shifts to an automobile assembly line.

"For foreign-owned factories like Japanese car plants, the devaluation means a fall in local costs, such as wages to assembly line workers, but a rise in the cost of imported parts. It also means that, if automakers want to build more factories here—and the government hopes to make Thailand the Detroit of Asia—their yen, marks or dollars will buy more local bricks and mortar."

Shot shifts to a textile factory floor.

"For locally owned factories, the picture is less clear. For companies with loans denominated in dollars or other foreign currencies, devaluation means it will cost them more baht to repay those loans. They may find that their exports increase, because the fall in the baht makes their goods cheaper in comparison to Chinese or Malaysian goods, but those countries may also devalue their currencies to stay competitive."

Shot shifts to a rice paddy with farmers in conical straw hats and water buffalo plows.

"Thailand is the world's biggest exporter of rice. Exporters who get paid in yen or dollars will find they're richer than before when they exchange their dollars for baht."

The shot shifts to a busy shopping mall.

"But as consumers they'll find that prices of imported goods, whether it's Ericsson phones or Levi's jeans or Martell cognac, are higher."

Shot shifts to a crowded tropical beach.

"Foreigners will find their vacation budgets stretch further in Thailand, as their dollars, pounds and francs buy more baht to spend on holiday fun. That could lead to a boom from the famous beaches of Phuket . . ."

Shot shifts to an interior with young women in bikinis dancing above a bar.

". . . to the infamous go-go bars of Patpong, a center of Bangkok's sex trade."

Shot shifts to stock market trading floor.

"Phoner graphic in," Quickie tells Laura.

"Thanks. Cue the VO for the interview," she replies.

"But the biggest impact may be felt here," Randolph reports, "on the Stock Market of Thailand, where foreign funds have been pouring in to support the growth of Thai companies and turn Bangkok from a financial backwater into a global player."

Shot shifts to Randolph on a busy Bangkok street.

"Honest," Laura says, "guest all set?"

"Yes."

"Okay. Tell him he'll be live when he hears Deng's voice."

"Overseas money has not just fed the expansion of Thai companies, it's helped create a financial services industry with thousands of jobs and stock market wealth that didn't exist five years ago. If that money leaves, those jobs and those paper profits will disappear. For the proud Thai people and their nation that's never been colonized by foreigners, their economic fate now rests in the hands of overseas investors and fund managers. That could be the most bitter medicine of all from the devaluation of the baht.

"From Bangkok, this is Brian Randolph reporting for FGN Asia."

"Cue," Quickie says.

"Now to look more closely at the impact of the baht devaluation, we have on the line from Bangkok, economist Paramat Sutonvika from Deutsche Bundt."

"Put him through, Honest," Laura says.

"Good morning, Khun Paramat," Deng says, using the Thai honorific.

"Good morning, Mister Deng," the guest replies.

"The wire services are calling this the biggest currency crisis in decades," Deng says. "Is that how you're seeing it?"

"Good," Laura tells Deng, "We can go three minutes if he's good." She releases the lever and says, "Put up the graphic, then go to the spilt."

"It's surely the biggest currency event in Thailand in a long time," the guest says. "But I think it's somewhat early to call it a crisis."

"What would make it a crisis?"

"You know the saying: in a recession, you lose your job; in a depression, I lose my job. It remains to be seen what the reaction of Thai industry and Thai markets will be, as well as that of foreign investors."

"What's the best-case scenario?" Deng asks.

"Excellent question," Laura says, depressing and releasing the lever. "Take the split. Nice job on the questions, Honest."

"I think the best-case scenario is that traders and investors see that things had indeed become overheated, that the Thai economy had come too far too fast and needs to pause for a breath before growth resumes."

"Where would the currency wind up in that scenario?"

"I'm not a trader," the guest says, "but I think a ten percent devaluation would not be unreasonable. . . ."

"That would mean that the currency would actually appreciate from where it is now," Deng says.

"Yes."

"So you think currency markets have overreacted to the Central Bank's announcement."

"Assuming the best-case scenario, yes."

"What needs to happen for the best-case scenario to play out?"

"Roll the VO," Laura says, then pushes the lever, "Nice, Deng."

"First, I think it's important that money managers assess the situation realistically. The economic fundamentals of Thailand haven't changed overnight. So if investors were confident about the situation here last week, they should remain confident about investing here today. And now the prices are even lower."

"We really need some new currency VO," Laura mutters, and sends a message to Nancy and Fiona.

"What does the Thai government or Thai business need to do to promote stability?"

"Kill the VO," Laura says, "Split." The screen shows Deng on the right and, on the left, a map of Thailand with a pin in Bangkok and the guest's name below it.

"The most important thing is for the Central Bank to signal that it will step in to stabilize the baht at some level through. . . ."

"You mean by market intervention, by buying baht?" Deng asks.

"Yes, precisely."

"But didn't the Thai Central Bank just announce it won't do that. . . ."

"It announced it will not intervene now," the guest says. "That doesn't mean it never will."

"What if the Central Bank can't support the currency?"

"Well, Mister Deng, the Bank has some four billion US dollars. . . ."

"What if the Bank has spent it all already?"

"Great," Laura tells Deng.

"None of us know whether the Central Bank has previously intervened. It's inconceivable that the Bank could have intervened at anywhere near that magnitude without having significant impact on the value of the currency. I'm sure that the determination to let the baht float was a strategic decision, not a move of desperation as some commentators have mistakenly portrayed it. In the days or weeks ahead, we'll likely see this float was the prelude to a more concerted, targeted market intervention. . . ."

"So," Deng says, "you're saying Thailand let the currency float in order to allow a market correction for the baht, and then the Central Bank will step in to support a new exchange rate?"

"Exactly."

"Well, assuming that's the case, Khun Paramat, do you think this is a buying opportunity for the baht?"

"I don't give investment advice, Mister Deng."

"But you think the fall of the baht has been overdone, that the markets have overreacted. . . ."

"I would agree."

"I'd call that a buying opportunity," Deng says, "even if our guest won't."

"Hello," Jeff says sleepily into the phone.

"Have I wake you up?" Yogi asks.

"Moshi-moshi. Yes. It's strange to wake up alone again."

"Nice to together for weekend holiday, but now you are back to correct bed."

Jeff doesn't know how to respond. "I'm sorry, but you know. . . ."

"Please do not always say you are sorry. This is situation," which Yogi pronounces sit-su-ay-son.

"Yes. But maybe next week, I can make a sourcing trip to China. . . ."

"I have called to tell you currency market move very sharply."

"Very sharply our way?"

"Yes. I am getting this news from your wife, so it must be correct."

"Ha."

"It was beginning from yesterday. Thai baht is falling. Korean won also falling. . . ."

"What about the rupiah?"

"Rupiah will also fall soon."

"So, that means it hasn't fallen yet. . . ."

"Economist on show of your wife say Thailand Central Bank will intervene in market, but I do not believe bank have foreign exchange for intervention. When this is known, will be panic. When is panic, rupiah will fall."

"But what if. . . ."

"You must patient."

"Okay," Jeff sighs. "I trust you. . . ."

"You must," Yogi giggles.

"I do, but let me ask you something. Did you invest any of your own money? Did you make any trades?"

"No, I cannot."

"Cannot?"

"Bank does not allow staff to trade for personal account. Is policy."

"And Yogi does not break the rules."

"I do not break this rule."

"When will I see you?" Jeff asks.

"I do not work today. . . ."

"But I have to be home for Laura. The office is closed, so I can't say. . . ."

"I understand. Perhaps we can play tennis Sunday."

"At night?"

"Yes, of course, after wife's bedtime. I know rule Jeffrey does not break."

"So he comes up to 28, and he's got his on air voice cranked up," Franklin tells Edie and Laura, seated on the stairway after her ten o'clock show, rain tattooing the landing above them, the only thing visible through the clouds the beacon at the top of the Central Tower rocket ship. "Mike says," and Franklin deepens his voice and makes it echo off the concrete walls, "'Pete, you know why I'm here. What happened out there last night was a disgrace, the greatest humiliation I have suffered in 44 years of award-winning broadcasting. I have here in my breast pocket my letter of resignation,' he tells me and my heart leaps," Franklin says in his normal voice, then switches back to imitating Old Hartman. "'And Pete, I was prepared to present this letter to you and terminate my relationship with this network, a relationship that began before you were born. But the devaluation of the Thai baht is a major story, potentially a watershed event,' he says, 'and I can't walk out on the network at a moment like this. I've stood by this network in every major crisis since the Bay of Pigs, and I'm not about to abandon the network now, when you need me most.' Then the blowhard pulls out the letter, rips it into little pieces, and lets them flutter down to the floor." Chook-koo. "So near and yet so far."

"But Peter, it was a disgrace," Laura says, "regardless of what the sponsors on your junk thought."

"There's a producer for you. Doesn't care about the sponsors—who pay for all this luxury," Franklin says, surveying the bare concrete decorated with damp cigarette butts.

"And what Deng said was pure ass-kissing crap, unadulterated garbage."

"Unadulterated, applause-winning garbage," Franklin reminds her. "He won't do it again."

"He did it again this morning," Laura says, "Puts a one-minute tag on a package instead of doing the SOT we'd hustled to pull from our guest the previous hour."

"I'll talk to him," Franklin assures her. Chook-koo.

"I'm afraid Mike could be right, though," Edie says, "about the baht."

"You really think so?" Laura asks. "Should I have done something when Brian called me . . . ?"

"There was nothing to do," Edie says. "He didn't have the story. . . ."

"But do you really think it's going to be that big?" Laura says. "Right now, everybody's nervous a little about the handover—stupid—so when the Thais float their currency, everybody jumps on it. . . . It's news on a quiet news day, gives them a fresh explanation for movement in quiet markets, and with the handover done, everyone's looking for the next big story from Asia."

"I'd much prefer to bask in post-handover afterglow, *mei-mei,*" Edie replies. "But in some of these tiger economies, the emperor has no clothes, and the baht may force them to look in the mirror."

"Which ones?" Franklin asks.

"The rest of ASEAN, and South Korea, too," Edie says. "There really isn't much reliable information available, but vast quantities of hot money have gone in there, because they've been told, by our network among others, that the Asian century is coming and no one wants to miss it."

"How bad could it get?" Franklin asks.

"Bad, I'm afraid," Edie says.

"How bad?"

"If I could answer that accurately, Pete," Edie smiles, "you'd have to pay me a far higher salary. But I can say this with certainty: it's a terrible story for us."

"Why?" Laura and Franklin both ask.

"It's terrible because we don't have good people where the story is. We had to rewrite the entire package from Bangkok, fake footage—if you look closely at the rice field, you'll see Candy in her Hakka farmer suit—and get Randolph to reshoot his standups," Edie says. "The *Journal* doesn't have good people on site either."

"They'll parachute people in," Franklin says. "I'm sure *Journal* reporters are already landing. . . ."

"They're not TV reporters, Pete," Edie says. "And there's a bigger problem. . . ."

"What?" Laura says.

"Asia's been a good-time girl for the company, as it has for investors. And now that the good time may be over, we'll see how they really feel."

"Sorry," Laura says, "I don't follow you."

"I'm sure Pete does: the worse the crisis gets, the less the people who run the company—and the people in the other three-fourths of the world—are going to care about Asia, or about us."

"I can't believe this week," Laura tells Jeff. "All that work for the handover, and it just disappeared into thin air." She takes a sip of white wine. "I also haven't heard anything more about Deng, my anchor. I told you about how on handover night he just went off on his own for the fifteen minutes after midnight, the most historic fifteen minutes of the whole night, the whole year. . . ."

"Right," Jeff says.

"Well, Peter just told him, 'Don't do it again' and that was it. But he keeps doing it again, Deng. It's really frustrating. I work to get the show a certain way, but then he just does whatever he wants."

"Have you. . . ?"

"Peter says he's going to talk to him. I used to think Peter knew what he was doing, but now. . . ." She shakes her head and sips more wine. "Edie's my friend, but she doesn't even have a degree, so how much can she really do? And now this crisis thing. It came so completely out of left field. . . ."

"Isn't that what makes it news?" Jeff says. "I mean, if you expect it. . . ."

"I understand what you mean. But that's a very simplistic view. For the handover story, we had resources and people in place to cover it. This story, because it's breaking in the places where we don't expect news, it's much harder for us to cover."

"What are you hearing, you know, about the exchange rates?"

"Everyone's still in shock, so it's hard to tell what's going to happen."

"But have you heard anything, like," casually, Jeff tells himself, casually, "about, say, Indonesia. . . ?"

"No," Laura says, taking another sip of wine. "But what's hard for us, the real challenge is to get past all these numbers and try to give the story a human dimension. This thing—whether you call it a crisis or not—is going to affect real people and their lives, if only we could find some of them."

"I didn't do anything about dinner," Jeff says, because he was glued to the television in Yogi's place all day watching the news now that he's figured out how to read the currency quotes that run across the bottom of the screen. "I can dash out and. . . ."

"No. I had some cheese sticks with Edie and I'm not really hungry." She takes a sip of wine. "Not for food, anyway. . . ." she says, reaching for Jeff's belt buckle.

Jeff tucks in Laura, dreading tomorrow, Saturday. She'll be home and will expect him to wake up there. He'll have to listen to her, and probably stay cooped up here in this shoebox all day unless the rain finally lets up, maybe head out for that overpriced dinner that Laura said she'd buy him once things calmed down after the handover, and put it on her charge card after they bring the bill to him, and go to sleep together, at the same time, like normal couples. All Jeff can think about is his currency gamble, and it is the one thing he can't talk to her about. Well, he realizes, one of the things.

He dials Yogi's numbers but she's not answering at home or the office or her mobile. He glances to the next building through the drizzle in the twilight. It's dinner time, so the Filipina probably is in the kitchen, all her clothes on. He feels very alone. He can't even take refuge in the JCC jacuzzi; it's closed for *shabbos*.

Jeff takes a fast shower, and changes into his khakis and a white button-down shirt with red pinstripes. He considers a tie, then dismisses the notion. No need to go overboard, he thinks.

He slides through the front door, locks the gate, presses the button for the elevator, grabs the umbrella Laura left outside, hears the scrape above eight on the way up and down, and opens the umbrella against the rain, which is heavier than it looked upstairs. He walks up the steps to Robinson Road, dodges the pedestrian fence to cross Seymour Road—Seymour who? Jeff wonders—and as he walks he keeps wondering about what's ahead, whether this is a good idea or whether he'll look back on this week as a chain of mistakes. He shuffles down the steps into the courtyard and enters the whitewashed colonial building with its two towers and an arch between them. He shoves his umbrella into the stand and approaches the crowd of dozens gathered for the JCC Friday night services.

From behind him, a familiar voice says, "I do not expect you here." Yogi smiles broadly as Jeff turns around. She has just come from work, dressed in a sea green suit with the usual short skirt, carrying her smart black leather bag with the built-in umbrella holder.

"What are you doing here?" Jeff asks.

"I come here quite often with Mitchell, my old boyfriend, before he go. He is more religious than you. . . ."

"It would be difficult to be less religious than me," Jeff chirps.

"Mitchell say services here very liberal, with playing guitar and permitting men and women to sit together. This is lucky for you: I can sit with you and teach you songs. Jew singing is quite lovely. Following services is delicious Jew food, and you do not need JCC card to enter. So before I meet you, this is my only opportunity for hummus. Thanks to you, now I get hummus more often. . . ."

"And I get *shabu-shabu*," Jeff says, adjusting to the idea that Yogi is here, and finding himself surprisingly relieved and happy about it.

"I think this is very fair. What has made you come here tonight?"

"My broker in New York advised me to pray. I'm still not sure if I'm supposed to pray for the currency markets or against them, though."

"Praying could be helpful," Yogi says. "But keeping close to me is most helpful for you."

CHAPTER 22

Before the Fall

"WHAT I WOULDN'T GIVE FOR A DONUT. . . ." Laura laments.

"I wish we had a donut, too," Edie agrees, "but no budget for idle bird time during the package roll. If we were at CNN, imagine the ad dollars rolling in with our wall-to-wall coverage of Diana, Princess of Wales. . . . "

"Still dead," Laura says in unison with her.

"We're going from the same location as the standup. It's the only place in town where I won't get drowned out by the bloody motorcycles or run down by one."

"All right," Laura says, cradling the phone on her shoulder and pressing the anchor lever. "Out of the package, we'll get the satellite link. Deng, you'll have Edie for less than three minutes."

"That's about standard for men having me," Edie says.

"How much time to the link?" Deng asks.

"Thirty," Quickie replies.

"Can I do a question on Suharto's future instead of this IMF junk?" Deng asks.

"Can Deng do a question on Suharto's future instead of the IMF visit?" Laura says into the phone.

"Sure," Edie says. "Exchange rate first, then Suharto's future and done, I reckon."

"Okay," Laura tells Deng. "Exchange rate first, then Suharto's future, and that'll be it. IMF as the backup."

"Ten," Quickie says.

"You're up now," Laura says into the phone, "in the split. Move a little left and tighten the shot."

"And lose these gorgeous legs?" Edie says before placing the phone on the ground in front of the elaborate doorway in the hotel garden serving as her backdrop, and motioning toward the camera. The shot closes tighter on Edie, starting from just above her waist. Laura nods and says, "Good," into the phone, though Edie can't see or hear her.

"Three, two, one, cue."

"For more on the crisis, Indonesian style . . ."

"Take the split," Laura says.

". . . we go live to FGN Asia's Edie March in Jakarta. What's brewing in Java with the exchange rate, Edie?"

"Within the past hour it's broken above ten thousand to the US dollar, Deng. Beyond the devastating impact on the economy described in my report, the other side of the story is hard currency rules in Indonesia. Exporters, currency speculators, and expatriates with dollars, pounds, francs or yen can get real bargains, because shop owners can't raise their prices as fast as the rupiah is falling. So people with dollars have been buying luxury items—electronics, cars, wine—at a fraction of their normal prices. . . ."

"What about. . . ?"

"Excuse me, Deng. . . . You can also find a lot of sad faces around town among people who bet wrong on the rupiah. When the rupiah moved from twenty-five hundred to five thousand, some expatriates thought it couldn't go lower, so they cashed in. Now they're lamenting their lack of patience, not to mention their faith in Indonesia's economic policy makers. People are crying in their beer, thinking it might have been champagne. Those tears emphasize that there's no limit to how low exchange rates can go and highlight the unprecedented volatility we're witnessing in currency markets throughout Asia, even now, more than two months after the collapse of the baht. This story is, it seems, still far from over."

"Two minutes," Quickie says.

"Two," Laura yells into the phone.

"Good point, Edie," Deng says. "Another big story brewing in Java and around Indonesia, the presidential election due in March. . . ."

"Right, Deng. General Suharto has been Indonesia's president since 1968, and before the crisis he was expected to be reelected handily to his seventh consecutive five-year term next March, even though he'd be 77 years old when that term begins. There's neither a credible opposition nor an heir apparent to Suharto. Markets plunged late last year when the president went abroad for a medical check up amid rumors of failing health. But the Smiling General looks fit these days when he appears in official media, distributing anti-poverty grants, golfing with fellow ASEAN leaders, and, since his wife passed away earlier this year, attending Friday prayers at Jakarta's central mosque."

"Minute," Quickie says.

"One minute," Laura screams into the phone, then adds "sorry" to the control room.

"The regime is notoriously corrupt, and Suharto's six children are increasingly brazen. There's even talk that one of Suharto's daughters, or a son-in-law speeding up the military ranks, is being groomed as a presidential successor. Such rumors are enough to keep investors scream-ing for Suharto's reelection."

"Thirty," Quickie says.

"Foreign investors face fewer restrictions in Indonesia than other countries in the region, and they largely accept the corruption, nepotism and authoritarianism in exchange for stability. The public at large in this predominantly Muslim country of more than 200 million has remained tolerant in exchange for decades of economic growth that has lifted tens of millions out of poverty. But as the economy slides backward, Indo-nesians may be less willing to overlook the dark side of Suharto's rule. After 30 years as an economic miracle worker, Deng, it looks like Suharto may need one more miracle . . ."

"Ten," Quickie says.

"Ten," Laura screams into the phone.

". . . to get his country out of this crisis and preserve his legacy."

"Thanks, Edie," Deng says.

"Lose the split," Laura says.

"That was Edie March, reporting live from Jakarta," Deng says, as the satellite picture from Jakarta goes black in the control-room remote monitor.

"That was close," Laura says into the phone. "Did you hear me?"

"I heard you," Edie says, bending to pick up the phone from the ground, "and I knew we'd make it. That's more than I can say for this shit hole of a town. And I hear Kuala Lumpur is bloody worse."

Jeff turns the television down, punches the numbers into the calculator, then calls Yogi.

"Yogi Takahara speaking."

"Moshi-moshi."

"Ah, hello. You begin to sound very Japanese. Perhaps tonight you will harder also like Japanese."

"I get harder whenever I hear your voice," he says, admiring the view from her terrace.

"How flattering. I will make talking for foreplay. . . ."

"You could make a little noise while we're doing it. . . ."

"Sure? Is wife make noise?"

"Actually, she gives stage directions."

"You still require direction from her?"

"Not to me. She's giving directions for some news program in her head. . . ."

"I hear some couple watch television while make love. . . ." Yogi giggles.

"I don't think she even knows she's doing it."

"Is odd to associate making love and making television."

"I think it covers her key interests," Jeff shrugs. "She's dedicated to doing both every day."

"Jeffrey is very busy man."

"Jeffrey is a very happy man when he is with you."

"Please, do not. . . ."

"I know I can't tell you how much I love you. . . ."

"You love *shabu-shabu* with me. Re-ray-son-sip cannot success with only that."

"I've heard that the most important sex organ is the brain."

"This would explain: I have small brain so also small vagina."

"I can't believe you talk like that in the office. What if someone hears you?"

"I have own office. Door is close. I am serious person, make serious decision for bank, write serious report. . . ."

"Earn serious money."

"Yes, but Beatles say, money cannot buy love."

"No, but it can help."

"You think you love me also because I help you make money."

"I loved you before that. . . ."

"But you now love me more."

"I love you more every day."

"Please. . . . You have called to ask again whether is time to sell. This is correct?"

"And to hear your voice. But yes, I see the rupiah got hammered again, and I figured out that there's about a half-million in the nineties, and more than a million in the one-twenties." Jeff stays at Yogi's all day now to watch FGN Asia's currency reports. "With the contracts I've already cashed, I think. . . ."

"Experienced investor know that when using profit to make profit, this is opportunity to increase wealth dramatically."

"I don't understand."

"You have already recover investment. Wife's collateral is safe. Now is time to take chance to make much more money."

"But what if the rupiah goes the wrong way?"

"There is some risk, but you must risk to make reward. . . ."

"Aw-main," Jeff says, amen in Hebrew. "But it's my money at risk, not yours. It's just a game for you. . . ."

"But I still play to win. Same for bank money."

"How much more can I make?"

"Is no limit. Rate can always fall lower. . . ."

"Okay, so how much can I lose?"

"I do not expect currency will return to previous levels. Even if IMF come, will not restore former values, only stabilize. Then currency maybe not go down further. But I do not think is possible to appreciate from level of today."

"So I just wait. . ?"

"Yes. When you patient, you get *shabu-shabu,* not only *shabu.*"

"But at some point, you get enough. . . ."

"You must trust me. I will say when is time to sell."

"I trust you with everything, my life, my love, and my money."

"You are hopeless investor and hopeless romantic."

"Now Singapore Airlines," Franklin says, inhaling Edie's smoke on the stairway and shaking his head. "The official airline of Fuggin Asia—

grounded. The official luxury sedan of Fuggin Asia—stalled. Our official business and luxury hotels—checked out. . . ." Chook-koo.

"No more flowers for Pussy. . . . Candy," Laura says.

"At least I got the hotels and SIA's official free flights for my crisis tour," Edie says.

"Yeah. Too bad we didn't have an official broadcast affiliate in each city for a crew and bird time. . . ." Franklin shrugs. "I must have been drunk when I approved that trip. I really thought this crisis would blow over in a few weeks, a month or two at most. . . ."

"We thought the same thing about the rain," Laura says, spying the light drizzle outside. "Maybe Old Hartman was right about building an ark."

"The crisis isn't going anywhere except straight for Hong Kong and anywhere else it hasn't hit yet," Edie says. "I wish we'd had a clue about the Peregrine thing while I was in Jakarta. Those tossers thought they ruled the world. I'm glad to see them get theirs."

"We're still on the story of their employees trying to collect their pay," Laura says.

"They'll never see a cent," Edie says. "It's because of that building. . . ."

"I thought it was loans to a taxi company with Suharto's daughter. . . ."

"Well, yes, but their building is cursed," Edie says. "Peregrine bought the Bond Center on Queensway."

"Which one is that?" Franklin asks.

"The beige monstrosity with the concrete koalas crawling up the side. . . ."

"So that's what those lumps are supposed to be. . . ." Laura says.

"Alan Bond, the Australian who commissioned it, went down in one of the biggest financial scandals in Hong Kong history, about five years ago," Edie explains. "Now Peregrine. . . ."

"Largest investment bank in Asia, ex-Japan," Laura says, "not."

"So we shouldn't buy the building in the bankruptcy auction," Franklin says, smiling.

"Whoever does," Edie says, "put them at the top of your bankruptcy watch list. And it wouldn't surprise me if other investment banks took the hint and started cutting back, offering severance packages, not renewing contracts. . . ."

"Can you imagine, though," Laura says, "showing up at the office and finding the place locked up, and armed guards telling you to go away?"

"Tell the truth, Laura," Franklin says, "how many mornings have you wished that would happen here?"

"I wish it would happen every morning—to Deng," Laura says. "Have you spoken to him yet, Peter? He keeps. . . ."

"God," Franklin says. "Let's get this settled, once and for all." Chook-koo.

"Exactly," Laura says, "let's. Please talk to him. . . ."

"What happened on handover night, whatever went on behind the scenes, came out as great television. . . ."

"But he disobeyed. . . ." Laura protests.

"Listen. Television is a medium of conflict, and that moment beautifully captured so many of the tensions inherent in the medium. . . ."

"What are you talking. . . ?"

"When Deng spoke, he put all those tensions, all those conflicts out in the open, laid them all out for the viewer. The age-old conflict between East and West, the conflict between capitalism and communism, that was all on the outside of the story. On the inside, you had the tension between the producer and the anchor and the pictures, which Deng handled beautifully. . . ."

"He. . . ."

"Let me finish. He made those pictures sing, better than the reporters—present company excluded, of course—could have." Chook-koo.

"Taa," Edie says.

"And, yes, he put across a point of view, and that gave our broadcast some flavor, some spice, some attitude. CNN had those same pictures we had, but they didn't have Deng, and we kicked their butt thanks to Deng. Viewers aren't idiots—at least not all of them—and they want to know what the anchor thinks, what's in his heart. Like Candy did with May's report. Like Cronkite did when he broke down announcing Kennedy's death, or with his tears of joy at the moon landing. . . ."

"You weren't even born when. . . ." Laura says.

"Exactly my point. Those are legendary moments, even for people who didn't witness them. They've been passed along in history, they are the history. They're what people remember, not some live shot from a reporter who doesn't know as much as the people in the studio or the audience, telling viewers what they can see for themselves with their own eyes. In a hundred years, when people want to know what happened on handover night in Hong Kong, do you think they're going to look at CNN with Judy Dandruff talking to that Filipina midget or watch Deng?" Chook-koo.

"What Deng did, what Deng does on the air is terrific. He's a great anchor, and you can learn a lot about television from him. And let's not forget, it wasn't Deng who got a heads up on a big, breaking story and just sat on it." Franklin gets up from the stairs and walks toward the fire door, then spins around. "Laura, the three most memorable moments in our handover coverage were May's package, Candy's reaction to it, and Deng's cover of the handover moment at midnight. You had nothing to do with the first two, and you tried to stop the third." He opens the door and walks out.

"Whoa," Laura says, still too shocked to be upset or angry. "Where did all that come from?"

"I've been telling you that you can't win against Deng, *mei-mei*" Edie shrugs.

"Deng hates me, Pussy hates me, and now Peter. . . ."

"And you're in love with him."

"What? *Et tu,* Edie?"

"Merely stating the obvious, *mei-mei.*"

"Are you kidding? Laura snaps. "I wouldn't touch him if he paid me. . . ."

"He does pay you. . . ."

"You know what I mean." Laura shakes her head. "Every night, my husband and I wind up panting like animals and for a little while—the only time all day—I manage to forget about the little wheel I'm running around on in this cage."

"Thanks for sharing, as you Americans like to say," Edie says, leaning back. "But that has nothing to do with love, though it's just like a woman to confuse love and sex."

"What are you talking about?"

"I'm saying that we women tend to place the heart a bit more than a foot below its actual anatomical location. Women link love and sex closely—most of the time they insist on having love with sex and often, too, too often wind up with neither—whereas men know that one doesn't necessarily have anything to do with the other."

"How romantic. . . ."

"It is, actually. Granted, men will screw anything that lies still," Edie sighs, "provided it's the most attractive thing in sight, of course. But when a man loves you, it's the kind of love that makes him spend three thousand Hong Kong on flowers that, if Candy even sees them, would only last a couple of days," Edie says. "It's the kind of love like in fairy tales—they lived happily ever after—that kind of love."

"Oh please," Laura moans. "I've been with enough men. . . ."

"Think of it this way, *mei-mei*. Would you define love as when you care about someone more than you care about anyone else in the whole world?"

"All right, yes."

"You don't just care about a handful—or, in some fortunate cases, two—of their organs, you care about everything they think and do. You think about them all the time. How they feel about you, their opinion of you, is what matters most to you in the whole world. More than anything else in the world, you crave their approval. Above all else, you want to please them. Can we agree that's a fair definition of love?"

Laura nods. "Yes."

"Well, that's how it's been with you and Franklin since the day he got here. Is there a man on earth you think about more than Pete?"

"Now wait a second. Even if that's true—and I'm not saying it is—that's not love. It's just because he's the boss. With the handover, he had something that I wanted and I needed him to get it. . . ."

"Keep talking. That sounds more and more like love to me."

"No. That's awful. You're reducing love to a professional transaction. . . ."

"As in, you give your everlasting affection and ask for the same in return. . . ."

"That's business."

"Call it what you will. But it has nothing to do with sex, and everything to do with approval. And, at the moment, I'm not getting one, and you're not getting the other."

"Hao jiao, bu jian, boychick," Moishe says, pumping Jeff's hand in the vestibule of the Ohel Leah Temple.

"That means, 'A long time don't see,'" Avi explains, as he shakes Jeff's hand. *"Shabbat shalom."*

"Shabbat shalom," Jeff replies.

"How come you don't come to look at samples no more?" Avi asks.

"Or for lunch to the factory?" Moishe adds.

"I just, I feel like this is my mother's thing with you now. . . ." Jeff says.

"At least come in and say hello once in a while," Avi says.

"Or come to jacuzzi," Moishe says.

"You often to services?" Avi asks.

"I started a few weeks ago," Jeff says, "first time in years. I haven't seen you before. . . ."

"Sharom areichem," Yogi says, joining the group, wearing a white linen suit with a microskirt, a black blouse, and string of pearls around her neck. It's the ninth straight Friday night she and Jeff have met at the temple, without either one of them mentioning any plan to attend.

"Areichem sharom," Jeff replies, while Avi and Moishe use the correct *aleichem shalom* pronunciation. "Avi, Moishe, this is Yogi." The three grin at each other. "Avi and Moishe are my business partners . . . well, my mother's business partners. . . ."

"So you make underwear in China," Yogi says. "How is business?"

"Has its ups and downs," Avi says.

"This is joke?" Yogi asks.

"Yes," Jeff says.

"I have hear before from Jeffrey, maybe," Yogi says. "I must learn many joke if I conversion to Jew."

"You going to make conversion?" Avi says, over Jeff's stunned silence.

"Perhaps," Yogi replies. "There are many aspects that I learn about Jewyism through my re-ray-son-sip that I find quite fascinating."

"And Yogi also loves chopped liver and pickled herring," Jeff says, trying to lighten the tone.

"What kind of work do you do, Yogi?" Avi asks.

"I am analyst with Bank International."

"A beautiful suit," Moishe sighs.

"Thank you."

"We are also in this business," Avi says.

"Also working for bank?"

"No, selling women's fashions," Avi says. "From this we had contacts for underwear also."

"I am wearing almost every day suit," Yogi says. "And underwear, also, almost every day." She smiles at Avi and Moishe, who smile back uncomfortably.

"How long have you been married?" Avi asks.

Jeff laughs. "Oh, this isn't. . . ."

"Is almost one year," Yogi says. "And why do you not kiss wife after hard day at office?" she asks Jeff before pulling his head down into a lengthy lip lock. "Ah, this much better, darling."

"I was saying," Jeff says, deciding it's simpler to play along with Yogi's gag, "that we haven't seen Avi and Moishe here before."

"Moishe has *yahrzeit,*" Avi says.

"That's the prayer for the dead on the anniversary of their death," Jeff explains to Yogi. "For close relatives only."

"My wife," Moishe adds.

"Your wife?" Yogi says.

"Yeah," Moishe says. "She died a bomb, six years ago."

"Sorry," Yogi says.

"That's awful," Jeff adds.

"Yahrzeit you have a lot in the family every year, father, mother, brother . . . but from all, wife is only one you make choose," Moishe says. "And she is only one for me every year always to *shul.*"

"It shows you made a good choice," Jeff says, putting a hand on Moishe's shoulder.

"So sweet," Yogi says. "I hope that for many years I will every year to *shul* for *yahrzeit* of Jeffrey." The three look at her, unsure what to say. "This is my joke," Yogi says. "Perhaps I am not ready to conversion yet."

"Let's go sit," Jeff says, hoping that will change the mood.

As they follow Yogi toward the seats, Moishe whispers to Jeff, "I can see why you not so much for lunch to factory with wife like this, *boychick.*"

Riding the up the escalator after work, Laura stands in place, too tired to push past the school kids, amahs, and sharp-elbowed old ladies, especially dangerous packing umbrellas on rainy days like this one. Laura thinks about how anxious she is to see Jeff tonight, just to have a glass of wine and lie there with him. She made a good choice. Imagine Edie, imagining I was in love with Peter. But maybe that's what he thinks, too. Maybe that was why he yelled at me on the stairs like that. He's jealous or mad, in some funny way, because I'm not in love with him, and he found a reason to take it out on me finally. Now that the handover's over and the network doesn't have to rely on me so much anymore. . . . Maybe he was trying to get me to quit there, save Fuggin Asia some money. He tried it with Old Hartman, why wouldn't he try it with me? Well, it's not going to work. I'm sticking with this story: it was the handover, stupid, now it's the crisis, idiot, and it's not about sponsors and donuts, it's about finding stories that come from the heart and digging down to the real emotions, finding what really touches people out there. That's what I'm doing, whether Peter likes it or not.

Of course, I think about him a lot. He's the boss; I thought about Dick my editor a lot, too. But that's not love, god no. I guess if you're the son of a billionaire, you probably expect every woman in the world to just fall for you automatically. He's good looking enough—though not nearly as good looking as John-John, back in New York—pretty smart, and, yeah, filthy rich. He can have any woman he wants. It's a reflection of his poor taste that he's chosen Pussy. Like Edie says, it's all the bottom line with him. He turned Pussy into the Chinese anchor he needed, now he's using her *guanxi* in Beijing. There's no denying that she's gorgeous, but that can't be enough. That won't last, especially since she's already my age, not some teenager. What's inside matters, too. That's why I'm so lucky with Jeff, he's so good natured, so understanding. But if Peter wants Pussy, that's his problem, not mine. I've got a husband. How dare any of them even think I'd be in love with Peter.

Jeff scrambles to get the phone on the first ring so it won't wake Laura. "Hello."

"Just tell me: did you know?" Tim asks, "Or was it unbelievable beginner's luck, like Hillary Clinton trading commodity futures?"

"Tim, thanks for calling."

"Listen, whatever it was, I hope you'll share your next bright idea with your buddy."

"Of course, but I think this was a one-shot deal. . . ."

"Some shot, pal. You're making more in a few months than I'll make in the next twenty years if I'm lucky. That's why I'm calling. Your trades on the sixties settled and that money's been transferred to your account in Isle of Wight. I'm sorry it took so long. You got the card for that account and the password and all that shit?"

"Yes. Thanks."

"Good. I took what you owe me out of those funds, for the upfront fees, the contract costs, the financing and everything, so we're square. The boat, she's still yours."

"Tim, consider the *Golden Beauty* yours, maybe rename her the *Floating Rupiah*. But send me the papers, whatever, and I'll sign them over. If there's taxes or anything, just take them out of whatever comes through on the next contracts."

"Hey man, that's very sweet, but I couldn't do that."

"I'm asking you to, Tim. In fact, I'm telling you. . . ."

"Jeff, it's already like I own the boat. I can do everything with it that I could if I owned it, so what's the point?"

"I want you to have her."

"I already do. You're gonna want it when you come back. . . ."

"I can't imagine coming back," Jeff realizes for the first time as he says the words. "At least not coming back the same way as before, doing what I used to do."

"Is it that Japanese girl? You still with her?"

"Yogi is part of it, but it's not just her. I don't know. But I know that it's better here than it was there."

"So you're gonna stay there?"

"I don't know. Maybe. Maybe not here. I hear there's a big world out there. . . ."

"And you've got the dough to have a look around, pal."

"But for now, here is good."

"It's weird to think of you living under the Communists there. . . ."

"There's no Communists in Hong Kong. Nothing's changed since the handover, not that I can see. But this currency thing. . . ."

"It's working for you, pal."

"Yeah, but it's big."

"We see a little bit of news here, but you want to stay, so it can't be so bad."

"The crisis hasn't hit here, at least not much, not yet. But things are miles long, but just a few inches deep. At the factories in China, they're just out of the freakin' rice field. Even here people here are just a generation out of sweatshops like that, and now they walk around with suits and big watches and mobile phones like they own the world and have a Filipina to pick up the laundry and the kids. But at night, some old lady still comes picking through your garbage for bottles and cans. I buy my bananas from an old woman in a straw hat and pajamas, like a freakin' Viet Cong. And I'm sure she doesn't buy them in a market, but picks them off a freakin' tree. . . ."

"Yeah, but look at my old man and yours, god bless their souls, I mean look at where we are compared to where they were. . . ."

"Tim, a few months ago, I was exactly where my old man was and didn't have any hope of getting out. . . ."

"But you're not now. I mean, look, pal, you're not just in Hong Kong, you're on easy street, if you don't mind me saying so."

"Maybe. I don't know. . . ."

"Jeff, get serious. If you cash out today, you're looking at over two million bucks, tax free. Which should mean you never have to look at another pair of ladies' underwear in your life again, except on your way to some hot pussy inside."

CHAPTER 23

National Days

"I DON'T UNDERSTAND what the problem is," Jeff says. "I go back there, and then a couple of hours later, I'm back here with you."

"Is like using same chopstick," Yogi says, wrinkling her nose to show disgust. They are naked, seated on her bed, on top of the cover, backs against the headboard, during her lunch break.

"Chopstick?" Jeff says. "Couldn't you at least say ladle. Or cleaver?"

"What is creaver?"

"It's a big knife . . . what do they call here? A chopper."

"This is what you think? Jeff have big chopper to cut up little Yogi. . . ."

"You're the one who started the analogy. . . ." Jeff protests.

"Analogy? This mean you want to in my bottom? I never do this. Can try, but only with the chopstick, not with the chopper."

"God, I love you." Jeff hugs her tight.

"Stop saying this," Yogi protests.

"But if you don't love me, why do you insist that I stay here all the time?"

"I must shower and back to work," she says, getting out of bed. "I enjoy have you here. Good *shabu-shabu*. This re-ray-son-sip, not same love."

"Whatever," he shrugs, watching her walk to the bathroom, tuck her hair under a shower cap and run the water. "I'll call her now," he says and goes to the phone in the living room, taking in the harbor view as he dials.

"Newsroom, Wellesley."

"Hi Laura, it's Jeff."

"So is my wandering Jew homeward bound?"

"Not today I'm afraid. . . ."

"Geez, what is going on up there?"

"You know what it's like trying to make a deal with the Chinese. I hope we can wrap things up today or tomorrow. . . ."

"You've already been saying that for a goddamned week."

"I know, I know. Believe me, I know. It's just . . . complicated, you know, and I need to be here. . . ."

"How much longer?"

"I don't know. There's also that problem with our production run in Foshan." As his absences have grown longer, Jeff has expanded his Golden Beauty of a lie. "I hope it will get straightened out, but if not, I may need to stay over the holiday on October first until they. . . ."

"Geez, just call me next time you plan to be in town. . . ."

"Be fair. I barely saw you for weeks before the handover. . . ."

"But at least I was in the same area code. We could talk by phone at least. . . ."

"What are we doing now?"

"Yeah, but I can only call through your office. . . ."

"They know how to track me down. Otherwise, I have to give you dozens of numbers and you'd have to dial them all and speak to Chinese operators and secretaries who won't know what you're talking about, probably won't know if I'm there or not, and won't care anyway. The girls in the office get through all that for you. . . ."

"But I can only call when your office is open. . . ."

"And you're asleep nearly all the time when it's closed. Besides, do you know what it costs to call China? Or to call from China, for that matter. Listen, I'll wrap things up here as soon as I can. Can't wait to see you. . . ."

"One thing before you go: I can't find my pass to the JCC. I should start working out again."

"It should be in the cabinet where you left it. Maybe you put it in the laundry. . . ."

"I haven't seen it in a long time. I thought maybe. . . ."

"Take a good look around, the cabinet, your gym clothes, gym bags, and if you really can't find it, we can get you a replacement card when I get back."

"Okay, I will."

"Love you."

"Love you."

"Bye."

"Bye."

Jeff hangs up and immediately checks his wallet to confirm that both the JCC member and spouse cards are inside. He's confident that Laura won't look seriously for the card, that she's unlikely to progress beyond thinking about an afternoon workout to actually choosing it over a bottle of wine and chicken wings with Edie. But the card is Jeff's assurance that she can't walk in on him and Yogi at the gym or pool while he's supposed to be making deals in China.

"I will call you later," Yogi says, putting her power suit back on after showering.

"It's like Superman turning back into Clark Kent when you get dressed," Jeff says, from the doorway of the bedroom.

"Is compliment?"

"Yes. I'm saying you look fabulous naked. It's like a secret identity you have: that beneath your clothes lie charms far beyond those of mortal women. . . ."

"Thank you. But you are not first one to discover my secret identity."

"I know that," Jeff says, "but I'd like to be the last one."

"I will call you later," Yogi repeats. "Is time to close currency positions."

"So you think the market has bottomed. . . ."

"Is time now," she says, kissing him on the lips and heading out the door.

"See you at the gym," he calls behind her.

"Director General Guofu makes a good point about combining the elements of the interview with Secretary Xunui into a VO-SOT-VO with footage from last year's parade for later shows," Franklin says. He's speaking from the temporary set of *AM Asia* at CCTV Beijing, seated between Candace Fang and Deng Jiang Mao, with the CCTV line producer and the CCTV director, each with their own names like eye charts, next to Deng, and Guofu, the CCTV executive producer on the project, sitting close enough to Fang to count her eyelashes, if he stopped staring at her bust. They're nearing the end of the post-mortem via satellite link for the week's first *AM Asia* show from Beijing, speaking live with Laura, Edie and Quickie sitting on the Hong Kong set, Helios and Honest Ho in the wings off camera. Everyone has earpieces for translation, but none of the CCTV people have spoken except for Guofu, and he speaks in English, though he waits for translations from English, by a CCTV translator in a booth somewhere there, before responding.

Deng says, "One of my professors always said that the addition of broadcast elements geometrically increases the impact."

Fang says something in Mandarin that's translated as "Maybe your professor has worked at CCTV network," and everyone in the Beijing studio laughs.

"My professor," Franklin says, "who most of you know as my father, is a very strong advocate of these meetings after a show—we call it a post-mortem, like with a dead body—as a way to deal with issues that come up during the broadcast instantly, to get things fixed before they get worse. It's like getting a minor repair on your car when you hear a strange noise, instead of waiting until you have a breakdown and need a major repair, or maybe even a new car. I want to thank you, Director General Guofu, for everything you have done and everything you are doing this week to make these broadcasts a success, and all the fine hospitality we are enjoying, such as the banquet last night—you should have been there, guys," he says into the camera for Hong Kong's benefit. "But also I think it's very significant that you have generously contributed CCTV satellite time for this post-mortem, and that you yourself are taking the time to be part of it. It demonstrates that you and your CCTV colleagues are professionals like us, and that, as it is for all professionals, it's the quality of the broadcast that matters, and that you are willing to put all your resources and energy and yourselves and your skills, into it to make it a success. I want to thank you for that on behalf of everyone at *AM Asia,* the entire team at FGN Asia, and from all of our partners in FGN around the world. I'm looking forward to the rest of this week, especially the historic live feed of the October first National Day párade on Wednesday.

"So, unless anyone has anything else, I'd like to. . . ."

"I'd like to mention one thing," Laura says, "about the live parade broadcast . . ."

"Careful, *mei-mei,* " Edie mutters, covering her lapel mike.

". . . news of which was broken on my show this morning. . . ."

"Her show?" Deng stage whispers.

"This may not be the right time to discuss. . . ." Franklin says.

"No, I think it is, Peter," Laura says. "I agree with all of what Director General Guofu said when he made the announcement. I think it is wonderful to give western audiences the opportunity to see this unique and important aspect of modern Chinese culture, and I am proud that FGN Asia can play a part in that."

"Thank you," Guofu says.

"Thank you, Laura," Franklin says. "Tomorrow. . . ."

"We've cut that bite from you, Director General Guofu, and the SOT will run throughout the day, I'm sure. But I just want to warn you, sir, that audiences may not react to the parade broadcast the way you expect them to. Viewers may not appreciate the opportunity or understand what they are seeing. That won't necessarily be a reflection on the quality of the broadcast or the worthiness of the event. It will just be a consequence of reaching a mass audience. As one of my professors said, 'You can't please all the people all the time.'

"Personally," Laura continues, "I want you to know that I am thrilled about our broadcast of the parade and will enjoy it enormously—because it means I have one less hour of news to produce." Laura smiles and waits for people to laugh at her joke.

"Thank you, Miss Laura," Guofu says after hearing the translation. "I will remember this."

"Okay then," Franklin says. "With your permission," he adds, looking at Guofu, who nods. "Until tomorrow, Hong Kong. Thank you everyone." The video link drops immediately, but the audio lingers with sound of people unclipping their mikes and dropping them on the desk and the sound of chairs scraping echoing off the satellite.

"You were right, Edie," Laura says, after they unplug and begin walking off the set. "Peter would be much better off letting Pussy blow Guofu instead of doing it himself."

Quickie, Honest Ho and Helios giggle loudly through their noses.

"Comrade Guofu was sitting rather close to Candy," Edie notes.

"And hanging directly over her tits," Laura adds.

Quickie honks, while Honest and Helios laugh out loud. They head for their spots in the newsroom as Laura and Edie walk toward the stairway. "You need to be extremely careful with these people," Edie says.

"Well, yes," Laura says, feeling the heat and humidity resist her push against the fire door. "I must remember not to make jokes to people with no sense of humor."

"You are, of course, livid about the decision to take the parade live. . . ."

"Of course. . . ." Laura says, imitating Edie's tone.

"A decision that was most likely taken under duress last night after too many glasses of *maotai,* while some powerful hand was within groping distance of Candy, or, worse, an influential party member mentioned her hotel room number. . . ."

"That's disgusting. . . ."

"With Pete vastly outnumbered, outgunned, and not prepared for this request because he doesn't recognize—and neither do Candy or Deng—that mainland officials make no distinction whatever between personal and business, so will ask for anything, anytime." Edie takes a theatrical breath. "So far, do you agree with my analysis?"

"Yes, I agree and, of course, I disagree with the programming decision on the parade. . . ."

"And, in point of fact," Edie continues, "if Pete were here on this staircase, you would be trying to convince him not to take their live feed. . . ."

"Yes. But since he's not here, there's no way I can fight it, so I accept it," Laura says. "After all, this is the post-handover . . ."

". . . stupid," they say in unison.

Laura continues, ". . . and a time of crisis . . ."

". . . represented by the Chinese characters for danger plus opportunity," they say in unison, "stupid."

". . . so one must put one's personal feelings aside," Laura continues, "to seize these opportunities and cope with the dangers of life in network television when the wolf is at the door—not the Broad Bottomed Wolf of the global FCC circuit, but a lean and hungry wolf, who may in fact be the only one still even remotely interested in your programming."

"Yes, that's how I reckoned you understood the situation."

"You were, as usual, correct."

"So what precisely was the point of your remarks to Guofu, in the context of being a loyal team player?" Edie asks, then lights her cigarette.

"That's exactly it, *jie-jie*. I did it for the team. I don't want Guofu to blame our team—or his—if this Fuggin worldwide broadcast of the parade winds up raining on CCTV. . . ."

"Meaning. . . ?"

"That instead of praise, the parade generates a storm of criticism and scorn. . . ."

"Oh," Edie says. "You still don't understand any better than Pete, do you?"

"What don't I understand?"

"Guofu and his team would never hear such criticism."

"But let's say it got so bad that we had to mention it on our air," Laura says, "from their studio. Or CNN did. They'd hear it then."

"No they wouldn't."

"I mean, there's no censor in their studio to stop their own employees from hearing the news. . . ."

"Laura, the Chinese practice history's most powerful form of censorship. . . ."

"But the news would leak out, no matter. . . ."

"And they simply wouldn't hear it," Edie says. "If you skywrote it across Tiananmen Square and spray painted it across the Gate of Heavenly Peace, it still would not reach them. Chinese simply do not accept or acknowledge unwelcome news. Suppose Candy told Guofu that if he gave her a hundred million dollars and they were the last two souls on earth, she still wouldn't open even the top button of her shirt for him. He simply wouldn't process that information and would continue to believe that there was something he could do for Fuggin Asia and/or for Candy, or something he could give her—I'm not certain whether he'd think in terms of jewelry or property or perhaps psychotropic drugs—that there was something he could do or say that would induce Candy become Guofu *Tai-Tai,* at least for a weekend. Moreover, he would continue to ask her to become Guofu *Tai-Tai,* since he would have never processed any of her refusals.

"It's a remarkable gift, really, *mei-mei,* this ability to ignore unwelcome information. CK and Lamont had it, and Pete has a spot of it, as well. It can be a quite useful leadership quality. The leader focuses on good news, concentrates on what's right, and leaves it to us drones to fix anything that might have gone wrong."

"Keep your eye on the donut, not on the hole," Laura says.

"Well put."

"My father, who wasn't a professor or a billionaire, used to say that to me."

"It works, so long as there's more donut than hole, so long as more things are going right than going wrong. Or at least some things are going right. Things fell apart for CK and Lamont because they ignored reality for so long and were such bad managers that nothing was going right anymore."

"There was no donut. . . ."

"Things may be getting to that stage here," Edie says, "so Pete needs a new donut."

"What new donut? I thought the crisis emptied the box. . . ."

"He's desperate to get us on the air in China. . . ."

"Of course. So was CK."

"Unless this bloody crisis turns, China's the only donut out there."

"I heard this from Peter, as an excuse for using Pussy as handover anchor. . . ."

"A big smile and big tits, particularly in close up, will help Guofu and his gang overlook her little crying jag that night," Edie says. "This visit is a good opportunity for Candy to rebond with the big motherland and reestablish her political reliability, by whatever means. . . ."

"But seriously, China's a good place for making underwear, but as a broadcast market. . . ?"

"You're looking too closely. Too much unpleasant reality. Try thinking like Lamont."

"That's an oxymoron."

"What's the future for Fuggin Asia? The suits in New York won't keep underwriting a network with no sponsors, no revenue, no viewers, broadcasting news no one wants to hear. If we can get on the air in China, if Fuggin Asia gets a toe in the door of the world's largest market, the world's most eyeballs. . . ."

"But what will they let us broadcast? Is there any market? Can people there buy Audis and nights at the Peninsula? There's no there there. . . ."

"You're being far too rational," Edie says. "This is television, not brain surgery, and television is everyone's lie. A foothold in China is something Pete can bring to the people in New York to keep the money flowing.

And as the rest of the region goes down the tube, it's possibly the only thing Pete can bring them."

"*Aiiiyaah,*" Laura says. "It's the post-handover . . ."

". . . stupid," they say together.

"So they're up there kissing ass. . . ."

"The right people in the right jobs. . . ."

"But about my *faux pas* in the post-mortem," Laura asks, "why wouldn't Guofu simply ignore the bad news I delivered? And it was just a warning about potential bad news, not actual bad news, plus my little joke that went over like a lead balloon. Why wouldn't he ignore that the way he would ignore other bad news?"

"Ah. It's all about face, giving face."

"As opposed to giving head. . . ?"

"Quite effective in tandem." Edie smiles. "A key element of giving face is to allow Guofu to continue to ignore the bad news undisturbed, to tell the emperor that his new clothes are beautiful, not that he's standing there in nature's own. What people in the west may really think about the October first parade is far away and not important to Guofu. What is important—and right here in front of everyone who matters in this case—is allowing Director General Guofu and his CCTV colleagues the fantasy that Guofu and CCTV—and their broadcast partner Fuggin Asia that Guofu has handpicked for the task—have enlightened and enriched the western barbarians by increasing their knowledge of China through arranging and executing this exclusive and unprecedented live global broadcast of the National Day parade. It's most important that nothing intrude on their fantasy that the parade broadcast will promote and enhance international understanding and peaceful cooperation based on mutual respect. Sustaining that image will be important to anyone that may want a favor in the future from Director General Guofu."

"So I made a big mistake," Laura says.

"Well, it depends on how you define big, *mei-mei,*" Edie sighs. "Let's just say that you would have done yourself and the network more proud if you'd spun your head around three or four times, puked green slime through the feed into their studio and said, 'Mao sucks Deng Xiaoping's cock in hell' instead."

The fire door swings open as Edie says the final half-dozen words, and a surprised Gladys Fung says, "Excuse me. I didn't think anyone was in here. I was just looking for somewhere to smoke."

"You came to the right place, Gladys," Edie says.

"But what are you doing down here?" Laura asks, smiling. "Slumming?"

"You didn't hear?" Gladys says, lighting up.

"Hear what?" Laura asks.

"We're all moving down here from 28 this week. You didn't know?"

"No," Laura says, and stares at Edie.

"More the merrier," Edie says.

"I liked things around here a lot better when we didn't have secrets," Laura says.

"So did I, *mei-mei,*" Edie says, opening the fire door. "So did I."

Jeff drops his copy of *The Far Eastern Economic Review* on the coffee table and answers the phone. "Hello."

"Hello," Yogi says.

"Moshi-moshi. I was about to call to remind you we have a tennis booking. . . ."

"Jeffrey, I am going home. . . ."

"Are you sick? Should I bring you some chicken soup? Jew penicillin. . . ?"

"I am going home to Japan. . . ."

"What?"

"The bank has offered severance package that is quite generous, and I have accept. So I will go home to Japan."

"But, but. . . ." Jeff stammers, then takes a deep breath. "Why don't you stay here? I'm sure you could find another job. Or maybe between your package and the money from the currency contracts, we must have enough. . . ."

"No. Is time to go home."

"Then . . . then," he gasps, "I can go with you. I'll leave Laura. . . ."

"No. Re-ray-son-sip could not stand this, for you to leave wife. I cannot responsible for that."

"But you're not responsible, I am. It's my decision. . . ."

"I am also decision. My decision is go back to Japan, to stay with mother, to have rest. . . ."

"Yogi, wait. I can't believe this. I can't believe you want to leave me, that you don't love me. . . ."

"Re-ray-son-sip is quite good. I have quite enjoy, just as I have enjoy live in Hong Kong, work in Bank International. But now is time to end and move to new. . . ."

"Yogi, come on, please. . . . I don't mean anything more to you than Hong Kong and your job at the bank?"

"Our re-ray-son-sip quite important, but is for fun. Now perhaps is time for me to more serious." She chuckles. "Maybe is time for me to married and baby. . . ."

"We can do that, Yogi. We can get married and have a baby." He listens for her reply but only hears gurgling on the phone. "Yogi, are you crying?"

"I remember many happy time with you," she says, sniffling away her tears. "I have enjoy quite much. . . ."

"But it doesn't have to end, Yogi. I'm asking you to marry me, damn it. At least think about it. We can talk. . . ."

"I have already think about it. Is not time to marry you. Is time to go home."

"When are you leaving?"

"I am call from Kai Tak"—the airport. "Flight is now boarding."

"Today?"

"Yes. Packers this morning to my flat. . . ."

"You told me it was the exterminator," Jeff says, and the coin drops further. "You knew when we sold the contracts, while you kept me staying with you. . . ."

"I will miss you quite much. I am sorry to leave, but I must. . . ."

"Give me your address, or phone number, or one of those computer mail addresses, so we can stay in touch. . . ."

"No, is better this way. You will keep with wife. Maybe," she giggles through her tears, "you will find new girlfriend also crazy for Jew food. I hope you good memory for Yogi. And Yogi good memory for Jeffrey. I must go now."

"Yogi, please. . . ."

"Good bye, Jeffrey. I must go. *Sharom areichem.*" She ends the call.

"Areichem sharom," he replies to the dead line. *"Aw-main."*

Jeff writes Laura a note—"Client in town. Must entertain. Back who knows?"—because he knows he's got to get out of the house, that he doesn't want to see Laura now when, if he talks about anything, he needs to talk about Yogi. He thinks about where to go and the JCC seems the best of his limited choices. Maybe he'll meet Avi and Moishe in the jacuzzi and they'll be sympathetic about his beautiful wife leaving him.

To Jeff, there was something heartless about what Yogi had done. It revealed something cold inside her he'd never noticed. But then Jeff thought about tears on that face like a doll, and about how she'd hoodwinked him into spending eighteen straight days playing house with her before she left. Maybe he'd done something during those eighteen days to disqualify himself from her long-term plans. Whatever it was, he was sure he'd meant more to her than she was willing to admit during that call. Yogi was right about one thing: it had been fun. And profitable, highly profitable, though, as she reminded him, money cannot buy love. And Yogi was right about something else: he still has his wife. Maybe he can even fall in love with Laura again. But he'll have to forget Yogi first.

Jeff looks across to the next building, where the Filipina is mopping the kitchen floor in jeans and a tank top. She works her way out of Jeff's view and returns half a minute later wearing a long sleeve shirt over her top. Somehow, she already can smell his blood in the soapy water of her wash bucket.

CHAPTER 24

Panty Lines, Party Lines

"AND THERE THEY ARE," Edie says brightly, turning from the bar at the front of Chinese Godown with a young Chinese guy at her side to face Laura and Jeff. "The famous *AM Asia* producer and her infamous husband in women's pants."

"Hi, Edie," Laura says, and mutters to Jeff, "You remember Edie, right?"

Jeff nods and shakes Edie's extended hand. He's really trying, but it's so difficult hauling this broken heart around when everything he sees and does pokes at the cracks. Edie, she's Yogi's friend. Here he is with Laura at the same bar where he met Yogi on handover night, where their currency play took shape. At Friday night *shabbos* services, he feels Yogi's absence far more acutely than any divine presence. When he uses the ATM to take out some of the money he has because of her, as the machine counts out the bills he hears that funny way she'd say, "Yeah, yeah, yeah, yeah, yeah," imitating a dog in some cartoon they both half remembered. It's a struggle for him to get out of bed these days. He's got no energy for the gym. He's got all this money, but it doesn't make him happy without her. He thinks of his mother, and how all her money—the money that she didn't tell him about and won't share—hasn't enriched her personality.

"This is Nelson Pang, brother of the guest of honor," Edie says, introducing the slender Chinese teen. "Nelson, this is Laura Wellesley, the *AM Asia* producer, and her husband, Jeff. . . ."

"Golden," Laura says.

"Of course. I should remember because he's so precious," Edie says. "Nelson was saying how happy he is to be going to the US with May."

Edie leads them away from the bar, into the crowd. A waitress approaches with a tray of drinks. "It's all on Pete's account, not the company's," Edie advises, "so drink up. And they're pouring top shelf at the bar." She drains her white wine and takes another glass. Laura takes a white wine, Jeff takes a red, and Nelson takes a soft drink.

"Nelson was asking me about America, about Boston, where they'll be living," Edie says. "Now these are Americans, as perhaps you could tell by their accents. . . ."

"If Edie ever lets us get a word in," Laura says, smiling, and sipping her wine.

"Right," Edie continues. "Genuine Yanks, yes, evident from how rude they are. Perhaps they can tell you about Boston."

"Is that CK over there, talking to Pussy?" Laura says.

"He hired May, and she asked if it would be all right to invite him," Edie says, then explains to Jeff and Nelson, "CK was our station manager until Pete fired him. I think May was concerned that Pete might have been embarrassed. . . ."

"That'll be the day," Laura snorts. "I'm just surprised CK managed to tear himself away from that brothel in Zhuhai to be here."

"A massage parlor in Shenzhen, according to the audit report," Edie says.

Laura shakes her head and drinks more wine. "You know, I never got a chance to tell that SOB what I thought. . . ." She turns to Nelson, "Pardon my French," then to Edie. "C'mon let's shovel some shit on that loser and have a couple of shots of Absolut. On Peter." She grabs Edie's arm, causing them both to spill some wine, and leads her across the room.

"What part of America are you from?" Nelson asks Jeff.

"I'm from New York. All I know about Boston is that it has a great ballpark, and the Red Sox haven't won the World Series since World War I, when Babe Ruth got traded." Jeff shakes his head. "That's baseball. I used to be a big fan back in the US." And, he thinks, my favorite player is still Yogi. "The other thing I know is that the weather stinks. It's really cold there in the winter. Coming from here, you probably won't be used to that."

"I've been going to school in England," Nelson says, "so I know something of cold weather. I hear America is warm in the summer, though."

"That's true," Jeff says. "It can be as bad as here, but only for a few months."

"Also it snows there, in Boston, doesn't it?"

"Oh yeah, and that makes everything a mess. You know the traffic, even walking, it's brutal when it snows. . . ."

"I'm a skier, so I love snow," Nelson says. "Are there ski areas in Boston?"

"Somewhere up there nearby. You didn't learn to ski here, did you?"

"Oh, no," Nelson laughs. "I took up skiing on visits to the Alps."

"The Swiss Alps?"

"Swiss, Italian, French. . . ."

"Wow, I didn't realize there were so many Alps."

"They're all the same Alps, actually," Nelson explains. "There's one mountain range, the Alps, with parts of it in different countries."

"God, I never knew that," Jeff says. "A young guy like you, and you know so much more than I do. . . ."

"Where did you attend university, John?"

"Jeff. It's Jeff."

"Oh, sorry. I wasn't paying attention. . . ." Nelson smiles, "I'm afraid I've developed a terrible crush on Edie. There's something about western women. . . ."

"That's funny. A lot of western guys feel the same way about Asian women."

"But they seem to me to be miniature copies of the real thing, cheap imitations," Nelson says.

"To some people, small is beautiful."

"Chacun à son goût," Nelson says. Before Jeff can ask, "Whuzzat mean?" Nelson repeats, "Where was it you attended university?"

"Well, I went to a state school in New York for a couple of years. . . . You would've loved it there. It was in the snow belt and there wasn't much to do in the winter except ski and . . . umm . . . snuggle."

"Sounds splendid," Nelson says.

"It had its moments. But then my father died, and I had to go back to run the family business. Women's lingerie—that's why Edie teases me about ladies' panties."

"You're the oldest son?"

"I'm the only."

"That's so Chinese, to put aside your own goals for the good of the family." Nelson smiles.

"That was like ten years ago. Then when Laura got this job, I came over here to arrange sourcing from China to try to expand the business."

"For you, China is a big land of opportunity. For me, it's America."

"I hope so, for both of us." Jeff lifts his glass toward him in a mock toast. "To greener grass."

"Excuse me?"

"It's a saying: the grass is always greener on the other side. Whatever you don't have seems better than what you do have." Now I don't have Yogi, I have Laura.

"I see."

"I'm just wondering," Jeff says. "You were going to school in England, but now you're switching to America. . . ."

"Since my sister's going to be there, my parents thought she could look after me. Our younger sister is also joining us. I think my mother believes in the years ahead it may be disadvantageous to hold a UK diploma."

"Pretty lucky, then, that your sister got a job in the US."

"I'd say it's particularly lucky that she didn't get a job in New Delhi or Accra. Paris or Geneva would have been nice, though." Nelson smiles. "May I ask you, in your business, do you source goods from China and distribute them through your family business?"

"That's it, basically. We get pieces made in factories in the mainland and ship them over to the US. Besides stocking our stores, my mother and another partner wholesale to US clients." Since Jeff has stopped trying to do this underwear business, he feels he understands it much better.

"How much are your markups on wholesale? If I may ask. . . ."

"Sure. It depends whether it's a stock item or special order, on who ships and. . . ."

"Assume stock goods to the US. You land them, and then sell them to shops. . . ."

"We manage 50, 60 percent. . . ."

"Fantastic," Nelson says. "Perhaps, if you'd like to try to expand your distribution. . . . I'll be in Boston, and your US operations are based in New York. . . ."

"That might be interesting," Jeff says with a smile. What a great kid, he thinks. He's eighteen, nineteen years old, probably never had to worry about money in his life, but here he is, he sees an angle and he can't resist playing it. "When you get settled. . . ."

"May I take your card?"

"Here," Jeff says, fishing in his wallet, then presenting it with both hands, thumbs on top.

"Thanks," Nelson says, and, as etiquette demands, reads the card. "Golden Beauties. . . ."

"That's the name of the line. . . ."

"I like it. Very good in Chinese, too. *Gum May,* simple yet elegant. *Gin Mai* in Mandarin. What's your mobile number?" Nelson asks, reaching into his pocket for a pen.

"Oh, I don't have one," Jeff says.

"That's quite unusual," Nelson says. "No email. . . ?"

"Not yet."

"Down the road, maybe I can help you get that established, as well as a website, so that you can put your catalogue online for customers. . . . What about your office in the States?"

No way I'm letting my mother near this new Jerry Lewis unsupervised, Jeff thinks. "Just contact me when you're settled, and I'll put you in touch." This kid could be perfect to *noodge* his mother and Jerry Lewis, shake things up a bit.

"All right, Jeff. Thanks. You'll hear from me." Nelson puts the card in his pocket. "I'm due to meet some friends in Ap Lei Chau. My going-away party, so I must dash. But I'm very glad to meet you." Nelson reaches out and pumps Jeff's hand. "Thank you very much."

"Good luck in the US, man. I think you'll like it there. And I'm sure you'll do okay for yourself."

"I'll be in touch." Nelson waves across the room toward his sister, scans the room for Edie, then disappears. Jeff smiles, realizing how much Nelson is like him ten years ago. Jeff didn't jump into Golden Foundations because he thought his family would be ruined if he didn't. He never even really thought about the money, except as an abstraction, a way of keeping score. It was all about playing the hand he'd been dealt, and not playing it or trying a different game never crossed his mind. He tried to make the business better because he couldn't imagine not trying.

It was about the opportunity—the challenge—not the money. Ten years later, it's clear that life will never stop dealing out challenges, fair or otherwise, and what he didn't think about back then—whether or not to accept the challenge and, of course, the money—are the things that matter most.

"You wife may insist on ignoring you, but I won't," Edie says from behind Jeff.

"It was that creepy kid," Laura says, as Jeff turns around. "He has a crush on me or something. I'm glad he's leaving town."

"Young Franklinstein at his most brilliant," Edie says. "Laura may disagree, but Pete is positively preternatural when it comes to identifying what someone wants, even before they know they want it, then giving it to them."

"Or maybe he just makes people think that what he gives them is what they want," Laura says.

"The essence of successful television, *mei-mei*" Edie says.

"And retailing," Jeff adds.

"Well, with some people you can give them shit, tell them it's chocolate, and they'll believe it," Laura says. "And too many people are convinced Franklin's Willie Goddamn Wonka."

"Hell hath no fury. . . ." Edie begins, smirking.

"Oh please," Laura hisses. "Truth is I was happy with what he did at first. . . ."

"You got your way then," Edie says, "Now it's different, and you're not."

"I'm just sick of this Peter worship. . . ."

"Sounds more like Peter envy," Edie says.

"Oh, please. . . ."

"Sending May to the US is pure inspiration."

"What's the big deal?" Laura says. "It's just another way to gut the news operation to save a few dollars. . . ."

"Yes, of course it removes quite a nice chunk of payroll from our books, including the crew we'll no longer be running around town with her. But there's more to it than that, *mei-mei,* quite brilliantly so."

"Like. . . ?"

"Sending May to the US demonstrates that Fuggin Asia is developing talent for the entire global network. She'll make quite a favorable impression in the US, I'm sure. She'll be the first Chinese in that market, and she'll get noticed, which means Pete and Fuggin Asia will get noticed for something other than bleeding red ink. She could even go national, May. She has the knack for those maudlin bits and pieces you Americans adore. So the brass will see there's something out here besides cratered stock markets and monumental cost structures. But the best part is, as you said, she's taking Nelson—who, I'll have you know, was trying to look down my blouse long before your blouse arrived. . . ."

"And you let him? He's not even old enough to shave. . . ."

"That's not where to look for fuzz," Edie chuckles. "But the true value for the network may well be Nelson and Kimberly, the younger sister, accompanying May."

"Who cares about them?"

"Patricia Pang cares, *mei-mei*. She's the head of the Legislative Council, Jeff, and she's May's mother. The transfer enables three of her children to go to the US and establish the basis for immigration of relatives."

"How do you know her mother wants. . . ?"

"You don't think it was May's idea to bring along her baby brother and sister?" Edie snorts. "So Pete builds *guanxi* with Madame Speaker Pang. She has clout around town, but the real help may be in her influence, or just her willingness to go to bat for us, with the central government. It's hard to say how much sway she holds with the mainland authorities— I don't reckon she knows—but there's no doubt that they respect her opinion and listen to her, when it comes to Hong Kong. I think Beijing already realizes that Chief Executive Tung has no idea what goes on here.

"But Franklin's real genius, the real inspiration," Edie continues, "is that if you'd asked May a month ago what job she'd fancy at the network, perhaps she would have said that she'd want to be the correspondent in Beijing or Shanghai or maybe Tokyo. Or she would have proposed some sort of Hong Kong commentary or human interest features. . . ."

"Wasn't that her beat?" Laura says.

"You mean back when we covered Hong Kong news?" Edie smiles. "May might have said she'd want one of those jobs, but it never would have occurred to her to ask to be a reporter in a highly competitive top-20 US market. But that's the response Young Franklinstein created for May, a response she never would have arrived at on her own, and it's a response that pleases May, pleases her family, pleases accounting. . . ."

"And it might please me and my mother," Jeff says, "because Nelson wants to sell lingerie for Golden Beauties."

"That's the only way he'll see any women's underwear in America," Laura snickers.

"Unless, of course, he does the washing at home," Edie adds.

"Or takes in laundry," Laura says, laughing. "Right around back of the takeout counter. . . ."

"Laura," Jeff scolds. "That's awful."

"But true," she replies. "Once he stops trying to look down my blouse, five minutes later that creepy kid is trying to make a partnership with you. You think it's a coincidence that he found you and you start talking business?"

"How many vodkas did you have?" Jeff asks.

"All I'm saying is that stereotypes don't just come out of thin air. That Chinese and Jews are always looking to make a buck, that the English are undersexed, that. . . ."

"I'm not undersexed, darl', just underserved," Edie says.

"There's nothing wrong with a kid being hungry and looking to make an honest buck," Jeff says, ignoring the other part of her remark. "If you aren't born with a silver spoon in your mouth, you've got no choice but to hustle. . . ."

"Well, you would. . . ." Laura begins.

"This place may require a large dose of hustle rather quickly," Edie says. "After all, Hong Kong is not immune from the crisis. . . ."

". . . stupid," Laura blurts.

The crisis, Jeff thinks, that made me a millionaire. Thanks to Yogi.

"C'mon, Edie," Laura says. "Hong Kong doesn't have the problems they have in Malaysia and Indonesia or the Philippines. . . ."

"We hold this debate at least once a week, Jeff," Edie explains. "With Pete included, when he and Laura are on speaking terms. No, Hong Kong isn't a basket case in that category. But there's been an impact here, and there's going to be a bigger impact as we go forward. For the past five years, people and money have been pouring in here at unprecedented rates. Now they've started pouring out."

"So it wasn't the handover—stupid—after all?" Laura says.

"It was the handover—stupid—but the handover is history, and now the crisis rules," Edie says. "We're not the only company around town that's cutting back. Do you remember my Japanese friend Yogi at Bank International? I brought her to the promo launch, Candy's coming-out party. . . .You came with Laura, Jeff. . . ."

"Maybe," he replies. This is torture, he thinks, absolute torture.

"I remember her," Laura says. "Very plastic looking little thing. Like one of those cheap dolls. . . ."

Jeff's right arm nearly slaps the back of Laura's head.

"Bank International offered everyone in the investment banking division a buyout. First offer was three months salary per year. . . ."

"Why?" Laura says. "There's no impact on China. . . ."

"But while everyone is laying the foundations for those megadeals in the mainland that have been mooted for the past 150 years or such, it's been business coming out of Manila and KL and Jakarta paying for those banquets at the Beijing World and the Shanghai Mirada, not to speak of the extraordinary overhead expenses here. Behind every dollar-denominated loan in default in the region, there's an international banking team that made it. . . ."

"They're punishing the people who made the loans?" Jeff asks.

"Not generally," Edie says. "The banks get all their fees up front, and those profits are booked. If they start firing people who didn't foresee the troubles in Asia, then there will be scads of empty offices in The City of London and Wall Street. But without more loans to make—and without a lot of funny money that people in high places and their friends skim off those loans to manage—there's hardly reason for bankers to be here. It's also a dirty little secret that investment banking is hardly brain surgery. . . ."

"Or television. . . ." Laura says, chuckling. "Inside joke," she tells Jeff.

"Most of the people on these project teams began as fresh graduates, and they can be replaced with new batches of fresh graduates when business picks up again."

"So how many at Bank International took the buyout?" Laura says.

"Dozens. Fiona's working on the story," Edie says. "The timing was perfect for Yogi. It was time for her to leave. Rather odd for the Japanese here. They have a community of sorts, so there's pressure to conform. But also, a lot of the men keep their families back in Japan, and I know Yogi carried on with a few. . . ."

"That's gross," Laura says.

"Perhaps," Edie says, "but it beats not carrying on at all, I must say. One of these married men left Yogi *enceinte,* it seems. . . ."

"Ancient?" Jeff says.

"Enceinte."

"It means pregnant," Laura tells Jeff loudly enough for some heads around the room to turn her way.

"Pregnant. . . ." Jeff mutters. "Pregnant she was. . . ."

"What are you, Mister Echo?" Laura says.

"Sorry, I just. . . ."

"Just stop, okay? Forgive him," she says to Edie. "I married a barbarian."

"Well, speak of barbarians, Yogi wouldn't let any doctor here touch her. I don't blame her for that. So she took the money and ran back to Japan."

"That is lucky," Laura says. "I could use a little luck like that. If somebody offered me. . . ."

"She's a clever girl, too, Yogi," Edie says. "She still holds the unofficial Bank International currency desk one day record: 37 straight winning trades, plus scoring at the old Hilton during lunch hour with the executive VP from New York, Ira Rothstein. . . ."

Jeff can't suppress a chuckle, but Laura doesn't notice.

"I've no doubt she'll do well in Japan," Edie continues. "But the point is that when the banks cut back, this place loses not just jobs, but top-end demand, for flats, for restaurants, clubs. . . ."

"But that's just one case. . . ."

"What kinds of shots are they pouring?" Jeff asks.

"See for yourself," Laura says.

"Pete's buying," Edie reminds him, and as Jeff walks toward the bar, says, "Nice bum."

"Touch it and you die," Laura says.

"Not even a two-on-one, *mei-mei?*"

"He'd die," Laura chuckles. "He's Mister Vitamin—he's a one-a-day."

"That would explain why there's room on your dance card for Young Franklinstein. . . ."

"Oh, please. . . ."

"If you hadn't lost him to a far hotter Pussy," Edie cackles.

"Keep it down," Laura scolds, then asks, "Do you think Peter really loves Pussy? I mean, is it love or business for him?"

"Well, Candy is quite a lovely young thing. . . ."

"She's my age," Laura snarls. "And she's stupid. . . ."

"I do think Pete cares for Candy, but he is all about the bottom line. He would never let himself love someone who couldn't help the family business. And with her looks, her on-air personality, her cachet up north, she is an asset, quite a Fuggin asset, as well as little tigress in the kip, I'll wager. . . ."

"Edie," Laura screeches.

"We love people because they make us feel good in one way or another," Edie says, "give us pleasure, and the thing that gives Pete the greatest pleasure these days is making Fuggin Asia successful. . . ."

"Well, in that case, he can't be very happy these days, can he?"

Edie shrugs and says, "We can let him buy a little happiness for us, can't we? Let's have another shot or three and ask Nancy which hot club we should liven up."

"Club?"

"It's Saturday night, *mei-mei*. We might as enjoy ourselves before the reckoning," Edie says. "You find Nancy, and I'll get us a couple of Absoluts."

"Make it a pitcher," Laura says as Edie heads for the bar.

Jeff waits for his red wine, elbows on the bar, pressing his palms into his eyes. She was pregnant, he thinks. That explains everything, but it explains nothing. Why not stay with him? Why not let their re-ray-son-sip grow along with their baby?

"Two shots of iced lemon Absolut," Edie says to a bartender. "Jeff, Yogi didn't tell you she was pregnant before she left, did she?"

"What? Who. . . ?" he says, uncovering his eyes, turning his head, and readjusting to the light.

"Yogi. She didn't tell you she was pregnant before she left?"

"No," he says, looking Edie in the eye. "Of course not. Why would she?"

"Yes," Edie says. "Of course not. Why would she indeed."

CHAPTER 25

Trick or Treat

"HI-DEE-HO."

"Hello? Michael? Michael Morris?"

"That's me. Call me Mike. Who's this?"

"Hi. I'm Jeff Golden."

"What's up, Golden boy?"

"We met the night of the handover. I'm a friend of Yogi, and you gave me your card. . . ."

"Got you, pal. Relax. 'Nuf said. So you want some books?"

"Books?"

"Yeah, you know, books. Special books. . . ."

"I actually wanted. . . ."

"We call it books. That's what we say. Books. From Thailand, Green-leaf Press, books. These days, they're running about a thousand per book. . . ."

"Wow. That's expensive books. . . ."

"But the reading is exquisite, man. I read just a little bit in the morning, and I'm buzzed until lunch time. . . ."

"Sorry, I'm not following. . . ."

"Whoa. Then maybe I should check out some of your books. . . ."

"Michael. . . ."

"Call me Mike. . . ."

"Okay, Mike. Like I said, I'm a friend of Yogi, and when she went back to Japan. . . ."

"Yogi, man, she went back to Japan. Smart chick, man. Hot, too. When she worked the trading floor, we called her "Tough Ticket" 'cause none of us ever got invited to her openings. . . ."

"Right. So I'm trying to. . . ."

"She went back to Japan, Yogi, like, ah dunno, a few weeks ago, maybe a couple months. . . ."

"Right. She told me she was going, but I lost the information she gave me about getting in touch with her. And now, I've got a friend in Japan who's looking for experienced bankers, and I thought. . . ."

"Gotcha, gotcha, gotcha. Gimme a sec'. I've got something around here. . . ."

"Thanks."

"Okay. Her email is—man that's simple: yogit at hotmail dot com."

"Sorry, I don't use that . . . yet. Have you got a telephone number for her?"

"Yeah. I got it all right here. There's something about that, though. . . . Let's see. Okay, it's 813, that's like the country code, then 71357508."

"Okay. I've got that. Thanks."

"I remember . . . yeah. She said that she's living with her mother, and her mother doesn't speak English. So if you want to call, Yogi said, you gotta speak Japanese. That was it."

"Oh. Okay."

"Your friend's Japanese?"

"Friend?"

"The one who wants to call her about the job. . . ."

"Oh yeah, yeah. He's not really a friend, just. . . ."

"Whatever."

"Thanks a lot for your help, Mike."

"No problem. And you ever want some books, you know, or you got friends who want some good books, you have 'em gimme call, awright?"

"All right. I will. Thanks. Take care. Bye."

"This can't be good," Gladys says, pulling up a chair next to Laura in the newsroom. "Last day of the month, Friday, HR drones lurking. . . ."

"You know I hate these meetings," Franklin begins, seated next to Edie in the slot, the chair formerly occupied by Lamont, then by plush toys sent to Candace Fang, "so we'll make it short and to the point." Chook-koo.

"Then everybody can enjoy the pizza," Edie says. "Pete's treat."

"And what's the trick?" Deng asks, adding, "Today's Halloween. You can tell from Edie's mask."

"As you know," Franklin says, "there's a regional economic crisis going on. I'm really proud of the way we've covered this story, with the same quality, insight and character that our Fuggin Asia team brought to the handover and to every other major story that's come our way in the seven months that I've been here. Our team is doing a great job, and you're all part of that team." Chook-koo.

"But. . . ." Gladys whispers to Laura.

"I'm proud of every one of you. From covering the story of the crisis, you know how devastating it's been. Some of the world's most dynamic economies, the engines of growth for the next century, have been thrown into reverse." Chook-koo. "And Fuggin Asia hasn't been immune. As you know, we've lost our flagship sponsors. I think it's important to understand that these sponsors haven't gone to some other network. We haven't done anything wrong . . ."

"That's his speech to New York," Gladys whispers.

". . . and when the economy recovers, these sponsors will come flocking back to us . . . and we'll charge them even higher rates when they do. But meanwhile . . ."

"Here's New York's speech to him. . . ."

". . . we have to adjust to this situation. Starting Monday, we are going to revamp our programming. Before I go into the details, I want to emphasize that no one will be fired because of these changes, and when we are out of this crisis, I want this team back together again, because this is a great team. But until then, we are offering some of you transfers to other jobs, either with Fuggin affiliates in other locations or new jobs here in Hong Kong if you choose not to relocate. The choice will be up to you in every case. When we're finished, go see Fairy Yeung and Jelly Lam. . . . Where are you, Fairy, Jelly?" Chook-koo.

The two women, Fairy, barely five feet, and Jelly, nearly six, wave meekly from the edge of the newsroom closest to their cubicles.

"Mutt 'n' Jeff," Laura says.

"Okay, there," Franklin says, spotting them. "So, after this meeting, see them for the details, for your choices of new assignments. That's for some of you. For others, we'll be keeping and expanding two of our shows, *AM Asia* and *Asia Market Wrap.* Everyone now working on those two shows will continue to work on those shows. That includes the tech crews and production staff. Edie has the details, but basically you'll be filling an extra hour on the air, so the shows will run four hours, six to ten for *AM Asia,* four to eight for *Market Wrap.* We'll continue to go with the fifteen live, fifteen tape format. So everybody on those shows, keep up the good work. Everybody else, see Fairy and Jelly. Thanks."

Questions in English and Cantonese fill the room, but Edie hushes them. "Everybody with *AM Asia* and *Market Wrap,* there's a note in the system with details about the new programming schedule and any changes in assignments. Everyone not associated with those two shows, see Fairy and Jelly back in the HR area. They will be working over the weekend in order to assist you with the paperwork and facilitate your smooth transition to your new jobs. But, please, first pick up your information packets, read them fully, and then ask your questions."

Fairy and Jelly are overwhelmed as they move toward the HR area at the end of the newsroom farthest from the studio. Laura skims the note in her computer that says she'll no longer be responsible for feature segments, so she'll still be producing the same two hours live, nods to Deng, says, "See you Monday," and heads home. For once, she's not in the middle of the madness at Fuggin Asia.

"Moshi-moshi," says the woman's voice that picks up the phone after four rings.

"Moshi-moshi. Jeffrey-to moushi masuga Yogi-san o onegaishima-su."

"Chotto mate kuda sa," the voice says, then the line goes silent.

Jeff has no idea what she's said—the only other Japanese phrase he was able to assimilate after asking around the JCC was *Yogi wa imasen*— Yogi is not here. Well, he'll wait another couple of dollars before he gives up.

"Moshi-moshi."

"Yogi-san?"

"Jeffrey-san?"

"Yes."

"How were you able to. . . ?"

"I asked your friend Michael, the guy with the emergency number. . . . I told him I had a friend who might have a job possibility for you. . . ."

"And he has give you telephone number?"

"Yes. And he also told me that I would have to speak Japanese to get past your mother."

"You were quite proficient. Mother did not say that there is stupid *gaijin* speaking poorly on telephone."

"How are you?"

"I am well. But did not want you to call me. Is time. . . ."

"I heard about the baby." Jeff waits for a reply, but Yogi remains silent. "Your friend Edie mentioned it at a Fuggin Asia party. She said you were carrying on with a married man. . . ."

"This only Edie's assumption. I never tell her about us. . . ."

"And you never told me about a baby."

"Edie is telling everyone this?"

"Not everyone, but she told me. And Laura."

"Do Edie and your wife believe that you and I. . . ?"

"Yogi, forget about my wife and Edie. Let's talk about you and me and our baby. I still want to. . . ."

"Sure it is your baby? This is funny. You married man, but you expect Yogi. . . ."

"Yogi, stop it. If you want to pretend it's not my baby, that's fine. But the point is that we were together, you got pregnant, you kept it secret, and you left. That wasn't what I was expecting, it wasn't what I wanted for us, and I still. . . ."

"Wife is not there now?"

"Yogi, forget my wife."

"You say this, but you do not forget wife. . . ."

"Yogi, I was ready to leave my wife for you when you called me from the airport. I still am ready to leave her. I asked you to marry me. . . ."

"And I have refuse. Do not want this sit-su-ay-son force decision for us. If do anything, must because we want to make lasting re-ray-son-sip, not for embryo."

"Yogi, I asked you to marry me. . . ."

"Married man never mean this. You say this because is proper thing to say when lover become pregnant. But you will never. . . ."

"Yogi, I didn't know you were pregnant. I know now, and I'm asking you again: please marry me."

"I quite happy with our re-ray-son-sip in Hong Kong. But I did not want to decision based on embryo."

"But, Yogi, that's exactly what you did. You left because you were pregnant. If you weren't pregnant, you wouldn't have left, would you?"

"I not prepare to decision. . . ."

"But you did make a decision, don't you see? You decided to go back to Japan and to leave me. . . ."

"The bank has made offer that was quite generous and I must think. . . ."

"But you said you wanted to stay five more years then go to Bali. . . ."

"With embryo, I do not have so much time to think, I must decision. . . ."

"Yogi, you say you didn't want to decide because of the baby, but that's exactly what you did. You left because of the baby. You ran away from me, away from somebody who loves you. . . ."

"There you say again you love me. You always say you love Yogi. But I cannot know if you mean it."

"I asked you to marry me. . . ."

"Is not right to marry for embryo."

"I didn't know you were pregnant. You knew, I didn't know, and you decided to run away. I don't understand. . . ."

"No, you do not understand. I have embryo, I must decision."

"So you decided to end things, to end a relationship that was making us both happy. . . ."

"Yes, was happy. But changing must happen in all sit-su-ay-son. In addition to embryo, there is changing at bank and in Hong Kong. Everything is changing. I must changing. We must changing. . . ."

"I agree. Relationships have to change and grow or they die. But we have to change together. With Laura, we've both changed a lot in the past year, but not together, and now we barely have any connection left. If a relationship is going to work, we have to face changes together, help each other through them. You can't just decide by yourself and run away, not if the relationship is going to succeed."

"I must thinking about this. I cannot allow embryo to decision for me. I must decision for myself."

"But if our relationship matters to you, then we should decide together."

"Perhaps cannot sure what is best."

"Perhaps you were trying so hard to solve this difficult problem, to see it from this angle and that one, with so many different sides to things, that you got all wound up and everything got so twisted around that you ended up doing exactly what you didn't want to do."

"Must say favorite word."

"What's that?"

"Sorry."

"I'm sorry, too, but we can learn from it, Yogi. Mistakes can be fixed. What matters more than what's been done is what we do next."

"You are sound like management consultant."

"Well, it's all about managing things. So how are you managing with the baby?"

"Is finish. In Japan is quite simple. Only 30 minute with doctor and finish. Only difficulty is I cannot sex for one months."

"You had an abortion?"

"Yes. Of course. You do not expect that I around Tokyo and stay my mother with no husband and Jewpanese baby?"

"I didn't think about. . . ."

"Of course not. Embryo not your problem."

"But it was my problem. I wanted it to be. . . . I would have wanted it to be. . . ."

"Is my problem and I must solve. I must leave Hong Kong before anyone know, and remove before mother can become aware. She think I am gain weight from her tempura and dumpling."

"But you're all right?"

"Yes. Now I am fine. Am thinking about what is next thing to do."

"I wish that things had worked out differently. . . ."

"Things now the way they are. Like name of bar in Lan Kwai Fong: Time Is Always Now. So is now, and I go ahead from now."

"Why don't you come back to Hong Kong?"

"This part is finish. I have left. Is time to move, to see what is next. Bank say this. Embryo say this. Jeffrey with his wife say this. . . ."

"I'll leave her tonight for you."

"You are quite fortunate, Jeffrey. You believe you know what you want."

"Yogi. . . ."

"Perhaps Yogi does not yet know what she want. . . ."

"But you shouldn't close the door on us, not without a good reason, not unless you're really sure. . . ."

"I am really sure I do not know. I am really sure I do not want to decision because of embryo. So now is no embryo. Now I am here and can think and maybe can decision."

"I hope you will think about me seriously as an option when. . . ."

"Now you are sound like finance consultant with option. . . ."

"I just want you to realize that I can be, I want to be part of whatever it is that you decide to do next. I love you and I want to be with you."

"Oh, so sweet. . . ."

"I mean it, Yogi. I love you and I will marry you in a minute, any minute you choose, anytime you say so. Do you understand?"

"Yes. . . ."

"You hurt me very much when you left. It also hurts me very much to know that our baby, our baby that could have brought us together broke us apart, that that was the reason you left. . . ."

"I understand. I am sorry. . . ."

"Now there is no baby, and that hurts, too. But I understand. I understand what you were thinking. I understand why you did what you did. I understand that you weren't sure, you weren't certain that you could rely on me. . . ."

"Yes, yes. . . ."

"Well, I don't want you to be uncertain about us any more, ever again. We belong together. Now that we've been apart, I know it for certain."

"So sweet. . . ."

"Yogi, I want to be part of whatever it is that you decide is next for you."

"Now I do not know. I have begin new re-ray-son-sip. Kobe Jewish Club is quite elegant, and next week can sex. After this perhaps. . . ."

Jeff hangs up. "Forget you," he says out loud. Women always manage to disappoint you, he thinks, always find a way. The closer they are, the more you love them, the bigger the disappointment. At least with Laura, all she does is ignore him. Maybe that's a start toward a relationship that works.

"It's like a ghost town out there in the newsroom," Laura says in stairway, lifting the top off her lunch container, fresh from the microwave.

"That smells great," Gladys says, taking a light from Edie's cigarette. Smoke rises in the bright sunlight of the stairway. Laura's lunch aroma competes with the smell of mud baking in the sun 25 stories below.

"It's boned chicken stir fried with onion, garlic and mushroom in a wasabi and light soy sauce."

"Lovely Japanese touch," Edie says. "You will please find a studio guest for the IMF deal tomorrow, please. If I see another phoner graphic from Seoul, I'll come in there and cut the line myself. . . ."

"Yes, thank you for the kind suggestion. If Honest can't dig up a guest, I'll have her impersonate one. She probably can speak Korean, too, that girl."

"I like your haircut," Gladys says.

"I convinced her to pass up the $99 special," Edie says. "Next is the wardrobe. . . ."

"Let's all go shopping together," Gladys says. "I know every back-alley fashion place in Mongkok."

"I was like that in New York. You should have seen me. . . ."

"Get accustomed to hearing this," Edie warns Gladys.

"In New York, I had the whole nine yards, from the DKs to the MBs, and JFK Junior had my office choking on flowers like we were in the old days here with Pussy. . . ."

"This story keeps getting better," Edie says. "From looking down your blouse to flowers. . . . In a couple of weeks, his mama will have broken his heart and your engagement. . . ."

"Before or after the love child?" Gladys adds.

"Television is my lie," Laura says, smiling. "I learned from the master." Laura smiles and chews a forkful of her lunch.

"You missed the days when Laura came in here with the balloon seat khakis and flannel shirts," Edie says.

"Thanks," Laura says. "If you were leaving the house at midnight, and the only people you'd see were Helios, Quickie, Edie and Deng, you'd go grunge, too. . . ."

"First time I saw her, I thought we were starting a camping show. . . ."

"And, you know," Laura says seriously, "now I don't understand why I'm still in the tent."

"Because we kept your show," Edie says. "Because you're our best producer."

"Thanks, but the way Peter blasted me about the handover, about how little I know. . . ."

"He was just angry, *mei-mei,* stressed. With him, it's all bottom line. . . ."

"And that's not a pretty sight these days," Gladys says.

"And you had been going on a bit about Deng . . ."

"But Deng. . . ."

". . . is the anchor, and the anchor is always right," Edie says.

"If Peter doesn't like me, then let him punish me," Laura says. "Transfer me, like Nancy. . . ."

"Some punishment," Gladys says. "London."

"That's winning the lucky draw," Edie says. "Fuggin London. . . ."

"Getting 80,000 Hongkies a month," Gladys adds. Edie and Laura stare at her. "My neighbors in HR leave everything out in the open. I can tell you anyone's salary, ID number, address, blood type. . . . I even know that Franklin's trying to get TVB to take me back if they'll just pay half my old salary there. . . ."

"But Nancy," Laura groans, "she went from being such a pill to the best, most cooperative. . . ."

"Fai Tak is fine," Edie says. "He's doing a good job."

"Quickie tells me his Cantonese is awful," Laura says.

"His editors don't speak much Canto either," Gladys says.

"And of course," Laura adds, "none of them speak English. . . ."

"As if you'd ever talk to an editor. . . ." Edie says.

"Hey, who was your field producer for the triumphant handover . . ."

". . . stupid. . . ." all three say.

". . . packages that they're still running on the US locals? I badgered and gestured and pushed and smacked enough editors who can't speak English to last a lifetime. . . ."

"Far easier in Mandarin than Cantonese," Edie says. "Fewer tones to get right with each smack."

"We are getting a bit of Beijing mafia out back, aren't we?" Gladys says. "The HR papers don't lie. I saw something else weird," she says, exhaling smoke. "Who is Lincoln Washington Lee?"

"The star-spangled banana," Laura, laughing and remembering that things were more fun when she wasn't at war with Peter.

"Some American minute man, we reckon," Edie says.

"Do you boil the chicken first?" Gladys asks.

"Oh," Laura says, snapped back to the present. "My husband does the cooking. Since that endless trip to China last month, he's gone back to being that sweet little homemaker I married."

"Feeling guilty, no doubt," Edie says, exhaling a long train of smoke.

"I only look at the bottom line," Laura says.

"Can I try it?" Gladys says.

"Sure." Laura hands her the container, and Gladys takes a forkful.

"Divine," she says. "Does he cater?"

"Only to Laura," Edie says.

"Slavishly, girls," Laura adds. "Eat your hearts out."

CHAPTER 26

Happy Anniversary

"T HIS IS NICE, REALLY NICE," Laura says, sitting at a plastic table covered by an Indian print cloth Jeff used as a bedspread on the *Golden Beauty*, on the roof of their apartment building with a couple of candles under hurricane lamps. To her left, she can see the lights of boats dotting Victoria Harbor, to her right the dark mounds of The Peak, and straight ahead, past Jeff, the towers and bright lights of Central, the moon rising above it all. They're working their way through a steamed whole sea bass stuffed with shallots and spinach. Jeff has just poured from their second bottle of that yummy New Zealand white wine, and put it back in their ice bucket, a plastic trashcan lined with a supermarket bag.

"I thought it would be better than going out," Jeff says.

"I still owe you a weekend at the Gold Coast. . . ."

"Whenever. No rush. I'm not going anywhere."

"No more thousand-and-one nights in China coming up?"

"You don't know how sorry I was . . . am . . . about that," Jeff says, more for himself than Laura. "Nothing like that is going to happen again." He sighs and takes sips wine. "I thought this might be fun up here. For a change. For a special occasion."

"This is even better than the view from Peak Bistro. And it won't cost us a couple thousand Hongkies, and then we stand on the taxi line hoping one shows up, and that some Chinese doesn't cut the line and take it. . . ."

"The apartment under here is vacant, and the table and chairs were up here," Jeff says. The last part is a lie; he bought the molded plastic table with detachable legs and the better grade of chairs with arm rests and backs, along with the lamps and candles, at a housewares store in Causeway Bay. The taxi driver bitched plenty about having to tie the chairs to the trunk lid.

"It's good. I mean the fish, the fish is great. But also it's a good idea to save a little money. Who knows what's going to happen with the network? Things are just so tough these days, with the crisis. . . ."

Jeff reaches under the table, and begins, "I wanted something special. . . ."

"The station has cut back, again, like I told you, so now I'm producing four hours in a row. At least I don't have to fight with other producers over packages and writers. And on days when there's no field producing, I get back here before noon. Next week I'll start at the gym again, and try to work off this Hong Kong ten. . . ."

"If you've put on any weight, I can't find it," Jeff says. "And I've looked everywhere. . . ."

"Good husband," she says, smiling. "You know those three little words every woman longs to hear: You're not fat. But how come you never bring me any of those fancy negligees anymore like you used to back in New York?"

"When I brought you the first-run Golden Beauties samples, you turned up your nose."

"That was just underwear," Laura says. "Besides, I didn't like the idea of everyone in your factory knowing my sizes. That robe you brought back from China isn't bad, but a nice sleek negligee. . . ."

Jeff reaches under the table again and smiles. "Well, you never wore any of that stuff very long. You'll wear these for a while, I hope." He hands Laura a small box wrapped in silver paper with string tied in a bow. "Happy anniversary."

"Holy shit," Laura says. "I completely forgot."

"It's okay. Open it."

Laura opens the box and sees a pair of earrings sparkling in the candlelight. "They're gorgeous." But she wonders why she isn't happier about receiving them.

"Try them."

Something deep inside Laura's head tells her not to. "I'm sure they fit. I just want to put them here and admire them." She places the open box on the table beside her plate and sighs. "God, I'm lucky to have you. Edie's always telling me I'm lucky to have someone here. Poor Edie, who claims she can't give it away, and, man, she sure does try. Must be tough here for a woman like Edie—and she's in good shape, she's smart, and it's not like she's ugly—but someone who's been around the block a few times, to be single here, with all these little Chinese hotties running around in their little skirts, shaking their little asses. . . . That girl who was Edie's friend . . . we met her at the Fuggin Asia promo launch. . . ."

Jeff realizes Laura expects an answer. "I met so many people that night. . . ."

"The Japanese girl, spoke very clipped English, had a face like a plastic doll . . ."

"No. . . ."

". . . and a funny name, like a cartoon character or something . . ."

"Bugs Bunny?"

". . . no, not Turner. . . . Yogi. That was it, Yogi was her name."

"No, I don't remember her. . . ."

"Anyway, Edie says a cute woman like that, with a really good job, smart—I guess she's smart if she's an investment strategist—this Yogi, the best she could do here was married Japanese men. That's awful. Man, I am glad to have you."

"I'm glad to be had," Jeff says, hoping the conversation is about to turn.

"I don't know where I'd be without you. When you were in China for that trip, like three weeks. . . ."

"I'm sorry, but at the time. . . ."

"At the time, I thought I was going to go out of my mind. It's not just the sex. . . . Don't get me wrong, I really like the sex. . . . When we're in bed, that's the only time of day I feel I can really let go, forget about all the other crap in my life for a while, to be someplace else, someplace where they've never heard of television. . . ."

"I'm glad." Jeff smiles and decides not to mention the camera cues.

"But it's not just that. It's really nice to be able to come home and to not have to think about things, not to have to worry about things with you. I'm glad this is one thing in my life that I don't have to put a lot of effort into."

"You do, though. . . ."

"God, that sounds terrible, but you know what I mean. I mean, this is the one situation I have that works, where I'm not worried that the whole thing could blow up in my face in a second, any second. Where everyone around me isn't looking to screw me first chance they get. I mean I work with some really good people, like Honest and Quickie and even Ashrami, who's a little slow but good hearted and really tries hard. But Deng, it's like the first thing he thinks about is how he can screw Laura and blame her for it and belittle her. And Edie.... I wouldn't have made it this far without Edie. But even Edie, I mean she works for Peter, and in the end that's who counts more for her. And she doesn't even have a degree." Laura doesn't notice Jeff's sour expression, just gazes at the earrings. "What are they?"

"What do they look like?"

"Well, they look like diamonds. . . ."

"Quarter carat each."

"Wow." Laura admires them again but still feels grim. "You must be doing okay."

"Things are going well."

"I'm glad they are for someone. I don't know what's going to happen with Fuggin Asia if this crisis keeps up. I mean Peter, he's awfully clever but he can be tricky, and all he cares about is the bottom line. I hope I don't wind up like those other people from the network, the ones on the other shows that got cut. . . . Did I tell you. . . ?"

"You mentioned. . . ."

"Peter promised everyone a job, see. Jobs in the US or in other Fuggin affiliates. And they all got a packet with job offers and forms to fill out. It all looked great." Laura takes sip of wine. "This fish is great, too," she says, taking another hunk. "The sauce is really nice. Light but tasty."

"Lemon, white wine, white pepper, thyme, shallots, plus a dash of horseradish. . . ."

"Whatever. I just care about the bottom line." Right joke, wrong audience, she thinks. "So Peter promised everyone a job, but he didn't promise anyone a visa, see?"

"I don't. . . ."

"So people have a job promised to them at Fuggin Minneapolis or Miami, but they can't get a visa from the US government to work there."

"Wow. That's sleazy."

"I'm not sure whether Peter knew that or not. You never can be sure with Peter. You think you know where he's coming from, what he's up to, then you realize, he's already a couple of steps ahead of you. So these poor people thought they had jobs but they can't. . . ."

"I don't understand, though. That party we went to for the woman going to America. . . ."

"May. Pang May Pau."

"She got a visa, right?"

"Yeah, but that was before, and she's different anyway, a different case. First of all, her mother's a big cheese here, so Peter isn't going to mess around with her. And May's a star, talent, and has a specific skill that's hard to find in the US. . . ."

"I don't understand."

"Well listen, okay? The company that's offering a job to a foreigner has to show that they can't get an American to do that job. That's how they get the government to grant the visa. So, if you're a TV reporter, well, they can say that she's the TV reporter we want, she's unique, and there aren't any others that will do. But if you're a tape editor or a graphics operator or a production assistant, there are hundreds, thousands of people in the US with the same skill, so there's no reason for the government to allow someone from Hong Kong to come in and take one of those jobs away from an American. Same thing like me. There aren't thousands of English-speaking TV producers in Hong Kong, so they could bring me over. Or at least there weren't when they did. Now, you probably can't walk through Central without tripping over a couple of unemployed producers. I guess I was lucky to get in when I did."

"It's more than luck. . . ."

"But who knows what'll happen next. I'm not even sure why I survived this round of cutbacks. I know Edie went to bat for me, and I know I'm good and that I put up with a lot, and I get the job done without too much bitching. But Deng doesn't like me, my anchor. Ex-Pussy, Peter's girlfriend, the one they call Candace Fang now, she hates me from back when she was my graphics girl and I dunked her mobile phone in her tea mug. And Peter said some really nasty stuff about the way I handled handover night, and we haven't spoken since then. So I don't understand. . . ."

"But like you say. . . ."

"With Old Hartman, he's got an ironclad contract. Peter is stuck with him. Same with Gladys, the sales VP. But with me, I mean, I cost him more than Andy because I'm on a package, so why didn't he get rid of me?"

"Maybe it's just because you're good," Jeff says. "I think you're great."

"But that's not because of my production skills." She smiles and eats more fish. "I have to work so hard, I'm under so much pressure, so much pressure that I don't even think of it as pressure anymore. I think it's normal to have an answer for everything in a split-second and keep track of a million different things. . . ."

"I think you worry too much."

"That's my job, to worry about everything. Do what I can, fix what I can, cover up what I can't, and worry about the rest. I make hundreds of decisions every day, and I'm never sure whether I've made the right ones." Diamond earrings should help, though, she thinks, and wonders why they don't.

"But you're doing a good job, and if they didn't think so, they wouldn't have kept you."

"I wish I could be so sure." She drinks some wine, and Jeff refills her glass. "There's something else. To tell you the truth, I don't get this crisis stuff. I understood the handover story, but not this one. I mean I understand how people are losing their jobs and companies are going bankrupt and can't pay their debts. But the stuff about currencies, I just don't understand that at all. I mean, why should it matter? If countries need more money, why don't they just print more?"

"Well, it's more complicated than that. After all, if they print more, then the currency value will go down. So they need to. . . ."

"With your high-school education, you're going to explain international finance to me?" Laura says, trying to temper the intemperate remark with a smile. He's your husband, not your PA, she reminds herself.

Jeff could tell her about how markets value currencies, about how demand is influenced by real economic factors such as interest rates and trade balances, as well as sentiment based on faith in government policies, expectation of the future direction of the economy and market movements, all the stuff he learned from Yogi and read and saw while he was worrying about his gamble with Laura's money. But that's not a subject he can touch. Instead he says, "Well, we deal with some of this stuff with the Golden Beauties shipments, but you're right. I don't really understand it either."

Laura sighs. "It's just so unfair. We were all watching the stupid handover, all focused on that, and we had it cold. We really kicked

CNN's ass, and that was my show. A hundred years from now, when people want to know what happened on handover night, they're going to watch my show, not CNN, not BBC, my show. We made history that night, and I wrote the script."

"That's why we came here. So you could...."

"But then this crisis came out of nowhere, blindsided us. Yeah, okay, I got a phone call from that freelancer in Bangkok—who's dried out now and gone back to the *Journal* full time. One lousy phone call and a note from a freelancer, and that only came a few hours before the shit hit the fan." Laura takes a sip of wine. "I mean, we're supposed to be a global newsgathering operation and that's the best we could do. The system—the Fuggin system let us down. But I know Peter still thinks that somehow it was my fault...."

"Calm down, Laura. I mean it's just a job...."

"No, it's more than just a job. It means a lot to me. I let down all these people. Peter, Edie, our viewers.... I mean when you reach into people's home into their lives, when you're a journalist.... You wouldn't understand...."

"Try me."

"When you're a journalist, you have a special obligation, you have to earn people's trust. And Peter, he trusted me, left me there without an SP, and let me handle the biggest story of the year, of the decade, and it turns out I got it wrong."

"In any business you have to earn people's trust," Jeff says, surprised at how much he sounds like his father. "When people come into your store, or when people take a shipment from you, they have to feel confident that they're getting what they want, what you've promised them, at the right price...."

"But it's different. When somebody's buying a nightgown, they can see it for themselves, they can see what's there with their own two eyes. When we report a story, the viewers can't see it for themselves, they have to trust us. Or when the boss leaves you solo in the hot seat...."

"When we send a shipment from China to New York," Jeff says, lapsing into the lie he's become so much more comfortable with than the truth, "people have to trust us. They can't see the shipment for themselves. And even in the store, with a nightgown or a bra, people can't see whether the material is really spun cotton or polyblend, they can't tell whether it was sewn with Sanforized thread so it doesn't shrink and bunch up along the seams after a dozen washings. There's a whole chain of trust that has to be established and lived up to." Realizing he's gone on too long, Jeff lifts his glass, "Like in a marriage."

"Like in a marriage," Laura says, clinking glasses with him. But sitting here at his glorious dinner for their anniversary that she forgot, looking at these gorgeous earrings that she can't bring herself to wear, Laura realizes something has gone terribly wrong and pledges to fix it.

"I felt like I had to find out where I stand with you."

"That's an interesting way to put it."

"I know," Laura says, sweeping her hand across a step before sitting, leaving room for Franklin to take the step below her. "It feels to me a little bit like junior high school. Did you have slam books?"

"What?"

"They put everyone's name down and you write what you think of them and pass it around, a different slam book every day or week or whatever, so you see where you stand . . ."

"Oh, like November sweeps. . . ."

". . .whether your stock is rising or falling, so to speak. And I feel like that's going on here. One minute, I'm total crap, the wicked witch of the handover who missed the crisis story, next I'm running half Fuggin Asia's programming day. So I wonder what's going on, Peter: what do you think of me, after all?"

"Answer to that will cost you a smoke," Franklin says. Chook-koo.

"Okay," Laura says, fingering the cigarette pack she just bought in the lobby.

"God, even that project is dead," Franklin says, looking at the twelve-story steel skeleton on the waterfront.

"Edie says they'll restart when they see demand or get more money. The kicker is that they'll restart where they left off, even if the plans change, or what they've put in already has rotted."

"Wait a minute," Franklin says. "Are we using that as VO for crisis stories. . . ?"

"Don't ask, don't tell," Laura says, lighting up.

"That's the quick thinking and strong ethical grounding that makes you our best producer. . . ."

"Thank you. But you said. . . ."

"When I worked assignments in LA, I fired a shooter because I told him to shoot a brush fire and when I went out to my car that night I saw the grass in the parking lot was burned. . . ."

"That's great," Laura says, blowing smoke his way.

"I didn't fire him because of the stunt, mind you. . . ."

"Well then why?"

"Because he was too stupid not to do it in someone else's parking lot, away from my car." Chook-koo. "Even your best people make mistakes. . . ."

"Even your best producers?"

"Especially them. The ones who never make mistakes are bound to be mediocre."

"Those things you said in the stairway to me. . . ."

"Laura, I was way out of line. I'm sorry about that, and I wish I could take it back."

"Apology accepted."

"You are our best producer. . . ."

"Thank you. After everything you said, I needed to hear that."

"You're welcome." Chook-koo. "We kept you even though you're on a package, and we could have saved some dollars—dollars we don't have—if we kept Andy instead. We may be in deep water financially, but we have to keep putting the best programming we can out there. My pop always says the quality of the programming is number one. It's the only thing we have complete control over, and our audience deserves our best. . . ."

"I do my best. . . ."

"And you do a great job." Chook-koo. "Of course, that doesn't mean that you do everything right."

"No, of course not. . . ."

"The thing with Randolph in Thailand, for example. Maybe you should have gotten it, but then again no one else did either. I'm sure he wasn't the only reporter in Bangkok who heard the bank rumor, and it didn't see the light of day anywhere."

"He didn't have the story. . . ."

"That's right. He didn't. But that doesn't mean he didn't have *a* story, that there wasn't something that we could have done. . . ."

"Like what?"

"Honestly, Laura, I don't know. It's impossible to look at it objectively now with the benefit of hindsight and knowing everything that's happened. . . . But the important thing is, next time you get something like that, to look for what you can use, look for reasons why instead of why not. . . ."

"But with everything else going on that night, starting with the Chinese costume party. . . ."

"Look, you had plenty of good reasons not to use it and plenty of other things to do. I understand that. But maybe that prevented you from seeing the reasons why you should have done something. That's all. It's something to keep in mind for next time."

"Yeah, for next handover night. . . ."

"Laura, in our business, the easiest thing to do, the easy choice is always no. When I got here, that was the standard answer from every department. Edie used to call Fiona Doctor No. . . ."

"That's great. She never told me. . . ."

"This isn't Nancy Reagan TV. We don't just say no."

"Understood. So what about midnight with Deng? Did I also make a mistake there?"

"Look, we both know that what Deng did was wrong . . ."

"I wish you'd tell him that."

". . . even though the television came out right."

"Well. . . ."

"But look, whether it came out right or wrong, there's nothing we can do about it now. It's not like a package where we can go back and reshoot or edit. It's done, it's over, and it's ours. It's got our name on it. . . ."

"It's got your name on it," Laura says with a smirk.

"Everyone's name here is Fuggin Asia," Franklin says. "What Deng did belongs to us, whether we like it or not. We own it. All we can do is try to make the best of it, use it to our advantage if we can. Make lemonade out of lemons."

"I see your point. But what about Candy?" Laura asks, blowing smoke toward Franklin.

"What about her?"

"If we admit that Deng was wrong, what about her?"

"Well, let's not get ahead of ourselves. What about Laura?" Chook-koo.

"What about. . . ?"

"You did a lot of things wrong, too. . . ."

"Like. . . ."

"You lost control of the show. And that's rule one: the producer controls the show. You didn't find a way to get to the remotes, not even to the pictures until I told you to. . . ."

"I was going to when you called. . . ."

"In that situation—to use you and Mike's favorite word, at that historic moment, seconds are like hours. . . ."

"So now I'm paired with Old Hartman. . . ."

"Well you are the two who've bitched the most about handover night. . . ."

"Because we both got. . . ."

"You want to let me finish, Laura," Franklin says, smiling. "First, maybe, you want to put that out," he adds, looking at the cigarette butt smoldering between her fingers.

"Oh, thanks." Laura drops the butt, steps on it, and reflexively lights another.

"Unlike Mike, in the end, you get a pass, same as Deng. The bottom line is you were the producer and it was great television, how ever it happened. And, you get credit for it just like Deng. It's kind of like what they say about chimpanzees and typewriters. You put enough of them together and you'll get *Hamlet.*"

"Now you're calling me a chimpanzee?"

"What makes you think I'm not calling Deng one?"

"He's talent," Laura says. "You wouldn't dare. . . ."

"In my experience, I've found that so-called talent is pretty fungible. . . ."

"So what about Candy?"

"What about her?" Chook-koo.

"Well, she had her great moment, I admit. But she was also a key contributor to the midnight fiasco. . . ."

"That we agree was great television. . . ."

"Yes, that we agree was great television."

"Even though everyone made some mistakes. . . ."

"Well, did everyone? Did you make a mistake by putting her out there?" Laura puffs smoke toward Franklin.

"No, I don't think so. She did everything we could have possibly expected her to do. She added real value with her reaction to May's report, and she looked . . . the way she looks."

"I just don't know what to think. . . ." Laura says, looking down and shaking her head.

"About what?"

"About Candy. It bothers me, what people say about you and her. . . ."

"It gets us a lot of publicity, though we both know that's not worth very much these days. . . ."

"I also understand about the *guanxi* that we get from her. . . ."

"They do love her in Beijing. She's a name up there. . . ."

"So, it's really just about business, isn't it?"

"She's a very valuable property . . . though please don't think I consider her, or anyone else here that way, as nothing more than properties. . . ."

"I understand, Peter." Laura sighs as she exhales smoke. "So what do I have to do to make myself as valuable to you . . . to Fuggin Asia as Candy?"

"Laura, that's a great question. I wish everyone on our staff would ask themselves that question every day. . . ."

"I'm asking you now. . . ."

"Well, you know what Candy does. . . ."

"Do I know everything that Candy does?"

"What do you mean?" Chook-koo.

"I mean her and you."

"Come on, Laura. . . ."

"I mean, you're not in love with her or anything like that, are you?"

"I'm not getting into that, especially with you."

"What does that mean, 'especially with me'?"

"I'm not going to sign your junior high-school slam book, and then sign it again next week. . . ."

"It's just between you and me, Peter. Off the record, no one else has to know. . . ."

"This is my fault, Laura. I never should have said all that stuff to you in the stairway. Sometimes my mouth gets ahead of my brain." Chook-koo. "That was stupid, and really inappropriate. . . ."

"Why do you say that?"

"Because I made it personal, and it never should be personal. That was the problem in Provo." Chook-koo. "And you don't need me getting personal with you, butting into your personal life."

"I'm not following. . . ."

"I mean anyone can see that you're a happily married woman. Who wouldn't be, with a husband who knows his way around a pair of panties inside and out?"

"Geez, Peter," she says, feeling a blush coming on.

"Sorry. All I'm trying to say is that it seems you made the right decision for you with your husband. I'm happy about that. Not just because it makes you happy, but because, when you come right down to it, I trust you to make the right decisions everyday. That's what a producer does, you make decisions and you live with them. . . ."

"Literally, in some cases."

"Well, when you marry your high-school sweetheart, somebody you've known a long time. . . ."

"Actually, I only knew Jeff for a few months before we got married. We did it because I was coming here. . . . My original travel papers from HR were for a single and it was a nightmare getting it all fixed before we left, along with having the wedding and everything."

"Oh, I didn't know that," Franklin says, and, for one of the few times he can recall, he wonders whether his lie sounds convincing.

"I'm telling you, with everything that was going on, moving, getting married, it was hard to know what I was doing sometimes, let alone make sense of everything. . . ."

"But as a producer, you're doing the same thing, making decisions on the fly, under pressure. . . ."

"And maybe not always the right ones. . . ."

"Maybe not. But like on handover night, you make a decision and it's done. You can't change it. . . ."

"Right, of course," Laura says, inhaling and exhaling a long plume. "But under different circumstances, if the situation was different, then you might make a different decision. . . ."

"Yes, of course." Chook-koo. "And I hope you would make a different . . . well, that you'd make the right decision for those circumstances. Otherwise you're not doing your job, you're not growing and learning and gaining from your experience. . . ."

"So the decision that you make in one case. . . ."

"Just because you're doing something this way now doesn't mean you should keep doing it that way forever."

"What's right at a specific time, may not be the right decision for different circumstances, at a different time, for a different situation . . ."

"Of course. . . ."

"So, Peter, what decision would you make about us. . . ?"

". . . and the great thing about this business is that. . . ."

"What about us, Peter?"

"The great thing about TV news is that there's a new show everyday, new scripts to write, brand new decisions to make every single day. . . ."

"So you always have new decisions to make, about everything. . . ."

"And, as things change," chook-koo, "we need to look at every decision we make in light of those new, different circumstances, based on how the situation may have changed, what we've learned. . . ."

"Your decisions have to fit the situation at hand. . . ."

"Especially now with the crisis, things are changing really quickly. Yes," he says, smiling and nodding his head slightly, "every day, new decisions. Every single day."

"About us. . . ?"

"About everything." Franklin sighs. "I'm afraid I better get back to the fray. . . ."

"And I should go home," she says, sighing then crushing her cigarette.

They both stand up together, and wind up with their faces about six inches apart.

"I guess we cleared that up . . . about you and Deng and making decisions. . . ." Franklin says.

"Yes. And what really matters now are the decisions we're going to make, you and me. . . ."

"Right," Franklin says, patting her shoulder, "exactly right. Our most important decisions are the ones in front of us." He smiles and holds the fire door for her.

"What's cooking, hon'?" Laura says, squeezing through the apartment door.

"I thought you'd be home earlier," Jeff says, "and we could have a workout. . . ."

"Oh, sorry. Peter asked me to go on a sales call with Gladys at Imperial Imports. They bring in Remy Martin, and I was hoping for free samples. . . ."

"Get any?"

"Only here," she says, pointing to her stomach. "No doggie bag," she adds, dropping her canvas carry bag on the floor in front of the credenza.

"No problem. We can still get in a quick workout. . . ."

"I'm not fit for anything but the jacuzzi," Laura says, flopping into the chair.

"Sorry, it's Friday, so you missed it."

"Oh, damn."

"That's why I said we should go early," Jeff says. "You can still do the steam room in the gym. . . ."

"Not the same," Laura says. "I'll survive a day without seeing the gym. What's for dinner?"

"Well, actually, I thought we could go out, have some Mediterranean food. . . ."

"Ummm. Mussels marinara, olives. . . ."

"How about hummus, baba ganoush, mutabak. . . ."

"Sounds like Lebanese. . . ."

"It's the dinner at the JCC after Friday night services. I thought tonight maybe we could go to services together. . . ."

"Are you joking?"

"No, I'm not," Jeff says. "I've been going pretty regularly the past couple of months. It's low-key stuff, and there are some non-Jews there. It only lasts about an hour, and the dinner afterwards is outstanding. . . ."

"You're serious," Laura says incredulously.

"Look, I'm not trying to convert you or anything. Hell, it was pretty surprising to me that I went in the first place, but I discovered I like it. The people are nice, the singing is good therapy, it's mainly in English, the building is interesting, you know, that one below the gym entrance with turrets. . . ."

"You really are serious." Laura laughs. "Hey listen, you go ahead. . . ."

"I'd like you to come with me. You mentioned that maybe we could. . . ."

"I did?"

"We can go to the gym first. . . ."

"I didn't come to Hong Kong to go to Jewish services and have a nice kosher dinner with a bunch of guys with beards and black hats. . . ." Laura says, no longer laughing.

"If it was like that, do you think I'd go?" Jeff says. "Why not just. . . ?"

"This is crazy. I can't believe we're having this conversation," she says, letting the anger stored during the week boil up. "I come home after another lousy week at the network with a couple of nice warm VSOPs in my tummy, and the last thing I need is more aggravation. . . ."

"Laura, I'm sorry, I thought maybe. . . ."

"I don't want any singing or Manischewitz wine. The only Jewish service on my mind was the usual, a little holy roll in the hay with you, but now I don't even want that. I'm going to pour myself a glass of dry white wine, go into my room, take off my clothes and drink it. You're free to go off and confess your sins, drink the blood of children or whatever you do at your services," Laura says, then takes a deep breath. "And maybe you can leave me a peanut butter and jelly on pita. . . ."

"White or wheat?" Jeff asks, heading for the kitchen.

In his 24th minute of pounding the stepper with the Ramones in his ears, Jeff feels a tap on his shoulder. He looks to the side and slips off his earphones.

"You are husband Laura, ya?" Candace Fang says, pronouncing his wife's name as RO-ra.

"I hate to admit I'm anyone's husband to a woman as beautiful as you." Jeff says, jumping off the stepper.

Fang giggles, letting her top teeth ride over her bottom lip, then bringing the fingertips of her left hand to the tip of her nose to cover her mouth, casting her eyes downward. Her long black hair is pulled back in a ponytail, and she's wearing a pink aerobics suit cut high on the leg that showcases her breathtaking figure. She could be a model for the outfit. "I am Candace from FGN Asia. We meet at party for video," she says, and before Jeff can begin to say anything, to see if she knows, and to let her know that he knows, she adds, "When meet first time, I am Pussy."

Jeff nods. "Yes, I remember." Casing the gym, he sees they're alone.

"Is very funny. Was after I with you I find out what is mean Pussy. I not understand why you think I want to go to room. Afterward, I ask friend why is." She giggles fetchingly again.

"You're not angry at me about that, are you?"

"I not angry. I not. . . ." She takes a breath and purses her lips. "English still for me difficult. I not must go with you."

"I was very glad you decided to go with me, Candace." Jeff sighs.

"I remember you very happy. . . ."

"You didn't tell anybody. . . ."

"Aaaiiiyaaah. I do not tell anybody. I with Peter, Fuggin Asia boss. Do not want make . . . not spoil with Peter."

"So Laura. . . ?"

"Cannot secret in newsroom. I never say anybody."

"That's good. I never say either." He smiles. "It was great, and I really. . . ."

"After this, many good thing happen to me."

"I'm glad it was good for you, too," Jeff says, knowing she won't get the joke. "One thing I wondered . . . you gave me back the money, didn't you?"

"I do not understand."

"The thousand Hong Kong dollars I gave you. . . . Did you put it back in my wallet?"

She covers her mouth again. "Yes, yes. But I can take now." She removes her hand and smiles. "This joke."

"Thank you," Jeff says. "For everything."

"We just move in building," she says. "Are in building, you and Laura?"

"We live around the corner. This place is too expensive for us."

"Peter say we save money here. Have apartment not yet finish to stay for one year. Sometimes he talk like he Chinese mother, always want to saving money. But if you not living here. . . ?"

"I'm a member of the Jewish Center, and we share the gym and the tennis court with the building. I spend a lot of time here. Do you play tennis?"

"No, I do not. . . ."

"How about swimming? Do you know how to swim? The JCC has a pool and a jacuzzi and I can. . . ."

"I know to swim. Building also have pool. For resident."

"I just thought, you know, if you're free in the afternoon like this. . . ." Jeff smiles.

Fang nods. "I am understand. For me, with Peter very good."

Jeff smiles. "I am very rich now. . . ."

"You cannot as rich as Peter," Fang says, then covers her mouth again. "Now I am talk Chinese mother. I very happy with Peter. Not just with romantic. Also with business. Peter have make me more than Pussy."

"I understand."

"For you is difficult with Laura?"

"Well. . . ."

"I know Laura difficult person sometime."

"Sometimes, yes," Jeff admits. "But I think it is also because I keep secrets from her."

"Secret about Pussy?" She covers her mouth again. "This not big secret. Wife say she happy you." Fang laughs, covering her mouth. "Much orgasm."

"Laura talks about us, about that. . . ?"

"Cannot secret in newsroom. But at home also cannot secret. When thing happen, if not so important, forget. Must. Cannot think. No good too much thinking."

"Yes, that is good advice."

"Is more secret for Jeff? Not only Pussy secret?"

"Well," Jeff sighs, "yes."

"Is big secret?"

"Yes."

"Is now finish?"

"Yes, it's finished, sort of. But I can't just forget it."

"Then you must tell to Laura. Secret is block communication, and no communication no good for together. Must tell."

"But. . . ."

"If is good with Laura, will forgive, can fix. If cannot, then perhaps must finish with wife."

"This is also good advice."

"Cannot half-half. Must all-all or not-not. Cannot secret. Except small secret," she adds, covering her mouth again and, to Jeff, looking good enough to eat. He wonders how is it that the beautiful ones are also the smartest? Or maybe they just seem that way when you're looking at them in a skintight, pink aerobics suit.

CHAPTER 27

Clear Air

I T'S A SUNDAY MORNING during that brief window of glorious weather on the Hong Kong calendar, the window Jeff and Laura failed to appreciate when they arrived a year ago. Humidity gone—perhaps on holiday to the Philippines—the air gently kisses the exposed skin beyond Jeff's shorts and tee-shirt instead of coating it in sweat. Under the cloudless blue sky, he spreads the Indian cloth over the table on the roof, ties the ends around the legs to secure it against the fresh breeze off the harbor and surveys the cityscape. He moves the chair with its back to Central around the table to face the harbor and enjoy the view all the way out to *Gao Long,* the hills called Nine Dragons near the border that inspired Kowloon's name. You couldn't have this in New York, he thinks, not in a million years, not for less than a couple million bucks. He does a complete turn, from Central to The Peak to the apartment towers concealing the synagogue to the harbor, thinking it's perfect weather for clearing the air.

Back in the kitchen, he squirts a little cooking spray in the bottom of the wok and adjusts the gas burner to medium heat. He cracks the first egg on the side of the wok. Amazing what you can do with this one pan, Jeff thinks, as he drops the egg's contents carefully into curved bottom. As the white sizzles, he gives the sauce a stir over its barely visible flame on the adjacent burner. You'll forget and burn the house down, his mother would say. As he flips the egg and the yolk remains unbroken, he feels a flash of relief. He takes that small victory as an omen that it's going to be okay this morning. He'll tell her, she'll understand, and things will start going the way they should between them. He counts to five then scoops the egg out of wok and onto half an English muffin, well toasted, topped with a slice of seared Canadian bacon. He gives the wok bottom another quick blast of cooking spray, cracks the next egg and deposits its contents gently, flicks on the coffee maker, stirs the sauce again, and keeps cooking. He hears the water in the shower stop as he turns the fourth egg. He counts five again, then scoops a final perfect over-light out of the wok and onto the last muffin half. He gives the sauce another stir then walks to the bathroom.

"It's a gorgeous morning, and the sun is behind Tycoon Court," he says, admiring his wife's pleasantly pulpy behind and then her handfuls of breasts in the mirror. I could do worse, he thinks. I've done better, I could do worse. It's worth fixing this. This morning in bed there weren't even any camera cues, at least none that he could hear. "Brunch on the roof?"

"Sure," Laura says. She rubs the towel over her hair then runs her brush through it. A husband who stayed in my bed last night and cooks breakfast on Sunday, she thinks, now this is living. She looks at herself in the mirror. Not so bad for pushing 30. Jeff seems to like it, last night and this morning, and that's what matters. Whatever happens at work happens or doesn't, for now her show is right here, and she can't see any glitches in this live shot.

Jeff puts a bottle of champagne, an Australian one, not as good as the JCC's brand, in their plastic wastebasket ice bucket. He takes that, along with the strawberries, already washed and drying in a plastic colander, on the first trip. He props open the front door with a magazine as he waits for the elevator. He rides up three floors, mounts the flight of stairs to the roof and props open that door with a cinderblock. He makes another trip to carry silverware, cups and glasses, then another with the fresh whipped cream and coffee pot. Back in the kitchen, he stirs the sauce again, and puts a lettuce leaf, tomato wedges, and a slice of orange on each plate.

"Is this okay for the roof?" Laura asks, modeling the blue and white silk fanny wrap he brought back for her from his long trip to China at Yogi's. He actually purchased it at the shop in Fortress Hill where Yogi bought her lingerie, at her urging. "If you do not bring your wife gift from trip, she will quite disappoint," Yogi warned. Jeff picked it because it reminded him of the outfits at the massage parlor in Shenzhen. He now realizes that Yogi was there that day buying Chinese gifts for her friends back in Japan. "Does it show too much?"

"I like what it shows," Jeff replies.

"As well you should. But what about the neighbors?"

"They can make up their own minds. . . ."

"Very funny."

"Nobody looks out their windows here," Jeff assures her. "Ready to eat?"

"You bet. Smells great."

"Okay." Jeff turns off the burner, stirs and then spoons sauce over the eggs on each plate.

"Don't be cheap," Laura says, so Jeff spoons more sauce for her.

He picks up the two plates with one hand and a bottle of water with the other. "You get the door and the elevator."

"Got keys? I wouldn't want to get locked out in this get up."

"Got 'em," Jeff says, and they squeeze through the door, Laura first.

In the elevator, after pushing the button for the top floor, she says, "With your hands full, you can't stop me from doing this," and gently cups his balls.

"If I could feel anything down there, your breakfast would probably be on the floor."

"I wouldn't mind it on the floor," she says. The elevator stops jerkily. They get out and climb the stairs to the roof. Laura surveys the scene and feels the air embrace her. "It's gorgeous up here," she says, taking a twirl. She looks at the table as Jeff puts the plates on it. "Nice spread."

"Well, don't just stand there looking beautiful. . . ." Jeff puts down the plates and pulls out a chair for her, the one facing harbor.

Laura curtseys and sits, her robe falling open as she does. She smiles and covers herself. God, she feels so sexy and special when he treats her this way. "I suppose you've seen enough of that for a while."

"One appetite at a time," he says. It would be easy to avoid this, let it slide. After all, things aren't so bad. They're weird, maybe, far from ideal, but not so bad. He grabs the champagne out of the bucket and begins unwrapping the foil top. "It's Sea Breeze, Australian. Not great, but appropriate for this morning."

"As long it has bubbles that tickle my nose," Laura says. "And alcohol."

He works the cork out by turning the bottle—the way Yogi always insisted—and it releases with a quiet pop. In memory of my father, Jeff thinks, as he fills her flute, then his, and then sits.

"Cheers," Laura says, lifting her glass.

He'd been reaching for his cutlery, so Jeff has to scramble for his glass. Couldn't she just give me a second, he thinks, pay some attention, then realizes that just wouldn't be Laura. He smiles and clinks his glass with hers. They both take sips. "Lovely," she says. *"Bon appetit."* With the first taste, Jeff thinks, the sauce turned out right. Nice and smooth, not too cheesy. He may not have learned much seamanship on the *Golden Beauty,* but he'd become an expert on Sunday brunch for two. He looks at the harbor and imagines cutting through the container ships and tenders under full sail, heading toward that beach he visited with Yogi on the junk trip, the day she must have gotten pregnant. Right or wrong, what's done is done. He could go on like this with Laura.

"This is good," Laura says. "Like eggs Benedict."

"It is eggs Benedict."

"Well, yes, except that the egg is supposed to be poached, I believe."

"We don't have a poacher."

"Good point. . . . Delicious."

Jeff thinks, yes, I could go on like this, with things the way they are. Things are good enough. But he's always settled for good enough, with the promise that something better will come. And maybe something better did come. But, whatever it was, it came and it went, and it left him just where he was before. All his life, he's been doing what other people expected, what other people wanted. Worse, it turns out that it was only what he thought other people wanted; he didn't even know the whole story, no one ever told him, and that led to serious mistakes. Like his mother said about the stores, he never asked. He just did what he thought was right, for her, for his father. Except for when Murray won a hand of pinochle or when one of his ladies left the store with a girdle that made her look 30 pounds overweight instead of 50, Jeff couldn't remember seeing his father smile. Everything was always for other people: I work this hard so you and your mother. . . . pop, you should have tried doing something for yourself while you had the chance, taken charge of things. You deserved better, pop. Yes, things could be worse, Jeff concedes, but they're not the way they should be, and he's going to try to fix it while there's still a chance.

"Laura, there's something I want to talk to you about. . . ."

"I know, I know," she says, dipping a strawberry into the whipped cream, and taking a bite, then a sip of champagne. "Look I'm a simple girl from the Maryland 'burbs. A little straight, I know. I never screwed in a dressing room. Fact is, I don't think I've ever done it anywhere but a bed. Okay, once in a sleeping bag, with a rock sticking into my shoulder. But I can change. If you want me to get on top, we can. . . ."

He can't help smiling. "That's not it." He refills both of their glasses with champagne and takes a sip of coffee.

"Oh. Well, we can try that anyway. Or even from behind, like I've seen in the movies. As long as it still ends up in the same place." She takes another sip of champagne. "It does, doesn't it?"

"That depends. But usually." He thinks of telling her Yogi's analogy story in a modified version. Well, here's one thing that's easy to fix. "C'mon," he says, getting up, taking her hand and leading her to the waist-high concrete ledge at the edge of the roof overlooking the harbor.

"This isn't some lovers' leap thing," Laura says, "or about the mobile phone. . . ."

"Just a small step," he says. "Lean against here and look at harbor." From behind her, he kisses the nape of her neck and reaches under her robe. He slips his other hand through the front of her robe to her breasts.

"People will. . . ."

"People will be incredibly jealous." He feels her getting moist and himself getting hard. He slips down the elastic waistband of his shorts. Laura puts her hands on the ledge and pushes back toward him. When he's hard enough, he slides inside her. He turns his head toward the skyscrapers of Central, then looks at the harbor, then closes his eyes and remembers the times with Yogi, on their knees in front of her living room window with this same view. He holds both of Laura's breasts, squeezing and pumping. She moans, "In three, two, one . . . cue," then her weight seems to collapse onto his cock. She moans softly as he continues to pump, as if he's on the stepper, and he remembers Candy in her pink gym outfit, pressing his mouth to her breasts in that Kowloon love hotel. He pumps faster, as if the stepper has speeded up. He doesn't shoot much, but it's a real orgasm this time, heart pumping, sweat dripping from his temples. He holds Laura, leaning hard against her as they both pant, opening his eyes, to see the harbor and her light brown hair that she's cut short again.

Laura tries to turn, but he pushes her back. "Just stay there a minute. Please."

"I'm not going anywhere," she says, reaching back to pat his ass, her vaginal muscles tightening as she does. "I don't know whether to say, 'What have we been waiting for?' or 'That was worth waiting for.' Got any other tricks up your, um, sleeve? Or should I say, up my sleeve?"

He pushes into her as deeply as he can again, but his feeling extends no farther than his pubic hair. He sighs and puts his hands on the ledge outside of hers. She pats his left hand with hers and says, "Nice work, mister. I'd keep smiling for the next week, if it wasn't for Fuggin Asia."

Soft now, he backs away from her and snaps his shorts back up to his waist. He pats her on the shoulder and hugs it as they stagger back to their seats like boxers after a tough round. He tops off their glasses with cold champagne. They each take a gulp and let out big sighs.

"Well, that took care of my issue," Laura says brightly. "I hope yours can be resolved so . . . rewardingly."

"Lee-law-ding-ree," Jeff mutters absently.

"What?"

"Nothing," he says and has another sip of champagne then some coffee.

"I hope no one called the police." Laura chuckles. "At least nobody from Fortune Towers threw a bucket of water on us." She looks at Jeff, who is still flushed. "Are you okay? Have some water," she says. He pours the dregs of his coffee into her cup, fills his cup with water and takes a long drink.

"That's better," he says. "Thanks."

"No, thank you," she answers, beaming. "So what did you want to talk about?"

"Maybe later."

"Okay, but sometimes later never comes."

Or it comes when you least expect it. The Time is Always Now. The idea is to make the other 23 hours, 50 minutes of the day as satisfying as those ten, and the only way that can happen is by telling her. Cannot half-half. If things are going to be right between them, ever, he can't keep holding it in.

"You're right," he begins. "There's something I haven't told you. Something important."

"All right," Laura says, nodding, as she dips a strawberry into the cream. "Whatever it is, tell me." She bites the strawberry. "Dee-lish."

Jeff sighs. "Laura, I'm rich."

"Well, I thought your family must be pretty well off. After all, you had a lawyer. . . ."

"Not my family. Me. I'm rich."

"Okay, fine. . . ."

"But it's about how I got rich. . . ."

"You rob banks?" She says, smiling and sipping champagne, still feeling a residual low hum inside her from the ledge. "I know your business is going well and that in China, well, you have to play ball with the right people. *Guanxi* or whatever. . . ."

"Please. Just listen." Jeff sighs. "My mother and her partner on Long Island and the two Israelis here are making all the money on the underwear. That doesn't mean they don't expect me to work like a dog. But I'm still just getting a lousy 500 bucks a week from my mother. . . ."

"But it's your business, your family's business, and some day, when your mother. . . ."

"Listen. I've had it up to here with my mother." He takes a sip of champagne. "She's screwed me left and right. It's a long story, and it's not really important now. The point is that I got cheated, used. And living here and seeing everyone else making a fortune and me with 500 lousy bucks a week—imagine trying to live on that here—I got jealous. So I wanted my own fortune. . . ."

"Don't we all?" Laura says. "But there's more to life. . . ."

"Yes, there is, and that's why I need to tell you this. So we can enjoy our life together without this thing between us."

"Now you're scaring me a little," she says, her smile receding. "Tell me."

"Okay," Jeff says, taking a deep breath. "Remember handover night?"

"Handover night . . . handover night?" she says vacantly. "I'm teasing. Of course I do . . . vividly. Did Deng really see you. . . ?"

"Remember during dinner you got a phone call on your mobile? From a reporter, a guy in Thailand. . . ?"

"Right. Brian Randolph, the freelancer. . . ."

"Well, I heard your conversation. You told me about what he said. About the bank in Thailand, about the baht."

"Yes," Laura says. "So?"

"So, believe it or not, I understood what you were talking about, and I asked some people about it. I didn't mention the conversation or you or anything. Most of them thought it was ridiculous, that Thailand would never float the baht. But I found out what to do, how to make money, if it did happen. Then I called my friend Tim in New York, the investment guy, and he helped me buy currency contracts. He even paid the fees for them, against the value of my boat back in New York."

"Geez," Laura says, still in a semi-haze of pheromones and alcohol. "So you shorted the baht with the boat...?"

"The Indonesian rupiah, actually...."

"And it worked? You made money?"

"Yes."

"How much?"

"A lot. More than four million.... US."

"Oh my god...." she shouts, emerged from the haze, her face reddening, the low hum in her belly rising to become a ringing inside her head.

"But you see, in order to make the trades, I needed collateral. My boat could cover the fees, but I needed collateral, and lingerie stores in Bethpage, Manhasset, Roslyn, Plainview and Syosset wouldn't work. Neither would the old homestead in Split-Level-Town. So I used your stocks as collateral."

"You didn't," Laura says. "How could you?" She thinks: This happened because I didn't know him well enough to begin with, because I expected it would work out just because I wanted it to, because it would be convenient if it did.

"I tried to ask you, but you were busy," Jeff says. "Remember? I called you at the station and said I needed money...." He thinks: This is what happens when a relationship stops, when it doesn't grow, when each person has a consuming passion they don't share with the other, and the two of them wind up with nothing important in common. "You said there was 500 Hongkies in your closet and hung up. I looked in the closet and saw your brokerage statements and used the account number."

"You betrayed me," Laura says. She thinks: He doesn't even understand my professional status, my position of trust as a journalist, the rules I have to follow. He's just a merchant, a shopkeeper, a little old Jewish shopkeeper. "You have no idea...."

"I'm sorry." He thinks: She thinks this is betrayal. If she only knew. He wants to tell her how hard he has tried in these past weeks to make things right with her, to fix everything, and how much he'd hoped it would be worth it.

"You abused privileged information," Laura says. "How can I tell Peter. . . ?"

"Listen, I checked with Jerry Liu, my mother's lawyer, the guy we call Jerry Lewis, and our pre-nup is very clear. You're clean, the money has nothing to do with you, even though I used your account numbers. You didn't consent to it, you didn't know. The deals were all mine, you're totally in the clear. But look, we can both share the money. . . ."

"I don't want any of your lousy, dirty money," Laura snarls. "Don't you understand about our company rules, about journalism, about integrity and public trust. . . ."

"Yes, and that's why I checked. . . ."

"You didn't just betray me as a husband with this awful thing, you betrayed me professionally. This could ruin my entire career," she says, shaking her head. "What did you need money for? You had a roof over your head, you had a salary, I pay for everything. You just couldn't resist. . . ."

"Laura, I was tired of relying on you and my mother. I wanted something that would be my own. . . ."

"Your own. Yeah." She shakes her head, gulps champagne and refills her glass. "With my information. From my job. And with my stocks for collateral."

"Like I said, we can share. . . ."

"You don't understand, damn it. If it was just between us, if you only betrayed me, then we could try to fix that as a couple. But this goes way beyond that: it's my career, it's the whole network's integrity. That stuff isn't just talk. We sign a contract that says we won't use any information we get for personal profit, that we won't do exactly what you did. This could cost me my job, you shit. I could even go to jail." Her mouth, Laura realizes, has leapt way ahead of her brain.

"Really?"

"I don't know. Maybe." Laura gulps champagne again. "How could you have so little respect for me?"

"Laura, it wasn't about you. It was. . . ."

"How can you say it wasn't about me? It couldn't have happened without me, none of it. You wouldn't even be here in the first place if it wasn't for me. . . ."

"Okay, okay. I didn't realize what I was doing to you. I was thinking about me. . . ."

"While you were screwing me," Laura says, shaking her head. "That's very impolite."

"Try to understand it from my side. I was tired. . . ."

"You were tired?!? Tired of what? I'm the one who gets out of bed at midnight every day and works until the next afternoon. How dare you even think about tired around me." She sips champagne and sighs, "I can't imagine anything more awful. . . ."

"I'm sorry," Jeff says, thinking she doesn't have a vivid enough imagination. "I hope that you can find a way to forgive me. . . ."

"Forgive you? I'm really angry at you. Really angry," Laura says, beginning to cry. Jeff puts his hand on her shoulder, but she knocks it away. "Don't touch me, you bastard. Just don't touch me." She sniffles. "I have to think about this, about what to do. And . . . and I don't want you in my face or poking me with your cock, as if that's some magic wand that can fix everything. Get out," she says, raising her voice. "Just get out. I don't want to see you, not for the rest of today at least. I need time to think. Just get out."

"Okay, okay. I understand," Jeff says, rising from the table, feeling, to his surprise, incredibly relieved. "I'll just take some of these dishes away."

"Do it fast, and get out," she says. "And leave the door downstairs open. I don't want to have to call the landlord because I'm locked out. Not in this Chinese whorehouse outfit."

She watches him go through the door, then looks at the harbor and the hills, paralyzed in her seat except for the hand that reaches for her champagne glass, then for Jeff's glass, then for the bottle. Laura wonders, who can I talk to? Edie? She'll tell Edie tomorrow. She can call her mother but she wouldn't understand. There are bumps in every marriage, dear, she'd say, just ride them out. Well, Jeff is the one who deserves the rough ride, not her. And fifteen minutes ago, looking out at this same harbor as if they owned it, losing herself around him, it was all so perfect. She could stand a lot more of that, and a lot less of all this other shit.

It's so unfair, Laura thinks. He doesn't deserve that money. How the hell did he figure it out with his goddamned high-school education. How could he figure out a way to make so much money? His friend in New York must have helped him. . . . But I have friends, Laura thinks, good friends. Why didn't somebody tell me how to make $4 million. How could this all happen? All of these people getting what they don't deserve: Jeff, Pussy . . . and me. I've worked my ass off. If anyone deserves $4 million, it's me. Instead, I'm humiliated again, this time by a little shopkeeper always sniffing for a buck who got lucky, incredibly lucky. He's lucky I put up with him, gave him a ticket to China and put a roof over his head, for what, so he can tell people my underwear sizes and play the currency market. All he's good for is sex and cooking, and I can get those from him or order out, whatever. The rest of my life is full enough. He's got his own bedroom. And the kitchen. He can keep cooking. Yes, he's a good little houseboy, the bastard.

But that full life she has is as Laura Wellesley, *AM Asia* producer, Fuggin Asia Hong Kong. When she tells Peter about what Jeff did, that life could be over. Peter's looking for reasons to fire people, and she just heard a damned good one for firing her. But she has to tell him; she can't not tell him. She could never manage it, carrying this secret into the control room along with all of her other responsibilities. No, she has to tell Peter. But what can she tell him? She can hear Peter say, "So what are you going to do about it, Laura?" If she says, "Cut his cock off and leave the bastard," Peter would say, "Well, maybe that's the right decision for you, but what does that do for Fuggin Asia? How does it help our bottom line?"

Indeed, it's all about the bottom line with Peter. What can Laura do for the bottom line? How can she turn this betrayal into something that's valuable to Fuggin Asia, to Peter? Money. Of course. Money. She can give him the money, she thinks, give Peter Jeff's money. That would teach the bastard. That would be the perfect decision. It would punish Jeff, it would compensate the network and, assuming she drove the bargain right, save her job. It would show Peter that she cares about Fuggin Asia, too, the way he does. Yes, she can give Fuggin Asia the money. Peter will be so pleased to see her making the right decision this time with so much on the line.

Right now, after squeezing the last of the champagne from the bottle and gulping it, Laura thinks the right decision for her is a little more sleep. She pushes away her plate and puts her head down on the table, the morning's clear air caressing her hair and neck.

Down in the apartment, Jeff carries the dishes to the sink and, reflexively, begins washing them as he tries to understand Laura's perspective. He doesn't understand why she thinks what he did was an insult to her. He also doesn't understand what makes her think that journalists are the only people in the world who need integrity, or that, somehow, their integrity is more important than anyone else's. She may be the expert on big business, but he doesn't understand what kind of financial logic tells her that a job that forces her wake up at midnight and work fourteen hours a day with an anchorman she hates, for a boss whose girlfriend hates her, is more valuable than a family fortune that amounts to a few decades' salary. He wonders whether to be happy or sad about her spurning the money. While he's tried to fix things these past weeks, really tried to fix things, he's never considered that she might prefer a wrecking ball, nor where that decision would leave him.

First, though, he has to consider what to do with the rest of today. He'd like to go to the gym and tell the former Pussy that her advice was lousy, as bad as her English. But he decides to leave the JCC to Laura—she's got her spouse card back—at least until dark. He takes his wallet and leaves the apartment. He nearly slams the gate shut, but remembers Laura's edict about leaving it open. He thinks about bringing her keys up to the roof to see if she's cooled down enough to discuss things reasonably, decides it's better to leave her alone. The harbor looked so gorgeous from the roof, a ride on the ferry to Lantau with the Sunday newspaper could be a good way to kill time until dark. Then a workout, jacuzzi, and home well past her bedtime. Let her think things over until tomorrow.

He hits the button for the elevator and rides down, ducking away from scrape above eight. The air at ground level feels as gentle as it did on the roof, and he walks downhill alongside the escalator, already running up, through blades of sunshine edging between the buildings. At Hollywood Road, he chooses the elevated walkway that follows the escalator, the quickest route to the Outlying Island Ferry Piers. At Central Market, he encounters his first wave of Filipina maids enjoying their Sunday off. Exiting the enclosed market arcade for the open air walkway toward the harbor, passing the Hong Kong Stock Exchange— they haven't swapped the bronze bull for a bear despite the beating the market's taking these days—he notices how splendidly organized these amahs are. Flattened cardboard boxes, sheets, straw mats or just leaves of newspaper mark out their territories, extending precisely to the poles dividing the walkway in half, half for the amahs, and half for everyone else, each world assiduously ignoring the other. Within the amah groups, there's food in plastic containers from their employers' kitchens or in plastic bags from the Park 'n' Shop, boom boxes, playing cards, Philippine newspapers and magazines, photo albums, Bibles, and beauty care items. Amahs give other amahs facials, massages, haircuts, makeovers, manicures and pedicures, all out there in the open but enclosed within their groups. Seeing one foot reflexology session in progress, he asks the amah receiving the rub, "How much you pay?"

She smiles and giggles. "Twenty dollars."

Jeff smiles back. "I'll pay you fifty if you let me do it."

CHAPTER 28

Laura's Donut

LAURA FEELS AS IF SHE'LL BURST by the time Edie arrives at 4:30 Monday morning, and instead of letting her go through the wires, Laura immediately tells her what Jeff did. "Four million US . . . I'd keep quiet and take the money," Edie advises, adding, "I never hold anyone accountable for anything they say before six a.m. or after nine p.m., so I haven't heard this yet. You can still decide not to tell me." She waves Laura away, turns to her computer screen, and begins reading in. But Laura knows she can't keep quiet about Jeff's betrayal. A good night's sleep, after a good day's nap, and another bottle of that Australian bubbly—the Jewish mother in Jeff had an extra on ice—has convinced her she has to tell Peter and turn over the money. Telling Peter and Edie not only protects her professional reputation but may help her find the right response to Jeff. Besides, she's just too upset to keep the news to herself.

In the control room, with these distractions occupying her mind, the show goes smoother than usual, the issues in the news seem small, this regional economic crisis less important. Laura ignores Deng's carping and instead notices how production values have improved in Pussy's feature segments, no longer Laura's responsibility. The B-blocks are now titled *From the Pages of the Financial Journal* and the Ds *Asia in Focus,* each with its own logo and background, as well as a different outfit from Color Me or Printemps for Pussy in each segment. Laura can see it won't be long before the segments become half-hour shows airing not just on Fuggin Asia but across the network—no reason why Pussy (or her equivalent on other continents) couldn't host a *Focus* show for every region and a global one. Laura can also see, with her professional eye, that the shows are taped as skeletons, with Pussy spending less than five minutes in the studio for each segment, the packages inserted later by editors between her lead-ins and tags; Pussy probably never even sees the reports she introduces so confidently. Laura wonders when and where they tape the segments, but she has to admit they're good, despite occasional rough edges in the scripts that would be easy to fix. Who writes them? she wonders.

"Pussy's cut-ins have turned into little mini-shows," Laura mentions in the staircase, after leaving Quickie to babysit the final one of the day at 9:45. "And they're pretty good."

"She works hard," Edie says.

"And she looks ... unbelievable," Gladys adds, taking a light from Edie's cigarette. "As good as she looks in real life, she looks even better on TV."

"Indeed," Edie says. "The exception that proves the rule."

Laura searches for something to say about Edie the glamorous field reporter versus Edie the sleep-deprived studio stairway smoker, but can't find the right mix of flattery and mockery. Instead, she says, "When you finish that cigarette, you'll come talk to Peter with me, right?"

"I don't think. . . ."

"For moral support, Edie, please. Just so I'm not alone in there. . . ."

"Excuse me," Gladys says. "Care to share?"

"We just. . . ." Laura begins.

"I think it would be good to ask Gladys' opinion," Edie says. "She'll keep the matter in confidence, I'm sure."

"Well?" Gladys says. "I won't tell a soul. Please. . . ."

"Okay," Laura says, happy to get another perspective. "My husband overheard a business conversation on my mobile and used information from it, without my knowledge or consent, to make money in the currency market. . . ."

"A lot of money," Edie adds.

"How much. . . ?"

"More than a year's salary," Laura says.

"More than ten years' salary," Edie says, "even your salary."

"Aaiiii-yaaaah."

"Thank you, Edie," Laura says. "He also needed to manipulate my accounts in order to make the money, which isn't relevant, except that it just makes me more pissed off at him. . . ."

"Why?" Gladys asks. "Why are you pissed off?"

"Because he abused my trust. Betrayed me and undermined my professional integrity to make a lousy buck."

"Oh," Gladys says.

"More than ten years' lousy bucks," Edie adds.

"So I'm going to tell Peter about it, and I want Edie come in with me."

"I think bringing Edie is a good idea," Gladys says, "if she can stop you from telling Peter. . . ."

"There's more," Edie says. "She wants to give the money to Fuggin Asia."

"What? That's ridiculous," Gladys says. "It's not their money. You didn't take it from them. . . ."

"No," Laura admits. "But I made it thanks to the. . . ."

"I don't think Peter Franklin needs your money," Gladys suggests.

"Yes, but the operation here does," Laura says. "And it's not about the money. . . ."

"If it's not about the money," Gladys says, "then why give it away?"

"I'm also worried about the legal issues. Peter and his father back in the US have lawyers just sitting around waiting to find people to sue. I see the money as a way to settle any possible claim against me, or Jeff."

"One item I picked up working in the law office," Edie says, "is that amateurs should never try to play at their game."

"You should go in to hold her hand," Gladys urges Edie, "and cover her mouth as needed."

"Well," Laura says, "shall we?" Laura gets up and looks at Edie.

Edie looks back, then looks at her cigarette, takes another puff, and sighs. "I'll warn you a final time: this is a mistake. All of it. Just ignore it."

"Come on," Laura says, standing and holding out her hand to Edie.

Edie shakes her head, grinds the cigarette under her shoe, and takes Laura's hand to stand.

"Good luck," Gladys says, remaining seated. "Don't forget me for the next bulletin here. It's far more interesting than anything on our air."

Laura holds the fire door open for Edie, and they cross the newsroom toward Franklin's office. "Thank you for doing this," Laura says as they approach the door. Iris Wong, Franklin's secretary, nods at them.

"Just go home," Edie says, stopping in front of the door. "It will be better—for everything, for everyone—if you simply go home. . . ."

"In Hong Kong, Fuggin Asia is my home."

"It's not," Edie says. "Go home, and fix things with your husband. . . ."

"Fixing things here matters more."

"That's not on," Edie says. "Simply not on. Your relationship with your husband is far more important than. . . ."

"It all starts here. I have to fix things with Peter first," Laura says, reaching for the door.

"Is it because you love him?" Edie says.

"It's got nothing to do with love. It's . . . it's all about the bottom line." Laura turns and walks though the door. Edie shrugs and follows.

Franklin looks up from his desk. "Ladies. Good morning. To what do I owe this pleasure?" Chook-koo. "Or should I say, how much is this about to cost me?"

Laura flashes Edie a grin as they sit down across the desk from Franklin.

"There's something I need to tell you, Peter," Laura begins. "I just brought Edie for moral support. She has nothing to do with it."

"Sounds serious," Franklin says, smiling, glancing at the two women then back down at the papers on his desk.

Laura sighs, thinking, okay, here goes. "Remember when I got that call from Brian Randolph in Bangkok. . . ."

"The tip about the crisis that you ignored. . . ." Franklin says, still happily distracted by the work in front of him.

"Yes. Well, I got that call on my mobile at home. My husband was there. And he pieced together what Randolph said, and he began trading currencies based on that information. . . ."

"He did?" Franklin says, giving Laura his full attention. Chook-koo.

"Yes, and, he says, he made money, a lot of money. . . ."

"Then I should have hired him as my producer for that night," Franklin says, and looks back down at his papers.

"Peter, I don't think you understand what I'm saying," Laura says.

"Yes, I do," Franklin says, fixing his gaze on Laura again. "Your husband recognized a tip on a major story and figured out what to do with it. Not just that, he figured out a way to profit from the story, profit from the crisis, which is more than anyone else around here has managed." Chook-koo.

"But he traded on inside information, my inside information, Fuggin Asia's inside information. He used my brokerage account as security for his contracts. . . ."

"So?" Franklin says, looking down again.

"So?" Laura repeats. "So, technically, I think. . . ."

"Technical stuff is for crews and lawyers," he says, looking up. "The bottom line is that he got the story, he knew it was important. You didn't. . . ."

"None of us did at the time, Pete," Edie says.

"Yes. But only one of us got a phone tip and was producing six hours of live news that night and the next morning." Chook-koo. "The fact that your husband got the story indicates that it wasn't impossible to see that something was up, something big. . . ."

"Peter, this sounds like more TV BS, like about Deng's handover night speech. . . ."

"Let's say we stick to the matter at hand," Edie says, kicking Laura. "If Peter has no problem with your husband's actions, and Laura has assured me that she had no knowledge of his trading, no involvement, and did not profit from it. . . ."

"How could she not profit from her husband's money?" Chook-koo.

"We have a very strong prenuptial agreement," Laura says, angry at Franklin but at the same time realizing she should be relieved. She was right about bringing Edie with her, and smiles. "A topic maybe you need to research. . . ."

"Thank you," Franklin says, smirking. "Touché. But it's true you got this story handed to you, you missed it, and your husband didn't. . . ." Chook-koo.

"Yes," Laura says. "We all missed it."

"And now all of us," Edie says, "especially Laura, are on it the way we were on the handover . . ."

". . . stupid. . . ." they all say.

"But the important part is that Laura missed it," Franklin says. Chook-koo. "She was the producer, and that's her responsibility. That's the point."

"Point taken," Edie says. "Right, *mei-mei?*"

"Yes," Laura says, sighing as she realizes she's getting off so easily, slightly disappointed that Franklin has denied her the grand gesture of handing over the money.

"But," Franklin says, "I want you to understand how serious a mistake it was." Chook-koo. "It would even be sufficient reason to dismiss you . . . if I didn't already have one."

"Excuse me?" Laura says with a nervous laugh. "You make it sound like you're going to. . . ."

"The memo won't go out until later this week, and I need Mike to think I told him first, so keep it quiet, please," Franklin says. "But as of December one, Fuggin Asia operations will be moving to Beijing."

"What?" Laura says.

"CCTV has agreed to a co-production deal and to carry the network in China," Edie says.

"Along with selected additional Fuggin International programming," Franklin adds. "And even if I wanted to take you with me to produce in Beijing, I couldn't get you a work visa."

"Your old chum Director General Guofu would block it, I'm afraid," Edie explains.

"Same problem for Mike," Franklin says. Chook-koo. "Tough choice for Old Hartman: sit out the rest of his contract and give up face time during some of his last ticks on the clock as a viable anchor, or take a major pay cut to stay on air in some second-rate US. . . ."

"The Information Ministry doesn't want many westerners mucking about," Edie says. "Chinese journalists are all spies, so they suspect the same is true of ours, despite our assurances. . . ."

"In your case, Laura, there's also Candy," Franklin says. "She's still not particularly fond of you, you know. Aside from the mobile phone incident and you trying to blame her for what happened between you and Deng on handover night, she thinks you're in love with me, or that your husband is. I've never quite understood. . . ."

"Please, slow down," Laura says, realizing they're serious, it's not a joke. "You're moving Fuggin Asia to Beijing, and you're firing me? That's so unfair. . . ."

"No one's getting fired," Edie says.

"At least not you," Franklin says.

"Then, what. . . ?" Laura begins, but can't think of what to ask. Things are happening too fast. "What about my show?"

"Wrong question, *mei-mei,*" Edie advises.

"Laura is a loyal employee. Been with the Fuggin group longer than you have, March." Chook-koo. "We'll keep, as you put it, your show and *Market Wrap.* We've been breaking in Honest Ho producing Candy's segments, and shooting them weekends at CCTV, as a shakedown up there for them and her. Their facilities are new, first class. They've built us a set. . . ."

"What about the anchors?" Laura asks. "Is Deng. . . ?"

"Deng's off *AM Asia,*" Franklin says. "Believe it or not, there's no shortage of English-speaking anchors up there, and they work for a song, comparatively."

This bit of news salves Laura's wounds. At least that bastard is going down, too. "You're not worried about credibility, working with CCTV? Working in Beijing, for Beijing. . . ?"

"What's more credible in Asia right now than China?" Franklin asks. Chook-koo. "It's the only country that isn't bankrupt. Even if Fuggin Asia wasn't going broke, I'd make this deal in a heartbeat. A partnership with the state broadcaster in the number-one market in the world. . . ."

"The butchers of Beijing," Laura mutters. "Edie, you will keep an eye on. . . ."

"I won't be there," Edie says.

"You're firing Edie, too?" Laura barks at Franklin.

"Lord, no," Edie replies. "Please, *mei-mei,* calm down. I'll stay in Beijing for a few weeks to train people and make sure the transition goes smoothly. Sara will be my successor as E.P. Then I'm off. . . ."

"Edie's going to be the new Christina Volpecello," Franklin says. "Based in London, trotting the globe. . . ."

"It's perfect. I've been training to be Queen Bitch all my life," Edie says. "And now I'll have a travel budget to go with the title. I'm sure, over time, I'll develop the requisite broad bottom. . . ."

"But no dog," Franklin says, smiling. "It's written into the contract."

"I could be your producer, like for the handover packages," Laura says excitedly.

"Benny Wilson still has that job," Franklin says. "He's too good to. . . ."

"At the beginning, one of us has to know what we're doing," Edie adds.

"Well, congratulations," Laura says, hoping she's able to conceal her sadness, hoping she's feeling loss and anger welling up in her throat because it's the end of the partnership between her and Edie, because Edie so easily kept it all from her, because Franklin has changed her life so radically without giving her the slightest say in it, and not because she's jealous that other people are succeeding so spectacularly while she's being fired. It's so unfair, she thinks, and the phrase reverberates in her head like a mantra.

"We're launching a new show from Beijing, an *Asian Evening News* that will go live here and also feed to the US. Candy and Deng will anchor it. Deng's finally getting his US network newscast, if not his millions just yet, and he didn't even have to change his name back. Peter Jennings, watch your ass."

"I trusted you, both of you. . . ." Laura stammers.

"And we trusted you, Laura," Franklin says, "and you helped us get to where we are now, and we appreciate it." Chook-koo.

"So that's why you keep your girlfriend Pussy, and fire me. . . ."

"Candace Fang is a lot harder to replace that you are," Franklin says.

"Speaking strictly in TV terms. . . ." Edie says.

"Right," Franklin says. "And you're not getting fired. . . ."

"If I'm not fired, then what's my new job?"

"Up to you," Franklin says. "Take your pick."

"And a US work visa won't be an issue for you, *mei-mei.*"

"US?" Laura says. "What about here?"

"You hate it here," Edie says.

"Tell you the truth, I hardly know it here," Laura says. "With my schedule, and our penchant for opening bars in Lan Kwai Fong, I've barely seen Hong Kong. I think I might like. . . ."

"I've been here more years than I care to remember," Edie says, "and I'm sailing off quite happily in the Fuggin royal yacht. Hong Kong is finished. In ten years, I expect this place will be like China, only far more expensive and far less interesting. Last one out, switch off the lights."

"You'll be much better off in the US," Franklin says. "You're a good producer. You're still just a beginner, really, even though you got thrown in the deep end here, but you're good. I'm not going to broadcast what happened here." Chook-koo. "You're leaving because of cost cuts, because you're on a package we can't afford anymore, because you don't want to go to Beijing, because we need to go local, or because we couldn't get you a visa. You choose the reason you like and that will be the story."

"That's how it is with TV, isn't it?" Laura says. "There's always a story. The truth is never good enough."

"A good TV story improves on the truth," Franklin says, "enhances it. . . ."

"Television is our lie," Edie says, smiling, for old times.

"You could learn a lot at a local," Franklin says. "We've got FGN affiliates in 54 US markets: LA, San Francisco, Miami, Provo. . . ." he adds, smiling.

"What about the *Journal?*" Laura asks.

"I talked to Dick Holmes in New York, and he said you could come back, general assignment."

"You told Dick you're firing me?"

"No, I told him we were restructuring here, possibly relocating, and might need to trim some people, and he mentioned you." Chook-koo. "Naturally, I said that you're one of the people we want to keep, but that it would be up to you, of course. . . ."

"Thank you," Laura says. "But I mean the *Journal* here."

"It's best that you get out of town," Franklin says, "out of the region, where people don't know about what happened with the handover and the crisis and everything. There'd be no escaping all that here." Chook-koo.

"Why not?"

"People here might make your past an issue. . . ." Franklin says.

"This is a very small town, *mei-mei,*" Edie says. "Everyone always knows everyone else's business. There are no secrets in Hong Kong."

"Guofu has lots of friends here," Franklin adds. "In the US, you'd start fresh. . . ."

"Oh my god," Laura gasps, anger that she showed Jeff yesterday now on display for Franklin. "Now I get it. That's why you kept me, you bastard. You bargained me and Old Hartman with CCTV. Bring Fuggin Asia to Beijing, and we'll get rid of the people on your hit list. Peter, you betrayed me. . . ."

"Whatever you call it," Franklin says, "it doesn't matter."

"All of it for your Chinese buddies. It's bad enough to think of you in bed with Pussy. You deserve each other, you deserve all of them, all your pals at CCTV. . . ."

"Stop it, Laura," Edie says. "Enough."

"It's okay," Franklin says. "Sometimes we all get a little personal." Chook-koo. "But what's done is done. First rule of live television: the next decision is the only one that counts. Look ahead. I'm offering you chances that other people would kill for. And, face it, Laura, Fuggin Asia doesn't owe you anything but a plane ticket home. . . ."

"Back to general assignment at the *Journal*. . . ." Laura moans, calming down as she realizes he's right.

"If you want to go back to print, that could be the best spot for you," Franklin says. "You'd get first crack at lots of stories and be able to find something to focus on. Once you get your teeth into something, stick with it."

"But that's what I did here, on the handover . . . stupid. Stupid me. I worked my ass off, and look where it got me."

"It's different at the *Journal*," Franklin says. "They've got dozens of reporters. You don't have to worry about anything but your story. When you're the producer, you're running the whole show. . . ."

"No pun intended," Edie says.

"No pun detected," Laura says.

"Or you can stick with TV," Franklin says. "Even in New York, if you want. We could slot you in there somewhere, I'm sure. But you have to understand that you're not going to produce the six or eleven show there right off the bat, the way you would in a smaller market. . . ."

"There's no need to decide this all just now, is there, Pete?" Edie says to both of them. "Laura, go home. . . ."

"I've got to book. . . ."

"Honest and I will take care of the show for tomorrow. . . ."

"Then maybe I should clear out my desk. . . ."

"There's no shortage of desks out there," Edie chuckles. "Just go home, *mei-mei*. Take the next couple of days off and talk with that gorgeous husband of yours over one of his gourmet dinners. Think things through." Edie puts a hand on her shoulder, "You'll begin to see the donut and not just the hole."

Riding the shuttle bus and the subway, Laura begins to see the donut and works on frosting it. Yes, this latest episode of "Television is My Lie" should convince her that it's time to get leave Fuggin Asia, get out of TV, go back to New York and the *Journal*. As crazy as that place could be, and as difficult as Dick often was, newspaper work on its worst day isn't half the ordeal TV is every day. Still, it would be a shame to waste all she'd learned about TV and take a step backward at the *Journal*. Maybe she could parlay her experience into working a media beat. Once she got back to New York and got her feet on the ground, she could pitch that. There ought to be a market, if not at the *Journal* then with Turner and the *Times* and the rest, for a media reporter who can dish the dirt on Franklin Global Networks, on Fuggin Asia and number-one son, in bed with the Chinese Communists every which way.

She's sure Jeff will welcome the opportunity to go home, go back to New York. He should be grateful there's no Fuggin lawsuit going after the money. She could even tell him that she negotiated this deal, to let them go back to New York and keep their money. They could get a nice place on Long Island, and he could go back to the stores, the way things were before. Or in the city, and he could go to school. He never talks about it, but Laura knows it bothers him that he doesn't have his degree. She'd encourage him to go back to school. If she's at the *Journal* and he goes to NYU, they could get a place downtown and be one of those totally hip couples that never go north of 14th Street without an invitation, except for her visits to Bloomingdale's. Yes, Edie's right, there could be a tasty donut around this hole.

Riding up the escalator, filled at this hour with old ladies coming back from the market, their bundles and elbows blocking the way, and women her age with their toddlers, Laura realizes Edie's right about Hong Kong, too. Laura accomplished her goal, she helped make history here, and now that's what Hong Kong is, history. Except for this one week a year, lousy weather. Lousy, greasy, tasteless food. Lousy, greedy people who can't even speak English. The Chinese can have it. She'll leave her lights on when she goes, and let Tung Chee-hwa, or Pussy's uncle the Premier, pay the bill.

Unlocking the front gate of Prosper Gardens—Proper Gardens, ha! the only proper part is leaving it—she thinks how refreshing it will be to move to an apartment with a front door she can open all the way instead of this $2000 shoebox. Only people coming from Hong Kong can look forward to better, cheaper apartments in New York, as the elevator scrape above eight reminds her. She opens the apartment gate and squeezes through the door. "Hello," she says tentatively, but there's no answer. She drops her bag on the chair. She could begin her farewell tour of the Hong Kong Jewish Community Center with a few laps around the pool and a lengthy soak in the jacuzzi. Those HKJCC chopsticks with the name printed in English, Chinese, and Hebrew are sure to be popular gift items back home. Maybe she can negotiate a bulk discount. . . . Geez, now she's even starting to think like one of them. Yes, it's time to go.

Laura goes up to the roof, where she'd napped until dark yesterday, to clear the glasses. But everything's already been cleaned up. Jeff must have been here, must have come back last night or this morning. Of course Laura expected he'd come back—after all, she's the one who got taken advantage of, the one who got used, he's the one who needs to come crawling to beg for forgiveness. Still, she finds it reassuring to see evidence of his return after she'd purposely been so vague about wanting him back. She was afraid maybe she'd been too harsh, said too many things that she'd regret. She'll see him tonight, and they'll sort it out. This time, she's the one with the startling revelation to share, and it's one that will make them both happy, one that will bring them together.

She takes a turn around the roof, drinking in the panorama. There's a lot to see here, Laura tells herself, and I should get out and see it while I've got some time and don't have to be in Chai Wan for dawn patrol. I've got to get up here with my camera before we go, she thinks. Aside from the rent, the only impressive part of the apartment is the view from up here, and she wants something to show people from this wild place she lived while making history during the handover—stupid—during the last, best days of Hong Kong. God, everything seemed so different yesterday morning, Laura recalls. In barely 24 hours, the whole world has turned upside down. She's about to land on the other side, on her feet.

But, first, maybe, it would be nice to have a nap.

Besides swimming a mile, taking three games off his tennis coach in their set after his lesson, reading two newspapers plus Laura's *Asiaweek* during his gym routine and in the jacuzzi, and calling to request information about the real estate course at Hong Kong Open University, Jeff puzzled all day over the right tone to strike with Laura.

Sunday in exile had reconfirmed there was no shortage of fun and games around town. His foot massage gambit had not only allowed him to caress a half-dozen nubile metatarsals—and he never had to pay—but brought him three reciprocal foot massages, including a surprisingly racy mutual one, four back rubs, a manicure, and a pedicure; lessons in two line dances to that "Sha-la-la" song he heard everywhere; a compare and contrast discussion of Moses and Saint Ignatius, the patron of the home district for one particular circle of Filipinas; and the phone numbers of fifteen young women starved for male companionship who would be thrilled to share a Park 'n' Shop barbecued chicken and a bottle of white wine with him on their next day off, or free night for the ones who weren't live-ins.

Very promising, indeed, but, Jeff wonders, is that really what he wants? He understands that Laura has a right to be upset with what he did, but he also thinks that she reacted unreasonably, that he'd been very generous to offer to share his money with her. All things being equal, he'd rather have his relationship with Laura work—and maybe occasionally stick a toe, or whatever, into these murky local waters—than have his marriage break up and need to overhaul his life again. He also can't help remembering what Laura said about jail: of course it's bullshit, but if there is anything to it, she wasn't the one who'd wind up behind bars. He needs to call Jerry Lewis again.

Jeff's been bouncing around Caine Road for nearly two hours—it's already after four. At Wellcome, he filled a cart with HK$200 worth of fixings for nachos and burritos before walking out. At the vegetable store, he scoped ingredients for a baby *bok choy* and tofu stir-fry. At the bulk store, he stared at a family-size Kraft Macaroni and Cheese, trying to find a dinner offering that would convey his desire to make things right and, at the same time, his conviction that Laura had been excessively harsh yesterday. He considers takeout from the JCC—hummus, baba ganoush, pita and a couple of matzoh ball soups, with a side green salad—with the implicit restatement of his invitation to Friday night services, but that message is too complex for a situation that demands straightforward simplicity. He could take her out somewhere nice—he can pay for it himself now—but what if she's still as mad as she was yesterday? They'd make a scene. . . . Finally, he settles on a Chinese barbecued chicken, a double side of water spinach, which Laura prefers to *choi sum,* rice, and, the inspiration to demonstrate he'd given the meal serious thought, that wasn't the usual takeout punt, one of those grilled squids shaped like a hot air balloon hanging in the window.

He brings the food up to the apartment, arriving as the fading sunlight, exploiting a crack between Fortune Tower and the escalator, filters in through the edges of the living room windows. "Laura," he calls. The response is grumbling from her bedroom as she uncoils from her nap.

She emerges from the bedroom straightening her clothes, the same outfit she'd worn to the newsroom. "What time is it?" she mutters.

"Time for you to get up from your nap and get ready for bed," Jeff replies, pleasantly. He's going to be pleasant and casual and go with the flow, the Asian way. It was him forcing the conversation yesterday, like a stupid *gweiloh,* that started all this trouble.

"Not tonight," she says, taking her bag off the chair in the living room, dropping it in her bedroom, and dropping herself onto the love seat. "Day off tomorrow."

"What happened? Nuclear holocaust on the Nikkei?" Jeff says, coming into the living room with a bottle of red wine, the corkscrew, glasses and placemats. He ponders sitting next to her on the loveseat, but settles for the subtlety of the chair and begins opening the wine.

"Well, we did have an explosion, and plenty of fallout," Laura says. Let him think it's about what he did.

"Did it have anything to do with. . . ?" he says, lifting out the cork.

"Well, the bottom line is. . . ." She sees his eyes fixed on her. "Let's have a little bit of this wine first. You don't have a tennis match or your Maccabee Games training tonight, do you?"

"No. Not tonight."

"Good, then pour. High, to aerate the wine."

Jeff fills two glasses from as high as he dares. He hands one to Laura, picks up the other, and says, "Cheers."

"To New York," she says. She smiles and takes a sip.

Jeff looks at Laura hard, brings the wine glass to his lips and tastes a drop. "New York?"

"We're going back to New York."

"We are?"

"Well, after I told Peter about your currency trading, he suggested that it would be a good idea to get out of here. So I negotiated a deal for them to send us back to New York. I'm getting my old job back at the *Journal,* if I want it. Or I can work at Channel Nine, the Fuggin New York local. They've given me a couple of days to decide. . . ."

"A couple of days to decide," Jeff says, staring at Laura.

"Right." She drinks more wine and keeps smiling. "I think I want to go back to the newspaper. TV is such an ordeal, and the agony is all about the wrong things. But maybe it would be good to try TV in a different place, one that's not so crazy, where everyone speaks English, and where I don't have to get up at midnight, and then see if I still think it's torture. There are a lot of things about TV that I like. . . ."

"So back to New York we're going," Jeff says.

Laura hears it as a question. "Right. I thought you'd like that." Laura smiles, but doesn't like this stare Jeff keeps giving her. "We don't have to give back the money or anything. No lawyers, no problems. Nobody's ever going to talk about what happened. . . ."

"Go back to New York and live happily ever after."

It still sounds like a question to her. "Yes, sweetheart." Laura sips more wine and refills her glass. "Here's to New York," she toasts, clinking his glass. Jeff moves the glass toward his lips, but doesn't drink. "We're going to live like a normal couple again," she says. "No more of this going to bed before dark stuff for me. We're going to see interesting people and do interesting things again, like before. . . ."

"Like before it will be," Jeff echoes.

"But better. I don't know if you want to go back to your stores. You can, of course. Or, I was thinking, maybe you want to go back to school. Finish your degree. Money wouldn't be a problem. . . ." Laura chuckles and takes another sip of wine. She feels like she's talking too fast and that her words belong to a different conversation, or at least not to one that includes Jeff yet. "If you want to, sweetheart. I'm not saying you need to go back to school. But you could. . . ."

"I could," Jeff sighs. "I could go back to New York and do all that. Or something else."

"Yes, you could," Laura says, relieved that Jeff has joined her conversation but now unsure where it's heading.

"Oh Laura," Jeff says with a shrug. "We both know this isn't about my stores or my degree. . . ."

"I'm just. . . ."

"It's always about you, your career, your business. You never ask about my business. My business is in Asia now. I need to stay here."

"But we can't."

"Why not?"

"That's not the deal I made," she says, and asks herself, what do I say now? It's at home in her living room with her husband and their dollhouse furniture, but she needs to make one of those split-second control room decisions. As on handover night, it's a historic moment but the show is veering away from her script. Does she keep talking up this deal she's cut, as if she's saved the day, made it possible for them to keep the money, or does she tell Jeff that the operation is moving to Beijing and that she's not invited, that she has to leave? Another sip of wine. Television is my lie, she reasons, but it's not Jeff's. "We can't stay here. . . ."

"I have to stay here," Jeff says. "If your station has a problem with that. . . ."

Laura sighs, "I'm sure Fuggin Asia doesn't have a problem with that. But, Jeff, I can't stay. My job here is done. It's finished. It's time to go. I have to go."

"Then go. . . ."

"How can I go without you?"

"It's easy. You get on the plane. . . ."

"You have to come with me."

"I have to. . . ?"

"I mean, I don't want to go without you."

"Boy, that sure sounds a lot different from a couple of minutes ago. And from yesterday. . . ."

"Jeff, yesterday, I said a lot of stuff that I shouldn't have. Things I didn't mean. Fuggin Asia really messed up my mind. Look, I understand now, I can forgive you for what you did. . . ."

"Forgive me?"

"Yes. I mean, you did take advantage of me. You did abuse my trust and my professional position. But I can see why you did it, I understand now."

"Good. Now we both understand."

She waits for him to say more, takes a sip of wine. But he doesn't continue, so she does. "The bottom line is that, out of everything, the final outcome is good, so I have no reason to be upset with you."

"Gee, thanks."

"You're angry," she says.

"No. Not exactly. Just surprised about how much has changed since yesterday. About how your tone has changed. . . ."

"Yes, I was being inconsiderate. I was all wrapped up in the job, and it's just a job, a lousy job. I realize that now. You're more important. You're more important to me than any job. . . ."

"That's not what you were saying a couple of minutes ago. When you said, 'We're going to New York.' You'd already decided. . . ."

"You're right. But . . . I can't stay here." She has to tell him. "The news operation is moving to Beijing next month. . . ."

"Beijing? I don't know if I could go to Beijing."

"I'm not asking you to." She takes a gulp of wine and sucks the overflow off her lower lip.

"You're telling me?"

"No. No. I'm not going."

"Sorry, I'm confused. Your station is moving to Beijing, so you're going to New York. . . ?"

"Right. I negotiated. . . ."

"Why not go to Beijing?"

"I can't. The Chinese government won't let me."

"Wow. I didn't realize you were that important."

"FGN Asia can't get me a visa."

"Oh." Jeff nods his head. "Like those people that couldn't get visas for the US. . . ."

"What's important is that, if I want to keep working for them, then I have to leave. Go to New York, or someplace."

"Okay, now I understand a little better," he says. "I understand that you have to go."

"Yes, because of my Fuggin job. . . ." she giggles because it's funny, not because she's already tipsy. "I can't stay here." They'd put out the story on her, Peter or Pussy or Guofu and her life would be hell, Laura thinks. She'd never get a job.

"I understand. You have to go, and I have to stay. It's one of those things that happen, one of those unfortunate circumstances that come up in life, like when my father died. Something we'll both have to deal with."

"Deal with?" Laura says, astonished. "How?"

"You have to go, I have to stay, so. . . ."

"You said yesterday that your mother and the Israelis are running the underwear thing. . . ."

"Yes. . . ."

"And you made four million dollars from the currency trades, so why do you have to stay here?"

"You really want me to go with you, don't you?"

"Well, yes. But I thought you'd want to," she says.

"I can't go back to New York," Jeff says, the idea forming as he speaks. "No way. . . ."

"Why not?"

"Because I came here to get away from all that, and I'm not going back, not because your boss says I have to?"

"What about if I say it?"

"I guess I'm through taking orders."

"What about the money?" Laura asks, draining her wine glass and swallowing her self-respect.

"Well since you're not in leg irons and you say they still want to give you a job, in New York at least, I assume you're in the clear. Your reputation and your integrity apparently survived my attempted sabotage."

"I mean, what about splitting it?" Laura says.

"Split the money?" The nerve, Jeff thinks, the fucking nerve.

"Yes. Like you said yesterday. I was being stupid yesterday. Unreasonable and stupid. That was Fuggin Asia talking, not me. My head was so deep into things there. . . . Forgive me. I can forgive you for what you did. I'm asking you to forgive me. . . ."

"I offered to share the money with my wife, at my side till death do us part, not somebody screaming that I betrayed her and her sacred professional integrity that she valued more . . ."

"You did. But. . . ."

". . . more highly than our relationship, than our marriage. Someone whose first loyalty is to some TV network that turns around and fires her for her trouble. . . ."

"They didn't fire me. . . ." Laura sniffs.

"Not to somebody who tells me what we have to do and where we have to go...." Jeff sighs. "Not to someone who calls me a louse for making money and then expects to split it...."

"Jeff, you know I didn't mean that. I was just upset. I'm sorry...."

"You have to go? Go."

"Jeff, I ... I've never heard you talk this way."

"We've never had to talk this way before. We've never even tried." He thinks, I should have had this conversation with my mother a year ago, or ten years ago. Better late than never. "Laura, everything could have been so good if you'd just opened your eyes, paid a little attention to me, to us, instead of that lousy station and Peter this, Peter that. I felt as if there were always three of us in the room. And this room is barely big enough for two. I tried to get rid of my elephant in the room, but you never tried to get rid of yours, not until it got rid of you."

"They didn't get rid of me. I can go the *Journal* or I can go any Fuggin station in the US. I just can't stay here, not with Fuggin Asia. Maybe I can stay here with you...."

"You're better off with them, I think."

"What are you saying?"

"I'm saying that you've always been a lot more interested in your career than you have in me. That's the relationship you care about, the one you're committed to. With you, the us is you and your career, not you and me."

"That's not how I meant...."

"Well, that's how I think it's been, that's how it felt to me."

"The money...?"

"Belongs to me. You have your career."

And I could destroy it by suing you to try to get the money, Laura thinks, telling the world how the producer of *AM Asia* missed the story of the Asian economic crisis and her husband the underwear salesman didn't. She imagines Franklin on the stand, testifying against her. Then Deng, Pussy, Old Hartman, maybe even Edie.... Or she could shut up and stay as Jeff's *tai-tai*, completely dependent on him. "So, this is it?" she asks.

"I don't know. It depends what it means, I guess." He feels his mouth turning into a smirk. "You have to go to New York. Go. I have to stay here. I'll stay. We'll both do what we have to do and see what happens from there."

"Oh god, fuck it all," Laura says, feeling genuine anger at the realization that yesterday she could have had a few million bucks and a husband who tirelessly tries to please her, and now she's got a ticket right back where she started from a year ago, with nothing except a huge sleep debt to show for it. "I don't deserve this. You took advantage of me, of my position, my information, and I'm the one who has to leave town. That's so unfair. . . ."

"When you find something fair in this life that'll be some real news for your TV show. . . ."

"Fuck you, too," Laura says, raising her voice for effect. "If you think I'm better off without you, then I might as well start now. You can just get out of here, out of my apartment this second. Come back and get your shit when I'm not here. . . ."

"Okay," Jeff says without moving.

"Get out. Now."

"Okay, okay, I'll just get my gym things," he says, retreating to his bedroom for his gym bag and tossing some clean clothes inside. He can come back tomorrow for his stuff. In the window across the way, the Filipina peels off a sweaty tee-shirt, showing her profile in a white push-up bra. Outside, before his workout, Jeff can call one of those Filipinas he met yesterday. He can call Yogi, tell her that Laura's out of the picture, and he can to come to Japan, or go to Bali, and buy a sailboat and tie a surfboard to the stern. Or he can go to Bali without Yogi and get his own sailboat. He can keep a little place here, too, if he goes, just in case he wants to keep an eye on Golden Beauties and his mother.

With his wife throwing him out and $4 million to burn, Jeff realizes he's done what he set out to do when he left Long Island a year ago. He's restarted his life, and he likes the way it's turning out. As night falls over Hong Kong, Jeff can do anything he wants, and he finally knows it. Watching him squeeze through the front door, Laura sits on the love seat with her glass of wine, already wishing she could reshoot this package with a new script.